Penguin Books

Upside Down Inside Out

MONICA MCINERNEY was born in the Clare Valley of South Australia and has lived in Australia, Ireland and England. Her first novel *A Taste for It* was a bestseller in Ireland and Australia. *Upside Down Inside Out* is her second novel.

Also by Monica McInerney

A Taste for It

MONICA McINERNEY

Upside Down Inside Out

Penguin Books

Penguin Books Australia Ltd
487 Maroondah Highway, PO Box 257
Ringwood, Victoria 3134, Australia
Penguin Books Ltd
Harmondsworth, Middlesex, England
Penguin Putnam Inc.
375 Hudson Street, New York, New York 10014, USA
Penguin Books Canada Limited
10 Alcorn Avenue, Toronto, Ontario, Canada M4V 3B2
Penguin Books (NZ) Ltd
Cnr Rosedale and Airborne Roads, Albany, Auckland, New Zealand
Penguin Books (South Africa) (Pty) Ltd
24 Sturdee Avenue, Rosebank, Johannesburg 2196, South Africa
Penguin Books India (P) Ltd
11, Community Centre, Panchsheel Park, New Delhi 110 017, India

First published by Penguin Books Australia Ltd 2002

1 3 5 7 9 10 8 6 4 2

Copyright © Monica McInerney 2002

The moral right of the author has been asserted

All rights reserved. Without limiting the rights under copyright reserved above,
no part of this publication may be reproduced, stored in or introduced into a
retrieval system, or transmitted, in any form or by any means (electronic,
mechanical, photocopying, recording or otherwise), without the prior written
permission of both the copyright owner and the above publisher of this book.

Design and illustration by Cathy Larsen, Penguin Design Studio
Typeset in 10.5/14 pt Sabon by Post Pre-Press Group,
Brisbane, Queensland
Printed and bound in Australia by McPherson's Printing Group,
Maryborough, Victoria

National Library of Australia
Cataloguing-in-Publication data:

McInerney, Monica.
Upside down inside out.

ISBN 0 14 029669 7.

1. Interpersonal relations – Fiction. 2. Ireland – Fiction.
3. Australia – Fiction. I. Title.

A823.4

www.penguin.com.au

For Mary, Lea, Marie and Maura

ACKNOWLEDGEMENTS

Thanks to my two families – the McInerneys in Clare, Adelaide, Jamestown, Hobart and Melbourne, and the Drislanes in Ireland and Germany; my two publishers – everyone at Penguin in Australia, especially Clare Forster, Ali Watts, Meredith Rose and Rebecca Steinberg, and to the Poolbeg team in Ireland, especially Paula Campbell and Gaye Shortland.

Thanks also to Max and Jean Fatchen, Karen O'Connor, Bart Meldau, Mikaella Clements, Rob and Stephanie McInerney, Steven 'Millipede' Milanese, Annie O'Neill, Janet Grecian, Christopher Pearce, Marea Fox, Jane Melross, Helen Chryssides, Leonie Boothby, Fiona Gillies, Anne Pett, Julie-Ann Finney, Mary Conlon, Eilish Conlon, Niamh Naughton and Eimear Duggan.

Big thanks to my friend and agent Eveleen Coyle in Dublin.

And once again, special thanks to two people – to my sister Maura for her insight, encouragement and patience, and to my husband John, for all that and more.

CHAPTER ONE

Dublin, Ireland

EVA KENNEDY had just stepped into the cold March air when a watermelon rolled across the footpath in front of her.

'Sorry 'bout that, Eva love,' a middle-aged woman called over. 'It's been trying to make a run for it all day, that one.'

Eva picked up the runaway fruit and passed it across to Brenda, who was surrounded by the remnants of her fruit and vegetable stall. There were boxes of cabbages and oranges piled high on the Camden Street footpath around her. Her son was dismantling the stall itself, loading the wooden trays into a van parked illegally beside the footpath, its interior light throwing out a dim glow.

'Howya, Eva,' Sean called from the back of the van. 'Any chance of a pint together tonight?'

'No chance at all, Sean. Haven't you given up on me yet?'

'Never. You've my heart broken, you know.'

Eva just laughed at him. Not even fourteen years old and he was already full of cheek.

She had just started pulling down the delicatessen's security shutter when she heard someone calling her name. It was Mrs Gallagher, one of her favourite customers, walking quickly down Camden Street and waving a shopping list like a small white flag.

'Eva, I'm so sorry,' she said breathlessly as she reached her side. 'I just couldn't get away from work before now. Am I too late?'

'Of course not, Mrs Gallagher. I wasn't going home yet anyway.' She pushed the shutter all the way up again and opened the front door, the bell giving its little ring as they walked in. The shop was warm, the air fragrant with the mingled smells of fresh bread, coffee, cheese and spices.

Mrs Gallagher gave an appreciative sniff. 'Thank you for this, Eva. I've friends coming over for dinner and I promised them some of your wonderful cheese.'

'It's no problem at all.' Eva went in behind the counter, tied on an apron again and pulled on some gloves. 'Ambrose and I are having a quick meeting after work in any case.'

'Now, that's the sort of meeting I'd like to have. I can just imagine what you two talk about. "What do you think of this cheese, Eva?" "Is this olive oil good enough?" "Are these chocolates chocolatey enough?"'

Eva laughed at the envious look on Mrs Gallagher's face. 'That's about it, actually. Now, which cheese were you after? We've your favourite here, this crumbly farmhouse one, or perhaps you'd like to try this new one? A smoked cheddar, from a small producer near Cork that Ambrose heard about. It's something special, I have to say.'

Mrs Gallagher took a taste, then smacked her lips in pleasure. 'Oh yes, I'll have a good wedge of that, Eva, thank you. Where is Ambrose, by the way?'

'In the Bermuda Triangle.'

'Where?'

'Our storeroom. It doesn't seem to matter how many times we reorganise it, things just disappear in there, never to be seen again.'

'Sounds just like my filing cabinet at work. And tell me, how will Ambrose cope without you while you're off gallivanting in New York with that young man of yours?'

'My cousin Meg is coming up from Ennis to help out. She's just finished a course at the Ardmahon House cooking school and really wants the work experience.'

'Oh, that's a marvellous place, apparently. I'll have to ask her for some recipe tips. Now, let me think, can I have some of that camembert? And some of the blue vein as well, while you're there.'

Eva had just taken out the wheel of camembert when she heard the front doorbell ring. She looked up, her smile fading slightly at the sight of a red-faced elderly woman. Mrs Lacey. The Terror of Camden Street.

'I know it's after six, but you're still here, so of course you can serve me,' Mrs Lacey said loudly as she rummaged in her bag. 'It's ridiculous the hours you shop people keep. You should be suiting us, your paying customers, not yourselves, if you ask me, Eva.'

Yes, Mrs Lacey. And may I say how especially toadlike you look today. A pound of our finest dried flies, was it? Or some of this pond slime flown in fresh from Galway this morning? Perhaps you'd just like to flick that long toady tongue of yours over the counter here and serve yourself?

'I'll be with you in just one minute, Mrs Lacey. Just as soon as I finish looking after Mrs Gallagher here.'

Mrs Lacey stared at the other woman as if she had magically appeared out of nowhere. 'But I'm in a hurry. Where's that uncle of yours? Surely he can serve me?'

What a good idea, Eva thought. She called over her shoulder. 'Ambrose, I wonder could you give me a hand out here for a moment?'

A tall, grey-haired man emerged from the store-room and took in the situation at a glance. 'Mrs

Gallagher, how are you? I see Eva is looking after you. So, Mrs Lacey, I have the privilege of looking after you. What a pleasure to see you. You're looking so well, too.'

Ambrose caught Eva's eye and gave her the quickest of winks.

Five minutes later, Eva followed both women out to make sure the *Closed* sign was firmly in place and the security shutter pulled right down. A gust of icy wind rushed in at her. She shivered. The end of March and it was still freezing. It was supposed to be spring, surely. What had her friend Lainey been boasting about on the phone from Australia the day before? Autumn in Melbourne and she was still going to the beach to swim at weekends. Eva wondered sometimes if Lainey just made these things up to make her jealous.

'You managed to see dear Mrs Lacey safely off the premises, then?' Ambrose asked as she came back in.

'Oh, now the truth comes out! "Mrs Lacey, what a pleasure to see you. You're looking so well, too." You're a silver-tongued devil, Ambrose Kennedy.'

'Years of practice, Evie. And haven't I always told you about the first law of shopkeeping? You can think what you like as long as you keep a smile on your face.'

'Mrs Lacey's a law unto herself, if you ask me. I don't suppose we could install a moat to keep her out, could we? That security shutter's useless.'

'No, I'm fairly certain she can swim. Now, are you still all right to stay back for a quick meeting? I won't keep you too long, I promise.'

'It's fine, I'm in no hurry.'

She'd been surprised when Ambrose asked her to stay back tonight. Their last catch-up meeting had been just three weeks ago. Still, maybe some problem had come up and he thought it better to discuss it with her before she went on holiday.

Eva enjoyed their meetings. They were a chance to compare notes on which products were selling well, which ones weren't, what requests they'd had. A laugh about some of the worst customers, generally Mrs Lacey. A moan about suppliers. A general chat about the shop's comings and goings. She suspected the meetings helped ease Ambrose's loneliness too. Since his wife Sheila had died suddenly of a heart attack four years before, Ambrose had stayed living in the flat above the shop on his own. It had been a very hard few years for him.

She made a pot of coffee and took out several freshly baked ginger biscuits from a glass jar on the counter. Then she settled herself on a chair at the edge of the storeroom, waiting while Ambrose put a folder of papers back on the shelf above his desk.

'You look very serious,' she said as he turned toward her. 'Don't tell me our olive-oil man has run off with the butcher's wife? Just as we beat him down on price and all?'

'No, oil's well that ends well there,' he said, smiling at his own joke. He took a biscuit and sat down opposite her. 'Tell me, Evie, how long have you been with me now? Six years? Or is it seven?'

Ambrose in reminiscence mode? She was surprised. 'Seven years all up. Those three years part-time while I was studying, and it's been nearly four years full-time now.'

He nodded slowly. 'Do you ever miss the painting, Evie? Miss being at art school?'

'Well, sometimes, I suppose. The painting more than the study, of course.'

'And that cover band you used to sing with? Is that still going, do you know?'

'It is, yes.' She often saw the band's name in gig listings in the newspapers. When she'd sung with them, they'd done mostly private parties and weddings. Now they seemed to be playing at lots of pubs around town.

'And do you regret having to give that up as well?'

'I did miss it at first,' she answered, even more puzzled. It wasn't like Ambrose to ask questions like these. 'But I couldn't work here full-time and do that too, I knew that.'

Ambrose shifted in his chair. She noticed then he didn't have the orders sheet in front of him as he usually did. She realised this wasn't a normal catch-up meeting.

'Eva, I need to discuss something with you and I've decided it's best to do it before you go on holiday with Dermot.'

It was bad news, she knew it. She had a memory flash of him wincing as he came down the stairs several weeks earlier. 'Are you sick, Ambrose? Is that what you want to tell me? Oh dear God, what is it?'

'Oh dear God yourself, not that,' he said, laughing at her expression. 'Haven't I always told you? I'm healthy as a young trout.'

Eva was relieved to hear it. 'Young trout? Sixty-four if you're a day, Ambrose. You're a fine old salmon, ready to be smoked, if you ask me.'

He smiled at her. 'No, I'm not sick at all, Eva. Not in health. What I am sick of is work. Sick of early starts, late finishes. I want to retire, Evie.'

'*Retire?*'

'I'm getting too old for this now. I don't want to spend what's left of my life behind a counter. I want to stop working, it's as simple as that. Stop working and go travelling again. Visit all the places that Sheila and I used to love visiting together. And start enjoying eating food again, not just selling it.'

She was completely shocked. 'But what about the shop?'

He looked steadily at her. 'I want to give it to you.'

'Give it? To me? You can't possibly.'

He laughed. 'Yes, I can.'

'But why don't you sell it, Ambrose? This building would be worth a fortune these days.'

'What do I need a fortune for? I've got all the money I need. I've got somewhere to live. Besides, the last thing I want is some stranger taking over the business and making a bags of it, ruining all the hard work we've put into it. Evie, you're the closest thing to a daughter I have. I want to give it to you.'

'But I don't know the first thing about managing a shop.'

'Of course you do. You've been working with me for years. You're so good with the customers, the window displays, everything. I'm sure you know just as much if not more about food than I do now. And I've never forgotten that you put your own life on hold for me four years ago.'

Eva felt the familiar stab of guilt. He still thought that. Because she'd never told him the truth. 'Ambrose, stop that, please. You're making me sound like a martyr. You pay me, this isn't a charity. And I love working here.'

'Oh, I know you do. But the fact is you went fulltime to help me out after Sheila died. And thank God you did. I couldn't see a day in front of me back then and I don't think I could have kept the place running if it hadn't been for you.'

He held up his hand to stop her interrupting. 'Please, hear me out. I've been selfish, I know. Once things settled down for me again, I should have suggested you go back to your studies, back to your music. I could have advertised for someone else to help me. But I liked having you here. And when you didn't mention your art or your singing, I didn't either.

'It would make me very happy if you took over the shop. It would make me proud, too. And this isn't just a spur-of-the-moment decision. Sheila and I often talked about it. How you were the sort of daughter we would love to have had. How we could both see you running this place, modernising it, making it your own one day. But it has to be solely your decision this time, nothing to do with me or what I might want. It has to be something that you really want to do, not something you're doing out of family loyalty.'

Eva felt the panic rise in her. *Of course I can't do it. This is your shop. I've only ever been your assistant. I can't do it on my own. I wouldn't know where to start. The customers would leave and never come back. I'd ruin everything.* 'Ambrose, I can't –'

'Eva, you *can*. I'm your uncle, yes, but I'm also a businessman. I know you can do it. You just have to realise that too.' He softened. 'I'm not expecting an answer from you now. I thought you could use this holiday with Dermot to think it all over. To decide if you want it. What you'd do with the shop if it was yours. How you'd refurbish it, modernise it, whatever you wanted. I don't want it to stay as some sort of museum piece. I've seen what's happening along Camden Street these days, new places opening, the old places changing. But I'm too old to be a part of it, Evie. I don't want to be part of it. But I'd give you all the help you needed, of course, financially and practically. To get you started.'

He was watching her carefully. 'Or perhaps you'll decide you don't want it at all. That you'd rather go back to art school. Finish your degree. Start singing again. Pick up where you left off four years ago.'

Eva blinked. *But that's worse. I can't go back to art school either . . .*

Ambrose took in her shellshocked expression. 'Oh, Evie, I've surprised you a bit, haven't I?'

She managed to laugh. 'Well, yes, that's one word for it.'

He made a sudden decision. 'A week's thinking time isn't really long enough, is it? Take another week off, Eva, after you get back from New York. You deserve it, you work very hard. I'm sure Meg would be happy with the extra work experience too. Have two weeks off and give it all plenty of thought.'

'Ambrose, are you sure about this? Really? I mean . . .'

'Yes, I'm sure. Completely sure. About all of it. The extra week off. The shop. Everything.' He stood up and rubbed his hands together. 'There it is now. All out in the open. Give it lots of thought, Evie, won't you? And when you get back from your holidays, we can sit down and hear what you've decided to do, can't we?'

She looked out into the shop, his words still sinking in. She knew every single inch of it – the long glass counter, filled each day with cheeses, meats, smoked fish, olives and dips. The shelves crammed with exotic oils, vinegars, chutneys and sauces. The baskets of fresh crusty bread. The handmade chocolates. The coffee, spices, biscuits, pasta . . .

'Evie? We can hear your decision then, can't we?'

'Yes,' she said, dazed. Oh God. She certainly hoped so.

CHAPTER TWO

London, England

'IMAGINE THAT, Joseph, the Sydney Opera House, one of the world's most recognisable buildings and yet the man who designed it has never actually seen it in the flesh, so to speak. He was a Danish architect, if memory serves me right. Won an international competition in the 1950s to come up with a design. Well, he won, no surprise there, it's a wonderful building, but then there was all sorts of bother, years of delays, you see, the costs blew out. Well, we know that scenario ourselves of course, but we're talking in the millions here . . .'

As his accountant kept talking, Joseph Wheeler began to regret mentioning that he was going to a conference in Sydney. He'd barely named the city before Maurice had launched into a history lecture. In the past five minutes Joseph had heard enough to set up his own tourist-guide business.

Maurice was the human equivalent of an Internet

search engine, Joseph decided. You just needed to give him a key word and off he'd go. Sometimes it was fascinating. But not today, not when there was this pile of paperwork in front of him. Joseph looked down at it. On top was the contract offer from the Canadian company. Maurice had checked through all the financial details. All it needed now was one more read-through and Joseph's final signature. All *he* needed was the time to do it.

What had the head lecturer at his university said when he recommended Joseph hire Maurice as his accountant? 'He can be a bit of a chatterbox, but if he's just working as a consultant you'll only see him occasionally. And he is fully qualified. Very experienced. It'll leave you free to get on with your designs.'

A bit of a chatterbox? Yes, and Bill Gates had just a bit of money. And The Beatles had been just a bit successful.

Joseph tuned back in just as Maurice moved on to another subject.

'Do you know, the Sydney Harbour Bridge set quite a few records when it was first constructed, as one of the world's first single-span bridges. There's actually rather an amusing story attached to the opening ceremony. You see, there it was, all planned, pomp and ceremony, when the whole event was hijacked . . .'

Joseph didn't have time to hear this today. Perhaps he could ask Maurice to speak into a tape recorder and he could listen to it later. He stood up. 'Sorry, Maurice, but I'll have to stop you there. I've a room full of work to get through before I go.' He walked over to his office door and opened it, standing expectantly.

Maurice didn't seem to mind in the least. He pulled himself out of the chair with a groan. 'In a bit of a rush today myself, actually, Joseph. That's the drawback of being a consultant such as me, lots of different clients. Like a family of children, baby birds, all calling to be fed, you lot are.'

Joseph kept moving, drawing Maurice toward the lift. His PA Rosemary looked up from her desk as they walked past. 'Goodbye, Maurice. Will I see you in two weeks as usual, even while Joseph's away? I'll need your help to prepare for the auditor.'

'Of course, Rosemary, of course. And you'll have some more of those lovely biscuits for me, I hope.'

'Oh, indeed, Maurice. If I have to stay up all night to bake them myself.'

He finally left, the lift making a satisfying ding as it carried him away.

Joseph waited a minute to be absolutely sure he'd gone, then turned to Rosemary. 'I don't suppose it's too late for me to do an accounting course?'

She smiled, pleased to see a glint of humour in his eyes. The first one in days. 'Would a coffee help?'

'More than you know. I'll be back in a moment. I just need to have a word with one of the designers.'

Rosemary carried the coffee and a bulging folder of paperwork into Joseph's glass-walled office and settled herself in one of the comfortable chairs. Wheeler Design took up a whole floor of this converted Hoxton warehouse these days. The computers in the middle of the open-plan room were all in operation, the designers working on the latest updates to Joseph's creations. The office itself was furnished with his prototypes – stylish chairs and sofas, desks, computer keyboards, all ergonomically sound. His most recent and successful design, the innovative backpack, was on display just beside the reception desk.

Rosemary took a sip of coffee and opened up the folder. They had a lot to get through this morning. They had a lot to get through every morning lately. She'd been working for Joseph for nearly three years now and it had never been busier. The fact that he was going to Australia for two weeks was adding to the pressure. She took out the glossy conference program that had just arrived from the Sydney conference organisers. They were certainly giving Joseph star billing. She skim-read the biography:

London-based Joseph Wheeler has a well-deserved reputation for excellence and innovation in the field of industrial and ergonomic design in the UK. Three years of research with physiotherapists led to his groundbreaking backpack design which features a weight carrying system that . . .

Good, it was all there and up-to-date. It was just a shame the photo of Joseph in the program was two years old – he hadn't had the time to get a new one taken. She looked over at the real thing, several metres away. Joseph was leaning down beside one of the designers, pointing out a detail on the computer screen, listening as the young woman explained a problem she was having with the new chair design. He didn't look that different these days, Rosemary thought. The only real difference was in the expression. In the photo he looked full of life, eyes alight, mouth on the verge of smiling. He hadn't looked like that in real life for months.

As she watched he ran his fingers through his dark hair, leaving a tuft standing up. He did this often, especially when he was getting stressed. She could tell his anxiety levels by the number of tufts standing up. So far, today had been a three-tuft day. Medium stress. Maurice's visit could probably account for two of those – his fortnightly visits were a waterfall of financial details, royalty statements, contracts and bank accounts. Joseph was working far too hard, Rosemary thought, and he didn't seem to be revelling in it as much as he used to. He seemed distracted. Preoccupied.

She doubted that anyone else in the office would have noticed. Certainly his outward appearance hadn't changed at all. He was as stylish as ever. Though he still wore far too much black for

Rosemary's taste. Just like her son. What was it with these young men? Didn't they believe in colours?

She'd often heard the young designers in his company – the men and the women – talk breathlessly about Joseph's appearance. 'But he's not conventionally handsome, is he?' they'd ask each other. 'No, he's *interesting*-looking. And those come-to-bed eyes of his . . .'

Rosemary had rolled her own eyes at that. Not so much come-to-bed as haven't-been-to-bed-enough eyes, she thought.

'Sorry for keeping you, Rosemary.'

She looked up as Joseph walked in and took a seat at his desk. 'Is everything on track out there?' she asked as she poured his coffee.

'We're nearly there with the chair design. But if we get the contract for the airline seats I'm going to have to take on at least two more designers. Could you please draft up an ad, just in case?'

Rosemary made a note. 'I heard back from the conference people in Sydney this morning, by the way. They've changed your flight booking as requested. They were astonished, I have to say. First time in living memory one of their keynote speakers has asked to be downgraded to economy class on an international flight, they said.'

She'd started to worry for Joseph's sanity herself when he'd suggested it. 'You want to fly to Australia economy class?' *Are you mad?* she hadn't said aloud.

Joseph had been decisive. 'It's an ideal opportunity. If I'm going to be designing new long-haul airline seats, I'll need that first-hand experience.'

'Can't you just walk through economy class on the way to your business-class seat?' she'd dared to ask.

He'd smiled at that. But he hadn't changed his mind.

Joseph flicked through the conference program. He'd be giving the keynote address and then running several workshops. He wondered when he was going to find the time to write that keynote address. The way his schedule was at the moment, it would be on the flight itself.

'Will I book a car to take you to the airport?' Rosemary asked, pen poised over her notebook.

'No, thanks anyway. I'm having dinner with my mother that night and she's offered to drive me out to Heathrow afterwards.'

Rosemary noted that. 'And how *is* Kate, Joseph?'

Joseph looked up from the letters he was studying and smiled briefly. 'She's much better, Rosemary, thanks.'

'Oh, that's good.' She didn't enquire any more about his mother's cancer scare. Joseph kept himself to himself, pretty much. She'd once dared to ask him how he was when she'd realised he and his girlfriend Tessa had broken up. It was as if a shutter had come down over his face.

'Now, I need your signature on these,' she said, getting back to business and handing over a pile of paperwork. 'And your answers to a few queries. There's a request from that new design magazine to do a profile on you, full-page photo, interview, you know the sort of thing.'

'No thanks,' Joseph said.

No surprise there, Rosemary thought. Joseph hated doing media interviews. The journalist would be disappointed, though. She'd sounded very keen indeed to follow Joseph around for a few days.

'Two requests from design students, asking about the possibility of work experience here.'

'That's fine. A week each, once I get back from Australia.'

Rosemary nodded. 'Next item. The website designer rang to say he's finished the updates to your site. I saw it this morning, it looks good. Lots of information, more photos. I think you'll be pleased.'

Joseph pressed a few keys on the computer beside him. There was a flash of colour on the screen then the Wheeler Design website came up. He quickly scrolled through, clicking from page to page. 'Great stuff. I'll call him later and tell him.'

'I've had an email from the Canadian company, too. Wondering if you've made a decision about their offer as yet.'

Joseph glanced at the paperwork again. 'I'll look at it again today, I hope. Can you please put them off for another few days? In fact, until I get back from Australia.'

'Of course.'

'Thanks, Rosemary. And are you sure you've enough time to help the auditor while I'm away? We can get a couple of temps in if your workload is too much.'

She smiled at him. Her last boss wouldn't have noticed if she'd been buried under her desk in paperwork. 'I should be fine, Joseph, thank you. That's all for the moment. I'll shut the door behind me, will I?'

He nodded. 'Thanks.'

After she'd gone he stood up, coffee cup in hand, and walked over to the big window. The rain was pelting against the glass, obscuring the view of the Hoxton shops and bars two floors down. He felt like he was in a carwash.

The paperwork on his desk was like a siren calling him over. He resisted it for a while longer, looking around the office instead. He'd designed it himself when he'd first moved in to the old warehouse five years before. Wheeler Design shared the building with ten other companies, everything from graphic designers to freelance journalists. The first couple of years had been great, like a social and work co-operative. But these days he hardly had the time to talk to any of the others, let alone socialise.

'You're on the high road to success now, Joseph,' Maurice had said that morning as he handed over the hundred-page document outlining the conditions and patent situation if Joseph were to take the job with the Canadian luggage company. They'd invited him to base himself in Toronto for six months to work with their team on a new version of his backpack. The work would be long and hard, but the money and prestige would more than compensate.

This was the high road to success? It was filled with potholes then, he thought. Exhaustion. Headaches. Meetings, contracts and paperwork. It was ironic, really. He was such a successful designer he didn't get time to actually design any more.

Joseph ran his fingers through his hair. What a day. And what a day yesterday had been. And the weeks and months before that. He felt more like sixty-four years old than the thirty-four he was. What had happened to his life? He was feeling more and more like he was barely clinging on. All this paperwork and all these details were hurtling past him and he was getting just a glimpse as they rushed by.

He had to concentrate. If this headache would go away, he could. He went back to his desk and started reading the tiny print of the Canadian contract again.

This document confirms the details of the proposed contract agreement between Joseph Wheeler of Wheeler Design of Hoxton, London, hereafter known as the Consultant and . . .

It was no good. He wasn't taking it in. He looked out the window again. Why was he putting it off? This was what all that hard work had been about, wasn't it? Finetuning his designs. Doing all the research. Making all the prototypes. So he'd get approaches like this?

Three years ago an offer like this one would have consumed him. Thrilled him. Sent his blood pumping.

But now? Today? He just felt like picking up the contract and throwing it straight in the bin.

CHAPTER THREE

'OH, EVIE, that looks *gorgeous*.'

Eva turned and smiled at her young cousin. 'Thanks, Meg.' She was very pleased with the latest window display herself. She'd been working on it all afternoon, carefully arranging a balancing act of shiny purple aubergines, bright red chillies and plump heads of garlic, surrounded by long, elegant bottles of olive oil.

It was like a still-life painting, she decided. But it just needed a few more bits and pieces. Some preserved pears, perhaps, all golden and round in their jars. The handmade chocolates? Or a selection of the freshly baked biscuits in their little cellophane-wrapped bundles?

Meg was inspecting the display closely. 'Could I try to do one of these while you're away, Eva? They look so artistic, don't they? I don't know where you get your ideas from at all.'

'Those three years I spent at art school, maybe,' Eva said mildly.

'Oh, that's right, I forgot about those. I only ever think of you as a shop assistant, I suppose.'

Eva blinked. Perhaps a person's tact gene only kicked in at the age of nineteen, she thought. Or perhaps Meg had missed out on hers altogether.

Meg was oblivious in any case. 'It's such great fun here, Evie. Not like work at all. Did I tell you a lady came in yesterday and asked me for quail's eggs, can you believe it? What size would they be, do you think? God, quails are tiny enough themselves, their eggs would be like peas, wouldn't they?' Meg gave a merry laugh.

'Then another lady came in and asked did we serve hot soup. She said she was freezing and walking past, smelt the bread and thought, Mmm, imagine a nice hunk of that bread and a big bowl of freshly made soup, not that packet stuff most of the pubs sell.' Meg took a deep breath, then kept going. 'I told her that, sorry, we didn't serve soup but I'd certainly talk to you and Ambrose about it. Bernadette and Maura, my teachers at Ardmahon House, always said you should never dismiss a customer's request out of hand. They said it's better to thank them for the idea and say you'd see what you could do. That way they feel like you really care about them as customers. Could we do that, do you think, Eva?'

Eva was trying to keep up. 'Do what, Meg, sorry?'

'Serve hot soup.'

'Where?'

'In the shop.'

'Where could we serve it?'

'Oh, I mean to take away, in the first instance. Unless we put a few tables and chairs in the storeroom.' Meg laughed. 'That'd be cosy, wouldn't it? "Yes sir, that table there is free, just next to those tins of tomatoes."'

Eva opened her mouth to answer, then shut it as Meg started talking again. 'And I just can't wait to start serving behind the counter. And helping Ambrose in the storeroom, too.'

'You're not still nervous of him, I hope?' Eva finally got a word in, keeping her voice low. 'His bark really is much worse than his bite.'

Meg whispered, 'I know. I think we just got off to a bad start with my tongue stud.'

'I can't imagine why. I thought it was absolutely gorgeous.'

Meg poked out her now plain tongue. Ambrose had taken one look at the silver stud the day before and grimaced. 'Isn't that remarkable. Now, take it out, please, before you scare our customers and put them off their food.'

'I don't mind really,' Meg whispered. 'I told him I'm happy to look just as ordinary as you while I'm working here.'

Ordinary? Every hackle on Eva's body rose again before she mentally pushed them all down. She looked at her reflection in the glass door opposite. Long straight black hair tied back in a plait. White shirt. Simple silver jewellery. Average height. Average build – well, definitely not thin, anyway. All right, she was hardly Claudia Schiffer, but *ordinary?*

The child is only nineteen, she reminded herself. Twelve years younger than you. She knows not what she says. She bit back what she wanted to say: 'I'll have you know, when *I* was your age, etcetera, etcetera. Do you realise I was wearing earrings and eye makeup before you could even *walk*, etcetera, etcetera.'

The shop telephone started to ring. 'That's Dermot for you, Evie,' Ambrose called out from the storeroom.

Eva walked over and picked up the phone behind the counter. 'Hi, Dermot.' There was no answer, just a lot of noise in the background, as though her boyfriend were in a bar. The property company he worked for was just off Grafton Street, surrounded by pubs, so perhaps that was exactly where he was.

'Hello? Hello?'

Still no answer, though she just could hear Dermot talking to someone. He seemed to be explaining the features of his new mobile phone. What was it with Dermot and mobiles? she wondered as she waited, not very happily, for him to put the phone back to his ear and actually talk to her. She hated mobiles herself, refused to get one, but Dermot was obsessed with them.

His latest party trick was guessing what brand a mobile phone was from the ring it made. He'd made a spectacle of himself in a restaurant two weeks previously. 'Don't tell me, don't tell me,' he'd shouted across to the table beside them, as one of the diners reached for a phone playing a butchered version of 'O Sole Mio'. 'It's a Nokia, is it? No? Then definitely a Motorola. Yes!' He'd actually punched the air in victory when the diner had shown him that, yes, it was a Motorola.

He finally came on the line. 'Eva? Are you there?'

'Well, yes, I thought one of us should be.'

'Sorry, babe.'

She winced inwardly. She wished he wouldn't call her babe. 'How are things?'

'Grand, grand. Except something urgent's come up at work and I need to see you tonight and talk about it. Can you come and meet me here at Archibald's?' It was a new wine bar off St Stephen's Green. 'Tonight? Now?'

'Hold on a moment.' She turned to her uncle. 'Ambrose, do you mind if –'

Ambrose interrupted. 'Off you go, Evie. It's nearly six anyway. Meg and I will close up shop here.'

She spoke into the phone again. 'That's grand, Dermot. See you soon.'

Moments later, she was walking down Camden Street. Pulling her coat in close against the sharp wind, she passed shops she knew like the back of her hand. The tailor, the charity shops, the hardware store, the photo gallery, the pottery shop. The old dark pubs were being joined by bright new bars these days, people spilling in and out of each of them, the air filling with the scent of tobacco and alcohol as she passed doorways, the noise from inside mingling with the traffic sounds.

She liked walking through the Dublin streets. In the early days she'd driven her battered old car to and from work each day. When she'd worked part-time, it hadn't been so bad. But when she'd gone full-time, she'd realised it was quicker to walk from one side of Dublin to the other than sit stranded each morning and evening in a traffic jam along the quays, looking down into the murky water of the Liffey.

Eva waited at the pedestrian lights, wondering again what the urgent work business was that Dermot had mentioned. And why he needed to talk to her about it. She smiled at the irony. Here she was dropping everything to talk to Dermot about his work and she hadn't told him about Ambrose's offer yet. She hadn't told anybody. Not her parents. Not her sister. Not even Lainey.

It was still early days with Dermot, though, she told herself. They weren't at the stage where they confided fully in each other, after all.

Which stage is that? The stage where you like each other? a voice piped up inside her head.

We like each other, she insisted.

Do you?

Did she? She thought about it as she walked on. The awful thing was she really wasn't too sure any more. She'd slowly been realising they didn't have anything in common. They didn't read the same books or like the same films. They didn't even laugh at the same things.

Perhaps she was just out of practice. Perhaps this was what relationships were like these days. After all, Dermot had broken something of a boyfriend drought. A long drought, in fact. In the past ten years she had gone out with only two other men, neither of whom lasted longer than two months – her decision both times. She was probably expecting too much. There were bound to be some things about Dermot that annoyed her.

Some things? Everything, more like it.

They'd met when he started calling into the shop nearly four months previously. She'd noticed him immediately, with his smart suit, groomed hair, quick movements. Like a glossy bird, Eva had thought. Preened and sure of himself. With great charm, he'd insisted she – not Ambrose – served him, each time he came in. Then, one Friday evening, he'd asked her out for a drink. Very flattered, she'd accepted. Then dinner. Even more flattered, she'd accepted again.

And again. They had fallen into a routine almost without her realising it.

They usually saw each other during the week. He was too busy showing properties to clients at weekends, he'd explained. They'd meet for dinner, a drink or a film. They'd kissed, but not a lot. Dermot always called a halt to that side of things too. 'Let's get to know each other first,' he'd always said. Eva hadn't known whether to be impressed at his self-restraint or disappointed at the lack of passion between them.

This holiday to New York had been his idea. His cousin had an apartment they'd be able to stay in. 'A bedroom each,' he'd said quickly, 'plenty of room for us both.'

'New York? Really? That would be brilliant.' She'd never been to New York. She'd always wanted to go there.

'You see, I've a little proposition I want to put to you while we're away.' He'd given her a meaningful look.

Eva's stomach had flipped in quite an unpleasant way. 'Proposition?' she'd repeated, not liking how close the word was to 'proposal'. She'd pressed him for details but he wouldn't elaborate. 'No, this is something to discuss when we're in a nice New York restaurant with a good bottle of wine in front of us, all relaxed.'

She'd fought back the sudden rush of panic his

words had given her. Was he talking about a marriage proposal? After just three months together? She didn't want to ask him outright in case he wasn't thinking in that direction at all. She'd be mortified if she'd misunderstood him completely.

Lainey had been delighted at the idea. 'Jaysus!' she'd shrieked down the line from Australia. She might have lost her Irish accent since she and her family had emigrated fifteen years before, but not her vocabulary. 'My friend the blushing bride! I can hear the wedding bells from here. I *have* to be bridesmaid. In pink taffeta. Promise me now, Evie.'

'Lainey, stop it! I might have it all wrong. I probably have. It's just he's been really secretive. Hinting that he wants to ask me something.'

'Oh, how romantic. But you can't marry him yet anyway, you know that.'

'Why not?'

'Because I haven't met him. And you can't possibly marry someone I haven't approved. Listen, forget New York, come to Melbourne instead. I'm off to Brisbane for two weeks in April for work – I can check him out and then the two of you can mind my apartment for me.'

Eva had just laughed at her. Lainey the steamroller. 'No, thanks. It's New York, New York or nothing, nothing.'

At the entrance to the wine bar she stopped and thought about it for a moment. Would Lainey approve of Dermot if she met him? And more to the point, would she want Lainey to meet Dermot? After what had happened last time Lainey had met one of her boyfriends? She put the thought out of her head and went inside.

He was sitting at a corner table, talking on his new phone. It was the latest model, silver-plated. He was very proud of it. As she took off her coat and sat down opposite him, he waved a finger at her, pointing to the phone with his free hand while he continued talking. After a second she saw what he was pointing at – he'd had his name engraved on the silver plating. 'Dermot Deegan'. Underneath it, in smaller letters, 'Play to Win'. Eva's heart sank. Motivational slogans were the latest trend in his property office.

'Hi Eva,' he greeted her, finally finishing his call. 'What'll you have, a G&T? A V&T?'

'Gin would be great, thanks, Dermot.' She watched as he went up to bar. He looked especially sleek tonight, she noticed. He was a very good-looking man. Out of her league really. She didn't normally attract men as successful and handsome as Dermot.

Beside her a small group of women were talking and giggling. They'd braved the weather in short dresses, showing plenty of skin, their heavy coats a jumble on a chair behind them. One of them had noticed Dermot and was whispering to her friend about him. The friend whispered back, then they both turned and shot a glance at Eva.

Eva shifted in her seat under their scrutiny, feeling a little dowdy compared to them. Dermot had tried to glam her up on a few occasions, before realising short glittery dresses and tight-fitting, low-cut tops weren't her style. She preferred simple clothes, coloured T-shirts, little jackets, long skirts and jeans. She glanced down at her clothes now – the white linen shirt and black skirt that Ambrose liked to see her in behind the counter. Definitely not the pop princess look Dermot favoured. Quite ordinary clothes, really.

That word again.

Looking around the wine bar, Eva surreptitiously opened the top button on her shirt, hoping that would spice up her look. Oh yes, instant glamour. Not. She was just contemplating opening another button and thrilling the winebar with her Marks and Spencer bra when Dermot came up behind her.

'One gin and tonic,' he said in a loud voice, putting a fresh drink in his place as well. 'So, how was your day?'

She had just started to tell him about Meg settling in so well when he broke in over her. 'Big things afoot in our place, Eva. Charlie in Commercial Property has resigned and you know what that means.'

She didn't have a clue. She didn't even know who Charlie was. Her blank look said as much.

'A reshuffle. There are places opening upstairs in the next few months and we are all officially Under Scrutiny.'

She knew he was worked up when he started Speaking In Capitals.

'Is that good?'

'It could be huge, babe.'

She tried to ignore the Americanism.

He shifted in his seat and gave her an unusual look. She had the same feeling she'd had with Ambrose several nights before. What was this – National Drop a Bombshell Week?

'Now, Eva, you might have wondered why I suggested we meet for a drink tonight. I mean, it's not our normal night to meet up, but well, with the situation changing so rapidly at the office, I realised that I had to keep things moving along. I decided there was no point waiting until we were in New York to ask you what I wanted to ask you.'

Eva went stiff. Oh my God, she thought. Was this the proposal? She wasn't ready for it. A sudden image sprang into her mind. Lainey standing beside her, dressed in a pink taffeta bridesmaid dress.

Dermot seemed uncharacteristically unsure of himself. He adjusted his tie, gave a little cough, even cast a glance at the mirror behind her to make sure he looked the part. There was another short pause while he took a sip of his pint, then he leaned in close toward her. 'You see, Eva, I've heard a few whispers that your uncle might be thinking about retiring.'

Eva's head shot up. How did he know that? Had he bugged her? Her thoughts raced. Surely Ambrose hadn't spoken to Dermot about this already? But no, of course he wouldn't have. In any case, what would Ambrose's retirement have to do with them getting married? Did Dermot want to work in the shop with her, after their wedding? She couldn't imagine that. She decided to say nothing, hoping she hadn't given anything away.

'As you know, Eva, property prices in this part of Dublin, Camden Street in particular, have been rising substantially in the past few years. Above all expectations, in fact. And all the signs are that the economy will continue to boom.'

Eva couldn't believe her ears. He was prefacing his marriage proposal with an economics lecture? In her mind's eye, Lainey-in-pink-taffeta started to make loud snoring noises.

'It's those indicators that have brought me to the point of our meeting here tonight.'

Eva was transfixed. *This* was his marriage proposal? And if she said yes, was this really the sort of romantic story she would relish telling her children and grandchildren about in the years to come? *Well, the way it happened was Dermot rang me up unexpectedly at work a week before we were due to go on holiday to New York, which was where I'd thought he was going to propose. And we met in a fashionable new bar and first he gave me a very fascinating lecture about rising property values in Dublin and then he said to me –*

'Eva, would you ask your uncle if I can handle the sale of his shop?' Dermot's voice rang out loud and clear through the wine bar noise.

Eva sat very, very still. Lainey-in-pink-taffeta disappeared with a pop. 'I beg your pardon?'

Dermot pasted a rehearsed engaging smile onto his face and leaned closer toward her. 'Evie –'

'Eva. Ev-a,' she said, her voice dangerously low. Only a few special people were allowed to call her Evie.

'Ev-a.' That smile again. 'Ambrose is due to retire, surely? What is he, sixty-five? Seventy? I mean, I've been keeping an eye on him for months now, before you and I, uhm, got together, and I've thought he's got to be thinking about retiring soon, and selling up. I mean, now is the right time, property prices are so high along Camden Street. Ambrose needs to seize the day.' He thumped his fist on the table with such force that their drinks and his mobile phone jumped.

Eva watched in a strangely detached way as her gin and tonic rippled then settled in its glass. She felt as though nine or ten layers of gauze had just been ripped, forcibly, from in front of her eyes. She spoke carefully, the words slowly forming themselves in her head. 'So is that what all of this has been about, Dermot?'

'What?'

'You calling into the shop. Talking to Ambrose. Paying me attention. Asking me out. The trip to New York? You've been going out with me to get to my uncle, haven't you? To try and get the commission on the sale of my uncle's shop?'

Dermot was immediately defensive. 'Of course that wasn't all it was. You're a nice-looking woman, Eva. Uhm, lovely smile. I'm sure plenty of your customers ask you out –'

Nice-looking? *Nice-looking?* Nuns were nice-looking. It was her turn to talk over him. 'How could I have been so stupid? This wasn't about me at all, was it? You weren't going out with me, Eva Kennedy. You were going out with Ambrose Kennedy's niece, whoever or whatever she happened to be, weren't you?'

She stopped short, feeling sick to her stomach. He wasn't denying a thing. Not any of it. He was just looking at her as though he was glad it was all out in the open and, now that it was, could she *please* ask her uncle if he could handle the sale? All sorts of things fell into place. Why he hadn't seemed interested in her – in her mind, her thoughts, her body. Why he'd allocated her specific times. She'd been just a project to him. Then she had another awful thought.

'Are you married, Dermot?'

'No!' he said quickly. But she noticed he seemed uncomfortable.

She knew without doubt that there was someone else. She stared at him in complete amazement. In a kind of wonder, even. 'How long did you expect it to take, Dermot? What was supposed to happen? That I'd be so flattered by your attention I'd get Ambrose to roll over and agree too?'

He said nothing. Again, there was no shame on his face. Just expectation.

Her temper rose like a geyser. 'You bastard, Dermot. You two-faced, deceitful bastard.'

The diners at the surrounding tables spun around at the sound of that. Eva noticed but didn't care. Let them listen. Let them hear what a creep Dermot had turned out to be. She stared at him, eyes blazing.

To her astonishment, Dermot rounded on her instead. 'Well, it hasn't exactly been a day at the beach going out with you either, do you know that?'

The other diners were making no bones about eavesdropping now. One of them turned his chair around for a better view.

'What do you mean by that?'

'Well, look at yourself. At least I'm actually doing something with my life, making something of myself. Not like you. You're just drifting along, not making anything happen. Three years at art school, but what have you done with it? Nothing. You talk about the singing you used to do, how you're an artist at heart, but I've known you for three months and you haven't so much as lifted a paintbrush or sung a note. Face facts, Eva, you're not creative. You're just . . .'

The whole wine bar waited.

'A shop assistant,' he finished.

Eva felt as though she was outside of herself watching all this happen. As though she was in a play or an opera. She half expected the diners behind her to burst into song.

> *A shop assistant!*
> *A shop assistant!*
> *He says she's just –*
> *[Gasp] A shop assistant!*

Eva could hardly find her breath. How dare he? How *dare* he talk to her like that? Hands trembling, heart thumping, she summoned every scrap of pride, stood and picked up her bag. There was nothing else to say. Feeling like a robot, she climbed the steps to the front door, opened it and started walking as quickly as she could.

Then, just a few steps along the footpath, she realised she did have something else to say. So she turned around and came back.

The other customers shifted expectantly in their seats. 'Excellent,' one of them said to her friend. 'Round two.' They settled back to listen.

Eva walked up to Dermot's table and stood right in front of him. She could feel her cheeks burning in anger and embarrassment. This time he had the grace to look uncomfortable.

'One last thing, Dermot. You can forget about the shop. My uncle isn't selling it.' *Because he wants to give it to me*, she was about to add.

But Dermot interrupted her. 'Oh well,' he shrugged. 'There'll be others.'

Somehow that hurt more than anything he'd said before. Standing looking at him, she thought of his deceit, his imagey ways, his American slang. All the things that had annoyed her rushed at her memory.

At that moment his mobile phone started to ring, playing a very loud tune. The sound reminded her of one of his particularly annoying habits. Moving quickly, she picked up the ringing phone, silver-plating and all, and upended it into his pint glass. The dark liquid gurgled and slopped around it.

'No, Dermot, don't tell me. Let me guess the brand by the sound it makes.' She waited a beat as they both watched the phone glug to the bottom of the glass. 'Ah yes, now I have it,' she said clearly. 'It's a Guinness.'

With that, she walked out again. And this time she didn't come back.

CHAPTER FOUR

AT THAT same moment in London, Joseph was driving around the block in his black Fiat for the fourth time, trying to find a parking space within walking distance of his apartment.

When he'd first moved into Shoreditch three years ago it hadn't been so bad. But in the past year every single warehouse seemed to have turned into a bar or a restaurant or an apartment block. Each of them was filled with people every night, taking up every available parking space for miles around. London was getting impossible to live in. Impossible to drive around, anyway. He could go back to the Tube, of course. Then he thought about it. No, he couldn't. He'd had enough of crowded carriages, delayed trains and broken escalators as a student.

He finally found a park three streets away from his house. Soon he'd need to carry a moped in the boot of the car, to get from where he parked to his house.

He walked into the apartment, flicking through his mail. The answering machine was flashing. Two messages. He pressed the button as he went past.

The first message was from his mother, her voice soft on the tape. 'Hello Joseph, I hope this thing is working. Just a quick call to say I've booked that Italian restaurant in Kentish Town for dinner on Friday at seven o'clock. That should give us plenty of time to get you out to Heathrow. I'm looking forward to seeing you, take care of yourself till then.'

The second was a marketing company wanting to sell him some double-glazing.

He was looking forward to seeing his mother, too, and he liked that restaurant a lot. As for the other message, he already had double-glazing. He pressed the button on the side of the machine, erasing both messages.

The phone started to ring just as he was heading into the kitchen. He answered.

'Joseph, you have to come and have a pint with me. Lou said it's the only thing that will save our marriage. It's on your head.'

Joseph laughed. 'George, how are you?'

'I'm fine, it's Lou I'm worried about. I don't know if it's twins she's having or wolf cubs.'

Joseph could hear Lou protesting in the background as George kept talking. 'She says she can't bear to be in the same house as me tonight, that I'm out of control and only you calm me down, make me humane. Come on, see you down the Rat and Leopard at eight, what do you think?'

'George, I can't. I've got work to do tonight.'

'Again? Joseph, have some fun. Have some lager. The entire British economy won't crash if you give yourself a night off.'

'I couldn't take the risk, George. How could I sleep at night, with that resting on my shoulders?'

'To hell with your shoulders. Think about my marriage. I've got some more T-shirts for you to take to Australia in any case. You have to see me before you go.'

Joseph looked at his computer, blinking at him on his desk. Yes, he should be starting on the conference presentation. But the thought of a pint with George was the best idea he'd heard in a long time.

'Okay. See you in thirty minutes.'

'The marriage lives on, Lou,' he heard George call. 'It's a miracle. Joseph's taking a night off. For us. The man is a saint.'

Joseph hung up. He hadn't seen George in months, a shame really. They'd gone through university together and kept in contact ever since, even going on holiday with their girlfriends once, George and Lou, Joseph and Tessa. He and Tessa had broken up just a few months later. George had been briefly sympathetic then very blunt. 'I'm not surprised, Joseph, really. Nice woman, but so serious. And much too tidy. You need more fun in your life. More mess, anyway.'

Tessa was an interior designer who took her work very seriously. His flat had driven her mad. The books especially. He wondered sometimes if that had been the final straw.

'They just look so untidy,' she'd said one afternoon, standing with her hands on her hips looking at the bookshelves.

Joseph had thought she was joking. 'Untidy? How can books look untidy?'

'All the different coloured spines. And the different sizes. Maybe it would be better if they were new. The second-hand ones just look so, I don't know, raggedy.'

Joseph didn't like new books. He liked second-hand books. Raggedy books. He always had done, since he was a kid. That had been his mother's treat each week. They would go down to one of the markets near their house in Kensal Green and Kate would announce that today was either a two-book Saturday or a three-book Saturday, depending on how much money she had spare that week. The two of them had spent hours rifling through boxes of second-hand books. Joseph's first art and design books had come from market stalls. His first copy of *Swallows and Amazons*. He'd got all the Penguin classics, bought as a job lot. Books on Incas. Books about the planets. About Africa, Australia, Asia.

'Some of them have even got other people's names written in them,' Tessa had said with some distaste.

That was another thing Joseph liked about them.

He liked the idea that other people had lived with these books, handled the pages, thought about their contents. He and Tessa had eventually agreed to differ on the books. There had been plenty of other things to disagree on instead. In the end, their parting had been a mutual decision. There hadn't been any huge, final row. Just the realisation one night, nearly two years ago now, that they weren't going anywhere together and it was better to start travelling in separate directions.

'She wasn't right for you, Joseph,' George had said. 'Lou said the same thing. She's got a theory about it, if you want to hear it. She reckons people are like onions, that there are layers and layers to them that you have to get past before you get to their hearts. And that's where it gets scary because you can't be sure what you might uncover each time you peel back a layer. That's the gamble.'

Joseph had thought at the time that the onion was one of Lou's madder theories. He remembered it again now. Perhaps there was something to it. In any case, what was the alternative? Skipping the layers and asking the big questions straight away?

Perhaps he should have asked Tessa the first day he met her whether she liked second-hand books or not.

He decided to shower and change before he went to meet George. On the way to the bathroom he switched on the television to get the news headlines.

It was tuned to the music video channel, showing a promo for a forthcoming eighties retrospective. All the bands he'd grown up with: Elvis Costello, Echo and the Bunnymen, Talking Heads, Dexy's Midnight Runners. Watching it, he imagined a retrospective on the past few years of his own life. That would really send the ratings skyrocketing. Man working in office, man working at home, man working in office, man working at home . . .

He pointed the remote control and changed channels to a re-run of an old British sit-com. Penelope Keith and some man with a hangdog face were sitting up in bed together, propped against their pillows. She was reading what looked like a manuscript, he had a book in his hands. As Joseph watched, the man said something, a wry, deadpan look on his face. Penelope Keith threw back her head and laughed. The volume was down but Joseph could imagine the sound of her laughter.

A rush of envy surprised him. That's what was missing in his life these days. Fun. Laughs. Like Penelope Keith and this man, he thought. Sitting up in bed having a laugh together. Good friends. Having fun. Not taking their work too seriously . . .

He suddenly laughed out loud. Oh, brilliant. Absolutely bloody brilliant. He was envious of some bloke in bed with Penelope Keith. Things were worse than he thought.

'They're causing us trouble before they're even born, Joseph. They're not even a foot long yet. What the hell are they going to be like when they're free, walking the earth? Marriage breakers, the pair of them.'

Joseph shook his head at his friend. 'George, I don't believe a word of it. Last time we met you were over the moon about having twins and Lou was the best woman in the world. I don't believe that much has changed in two months.'

George took a sip of his pint then grinned, a little shamefaced. 'It hasn't. You're right. I am happy about it, I really am. I just needed to vent some spleen. I was starting to feel like I was being buried under a pile of baby blankets. See, Lou was right. She said you're good for me, you calm me down, she says.'

'I'm glad. The Valium friend. Everyone needs one.'

'No, she has a theory about you. She says that growing up without a father means you're a nicer person. That you've been taught to respect women. Be kinder.'

'Thank her for that, won't you. I'll be sure to let Kate know her divorce was the making of me.'

'Well, it's a theory, anyway. You know Lou and her theories.'

'One for every occasion, as I recall,' Joseph said with a grin. He liked Lou.

'Where is your father these days? Lou was asking me that tonight and I couldn't remember.'

'Still in Australia, last I heard,' Joseph said shortly.

'Australia? So are you going to meet up with him while you're there?'

Joseph shook his head. 'No, it's a business trip. I've no idea where he is anyway.'

'But aren't you having a holiday after the conference? Couldn't you track him down?'

'No need to. Another pint?'

George laughed. 'Ah, that old Wheeler nifty change of subject. Sure, thanks. You know Dave Grey, old Boomer Boy from university, is living in Sydney now. You should look him up at least. I'll email you his address, will I?'

'Great. Two pints, I'll be back soon.'

A few minutes later Joseph returned with two brimming pint glasses, holding them high out of reach of the crowds in the busy Shoreditch bar. They talked about the latest soccer results for a while. Then George leaned back in his chair and fixed Joseph with a look. 'So, that's sport covered. Any women on the horizon?'

'Lou wants to know, doesn't she?'

George gave him an innocent look. 'She just wants you to be happy, Joseph. She's always on to me about what a catch you are, how she's got a whole line of friends waiting in the wings to meet you, just as soon as you give her the go-ahead. So, how about it?'

Joseph just laughed.

George shook his head. 'I told her you wouldn't answer me. "We're men, Lou," I said to her. "We don't talk about feelings, about our emotions, we talk about sport." "What is it with you," she asks me sometimes. "Are you made of stone? Are you granite-man? Easter Island statue man?" "Of course I've got feelings, Lou," I tell her. "All men have feelings. We just don't go on about them as much as women do." Bad mistake. Now she knows I've got some feelings she wants to hear about them all the time. Honestly, what is it with women, they say . . .' Joseph waited for the rant to end.

George stopped himself finally and laughed out loud at the expression on Joseph's face. 'All right, all right, I know. Enough of that stuff. Back to business.' He handed his friend a big plastic bag. 'Here are those T-shirts. A month's supply at least. Just what you need to impress the Aussies.'

'Thanks, George.' Joseph flicked through the pile of T-shirts. Since George had started his own printing company, he'd kept Joseph supplied with T-shirts promoting every new band that had come onto the London scene in the past few years. 'You couldn't give me a crash course on who the bands are as well, could you?'

'There's no point. Half of them will have split up by the time you get back from Australia anyway. Two weeks in the sun, you jammy thing, I'm very jealous, you know. Flying business class, I suppose?'

'No, economy class actually.'

'Economy? Those cheapskates.'

Joseph smiled. 'No, it's voluntary. I've been asked to submit a design for a new economy-class seat. You know, to combat all this DVT business. This is part of the research.'

'You're not just overworked, you're seriously ill. No-one in their right mind swaps a business-class ticket for an economy one. Not on a 22-hour flight.'

'It can't be that bad, surely.'

George had first-hand experience of a long-haul flight. He gave a strange, enigmatic smile then took another sip of his pint. 'You'll find out, Joseph my lad. You'll find out.' He held up his glass. 'So. To your trip.'

'To my trip.'

Their glasses clinked.

CHAPTER FIVE

IN DUBLIN, Eva Kennedy had just climbed out of a taxi and was letting herself into the small mid-terrace cottage she rented in Stoneybatter.

She was in a very bad mood. She'd had to wait nearly an hour in the taxi queue down from the wine bar. Her umbrella had become more and more bedraggled by the wind, while she got angrier and angrier about Dermot. As she opened the front door, she half hoped Meg would be there to distract her and half hoped she wouldn't be, so she could lick her wounds in peace.

Meg wasn't home. The living room was quiet and warm, a small fire burning in the grate. Meg had left a note letting Eva know she'd gone out to see a film with some old schoolfriends. 'Back late I hope!' she'd written.

Eva prowled the house, a shaken-up mixture of anger and hurt. That creep. The foul, stinking creep.

Sneaky, conniving, dishonest bag of –

But you weren't honest with him either, a small voice inside her piped up. *You were only going out with him because you were flattered and because there was no-one else on the scene.*

That's different, she snapped back.

Why? the voice said.

Because I wasn't going out with him for financial gain.

He paid for your dinners. He took you out. Money was involved then, wasn't it?

That is not the same thing. He was just using me.

And you weren't using him? To break a boyfriend drought? He hardly kidnapped you and dragged you out on dates at gunpoint, did he?

No, but –

In actual fact, you're feeling relieved it's all over between you and Dermot, aren't you? You knew in your heart he wasn't right for you. And now he's even saved you the bother of making the break-up happen. You didn't even have to make that decision for yourself. And it's not his deceit you're most upset about. You're just cranky because he hit the nail on the head. He was right. You aren't creative any more. You are only a shop assistant these days.

Eva stopped the conversation right there. There was nothing else for it. She'd drown that small voice. In a gin and tonic.

With the drink made – not so much a gin and tonic as a gin-gin-gin and tonic – she wandered into the living room. She needed to do something, quickly, before she started remembering again what Dermot had said about her. It was much more satisfying to just feel outraged. The last thing she wanted was to find any truth in his words.

She set eyes on a pile of books under the computer table in the corner of the room. She'd picked them up at the second-hand shop on Camden Street the week before and still hadn't got around to either reading them or putting them on her bookshelves. The very thing, she could sort them out.

But it was no good. She'd no sooner sat down on the floor in front of the bookshelves, doing her best to banish Dermot's words from her memory, when Meg's words popped in for a visit.

'I told him I'm happy to look just as ordinary as you while I'm working here.'

What was going on this week? Was there some conspiracy to completely destroy any self-confidence she had?

She decided to forget about the books. Gin and tonic in hand, she walked into the bathroom and gazed at herself in the mirror. A pale, dark-haired woman looked back. Two eyes, a nose, a mouth. Yes, that was fairly ordinary. *Ordinary*. An ordinary body. An ordinary, nice enough face. She had a good smile, people had told her that. Even Dermot had told her that. But she wasn't striking-looking. Not model material. She wouldn't stand out in a crowd.

What did those magazine articles say? Everyone has good points. She looked for hers. They must have taken the night off. She looked again. All right, her skin was clear. Clear-ish. She blushed a bit too often, two sudden spots of colour on her cheeks. Clown-girl. But there wasn't much she could do about that. She had an occasional dimple, but that couldn't be relied upon; sometimes it would appear, sometimes weeks would go by and she wouldn't see it. Her straight black hair was shiny. That was good, wasn't it? A sign of good health, like a dog's wet nose? It was tied back in a plait tonight. It was usually tied back in a plait. Just the thing for a shop assistant, nice and neat. Except for the one piece that always worked its way loose and would wave around her face. She tucked it behind her ear again now.

'Lovely eyebrows,' a maiden aunt had said to her once. Well, that was a real plus. If Brooke Shields ever needed a stunt double.

Her eyes were hazel. Not stunning green, not deep and mysterious brown, just somewhere muddled in between. She'd tried life with purple eyes for a short time a year ago, when her sister Cathy, an optician in Manchester, had sent over a trial pack of coloured contact lenses for her to try. But it had been a disaster. The customers in the shop couldn't decide if she was suffering from some tropical disease or pretending to be Elizabeth Taylor.

Even her height was average. If she was tiny, petite, that would be a talking point. She could be feisty, aggressive to make up for her lack of height. Or if she was tall, like her friend Lainey, she could be authoritative, confident. But what could you do with average height? Just stand around and wait for the short and tall people to let you get a word in?

Her build? Average. Well, perhaps a bit more than average, more curves than fashionable straight lines, but she could hardly work in a delicatessen and not eat, could she?

Average. Average. Average. Ordinary. Ordinary. Ordinary.

And she didn't want to be just ordinary. She'd actively fought against it when she first started art school. She'd felt so self-conscious, the country girl from Dunshaughlin lost in a sea of Dublin city cool. She'd studied the trendsetters, trying their looks out for herself. She'd been a Goth for a few months, teasing her hair until she was in danger of picking up television signals. Then she'd tried the torn clothes and lace look, until the chill November wind had sent her rushing for a warm jumper. She'd tried ripped jeans. New jeans. Dyed hair. Permed hair. Big earrings. No earrings. No make-up. Lots of make-up.

Ambrose and Sheila had put up with her erratic appearance at first. Then one Saturday after the shop had closed Ambrose called her in and laid down the line. She was scaring off his regulars, he said. The black lipstick had been the final straw. She had to choose – the wild looks or the job.

Mindful that she was now an art student and supposedly at the cutting edge of society, she had half-heartedly protested that if the boring, rigid conformists of Ireland's narrow-minded society couldn't face up to the vibrancy of . . .

Ambrose had listened patiently for a minute or two, then stopped her flow with a hand held up. 'Eva, please, do you want this job?'

She hadn't just wanted the job, she'd needed it desperately. She'd been studying part-time as it was, supporting herself with the delicatessen work and the few pounds she got singing in a cover band once or twice a month. But that wasn't reliable. She'd thought about her tiny bank balance and the drudge of going out looking for work again. And she'd thought about how much she enjoyed working in the shop. It didn't feel like work to spend hours surrounded by fresh-smelling herbs and good cheeses and exotic oils and breads. And she certainly ate better than any of her fellow students.

'The job, please, Ambrose,' she'd said quietly.

The following Monday she'd arrived into work looking like a different woman. Her face was free of make-up except for a warm red lipstick. Her long dark hair was tied back in a sensible plait. Her white shirt and dark skirt were stylish and simple. And that was pretty much how she'd looked since. Ordinary. She looked like an ordinary shop assistant. Because Dermot was right, she *was* an ordinary shop assistant.

She'd had such high hopes once. To be a great painter, or even to make a career out of singing. But what had happened to those dreams? She just didn't know any more.

She walked back to the living room and put her glass down on the coffee table with a bang. That was enough introspection. Enough tripping down memory lane. Stumbling down it, more like it. She needed to *do* something. She spied her computer in a corner of the living room. Perfect. That's what she'd do, pick up some emails. Distract herself with the flickering screen.

A few clicks and several minutes later she watched as three new emails arrived. One was from her mother and father in Dunshaughlin. They were still learning their way around the computer Eva and her sister had given them for Christmas. Eva clicked on the envelope to open their message and almost jumped as the type fairly leapt out at her.

Hello Eva. How are you? Everything's grand here. Love Mammy and Da

Eva smiled, despite her mood. They'd obviously reached the Adjusting Font Size section of their instruction manual. Last month they'd learnt how to send an attachment. The week before they'd discovered you could jazz emails up with borders and decorations and Eva had been bombarded with everything from balloons to ivy. No messages, just the borders. At least she'd got a message of sorts this time. She sent back a quick reply in normal font size, without borders or attachments:

Aren't you both clever! All well here too. Love Eva xxx

She clicked on the second message – a corny joke forwarded on by Dermot. She deleted it with some force. The third was a chatty, newsy email from Lainey. She was really looking forward to her trip to Brisbane, to set up a new office for the event management company she worked for, she'd written. Lainey's career was moving ahead in leaps and bounds by the sound of things. Eva read on to the end of the message.

Are those wedding bells still pealing???? (I've found
THE perfect shade of pink taffeta, by the way.) Keep
me informed At All Times please. Love L xxxx

Wedding bells? No, not exactly. Bells were tolling,
but not with good news, that was for sure. She
tapped out a quick message.

Lainey, put the pink taffeta back on the shelf. I'm
back on the shelf. The wedding is off. New York
holiday is off. Dermot is COMPLETELY off. Now what
do I do with two weeks holiday? Answers on a
postcard please. Have gone swimming in a sea of
gin, will write again soon. Love Evie xxx

As Eva pressed Send, she realised that she and
Dermot hadn't actually agreed that the holiday to
New York was off. Somehow it had gone without
saying. Call it a mad hunch, she thought. She'd have
to go into the travel agent at lunchtime the next day
and cancel her ticket. Thank God she'd insisted on
paying her own way.

What would she do now with her time off? What
could she do? Stay in Dublin? Hide in her room?
Postpone her holidays and send poor Meg back to
County Clare? Perhaps another gin and tonic would
help her make up her mind. She was just pouring it
when the phone rang, making her jump.

She'd barely had time to say hello when the voice

broke in. 'Evie, I just got your email. What do you mean the wedding is off?'

'*Lainey*? What time is it over there?'

'The crack of dawn. I'm up early, checking my emails before I go for a run. What on earth's happened with Dermot? Or are you too far gone in the Sea of Gin to tell me?'

'Have you got time to hear?'

'Of course I have. Tell me everything.'

Eva did so with great relish, buoyed by Lainey's roars of laughter as she described the mobile phone going into the pint of Guinness. Then she became serious again. She decided she didn't want to talk about Dermot any more. She didn't even want to think about Dermot any more. 'Lainey, let's forget him. The real problem is my holiday. What am I going to do now?'

'Well, I'd have thought it was perfectly obvious.'

'What's perfectly obvious?'

'Come here instead.'

'Come here? Come where?'

'Here. To Melbourne. To Australia.'

'To *Australia*?'

'Yes. Glorious beaches, cafes, restaurants, food, wine, sightseeing, incomprehensible accents, TV soaps, Irish theme pubs. You'll love it. It's perfect, can't you see? If you got here as quick as you could, we could have some time together before I go to Brisbane, then you'd have the whole apartment to yourself for a week or so.'

'Lainey –'

'And I'd ring you from Brisbane every single night and try and get back as quickly as I could to see you. I mean it, Evie. Come to Melbourne instead. Seize the day. *Nil bastardo desperandum* or whatever it was Robin Williams said in that film. It makes sense, don't you –'

'Lainey, stop. I can't.'

'Why can't you? Seriously. Why can't you?'

'It's so far away.'

'It is not. That's just a fallacy. Honestly, you'll hardly notice the plane trip. And loads of airlines fly to Australia. You'll have no trouble changing your flight.'

'I'd need a visa, wouldn't I?'

'You'd get one easy-peasy. Lickety-split. It's all electronic these days.'

'It costs a fortune.'

'No, it doesn't. Compared to New York, Australia is cheap.'

Eva ran out of excuses. *Could* she go there instead? Her mind raced. Did it make sense? She had a strange excited feeling all of a sudden.

'Evie? Are you still there or have you nodded off into your gin?'

'Sshh, I'm thinking about it.'

'There's nothing to think about. Just do as you're told.'

'Lainey, I'll call you back.'

'When?'

'Soon. I promise.'

Eva hung up the phone and started pacing around the house, feeling the bubble of excitement rise again. She walked into the kitchen and looked at the pinboard, her eyes drawn to the photos of Lainey stuck on it. Her friend's bright-eyed, open face smiled at her. Challenging her to come.

Could she go to Australia instead? It wasn't ideal, not by any means. Not with Lainey going away from Melbourne. And it was a long way to travel for just two weeks' holiday. It would cost more, too – but she did have some extra savings. And if she went into the travel agent first thing tomorrow morning, begged a favour, asked for help with the visa and booked the earliest flight possible to Australia, she and Lainey would have a few days, maybe more, together in Melbourne before Lainey went to Brisbane.

And it would do her good to spend some time in Melbourne on her own, Eva thought. She'd always enjoyed being in a new place, looking around, exploring. Not that she'd done much of it recently, apart from a day trip to Belfast last year to do some shopping, and a couple of weekends in London staying with friends.

Ambrose had asked her to use her holiday to make a decision about the shop too. Could she try and make up her mind in Melbourne rather than New York? Lainey was always talking about the wonderful food in Melbourne, all the delicatessens and markets and cafes. And the art galleries as well. Perhaps seeing them all might help her decide what she really wanted to do with her life?

Should she sleep on it? Make a rational decision in the morning, when Dermot-anger and gin had gone from her system? She thought about it for a second. No, she couldn't wait. Not another minute. She pulled her address book out of her bag. With shaking fingers, she dialled Lainey's work number.

'Lainey Byrne speaking.'

'Lainey, it's me again.' She took a breath. 'Would you be able to pick me up from Melbourne airport? Next week sometime?'

Lainey's shriek down the phone was all the answer Eva needed.

CHAPTER SIX

One week later . . .

JOSEPH WALKED into the warmly lit Italian restaurant in Kentish Town, carrying his backpack. His mother, Kate, was seated at a side table, reading the menu.

She was looking well again, Joseph thought as he crossed the room toward her. The strain of her illness had nearly disappeared from her face. Her newly short hair was expertly cut, and she still had that – how should he put it? – individual approach to clothing. Tonight she was wearing something with an Asian influence, a jacket in a rich red brocade with an embroidered collar and long flowing sleeves.

She looked up as he approached and gave him a big smile. 'Joseph, it's so good to see you. Will I order you a glass of wine? Or a beer?'

'It's great to see you too. I'll have a beer, please.'

Kate gave the waitress the order, then turned back to him. 'So you're all packed and ready to go?'

'By the skin of my teeth,' he said, moving the backpack out of the way. 'How are you, Kate?'

'Is that a normal "how are you?" or a "how *are* you?"'

He smiled at that. She'd told him previously that some of her friends had reacted strangely to the news that she was being treated for cancer. They'd started speaking to her in new low voices, their faces a constant study of concern. 'How *are* you, Kate?'

'You're still getting that?'

'No, not so bad any more. Now they've realised the treatment has worked and I'm not going anywhere just yet. I quite miss the attention, actually.'

'Do you?'

'No.' She smiled at him again. 'And how are you, Joseph? And that's a normal "how are you".'

'I'm fine.'

She took in every detail of his face. 'You don't look it. You look exhausted. What's happening at work, has it settled down at all?'

'Settled down? Got busier, I think. I've taken on two new designers to handle the updates of the office chair designs, I didn't have the time to do them myself. The auditor is due in a fortnight, so there's been a lot of preparation for that as well.'

'You're still drowning in meetings, are you?'

'No, just staying afloat.'

'And the Canada project?'

'I still haven't decided. I'll look through the offer

again while I'm in Australia.'

'And tell me, have you managed to stay off the cigarettes?'

'I have. It's been nearly six months now. I look back now and remember them sometimes and I think, Yes, they were the good old days. Those happy times . . .'

She didn't smile. 'Anything new in the pipeline? Any new projects?'

He paused for a moment before answering. 'No,' he said simply.

'Are you all right, Joseph?'

'Yes, of course I am.'

'Are you happy?'

'Deliriously.'

She looked doubtful. 'Am I allowed to ask if you are having any sort of social life?'

'Of course you can ask.'

There was a pause.

'Well?'

'You expect me to answer as well?'

She just shook her head and laughed. 'Let's order, Joseph, will we?'

They were just finishing their coffee when Kate switched the topic of conversation.

'You are still staying on in Australia after the conference, aren't you? You haven't changed your mind?'

He nodded, puzzled by her tone of voice.

'How long will you be there, have you decided that? Or where you'll be going, after Sydney? Have you made any plans to travel around?'

'Are you working undercover for the Australian Tourist Board?'

She gave a soft laugh. 'No, Joseph, that's not why I asked.' She paused. 'I need to talk to you about something before you leave. Something important.'

He was immediately on edge. 'Is it the cancer again?'

'No, it's not about me.' She reached into her bag, withdrew a photograph and handed it over to him. It was a colour print of an elderly man, smiling into the camera. Tall, tanned, with greying hair, dark eyes. 'Do you recognise him?' Kate asked.

Joseph looked closely. 'It's Lewis?'

She nodded.

Joseph thought of the other photos he'd seen of his father. They'd all been taken more than thirty years before, when Kate and Lewis looked like cast members from the hippy musical *Hair*. Joseph himself had looked more like a little Josephine, with a shock of curly dark hair. 'This looks very recent.'

'It's just a few months old.'

'A few months? Where did you get it from?'

'Lewis sent it to me.'

'He sent it to you?' He couldn't stop echoing her. A pause. 'We're in touch with one another again.'

'You're in touch with *Lewis*?' All his life Joseph had heard that his father wanted nothing to do with either him or Kate. After they'd divorced he'd moved to Australia, started a new life. Married again. 'Since when, Kate?'

'Since about twelve months ago.'

Since about when she was diagnosed with cancer. Joseph watched her, waiting for more.

'When I thought that . . . well, you know what I thought might happen, I realised there were a lot of things in my life I needed to sort out. Lewis especially. So I wrote to him. He wrote back. There were a few letters, then we spoke on the phone. We've been ringing each other regularly for the past few months.' She stopped there.

Joseph glanced at the photo again. 'And how is he? Where is he? Is he still in Western Australia?'

'No. He moved from there three years ago. He lives in South Australia now. In a wine-growing area. He lives out in the countryside, with a few vines himself. And some olive trees.'

'And his new wife?'

'That marriage ended. Quite a few years ago.'

'So he's a farmer now? Growing grapes?'

She shook her head. 'No, he's still an artist. He makes tables now, by hand. From wood.' Kate took a breath. 'Joseph, I told Lewis you're going to Australia. He would very much like to see you. To meet you.'

'He's remembered he has a son? After all these years?'

'It was never as simple as that.'

'Wasn't it? I thought it was exactly that simple.'

'I wish it had been. If I could have changed any of it, I would have.'

'Changed what? Stayed together, do you mean?'

She shook her head, looking deeply sad. 'No, we couldn't have done that, I'm sure of that. But perhaps this is a second chance. A chance for you to get to know him.'

'A second chance?' Joseph gave a hollow laugh. 'I'm thirty-four, Kate. It's a bit late for us to bond, isn't it? Though we could kick a ball together, I suppose. Or go bike-riding. You know, the normal father–son activities. That would be a nice sight, wouldn't it? Two grown men –'

'Joseph –'

'No, it's a bit late for that too, isn't it? There really isn't any point meeting him.'

'I think there is a point, I think it's very important.'

He shook his head. 'After all these years? I don't think so. In any case, this is a work trip. It's not the right time for something like this.'

'What would be the right time? And how much time have any of us got, to do what we want to do, what we need to do? What we should do?'

She was talking about her cancer, he knew that. He was quiet.

'That's why I've decided to go and see Lewis again myself. In a few months. Even sooner, if I can.'

'You're going to go to Australia?'

She nodded. 'We need to see each other. The phone calls and letters aren't enough for us now. I've always wanted to see Australia, so I'm going to go to him.' She paused. 'What's happened has surprised us both, Lewis and me. It wasn't what he expected to happen, let alone what I expected. Not so many years later. It's funny, looks fade, you age in many ways, but I've discovered a sense of humour never changes.' She gave a sudden, beautiful smile. 'I'd forgotten the way Lewis could make me laugh.'

'He used to make you laugh? I don't think you ever mentioned that before.'

There was another long pause. 'I'd forgotten it, I think.'

Joseph knew his father was an artist. He'd obviously inherited his design ability from him. Joseph knew he took after his father in appearance too. The height, the dark hair. But he hadn't known his father had a sense of humour.

He picked up the photo from the table again. Lewis must be in his mid-sixties at least, he realised.

Kate was watching him very closely. 'Can you extend your holiday? Take more time off work if you have to?'

He shook his head. 'There's too much on.'

'But this is your first holiday in years. You haven't been away since you and Tessa broke up, have you? Taken any time off work since then?'

He didn't answer.

'I'm so proud of you, Joseph, you know that. Of all your success, all you've done. But you seem so serious these days. Preoccupied. Working all the time. I'm worried about you.'

'You've much better things to be worried about than me.'

'Perhaps I have. But you'll always be my favourite subject.' Kate's voice was soft. 'Do you want to go and see Lewis?'

He felt the fight in him start to dissolve. 'I don't know.'

'You wouldn't even have to ring him beforehand, he said. He works from home, he's there most of the time. You could just go there when it suited you. Stay as long or as short a time as you like.'

He turned the photo over. There was an address written on the back: 'Lewis Wheeler, Spring Farm Road, Sevenhill, Clare Valley, South Australia.'

Another moment passed. She tried again. 'South Australia isn't that far from Sydney, is it?'

'I don't know. It's a very big country.'

'But they have planes, don't they? Trains? Cars?'

'I've only got ten days off after the conference.'

'It would only take one day to meet him. An hour, even.'

He smiled, despite himself. 'You've an answer for everything, haven't you?'

'I had to have, bringing you up. Always so curious, about things, about people. "How do I do this?" "What makes this happen?" "How does this work?"'

The tension between them eased a little.

'I know I can't make you go there, Joseph, but I really do think it's important. Not just for you. For me. And for Lewis.'

'I'll think about it. I can't say more than that yet.'

She gave her sad smile again. 'Then that will do for now.'

CHAPTER SEVEN

EVA RAN through Heathrow airport, cursing the weather for delaying her flight from Dublin, cursing the distance between the terminals. She wasn't just late for her flight, she was *very* late.

'Sorry,' she called over her shoulder as she narrowly missed running into a young couple. In her mind's eye she was competing for Ireland in the Olympics. She pictured the crowds lining her route, cheering her on. She could almost hear their shouts: Hurry, Eva, hurry, you can make it.

She finally saw the sign for the right terminal. At last. Now she just had to find the right check-in desk.

Joseph stood in the queue, waiting to check in. He glanced around the terminal, hardly noticing the crowds and the bustle, still preoccupied by his conversation with his mother. The subject of Lewis had hung heavy in the car on the way to Heathrow. As Kate dropped him outside, leaning across to hug him goodbye and wish him well, the photo of his father seemed to be burning a hole in his pocket.

At first he'd joined the business-class queue, out of habit. The desk clerk had politely pointed out the economy queue to him. 'Unless you'd like to upgrade, sir?'

Joseph had thought about it fleetingly, remembering all the horror stories about the 22-hour flight. But he'd dismissed the idea, he needed to do this research. 'No, thank you. Economy will be fine.'

He finally reached the check-in desk and handed over his tickets, passport and backpack. The middle-aged clerk dealt charmlessly with them, hardly meeting his eye as she issued instructions. 'London to Singapore, change planes at Singapore for Sydney. Your luggage is checked all the way through. Here are your boarding passes. Proceed directly to gate thirty-one for boarding.'

Yes, *ma'am*, Joseph thought, fighting a temptation to click his heels. He turned away and headed past the long queue toward the departure gates.

Eva stood in front of the banks of monitors, her heart skipping as she saw the boarding message flashing beside her flight. Oh God, which check-in desk was it? Number fifteen. Back the other way. She turned, bumping into a dark-haired man coming from that direction. 'Oh sorry,' she called back over her shoulder, not daring to stop.

Joseph looked back as the woman rushed past him, her long plait bouncing against her back. She seemed quite distressed. An anxious first-time traveller, perhaps. He hitched his daypack onto his back and kept walking.

Eva counted at least ten people in the queue ahead of her. 'Oh come on, come on, please,' she urged under her breath. She could feel her heart beating, her blood pressure rising. She tried to calm down. She was in the right terminal, at the right desk. Everything was fine now, surely.

She mentally checked that she'd brought everything – tickets, passport, purse . . . She'd been doing nothing but run through lists in her mind for the past few days. She felt like entering herself in the Guinness Book of Records: 'World's Most Efficient Traveller – Eva Kennedy, aged thirty-one of Dublin, Ireland. Booked and packed for a holiday to Australia in less than a week.'

Meg had followed her around like a puppy, more excited than Eva herself. 'I just think it's deadly! Off to Australia to recover from a broken heart. And I get your whole house to myself.'

'Meg, I don't have a broken heart.' She didn't. She had an annoyed heart, not a broken one.

'Oh, you know what I mean. Do you think you'll have a holiday romance? To help you get over Dermot?'

'Not unless Lainey has a few spare men tucked away in her flat for me, no, I don't think so.'

Lainey had rung daily with travel tips. 'Drink plenty of water during the flight so you don't dehydrate, that causes jetlag,' she'd advised. 'Move your legs a lot, you don't want to get a bloodclot. Bring your own blow-up neck pillow, the ones the airlines supply are like after-dinner mints. Be sure to eat a banana just before you land.'

Lainey hadn't actually explained what good the banana might do. In any case, Eva had barely been able to fit in what she did want to bring without worrying about a bunch of bananas.

Ambrose had given her a big hug and wished her well. 'With your holiday and your decision-making,' he'd said quietly.

She reached the top of the queue at last, and handed her travel documents over with relief. 'I'm sorry, I know I'm late, my flight from Dublin was delayed. Honestly I thought I wouldn't make it, I can't tell you how glad I am to see you.'

Behind the counter, the woman was ignoring her, tapping away at the keyboard, her long fingernails making rhythmic clicks against the plastic. 'I'm sorry, madam, but that flight is fully booked.'

Eva felt a cold rush down her spine. 'I beg your pardon?'

'There isn't actually a seat available on that flight at the moment.'

'Oh please, there must be. It wasn't my fault the plane from Dublin was delayed. My ticket has been confirmed, there must be room for me.'

Another clickety-click of fingertips on the keyboard. 'I can get you from Singapore to Melbourne, it's the London to Singapore leg that seems to be oversubscribed. You're on a waiting list, there's every chance you'll get on.'

Waiting list? Every chance? This was some start to her big adventure. She couldn't even get out of Heathrow. Eva started to blame herself, thinking she should have got an earlier flight from Dublin. She shouldn't have run with this crackpot idea in the first place. She should have stayed put in Ireland for her holidays. Kilkenny was supposed to be nice this time of year –

No, don't think like that. Stand up for yourself. This problem with the seat isn't your fault. You've paid for your ticket. Surely they can find room for you?

Exactly. Eva had worked in the delicatessen long enough to know that politeness would get her much further than aggression. 'I really do need to be on that plane to Australia tonight. And my luggage is already on its way through to Melbourne. Surely it would be far too inconvenient to unload it at this stage?'

The woman sighed, looked at the queue stretching behind Eva and called over to a young man in a suit passing behind the counter. 'Ray, can you deal with this? A seat allocation situation.'

Eva flashed the young man the biggest smile she could muster, praying that her dimple had chosen this moment to appear. She needed all the help she could get. She'd even waggle her lovely eyebrows at him if she had to.

The young man looked solemnly at her, then at her ticket and passport. 'Miss Eva Kennedy, travelling from Dublin, is that right?' He had an American accent. She nodded.

'I'll take over here, Janice.' He moved to the neighbouring computer terminal, unattended at that moment. 'Now, Miss Kennedy, let's see what we can do here. I'm actually hoping to get over to Ireland for a long holiday next month, when my placement here finishes. My grandmother was from Tipperary and my great-grandfather on the other side was from Offaly, he came out to the States in the 1840s . . .'

Oh holy God, Eva thought, fighting a growing feeling of panic. Was this really the time to hear about his family tree? She smiled fixedly as he told her about his great-aunt Tilly who had traced all his ancestors several years ago. He was certainly very well informed. 'It's A Long Way To Tipperary' started playing in her head.

The young man finally finished the story of his family tree, clicked away at the keyboard then beamed at Eva. 'Now, ma'am, you'll need to be quick. Take this card and run as quickly as you can to that counter down there. Ignore any queues. Just give them this and tell them Ray said they should look after you.'

She smiled in huge relief. 'Thanks, Ray. And I hope you enjoy Ireland when you get there.'

The other counter was halfway to the end of the departure hall. She was breathless by the time she got there. 'Ray said . . .'

The middle-aged woman listened to her explanation, took the card and tapped at a keyboard. 'Yes, Miss Kennedy, we have managed to find you a seat. An upgrade. I'm sure you won't mind. You'll be travelling to Singapore business class this evening. Boarding through gate thirty-one at this moment. Have a good journey.'

There must have been a terrible mistake, Joseph thought. They must have accidentally put him in the children's seats. Surely they didn't think an adult could sit in this position for more than twenty hours? He'd come out atrophied, like one of the Pompeii earthquake victims, frozen solid in a bent position for the rest of his life. He moved around again, trying to stretch his legs. He could hardly feel his feet and his neck was aching. And they hadn't even taken off yet.

At least he had the window seat, through some minor miracle. And the two seats beside him were free. He might manage to contort his body in such a way that he could half lie down.

A loud racket at the front of the plane broke into his thoughts. Over the headrests in front of him he watched as two twenty-something males weaved their way down the aisle. One was dressed in a Princess Diana commemorative sweater, the other in a dirty yellow T-shirt bearing the slogan 'I went to London and all I could afford was this bloody T-shirt'. Joseph ducked as one of them threw something in his direction. The object bounced into the empty seats beside him. It was an oval-shaped red leather ball.

One of the pair scooped it up in big, shovel-sized hands. 'Sorry about that, mate,' he said in a broad Australian accent. Joseph was about to say something in return but he was already being ignored. He watched as the young man held the ball aloft while his friend took a series of photos with a battered-looking camera.

'This footy's been right round Europe with us,' one of the pair explained to a harassed flight attendant.

'How lovely,' she said in a distracted voice.

'Please take your seats, gentlemen. We're about to commence take-off.'

'Gentlemen? Us?' The pair fell about laughing at the idea as they threw their duty-free bags with a clank into the overhead locker, then settled into the seats beside Joseph.

The blond-haired one leaned across. 'Gidday, mate. Better introduce ourselves, seeing as we'll be sitting next to each other on this flight, eh? I'm Doug from Melbourne and this is my mate Shorts. Cos he's so tall, geddit?'

In the business-class section fifteen rows from Joseph's seat, Eva stretched luxuriously. What next, a long bath in asses' milk? A flight attendant feeding her peeled grapes? She felt like the Queen of Sheba. A supermodel and royal princess rolled into one.

Not that she had much to compare it to – a few three-hour flights to Mediterranean holiday resorts with some school friends had been the extent of her long-haul travelling. But she'd heard plenty of horror stories from customers when she told them she was flying to Australia.

'You'll need a week to get over the flight,' one had prophesied. 'It's endless,' another had added. 'Apparently all you do is eat plastic food and sleep with your head in your neighbour's armpit.' 'It'll be horrific,' they'd said as one.

Oh no it wasn't, Eva thought, smiling serenely as the flight attendant offered her a choice of champagne or wine.

'Champagne would be just perfect,' she said graciously.

Joseph now knew he was in Dante's inferno. His hopes that the flight would be a time of quiet contemplation about his father, the Canadian offer and the seat designs had dissolved hours ago. It was just as well he'd finished writing his conference speech the night before, rather than write it on the plane, too. The two Australians beside him were now into their fifth round of a drinking competition. Their seat trays were overflowing with beer cans and miniature whisky bottles. Shorts was virtually unconscious, his mouth open, his loud snores punctuated by burps.

The two were on their way home after twelve months backpacking around Europe, Shorts had explained to Joseph just before they'd begun their drinking spree. 'These are our last hours of freedom, Joe, so we're making the most of it. Doug's off to medical school, I'm studying to be a vet. We turn back into grown-ups the moment we get off this plane.'

He'd never really had those carefree days himself, Joseph thought now. Never had a year off to do what he liked, travel around, take it easy. He'd gone straight from school to university to starting his own company. And the success of his very first design, the ergonomic office chair, had meant he'd been pushed into the world of business straight away, dealing with manufacturers keen to buy his designs, managing projects, hiring staff. At the start it had just been him in a small office. Now he had a PA, a financial consultant and a team of designers working for him.

He felt exhausted again just thinking about them all. Covering his head with the complimentary paper-thin blanket, he shut his eyes and tried, once more, to sleep.

'That's wonderful, thank you,' Eva said as the flight attendant helped her convert her comfortable seat into a completely flat bed.

'You're welcome, madam. Pleasant dreams.'

Eva settled herself under the blanket. She felt a little bit odd, all tucked up, with the other business-class travellers lying around her. It was like being in a boarding-school dormitory. If she started a chant or a singsong, would they all join in? she wondered. She surreptitiously looked around. No, she seemed to be the only one who hadn't done this a hundred times before. Certainly the only one who was thanking the flight attendant for every little thing.

She couldn't wait to tell Lainey about it. Mind you, Lainey probably wouldn't be surprised. She'd no doubt talked her way into upgrades plenty of times. Lainey was very good at things like that. Taking control. Getting things done. She always had been, even when they were children, growing up in the same street in Dunshaughlin. Lainey had been the one in charge from the beginning, inventing games, making the decisions, never short of ideas. They'd be world-famous child popstars, she'd decided at the age of ten. An Irish version of The Osmonds or the Jacksons. Unfortunately Lainey was tone deaf and couldn't play an instrument. But Eva loved to sing, and the teacher at school had once publicly praised her singing voice.

'I'll be the brains behind it instead,' Lainey had said confidently. 'I'll write the lyrics and be the manager and you write the music and sing.' Their first joint effort was 'You Threw Me Away (Like A Tissue)', performed to an audience of their parents. Lainey had been disgusted at their reaction. 'You'd think they could have at least *pretended* to like it, wouldn't you?' she'd said to Eva. 'Your mother was nearly *crying* laughing.'

Too bad, Lainey had declared then. We'll be writers instead. The new Jane Austen and Emily Brontë. They got to chapter three of *Love is Leaping*. Then the Olympics had sparked an interest in gymnastics. Which led to ballet. Which led to fashion design. Which led to painting. They'd both been taken aback to discover that Eva had real artistic talent. Lainey had noticed it first.

'Yours really does look like the landscape,' she'd said with surprise after they'd spent the day painting at the Hill of Tara. 'Mine just looks like the bottom of a pond.'

Eva had shyly agreed. It wasn't often that she was better than Lainey at something. But her painting did look good, the different shades of green and brown and light blue and muddy white nearly mirroring the panoramic view in front of them.

They had to exploit this new-found talent, Lainey decided. Eva could paint a Hill of Tara series. They could sell them to the tourists at weekends and during the summer holidays. 'We can set up a little stall, dress up in Irish dancing costumes so we look like the real thing, sell the lot and make an absolute fortune. What do you think?'

But then Lainey's parents had dropped the bombshell. The family was emigrating to Australia. Her father had decided that his building skills would be much better appreciated in Melbourne than they were in Ireland. Despite huge opposition from Mr Byrne's much older sister, who said he was a traitor for abandoning Ireland, the decision was made. The whole family was going: Mr and Mrs Byrne, fifteen-year-old Lainey and her three little brothers. They were leaving in a month's time.

It hadn't been the end of their friendship. They'd written letters, made phone calls and then, more recently, sent emails. Lainey had been back to

Ireland twice, once with her family at the age of eighteen, then again on her own when she was twenty-three. Eva thought about that trip again now, the last time she'd seen Lainey. Eight years ago. It had nearly been the end of their friendship . . .

She stopped her train of thought right there. There was no point dwelling in the past. That was all behind them now. It would be completely different this time. They were both older, for a start. More settled. It would be just great, she decided. Two weeks of fun and laughs. She was really looking forward to seeing how Lainey lived and hearing all about her job with the event management company. Seeing her family again. Asking her advice about Ambrose's offer.

And finding out once and for all exactly what happened between her and Martin eight years ago?

No, no, there was no need to bring any of that up. It was a long time ago. She'd got over it. And she was sure Lainey wouldn't want to talk about it anyway.

Chicken.

She wasn't being chicken. She just didn't want to spoil this holiday, for either of them.

And besides, the issue wouldn't arise anyway. There'd be no men to come between them this time, would there?

Joseph shifted in his seat again, trying once more to find a comfortable position. Was Australia on the other side of the planet or the other side of the solar system? They'd been flying for more than ten hours already and were still nowhere near Singapore. It would have helped if he'd been able to unscrew his legs and put them in the overhead locker. Or if he'd been three foot tall rather than six foot tall. He felt like a battery hen.

At least he'd finished his research into the comfort level of long-haul economy seats. It had been very simple. There was no comfort level. Perhaps he should have followed Doug and Shorts' example and drunk himself into alcohol-induced unconsciousness. They were now snoring loudly beside him. He reached up and switched on the overhead light. If he couldn't sleep, he'd read.

Twenty minutes later he put the book down again. It was no good. He wasn't concentrating. He'd read the same page five times. There wasn't room in his head for a story. It was already filled with thoughts about his father.

He leaned down, took out the photograph of Lewis from the bag at his feet and looked at it again. He wondered where it had been taken. Who had taken it. There was countryside in the background, the edge of a building, but it was difficult to make out any details.

He could see a resemblance between them. The

eyes, was it? Or the shape of the face. Something, in any case. What would Lewis's voice be like? he wondered. He'd been living in Australia for many years now. Would he have an Australian accent?

He should have asked Kate more about him. As a child he'd had plenty of questions about Lewis, about why they'd divorced. Sometimes Kate had answered, sometimes she'd seemed too upset. 'It was very complicated, Joseph. But it wasn't your fault, I promise you that.' It was all she'd say. If it wasn't his fault, why hadn't Lewis been in contact with him then? He'd asked that question more than once. 'It was very complicated,' Kate would repeat. He'd finally stopped asking.

But now here was his chance to get some answers. He looked at the address on the back of the photograph again. The Clare Valley, South Australia. He made his decision. He was going to go there.

Eva looked at her watch. What a shame, only another two hours to go before they reached Singapore. Then she'd hit the ground with a bump, in more ways than one. How on earth would she cope with economy class from Singapore to Melbourne now she'd had a taste of the high life?

'Orange juice, madam?' the flight attendant said beside her.

She smiled up at him. 'Would a glass of champagne be completely out of the question?'

As they started the descent into Singapore and Doug gave another shuddering snore beside him, Joseph made one more decision. As soon as they arrived in Singapore, he was going to the ticket desk and paying for an upgrade for his flight to Sydney.

And he was never flying economy class again.

CHAPTER EIGHT

EVA SPOTTED Lainey just seconds after she came through the automatic doors into Melbourne airport. Lainey was hard to miss, waving wildly from the back of the crowd.

Several people turned to watch as they hugged each other: the tall, tanned woman, her dark brown hair cut short to frame her face; the shorter, pale-skinned, dark-eyed woman with the long black plait.

'Look at you, you gorgeous thing. I can't believe you're actually here.' Lainey was nearly in tears.

'Get away out of that,' Eva laughed at her. 'Didn't I always threaten to do it? And look at you. Have you just come from the Businesswoman of the Year Awards, or do you always look like this?'

Lainey had come straight to the airport from her office. She glanced down at her work clothes, a modern tailored suit and very high shoes. 'These old things? Oh no, this is my jogging outfit. Now, come on, let's get you home. I'm sure that flight was murder.'

'Not all of it, actually.' Eva quickly filled Lainey in on her business-class experience. 'It made the last leg bearable, I just kept reminiscing.'

'Well, now, don't you be getting any high and mighty ideas with me,' Lainey laughed as she grabbed Eva's suitcase and went striding out to the carpark. She started climbing up the stairs to the third level. 'Come on, Evie, the lifts here take years,' she said over her shoulder as she set a cracking pace, talking all the while.

They walked past two rows of cars before Lainey stopped next to a very flash sports car and started fumbling in her bag for keys. 'Hold on a second, I'll just open up the boot.'

She noticed Eva's expression. 'Go on, you're impressed, aren't you?'

'Very.'

'Then I'm sorry to disappoint you.' Lainey turned to the car parked beside it, a small red hatchback. 'This one's actually mine.'

As they drove out of the carpark onto the freeway, Eva felt like a child on her first car trip. She waited for her first real glimpse of Australia, her nose practically pressed against the window. The sky was huge. The trees outside looked different. The light was brighter.

Lainey smiled at her. 'Well, Miss Newly-arrived-from-Ireland, your first impressions?'

'That blue stuff, up in the air, what's that called? I don't think I've ever seen it at home.'

'We call it the sky here in Australia. Pretty, isn't it? You have a grey version of it in Ireland, I believe.'

'Oh yes, so we do. Ours produces water, as well.'

'Really? How clever.'

It was how Eva had imagined America to look, not Australia. The big blue sky. Wide freeways. Beyond them groups of detached houses, each of a different design, all with their own good-sized garden, not like the rows and rows of identical houses that made up many of Dublin's housing estates. But not a kangaroo or red sandy desert in sight. It was quite a disappointment.

The half-hour drive was a jumble of quick conversations, half-sentences, rushes of questions. Speaking in headlines, Lainey called it. As they got closer to the forest of tall buildings in the city centre, she finally put a stop to it. 'I can't drive and concentrate at the same time and I'll just ask you all the same questions tonight anyway, I know. Will I take you for a quick tour instead? You're probably so jet-lagged you won't even remember it, but I'm trying to be the ideal hostess.'

'That'd be brilliant. But just speak slowly, will you, till I get used to that Australian accent coming out of your mouth. I keep thinking you've been taken over by an alien being.'

'Oh, sure now, love, is this better? I can speak in

the tongue of the auld country at the drop of a hat, you've only to ask now, do you hear?' Lainey answered in a stage Irish accent.

Eva laughed. She remembered the first time she'd heard Lainey's new Australian accent, during a phone call years before. 'I had to do it,' her friend had explained from Melbourne. 'You try and survive in an Australian school with an Irish accent. All the teasing. Tirty-tree this and tirty-tree that. It was driving me bananas.'

Lainey's tour of Melbourne's city centre went past in a flash. She pointed out gracious old buildings with iron-lacework balconies, surrounded by gardens and parks. The long streets were lined with leafy oak trees, alluring shops side by side with elegant restaurants. The footpaths were crowded with people. It reminded her of London, Eva decided, all stylish and bright and bustling. London with bright green and yellow trams. And clean streets. And much better weather.

Lainey was watching Eva's reactions with great enjoyment. 'It's not as speccy as Sydney, I know, but I love it.'

'Speccy? As in speccy four-eyes?'

Lainey laughed. 'Lesson one in how to speak like an Australian. Abbreviate everything. Speccy is short for spectacular. Now, whistlestop tour over, time to see your home for the next couple of weeks.'

She expertly turned the car back in the other

direction, whipping along to get past a tram and calling out more landmarks as she drove past them. 'You won't remember any of these but at least I'll know I've done my job properly. That's the Melbourne Cricket Ground there and the Tennis Centre to the right, that big white thing. This city is sports mad, you'll discover. And that's the river there. If you think the Liffey is bad, wait till you have a good look at the Yarra. It flows upside down, with the mud at the top.'

A left turn and a right turn and they were driving down another street, this one lined with Asian shops and restaurants. Piled outside the shops were brightly coloured displays of fruit and vegetables – mangoes, bananas, pineapples and green leafy bunches. The windows were covered in handwritten signs in Asian lettering. Roast ducks and chickens were hanging in the spotlit front windows. There were family groups strolling along, dark-haired kids playing up, running in and out of shop doorways past elderly women sitting on low chairs in the shade.

'This apparently used to be a real Greek area in the fifties,' Lainey explained, slowing the car so Eva could take it all in. 'Then the Greek families moved on to other areas of the city and the Vietnamese people moved in here and took their place. This street's like a haven for each new wave of immigrant groups.'

'And where's the Irish haven?'

'Every pub, Evie, surely you know that yourself.

No, we've infiltrated their very marrow by this stage. Scratch most Australians and you'll find a bit of green blood.'

Minutes later Lainey pulled into the kerb in front of a row of three-storey apartments. Eva guessed it had once been an industrial area, with old warehouses now beside newly built apartment complexes.

Lainey climbed out, moving around quickly to open Eva's door for her. 'Welcome to the very fashionable suburb of Richmond. I usually park in the underground carpark, but three flights of stairs will be enough with your case as it is. What have you brought with you, for God's sake – the Rock of Cashel?' All this was said as Lainey dragged the case out of the boot and started hauling it up the stairs to the third floor. She stopped at the final landing, unlocked the door and threw it back dramatically. 'Here it is, Evie, home sweet home.'

Eva leapt back as something small and black brushed past her legs and ran out through the door.

'Oh, bloody hell, not again. Hang on, Evie.' Lainey turned and ran down the stairs, shouting something that sounded like 'Hexie' to Eva's ears. A few minutes later she was back, clutching a little black furry bundle against her chest. She grinned. 'Well, that's a more dramatic introduction than I'd planned, but here he is – my new pet. What do you think?'

Eva took a very big step back.

'Oh, I'm so sorry,' Lainey groaned. 'I completely forgot. You're scared of cats, aren't you?'

'I'm not scared.' Eva was indignant at the idea. 'Just . . .'

'Nervous? Uneasy? Shall I get the thesaurus?'

'Very funny. No, it's none of those things. I'm just not used to them, that's all.'

'It's your sister's fault, if you ask me. Her and her asthma. Depriving you of pets as a child. A terrible state of affairs.' Lainey was now holding the purring kitten with one hand and Eva's suitcase with the other. 'I reckon it was just attention-seeking behaviour. Do you remember she used to make me take my coat off before I came into your house? She said I was always covered in so much fur, she was never sure if I was all human or half-beast. But never mind, here's your chance to have a pet at last. And such a perfect specimen to start with, aren't you, Rexie?' She rubbed her face against the kitten's fur.

Eva pulled a face. How could Lainey do that? 'Rexie, did you say? I thought you were calling him Hexie. That you'd joined a witches' coven and just hadn't broken it to me yet.'

Lainey laughed. 'Hexie? Oh no, it's much more interesting than that. When I first got him, you see, sometimes he would try to mew but no sound would come out. You'd just see this wide-open mouth and spiky little teeth. And he reminded me of those old dinosaur movies – you know, the ones using time-lapse photography, with the plastic models opening their mouths and giving those long roars?'

Eva slowly nodded, wondering if she could blame the jetlag for this conversation.

'So that's why I called him Tyrannosaurus Rex. Rex for short.' Lainey beamed at her.

Eva had thought she knew Lainey well. Strong, authoritative Lainey. No-nonsense Lainey. The sort of woman who would have an alsatian for a pet. Or a forthright toucan. But a small black kitten? Called Tyrannosaurus Rex?

'Well, Evie, what do you think of him? Isn't he sweet?'

Eva looked at Rex. Rex looked at Eva and gave a slow blink. 'Oh yes, he's gorgeous. Adorable. Straight off a chocolate box.'

'And you could grow to love him, couldn't you?'

Rex was now looking right at Eva, his tongue sticking out, halted mid-lick. Eva was tempted to poke her own tongue back at him. 'I'll certainly do my best.'

'And you wouldn't mind looking after him while I'm away?'

Lainey hadn't mentioned *this* in any of the preflight phone calls. 'You want me to grow to love him *and* look after him? What does look after mean, exactly? Feed him? Talk to him? Pat him?'

'Could you? Would you? Please?'

'Tell you what, Lainey, how about I pay to put him in a cat holiday home while you're in Brisbane?

I could go and visit him every week. Bring him photos of you to look at.' Eva was only half-joking.

'No way. I've only had him a few weeks. He's only just learned this is his home. If he went to a cat home I'd have to start from scratch all over again when I came back. He'd be psychologically disturbed.'

'Lainey, Rex is a kitten. Not your five-year-old son.'

'I can't even joke about it. That's why I was especially delighted that you decided to come here.' Lainey groaned. 'I'm sorry, that sounded terrible. The main thing was seeing you, of course. But it also meant Rex could stay here, in his new house. It really would have set us both back if he'd had to leave home so soon.'

'What would you have done if I hadn't come over? You weren't seriously going to take him to Brisbane with you?'

'Well, actually I did consider it. Then I did a deal with my neighbour Adam downstairs. He'd take Rex down to his flat while I was away and look after him there. The layout's the same, and the view from the window is almost the same, so I hoped it wouldn't be too disorienting for Rex. And in return I'd invite Adam up for dinner when I got back. He says he feels like he's at my dinner parties anyway, we're always so noisy, so he may as well come up and enjoy the food. And he's always telling me he loves cats.'

'That cat-sitting just sounds like a ruse for him

to get to know you better. It sounds to me like he fancies you.'

'Yes, I think he does.'

Eva noticed Lainey wasn't even surprised at the idea. It was as if she expected it. But of course she did, because men always fell in love with Lainey, didn't they? In Ireland as well as Australia. Eva pushed down a memory that was trying to force itself to the surface.

'But now poor Adam has missed his chance because you're here, you gorgeous thing,' Lainey said as she put Rex on the floor. 'And you *don't* mind looking after him, do you? Not really?'

Eva knew full well she didn't really have a choice. She looked at her friend, all beaming good humour and enthusiasm. 'Of course I don't mind,' she said, giving in. It was usually simpler in the long run.

'You're a star, Evie.' Lainey hugged her again. 'And look at you. You look great, really great. That skin of yours is like fresh cream. I'm all leathery like a crocodile now, too much sun.'

Eva shook her head. Lainey was not in the least bit leathery. 'You look fantastic. Like you should be a model in an ad for a new deodorant or track shoe or something.'

'Enough of that flattery. Come on, let me show you around.'

Eva's house in Stoneybatter could have fitted twice into Lainey's apartment, which took up the entire floor of the building. Lainey proudly showed it off – a large kitchen and dining area, her bedroom, with an ensuite bathroom complete with spa bath.

'And this is your bedroom.' Lainey took her by the hand and opened the door with a flourish. It was a large room, with a big window overlooking a park opposite, with factories and storage buildings beyond. The double bed was piled with pillows and cushions, the wardrobe open, showing plenty of empty coathangers and hanging space, ready for Eva's things. There were three vases of flowers.

'This is just fantastic, Lainey. Thanks a million. For all of this.'

'It's my pleasure. My house is your house. Now, come out here again, I want to show you the best bit.'

As they walked back through the kitchen, Lainey pointed at one of the shelves, covered in framed photos. 'I'm dying to show you all those as well. They're all of you and me, through the years. I had a ball going through all the photos, choosing the best ones of us.'

Eva picked up the closest one, a black and white shot of the pair of them, aged about six, dressed in their school uniforms and staring solemnly into the camera. Beside it was a Hallowe'en night photo, Eva dressed as a witch, Lainey as an angel, both aged ten. Another of them as teenagers, dressed in sunglasses and lipstick. They'd probably been pretending to be famous popstars or actresses.

Lainey was practically skipping with impatience. 'Evie, later, there's plenty of time for photos, come and see this first.'

Eva had just turned in Lainey's direction when a large frame at the back caught her eye. She picked it up. She hadn't seen this photo in years. Not since she'd ripped her own copy up.

Lainey came back and glanced at it. 'Oh yes, that one. That was when I was back in Ireland last, do you remember? What age were we? Twenty-one? Twenty-two?'

'Twenty-three,' Eva said firmly. They both looked down at the photo – Eva in unbecoming pigtails, Lainey beaming confidently at the camera, and in between them a young, good-looking man, his arm around them both.

'What was his name, Evie, do you remember?'

Eva blinked. Had she heard that right? She turned to Lainey. 'What was his name? Are you joking me? You can't remember?'

'Come on, it was years ago. God, my memory only lasts about a month these days. Anyway, let's look at those later, I've heaps to show you.' Lainey had lost interest in the photo already, eager to continue her tour.

Eva felt a bit strange. It wasn't just the jetlag. Surely Lainey hadn't meant to be so dismissive. Of course Lainey could remember his name, she probably just hadn't tried hard enough. Or she'd blocked it out. Or something.

Lainey's voice floated over from the living room. 'Evie? You haven't fallen asleep, have you?'

'Sorry, no, I'm coming.' She came out of the kitchen, willing herself to smile, to relax, not to be upset about it. Come on, Evie, you're in Melbourne, she told herself. This is Australia. Enjoy yourself. Forget about all that business. Think of it as maturity, knowing when to say something and when to stay quiet.

Maturity? That's one word for it.

And what's another word?

Cowardice.

Oh, shut up, Eva thought.

'Ta-daaa!' Lainey declared as she opened up two glass doors and stepped outside onto a balcony.

Eva followed her out, uncomfortably conscious that Rex was close behind her. She gazed around. 'Oh, Lainey, this is gorgeous,' she said. 'You lucky thing.' It was like being in the country, not just a few minutes from the centre of the city. The balcony looked out over a big mass of trees. Just beyond the greenery was the River Yarra, flowing quickly past and then disappearing around a long bend. As they stood there, they could hear shouts from passing rowers floating up. Listening hard, Eva could hear the rumble of trams in the distance.

Lainey clapped her hands then, giving both Eva and Rex a fright. 'Come on, Evie, have a shower, put on some fresh clothes and I'll take you on another tour. Frighten that jetlag out of you. I know you're tired but I'm not letting you go to bed for *hours*.'

They were soon back in the car, once again zipping through the traffic. 'We're off to St Kilda, Evie,' Lainey announced. 'The groovy part of town. And my second home, of course.'

'Of course.' Eva saw a row of palm trees ahead. Then a sudden blue flash of water – the sea, glinting and flashing in the bright sunlight. They drove along the Esplanade, past a big white pub, a multi-storeyed hotel and an assortment of colourful and quirky-looking apartments.

Trams sped past them, halting here and there, passengers casually clambering on and off, strolling across the road as the traffic stopped for them. Eva took in every detail – the relaxed mood, the music blaring from cars and shops, the stylish crowds. Tattoos and nose-rings seemed to be the look of the day. Dreadlocks. A few shaved heads. And lots of tanned and toned skin.

They had just parked and started walking along the street when a sudden collection of squeals flashed through the air. Eva jumped, while Lainey just walked on unperturbed. She smiled at her friend. 'It's the kids on the fairground ride. At Luna Park, just over there.'

She pointed beyond a fast-food restaurant to a brightly coloured gateway.

They finally reached the bar and cafe Lainey had in mind. Two streets back from the main shopping street, on the far edge of St Kilda, it took up the ground floor of an old stone building. Ivy and flowers spilled over from planter boxes outside.

'The owner of this place is actually a friend of mine,' Lainey whispered as she and Eva waited at the reception desk in the centre of the bar. Eva looked around, taking a few moments while her eyes adjusted from the bright light outside. It was a very large room, filled with people. She turned in a circle, taking it all in. Each corner of the cafe was decorated in a completely different style. One corner was tropical, like a Hawaiian bar. The next was a stark and stylish black and white. The third was like a 1970s lounge room, all funky sofas and lampshades. The fourth was straight off the *Casablanca* film set, all whirring overhead fans and a big piano, currently silent.

As the receptionist found a table for them, Lainey spoke to Eva in a low tone. 'My friend made his money running one of those Irish theme pubs, then sold out of that to start this. He's about to open another one in Carlton, on the other side of town. Can you work out what it's actually called?'

Eva stared at the logo. It was the number four over the number four, like a mathematical equation. 'Four out of four?'

'It is a bit obscure, isn't it? It's actually Four Quarters, do you see?'

'No, not really. What does it mean?'

'This city is completely football mad – Australian Rules, you know it?'

Eva nodded.

'Each game has four quarters, so he picked up the idea and called it after that. His designers change the look of the four quarters every few months, to keep people interested. The last lot were great – a space-age area, a French cafe, a florist's shop and a 1950s milk bar. People give him suggestions too, for what they'd like to see. It's like a grown-up version of the lands at the top of the Faraway Tree, don't you reckon?'

Eva nodded. It was a very simple idea that could have looked very odd. But it obviously worked – each quarter was jammed with people.

'He even serves different sorts of food in each quarter,' Lainey said. 'It's really taken off. Especially at night-time. People start in one corner and work their way around.'

They were shown to a table in the Hawaiian section. Eva sat back while Lainey went to the bar. She felt half drunk already. Jetlag was actually quite pleasant, she decided. As though nothing around you was real.

Lainey came back with the drinks. 'Cosmopolitans, just the thing for us international gals.

Now, shall I quickly bring you up to date with my boyfriend sagas, just to set the scene?'

Eva smiled. These were exactly the sort of conversations she'd been looking forward to. That other stuff, the photo, all that had happened ten years ago, it was in the past. She'd leave it there, she decided, where it belonged. She nodded. 'Yes, please. Every one of them.'

'Well, you know about Peter, from two years ago. Short but very sweet. Him, not the relationship. But no zing, so we broke up. Then I had a long-distance fling with a fellow from the Sydney office. But then I was promoted and he wasn't, so that ruined that. I've had a few dates since, and dear old Adam downstairs is eager and hopeful, but as you can see, I'm actually single at the moment. Have been for a year now. Criminal, isn't it?'

'What's wrong with the men in this city? Are they blind?'

'Oh, I've had the offers,' Lainey said. 'But I don't want quantity, I want quality. I'm too old to waste time dilly-dallying around, trying new ones on for size and finding out too late they don't fit properly. I'm waiting for the real one now, I've decided. Mr Gorgeous. The one that makes me weak at the knees. Makes my heart skip a beat. Makes my stomach swirl –'

'You're not waiting for Mr Gorgeous. You're waiting for Mr Cholera.'

Lainey laughed and held up her drink. 'Exactly.

To Mr Cholera! Now, what about you and a nice holiday romance? That's what you need, isn't it? What about I ask Greg to the dinner party and you can see what you think of him?'

'Who is Greg? And what dinner party?'

'Didn't I tell you? I'm having a dinner party the night before I go to Brisbane so some of my friends can meet you. I just hope Greg will be able to make it at this short notice.'

'Lainey, slow down. Who is Greg?'

'The guy that owns this cafe. He's mad about anything to do with Ireland, I know he'd love to meet you. And now I think of it, I reckon he's exactly what you need to get over Dermot.'

Eva looked at her friend and shook her head. 'Exactly when *did* you become a matchmaker, Lainey Byrne?'

Lainey grinned and held up her glass in a toast. 'About ten seconds ago.'

In Sydney at that same moment, Joseph stood at the window of his hotel room, his mobile phone to his ear. In front of him was the harbour, all blue glinting water and white sails. To his right was the Sydney Opera House. To his left he could just see the Sydney Harbour Bridge. This felt more like a tourism commercial than a work trip, he thought.

'Joseph? You there?'

'Sorry, Dave. Distracted by the view from my window.'

His university friend gave a booming laugh. 'Wait till you see what I'm organising for Friday night, then. The finest wine, women and song Sydney has to offer. So I'll see you at my place at Bondi, okay? Around nine?'

Joseph noticed the upward inflection at the end of each sentence. 'Dave, is that the beginnings of an Australian accent I hear? Already?'

'If you can't beat them, join them, that's my motto. Anyway, better go. Welcome again, enjoy your conference and see you Friday. *Ciao!*'

'You're speaking Italian as well as Australian?'

'German as well. *Aufwiedersehen!*'

Joseph laughed. 'Goodbye. See you Friday.'

He checked the time. He'd been in Australia for four hours and had already managed to get some work done, before he'd even left the airport. Standing at the luggage carousel, he'd watched bags of all shapes and sizes emerge through the rubber curtain and begin their sashay on the moving catwalk. The designer in him had dismissed key elements in most of them. Too gaudy. Too rigid. Too unwieldy. Some were just dead ugly. He kept a particular watch for backpacks, though there were few brands he hadn't already studied in great detail. Some were so full they were nearly bursting. One or two actually had rips. The material he'd used in his backpack made a rip nearly impossible. He saw one backpack with what appeared to be a nappy taped onto the backstraps, presumably for extra comfort. He'd thought of that too. His design had cotton wadding built into the strap material.

A driver had been waiting for him at the airport concourse, holding up a sign bearing his name. Twenty minutes later he'd arrived at this stylish waterside hotel, where two porters, speaking into headsets, had been waiting to greet him at the lobby. He'd been checked in before he even reached the desk, his key being passed over with a flourish. His room was more like a fashionable apartment than a sterile hotel suite. There had been a welcome card awaiting him from the conference organiser, with a reminder about the technical rehearsal at the nearby venue later that afternoon.

He checked the time. He wasn't due there for another two hours. But he'd slept well in his business-class seat from Singapore to Sydney, he didn't need to go to bed. And he was in work mode now. He might as well go there and get it under way.

What was he talking about, he was in work mode now? He was always in work mode these days. He picked up his presentation notes and headed out the door.

CHAPTER NINE

IN DUBLIN, Meg was taking herself on a tour around the contents of the front-counter display cabinet, notebook in hand.

Sitting in the storeroom, Ambrose overheard her muttering to herself.

'Goats' cheese. Artichoke hearts. Anchovies. Semi-dried tomatoes . . . what's this one, Uncle Ambrose?'

He peered out. She was holding something up in a pair of tongs.

Standing up with a small groan, he walked closer. 'That's pickled ginger. You use it in Chinese food.'

'Oh, right. I *love* Chinese food. We did a few classes at Ardmahon House about international food and my teacher Maura said that one day there won't be such a thing as regional cooking. That as the world gets smaller, as people keep travelling the world so much, all the different cuisines will get mixed up. And it's getting like that in Dublin already, isn't it, with all those new restaurants? And here too, Uncle Ambrose – in fact, you're a trendsetter, aren't you? Bringing in lots of Italian and Greek and other foreign food to Ireland, don't you think?'

By God, this young one could talk, he thought, watching as she moved across to the olive oil section of the shop. She was like a wind-up toy. An over-wound toy, sometimes. So different to Eva's grown-up ways and ever-ready humour. As he walked back to the storeroom, Ambrose thought of Eva's surprise when he offered her the shop. What would she decide? he wondered. To stay with the shop or go back to her art studies? He really didn't know. It was so hard to tell with Eva sometimes. She was one to keep her thoughts to herself. He liked that about her. He liked a lot of things about her. She was a lovely girl, warm and friendly, terrific with the customers. Such a shame she had so little confidence in herself. Ambrose knew she had it in her to run the shop, manage the whole business. He just hoped she knew it too.

With a sigh, he took out the stepladder. Time to get back to work. He'd climbed two steps when Meg's voice behind him made him jump.

'Uncle Ambrose! What are you doing up there?'

'The storeroom clean-up, Meg. The job Eva and I dread each year.'

'Oh, can I help you to do it? I love this sort of thing. I could even set up a system, reorganise it a bit, if you like.'

Ambrose looked around the little room. The storeroom had never been in any particular order but they had all muddled along very happily. So what if it sometimes took a bit longer to find things than it should? What was the rush? But there was Meg, itching to get stuck into it. Oh why not? he thought. If Eva came back and agreed to take over the shop, it would be a good thing for her. And if Eva came back and said she didn't want to take over the shop, then it would make it easier to pack everything up in readiness for selling.

'Yes, you can, Meg. Let me get myself a chair here in the doorway. I'll be the general, directing from afar. You be the soldier on the battlefield.'

Meg beamed at him. Now she really felt like she was helping out. She put her hands on her hips and looked around. 'It is in a bit of a mess, isn't it? But I'll have it all sorted out in no time. Now, what about I put all the pasta and grain in one corner? And the dried produce and all the fruit and nuts could go together too. That way you could come in and get just what you needed, quick as a flash, couldn't you?'

Ambrose nodded weakly. He wondered if he'd made a mistake giving Eva that extra week off after all.

CHAPTER TEN

'FEEL LIKE a nightcap, Evie? Out on the balcony?'

'Great idea.' Eva opened the double doors and went outside, breathing in the cool night air, listening to the sounds of Melbourne filtering over.

The city was becoming more familiar to her each day. While Lainey was at work she'd turned into the Queen of the Tourists, catching trams and visiting the zoo, galleries and museums. She'd read the Melbourne restaurant guide from cover to cover, her mouth watering at the descriptions. 'Make a list,' Lainey had urged her. 'We'll try and get to as many as we can.'

Eva liked the sound of the lively Greek taverna in Collingwood. The casual Vietnamese restaurant in Richmond. One of the Spanish tapas bars in Fitzroy. And the tiny bar in a city-centre laneway that sounded like it was all low lighting and high attitude.

Tonight they'd been to Lainey's parents' house in

the outer suburbs for a barbecue. On the way there, they'd taken a detour through the inner-city area of Carlton. 'You've got to see this,' Lainey had said. 'It's called Lygon Street. We're in Carlton, Melbourne's Italian area. You'd swear you were in Milan or Rome some nights.'

Lainey was right. All the footpaths were crowded with tables. Young Italian men were driving slowly up and down the road in hotted up cars, calling out to big-haired, glamorously dressed young women who were doing their best to pretend they were ignoring them.

'It smells like garlic and coffee and something, doesn't it?' she said.

'It's garlic and coffee and sex, if you ask me,' Lainey asked. 'This street is like a mating pen.'

From there they'd driven on to Lainey's parents. Mr and Mrs Lainey, Eva called them. She had since she was five. Her mother had once heard her calling them by their first names and been horrified. 'You have to call them Mr and Mrs,' Mrs Kennedy had said. 'It's only polite.'

Mr and Mrs what, though? Eva had wondered, too young to understand about surnames. She'd decided on Mr Lainey and Mrs Lainey and it had stuck ever since.

Eva had handed over the presents she'd brought them from Ireland – shortbread and giant bags of Tayto crisps – and caught up on the news since she had last seen them during their first and only holiday back to Ireland, many years previously. Mr Lainey's building company was still doing well, he said, hard work but good. Mrs Lainey was working in the library, assistant to the chief librarian now, and loving it. They hadn't lost their Irish accents at all. The Meath tones were as strong as ever.

Lainey's three brothers were a different story. Eva couldn't believe they were the same three boys. She remembered Brendan, Hugh and Declan as cheeky schoolkids, knock-kneed and pale-skinned. Certainly not the three strapping fellows alternating tossing a football around the back garden with cooking platters of chops and sausages on the enormous barbecue.

Over dinner Mrs Lainey asked what Eva was up to in Dublin these days. She seemed surprised at her answer. 'A shop? I thought Lainey said you'd been to art school.'

Eva remembered then that Lainey had inherited her bluntness from her mother. 'Well, yes, I did go to art school.'

'But you're just working in a shop now?'

Eva nodded. She was tempted to say that perhaps it might soon be *her* shop, but it was still too soon to talk about it. She hadn't even told Lainey yet. She wanted to keep mulling it over in her own head, let her ideas about it settle before she opened them up for scrutiny.

'So you weren't really creative, after all, then? Was it just a phase, do you think?'

Eva had forgotten Mrs Lainey could also be so tactless. 'Well, no, not just a phase. I really do like to paint. And sing, actually. I'm just not doing it for a living at the moment.'

'Oh dear, don't take offence,' Mrs Lainey said quickly. 'There's nothing wrong with working in a shop. What would we do without you shop assistants?' She'd changed the subject then. 'You know, Lainey is practically running that event management company she works for. She's just great. She's worked her way right up to the top, so she has.'

'She's great,' Eva had agreed. But the comparison had been obvious. Lainey had gone from success to success in Australia, while Eva still worked in a shop. Lainey was successful, Eva wasn't.

As Lainey came out on to the balcony now with their drinks, Eva turned to her and blurted out what was on her mind. 'Did *you* always think I was fooling myself about my painting and my singing, Lainey?'

'What?'

'Your ma said perhaps I'd just been going through a phase. When I went to art school. That I wasn't really creative. Dermot said the same thing to me, actually, the night we broke up.'

Lainey flinched at her mother's words. Her mother could be terrible sometimes, speaking without thinking. 'I always loved your paintings. But how long is it since you've done any?'

'A while.' Four years exactly, she thought. Since the day she left art school.

'Why is that, do you think?'

Eva paused. She knew exactly why. 'Oh, I don't know really,' she lied. 'A million reasons. I mean, writers have writer's block –'

'Butchers have butcher's blocks.'

Eva's hackles went up. 'Are you taking this conversation seriously?'

'I'm sorry. You have artist's block, is that what you mean?'

'Yes, I think that's it.' That would do fine, she thought.

'Well, what about your singing, then? You've still got a great voice, haven't you? What happened with that band you used to sing with?'

'I had to give it up when I went full-time at the shop. And it wasn't really a proper band. We just sang everybody else's songs.'

Eva had once sent Lainey a video of the band performing. She had been very impressed. 'So? A cover band's still a band. And I thought you were really good, much as it kills me to say it. I still sound like a howling dog when I sing.'

'You do not.'

'I do. Anyway, you're happy in the shop, aren't you? Or would you like to do something else?'

Eva took a breath. This was the moment to tell her about Ambrose's offer. She told her everything.

Lainey was delighted. 'Evie, that's fantastic. Absolutely brilliant. What a compliment.' Then she noticed her friend's expression. 'Aren't you excited about it? Why do you look like he's handed you a dead fish on a plate?'

Eva laughed at that. 'I *know* Ambrose's offer is fantastic, Lainey, of course I do. But what if I make a mess of it? What if it doesn't work out?'

'Well, you get tried under section two of the Failure to Run a Shop Act and sent to prison, of course. Evie, would you listen to yourself? Of course you can do it. Have some faith, will you?'

That was easy for her to say, Eva thought. The woman who'd never had a moment's self-doubt in her life. 'It's not as simple as that.' She stopped there, wishing she could explain why she hadn't immediately accepted Ambrose's offer. Why it had been going round and round in her head for days. She tried to put some of her thoughts into words. 'It's not just a matter of whether I think I can do it or not. I suppose it's realising that if I do accept it, then I've decided finally, once and for all, that I never will be a success as an artist or a singer. After all those years of thinking that was exactly what I wanted to do, what I wanted to be.' She laughed briefly. 'Someone should invent a machine to show you what your life would have been like if you'd taken a different path, don't you think?'

Lainey smiled. 'Like those machines some hair-dressing salons have, do you mean? Where you give them your photograph and they show you what you'd look like with all different sorts of hairstyles?'

'Exactly. But it would have to be a video, wouldn't it? A one-hour special of edited highlights of your alternative life. Showing the house you'd have lived in, the people you'd have met, the sort of work you would have done.'

'So what would your alternative life have been?' Lainey asked, leaning back in her chair. 'The struggling artist living in the garret, traipsing from gallery to gallery? Or the husky-voiced singer dragging herself from low-paid gig to low-paid gig, bottle of scotch in one hand, cigarette in the other?'

'Oh, neither. I'd have been hugely successful, of course. Gone straight to the top. There'd be no point splashing about in the shallows. Anyway, haven't you always thought I'd make a wonderful famous person? I'd be so kind to my fans. So generous with my wealth. Friend and confidante to the great and the good, sought after by all the TV chat shows . . .'

Lainey grinned in recognition. They'd played this game a lot when they were children. Pretended to be famous popstars or actresses for days on end, swanning about in make-up and fancy dress, talking in fake accents, driving their parents mad. 'Oh, *absolutely*. And I can just see your paintings –'

'No, no, *no*, Lainey, not paintings. I'd have

moved on to sculpting, I think. With my singing as a sideline.'

'Of course. And your name? Would you still be called Eva Kennedy?'

'Oh, no,' Eva said emphatically, 'that's much, much too ordinary. I'd trade on my very fashionable Celtic roots of course. Use an Irish name. An ancient name, dripping in historic significance.' She thought for a moment, before turning to Lainey. 'I'd call myself Niamh. Niamh Kennedy.' She pronounced the Irish name slowly and dramatically – Nee-av.

Lainey sat up straight and started speaking with a very refined English accent into a pretend microphone. 'Welcome back to *Gushing Interviews with Famous People*. We're delighted to have the especially famous and international award-winning Irish sculptor and singer in the studio with us tonight. A big hand please for Miss Niamh Kennedy.'

Eva inclined her head at the imaginary applause.

'So tell me, Niamh, where are you living these days?' Lainey held out the pretend microphone in Eva's direction.

Eva gave a gracious smile. 'Well, I do of course spend part of the year in my castle in Spain. I find the air and the light there agrees with my artistic temperament. But in fact most recently I have been exploring my Celtic heart and soul and I'm currently living and working in a small caravan in the west of Ireland. I find the rugged coastline, the crashing of the seas and the almost tangible mystery in the air,' her voice was now a breathy whisper, 'inspire me so much my sculptures nearly sculpt themselves.'

'Oh, how marvellous for you. And you've had a number of very successful exhibitions recently, I believe?'

'Oh, yes,' Eva said huskily. 'My retrospective, entitled "The Sea: Oh How Dark and Mysterious", has just closed at the Guggenheim in New York and I believe the Tate in London achieved record attendances with my new collection called "Away, Clouds, Oh Airy Beings of Mystery, and Leave My Soul in Peace".'

Lainey nodded solemnly. 'Isn't that splendid. And your music career, Niamh, have you put that on hold?'

'Oh no, not at all. How could I when I have the world's great lining up outside the door of the caravan? It would be almost criminal to turn them down, surely? It's been a busy year for me indeed. In fact, I've only just finished the backing vocals for Enya's new album.'

'Really? Good Lord. I thought Enya did them all herself.'

Eva gave a merry laugh. 'That's what everyone thinks. God help her, the poor woman does about four hundred layers per song, she hasn't the time to do them all herself. No, I slipped into her studio just last month and did a few dozen of them myself.'

'That really doesn't surprise me at all. Niamh Kennedy, you are a living saint and a national living treasure.'

Once again Eva inclined her head to the rapturous applause. Then she turned back to Lainey and laughed out loud. 'Thank you,' she said.

Later, they stood side by side in the bathroom, taking off their make-up. Rex had wandered in after them. He was now in the bathtub, licking up a puddle of water near the plughole. Eva tried not to react. She had been getting used to him, slowly. She now agreed with Lainey that yes, he did look sweet when he was curled up in a ball on the couch, fast asleep. And he did indeed look funny when he chased his own tail, and when he scampered up and down the curtains. But she still couldn't pick him up. She hadn't patted him, either. And she definitely drew the line at sharing a bath with him and his fur. She'd stick to the shower from now on.

She took her hair out of the plait and shook her head. Her black hair fell in a long and silky swathe down her back.

'Wow,' Lainey said, in the middle of putting toothpaste on her toothbrush.

'Wow what?'

'Wow, your hair. That's the first time I've seen it out since you got here. You've always got it in that plait. You look completely different with it down like that. It looks amazing. Why don't you wear it out all the time? Or tomorrow night at the dinner party at least?'

'No, I don't think so.' She'd got into the habit of tying it back. Especially at work, serving food as she did. 'Anyway, the mad gypsy look's too wild for a boring old shop assistant, don't you think?'

Lainey rolled her eyes, unable to speak with the toothbrush in her mouth. Still brushing, she waved when moments later Eva yawned, said goodnight and went into her bedroom. But as Lainey finished in the bathroom and walked through the apartment turning off the lights, there was a thoughtful look on her face.

Followed just minutes later by a mischievous smile.

CHAPTER ELEVEN

IN SYDNEY, Joseph was walking up the last fifty or so steps to Dave's impressive Bondi Beach apartment, feeling a slight ache at the back of his legs. It was hardly surprising, really. This was the first time in ages that anything but his vocal chords had been getting any exercise.

He stopped for a moment, leaning out of the wide window in the stairwell that overlooked the beach itself. The air was filled with tangy spice scents from the restaurants down below, mixed with the salt air. He could hear conversations and bursts of laughter from the diners.

He'd caught a taxi to Bondi direct from the conference's final-night dinner. It had been a big success, the organiser had told him eagerly as she'd said goodbye. She'd had plenty of feedback from all the delegates, who'd found his keynote address and workshops inspiring and informative. Joseph had been pleased to hear it. But after the three days of speaking and demonstrating ergonomic design he'd felt like nothing but a fraud. That he was there under false pretences. Because he wasn't a designer any more, he realised. He was just a businessman now, conducting meetings, dealing with suppliers, signing deals . . .

He turned away from the view, climbed the final steps to the front door and knocked several times. The door was flung open by Dave himself. He grabbed Joseph's hand in a firm, vigorous hand-shake, then slapped him on the shoulder for good measure. 'Joseph Wheeler! Come in, come in, my old mate. Great suit, by the way. Paul Smith, is it? Very hip. And that shirt? Linen, is it? Come in. What'll you have to drink?'

Trying to make conversation over the loud music blaring from the stereo speakers, Joseph followed Dave through the stylish living room and out onto the long, wide balcony. Lights were strung in the trees all around. And the smell – it was intoxicating, a mixture of sea and salt from the beach and some sort of tropical flowers. Was it jasmine? Joseph wondered. It was so breathtaking it was almost too much.

The women at the party were just as gorgeous. Groomed and tanned, wearing slinky dresses, lots of jewellery and even more attitude. And they were all so skinny, he noticed. How did all their internal organs fit into such small bodies? He soon felt like a magnet attracting iron filings, as one after another of the beautiful glossy creatures glided over towards him. Dave had obviously filled all his friends in on Joseph's life story.

'Dave tells us you've got your own design business.'

'Dave tells us you're very, very successful.'

'Dave tells us there are companies lining up to buy your designs.'

One of the bolder ones cut to the chase. 'Dave tells us you're single and straight.'

An hour later, Joseph decided he'd had enough. He was keeping up, managing to trade some banter, even flirt a little with one or two of the women, but his heart just wasn't in it. The conversation hadn't extended much beyond property prices, share markets and business deals. He needed some fresh air.

Then he remembered he was already in the fresh air, on the balcony. What he needed was some not-fresh air. He excused himself from the trio of glamorous string-beans around him and went inside to get a glass of water.

The kitchen wasn't empty. A red-haired man was washing a big collection of glasses, whipping through them with great efficiency.

'Could I just get a glass of water?' Joseph asked.

'Water? I'd say you're the first person to drink water in this flat for a long time.' The man gestured to the bar in the corner. 'Champagne, vodka, gin, ten brands of beer . . . But you want water. I've heard it all now.'

Joseph had spotted his accent. 'You're from London too? What part?'

'South London, me. Just here on a holiday, back-packing around, picking up work here and there. No real hardship, this, is it? Turn up at a ritzy place like this, wash a few dozen glasses, drink as many dregs as you can,' the grin again, 'then back to the hostel with a pocketful of cash, ready to head off travelling again.'

Joseph leaned against the kitchen bench, very interested. 'So where have you been in Australia so far?'

'Everywhere. The north, the west, the south, the east. This is my fifth trip to Oz. And you?'

'First time. I'm thinking of moving on from Sydney myself in the next few days. Got any tips on where to go next?'

The man stopped washing glasses for a moment while he thought about it. 'It depends what you're after. Broome is incredible, all red sand and blue sky and sea. Or there's Byron Bay, hippies and rainforests on tap. Are you heading in any particular direction?'

'To South Australia.'

'In that case, make sure you go via Melbourne. Definitely. It's a great city. A brilliant city.' He lowered his voice. 'I wouldn't want anybody here in Sydney to hear me say this, for fear of execution, but I think

Melbourne's better than Sydney. Streets ahead of it. Sydney's all flash and glamour, like the beautiful younger sister. She catches your attention first and you're beguiled, seduced in a moment. But then your attention slowly starts to wane and suddenly you notice Melbourne. The quieter, more demure sister, on the surface. Until you discover that still waters run deep and Melbourne's the one you really fall in love with.'

The man laughed at the expression on Joseph's face. 'And you thought I was just a thick dishwasher, didn't you? I used to be an English lecturer. Straight out of school, into teacher training, then schools, colleges. Twenty years of my life – routine, pressures. Then I had a heart scare three years ago, a month after I turned forty. Slow down, the doctor said. Change what you can. So I took him literally. I changed everything.'

'Everything?'

'I resigned. I sold my house. I work in the local pub now, save like mad and take six months off every couple of years and come here and travel around. I stay in hostels, wear whatever I want, go wherever I want, do whatever I want, and it's the most relaxing thing in the world. If I wanted to go to parties like this I'd stay in London. It's much better in here.' He gestured around the kitchen. 'Peaceful. The only problem is I get terribly rough hands.' He held them up and laughed. 'A small price to pay.'

'And you enjoy yourself?'

'Sure do. It's good fun. Really good fun. Pressures, deadlines, who needs them?'

Dave poked his head in then. 'Joseph, there you are. Leave the hired help alone and come back out here. A gang of us are talking about going up to Queensland in the next few days, spur-of-the-moment thing. Fancy coming along?'

Joseph made a snap decision. 'No, thanks anyway, Dave. I'm going to head for Melbourne.'

The hired help smiled into the sinkful of glasses.

CHAPTER TWELVE

IN MELBOURNE the following evening, Lainey looked up from her refrigerator and groaned. 'Oh, damn it, I forgot to get champagne for tonight.'

Eva glanced over from the dining area where she had just finished laying out the place settings. 'Do you want me to drive down to the off-licence and get some? You've still got the food to finish, haven't you?'

Lainey was at the kitchen bench, which was covered in bowls of cut-up vegetables and delicious-smelling sauces. She was making an Asian-style banquet for them all. 'They're called bottle shops here, remember, not off-licences,' she said automatically. 'Would you mind, Eva? Are you sure you're okay with the trams?'

'Just give them right of way at all times, is that the general rule?'

Lainey nodded and tossed her the car keys.

'That'd be brilliant, thanks a million. Can you get half a dozen bottles?'

'Half a dozen?'

'Well, you know the saying. You can never be too thin, too rich or have too much champagne in your fridge.'

By the time Eva had got lost, then found the bottle shop, found a parking place then chosen six bottles from the many varieties of Australian champagne, nearly an hour had passed. Back at the flat she struggled up the final set of stairs carrying the box of bottles in both arms. The front door flew open. She nearly jumped out of her skin to find Lainey standing right there.

'They're all here,' she whispered, a strange glint in her eye. She took the box out of Eva's hands and put it in the hallway beside her, then tugged at Eva's hair tie so her hair flowed around her face and down her back.

'Oww!' Eva was completely taken aback. 'What on earth are you doing, Lainey? Give that back.'

Lainey pocketed the hair tie and pulled a bright silk flower out of another pocket. She deftly pinned it in Eva's hair. 'Trust me,' she hissed. 'It'll be fun.'

Bewildered, Eva followed her into the apartment. As they reached the entrance to the dining room Lainey stopped and spoke in a loud voice. 'Oh *Niamh*, here you are. Come in, I've just been telling everyone all about you.' She caught Eva's eye and winked.

In a quieter voice she spoke quickly to Eva. 'Yes, I've just been telling them all about your sculpting and that caravan in Galway you live in and your wonderful singing and the fact that you've just finished working with Enya on her new album.'

Her voice rose again. 'Everyone, this is my friend Niamh Kennedy, all the way from Ireland.'

Eva understood then why Lainey had played those tricks with her hair. To get the wild gypsy look to match this wild artist's story. She started to smile, about to confess it was all nonsense and that Lainey had always been a madwoman. Then she noticed how interested everyone seemed in her.

The four people in the living room had stopped their conversations. They had turned to look at her, smiling expectantly. Curiously, even. Eva wasn't used to this sort of reaction at all. People in Ireland certainly didn't react like that when she said she lived in Stoneybatter and worked in a delicatessen on Camden Street, that was for sure.

She caught Lainey's eye. Out of sight of her friends, Lainey was winking madly. 'Go on,' she mouthed.

Eva's mind worked quickly. Would she or wouldn't she go along with it? A long second passed. Then, smiling warmly, she moved into the room. 'Hello, everyone.'

Two hours later, the dinner party was in full swing and Eva was having the time of her life. The food was delicious. The entrées of deep-fried spiced tofu and cold Vietnamese rolls had disappeared in minutes. Now the steamed salmon in black bean sauce, grilled prawns with coriander and spicy rice noodles were being passed around from guest to guest.

The wine was plentiful. They'd managed to assemble quite a collection of empty bottles already.

Eva had answered lots of questions about her first impressions of Australia. And with Lainey's help, she'd answered lots of questions about her sculpting and singing too. She was usually nervous about meeting new people – when she was Eva Kennedy, at least – but she didn't feel half as nervous being Niamh Kennedy. She actually felt quite confident. It gave her something to hide behind.

Greg Gilroy, the owner of the Four Quarters bar and cafe, had been particularly attentive. Lainey had been right, he did have a thing about Ireland and all things Irish. Early in the evening he'd managed to manoeuvre things so that he was sitting next to Eva at the table. He'd been minding her closely since, refilling her wineglass, passing dishes of food, and leaping to explain any Australian terms or the background to any Melbourne stories that came up in the conversation.

She wondered if he had any Irish blood in him. According to Lainey, loads of Australians did. No, if anything, Greg looked Scandinavian. Tall, brown-skinned, his blond hair cut fashionably short. He was asking her now to describe the area in the west of Ireland where she lived. He listened with rapt attention as she spoke vaguely about wild beaches, dramatic cliffs and stormy skies.

'Oh, I loved Galway,' he said with feeling. 'I think it was my favourite part of Ireland.'

Oh no, Eva thought. Lainey hadn't told her he'd actually been to Ireland. Thank God she hadn't tried to be any more specific. She'd only been to Galway a few times in her life. 'When were you there?' she asked politely.

He proceeded to tell her in great detail everything he'd done on a trip to Ireland five years previously to source ideas and props for his Irish theme pub. He also managed to namedrop shamelessly, telling her about every minor brush with every minor Irish celebrity he'd met during that time.

'I wish I'd known you back then as well, Niamh,' he said with a slightly oily smile. 'I could have commissioned you to do a sculpture especially for my pub.'

Lainey overheard and winked at Eva. 'Oh Greg, you wouldn't have been able to afford Niamh's work. She's far too exclusive for a pub and cafe owner like you.' She flashed him a wide smile. 'No offence, of course.'

'None taken, of course,' he said. A little huffily, Eva noticed.

One of the other guests, a woman called Christine, turned to Eva. 'Niamh, do you mind me asking, how do you actually spell your name?'

Another woman spoke up too. 'I was about to ask the same thing. When Lainey rang to invite us to meet you, I thought she said your name was Eva, but I must have misheard.'

Lainey interrupted. 'It's spelt N-i-a-m-h, but pronounced Nee-av. The 'mh' is pronounced as a 'v' sound in the Irish language, isn't that right, Niamh?'

Eva just nodded. She felt foolish, as though she had formally appointed Lainey as her spokeswoman for the evening. But she didn't dare open her mouth in case the charade came tumbling down around her.

Greg was listening intently too. 'Could you spell that again, Lainey?' he said.

As Lainey did so, Eva watched amazed as Greg wrote it down in a Filofax he'd taken from his jacket pocket. He noticed that she had noticed. 'Such a beautiful name, I'd hate to forget it.'

'But it must drive you crazy having to spell it out all the time to people like us,' Christine said. 'Are you ever tempted to shorten it or change it?'

'You Aussies, what are you like!' Lainey turned to Eva. 'Didn't I tell you, Niamh, they – or I should say we, shouldn't I? – shorten everything here. Football is footy. Breakfast is brekky. How could we shorten your name though? Call you Knee, perhaps?'

Eva laughed with everyone else, feeling more and

more uncomfortable as the centre of attention. She decided to excuse herself. 'Look at all those empty bottles. I'd better go and see if I can find a full one. I'll be right back.'

Lainey waited until Eva had gone to the kitchen, then leaned towards the others. 'Just between us, Niamh would *never* change her name to anything else. She is very particular about her Irish heritage. You know of course that the English came in and anglicised so many of our names.'

Christine glanced over at Eva in the kitchen and whispered too. 'Is that what the Troubles and all those other things we hear of in Ireland are all about? The English changing your names?'

'Well, that's part of it,' Lainey said diplomatically, not keen to launch into a full explanation of Irish history tonight. She spoke quickly as Eva came back toward the table with the new bottle. 'But trust me, it's just better not to talk about any of it in front of Niamh. She can get very passionate about it. And you know these artists, they can get very hotheaded. Niamh has an absolutely *wild* temper.' She smiled innocently across at her friend as Eva sat down.

Next morning, Eva took over the kitchen, cooking up a huge fry – bacon, eggs, sausages, the works. Rex sat at the kitchen door, waiting for a rind, flicking his tail from side to side.

Eva threw him a piece, smiling as he caught it in his tiny teeth. Who'd have thought the day would come? Next thing she'd be thinking about getting a cat herself. Though perhaps that was jumping too quickly into the wonderful world of pets. She'd start with something smaller. A moth, maybe.

'Hurry up,' Lainey called over from where she sat surrounded by the weekend papers. 'My hangover's getting worse by the minute. I need a big dose of grease. God knows how I'm going to finish packing in time for my flight tonight.'

'You deserve every atom of that hangover,' Eva laughed, flipping the eggs. 'I kept waking up during the night thinking about that whole Niamh business. You're a brat, Elaine Byrne.'

Lainey just smiled. 'It was a bit of fun, though, wasn't it? And no harm done. I'll tell them all the truth next time I see them.' With that she started singing very loudly and off-key. '"When Irish tongues are fibbing, the world is –"'

'Lainey, stop that, you'll shatter the windows. Are you sure they won't mind? Won't think we were taking them for a ride?'

'Of course not. Anyway, we weren't that far from the truth. Niamh could *almost* be a long version of Eva. Spoken by someone with a bit of a stutter. And you are an artist. And a singer. You're just not practising at the moment.'

'No.'

Lainey stretched. 'I have to say I thought Greg was very taken with you. I reckon my story about you and Bono from U2 really clinched it, though. Greg's such a namedropper himself.'

Eva stopped cooking. 'What story about me and Bono?'

Lainey turned innocent eyes at her. 'Oh, I told Greg you'd done a sculpture for Bono's garden.'

'Lainey! When did you tell him that?'

'I think you were in the kitchen,' Lainey said vaguely.

'That was taking it a bit far, wasn't it? The Enya story was bad enough.'

'Darl, it was just a joke. Don't take it so seriously. Just be flattered by Greg's interest. And he was interested in you, wasn't he?'

Eva blushed.

Lainey pointed. 'Aha, didn't I tell you! Your Irish accent was driving him wild! He was so disappointed when he first met me and learned I'd actually had one but lost it. "But Lainey, have you any idea what an Irish accent does to a man? So, so sexy."'

Eva smiled. Lainey managed to take off Greg's slightly pompous tone very well. 'Well, he did say he might give me a call, take me out while you're up in Brisbane.'

Lainey clapped her hands. 'Oh, excellent. That's exactly what you need, a little holiday romance. And

he's a nice fellow, even if he is a bit of a tight-arse.'
She laughed at Eva's expression. 'Tight with his
money. And he can be a bit of a bloke, especially
when he's had a few too many. And he gets a bit pos-
sessive of his girlfriends, from what I've heard. But
that won't be a problem for you, you'll be gone
before he has a chance to get too weird.'

'Never start up a dating agency, will you, Lainey?
That's the worst character reference I've ever heard.'

'Well, nobody's perfect. But he's okay, really,
despite all that. Very rich too. Now, come on, hurry
up with that fry. I swear my head is about to
explode.'

Chapter thirteen

Joseph looked out at the view from his South Yarra hotel. The English dishwasher at Dave's party might have been eloquent about Melbourne, but had he been truthful?

From his vantage point on the fourth floor, the scenery wasn't exactly breathtaking. An inner-city street of clothes shops, cafes and restaurants. The sky was grey. The mist was so thick he couldn't see much beyond two streets away. There was a faint drizzle trickling down the window glass. Not a harbour to be seen, though he had glimpsed a muddy-looking river as he'd ridden in a taxi from Melbourne airport that morning.

Joseph was very impressed with his hotel, though. If he'd been an interior designer rather than an industrial designer he would have been even more impressed. His studio room looked like it had been styled for a magazine feature. Polished wood everywhere. Two large windows, one looking into a small central atrium designed to resemble an Asian garden, with running water, simple plants, polished stones. The other window overlooked the street. One of Melbourne's best shopping streets, the receptionist had told him. It was like a fashion parade there some days, she said. A shame the rain was spoiling the view. The only movement he could see from his window were the cars and the trams, adding some colour to the grey and gloomy scene.

He caught sight of his reflection in the window. He was wearing another of George's T-shirts and his favourite old black jeans. He needed a haircut. He could almost be mistaken for a normal person on holiday, he decided, instead of the overworked, stressed businessman he was.

He'd checked in with his office the night before.

Rosemary had answered. 'Joseph, you're supposed to be taking a break, not worrying about us.'

'Just checking everything's fine.'

'No problems at all. Maurice's been in, picking up some paperwork. The designers are all happy. I'm taking messages for you, but nothing that can't wait. Now, forget about us. Goodbye. And enjoy your holiday.'

He would, he decided now. Just as soon as he got some more work out of the way. During the one-hour flight from Sydney, he'd decided to visit some of the backpacker hostels in Melbourne, talk to some of the travellers, see if there had been any changes in design since he'd developed his own backpack. Maybe getting out and about would set the ideas flowing again, spark some inspiration, help him decide whether or not he wanted to go to Canada.

And then in a few days he'd go to South Australia. He picked up the travel brochure he'd collected at Melbourne airport and looked at the section on the Clare Valley again. There were two pages of photographs – glossy green rows of vineyards curving over hills under bright blue skies, sunwarmed stone cottages surrounded on all sides by vines and gum trees. Photos of laughing couples sitting by fireplaces, toasting each other with wine, plates of fine food close by. More couples walking hand in hand down tree-lined paths, bottles of wine tucked under their arms.

Was this how his father lived? Roaming over hills with a bottle of wine in one hand and a basket of food in another? Merrily building log cabins? What else had his mother said? That Lewis had a small vineyard, some olive trees? He started to form a mental picture based on the photographs in front of him. His father outside, working in a garden. Looking up as Joseph walked toward him –

He stopped his thoughts right there and picked up the telephone.

Forty minutes later he had spoken to three travel agents and knew all his options. He could drive all the way to South Australia, or fly to Adelaide and hire a car there, or take the overnight train. He liked the idea of the train. Something about arriving there slowly appealed to him.

He went over to the window. The clouds were disappearing, leaving behind a deep blue sky. Now he could see a great swathe of the city. Where there had been mist before there were now parks and gardens. On the horizon he could see the glint of the ocean. The grey buildings were starting to dry off, their natural warm stonework shining through. Even the trams seemed brighter, he thought, looking down to the street below. Stylish young people were stepping out of the designer boutiques, confident and self-conscious all at once.

That was more like it. He thought back to the English backpacker's comments about Melbourne and Sydney. It seemed the dowdy older sister had just put on a very bright dress.

He was just on his way out when he remembered the phone number Dave had given him of a financial-journalist friend who'd moved from Sydney to Melbourne. 'Aaron's a nice bloke,' Dave had boomed. 'You'll like him. He'll be able to give you some Melbourne holiday tips. Take you out for a beer or something. I'll let him know you're coming.'

Joseph rang the number and introduced himself.

'Oh hi, Joe. Dave said you might call. Welcome to

Melbourne.' He had quite a distinctive voice. A cool-sounding drawl, somewhere between an Australian and an American accent. 'Listen, I'm actually going to a party tonight, at a friend's house in Brighton. Do you want to drop in and meet a few people? It's all pretty caj.'

'Pretty caj?'

'Yeah. Caj. Casual. Got a pen? I'll give you the address.'

Joseph wrote it down and then repeated it back. 34 Warner Street, Brighton.

'That's it. Sorry, I'm right on deadline, can't talk. But we'll see you at the party? Nine-ish? Okay, bye.'

'Thanks, Aaron. See you then.' Joseph threw on his coat and went downstairs.

Chapter fourteen

A few kilometres away, Eva let herself into Lainey's apartment and put down her bag and umbrella. This morning's downpour was the first rain she'd seen in days. Coming from Ireland, that was some going.

It was blue skies and sunshine every day in Brisbane, Lainey had told her on the phone the night before. And her work was coming along very well, she'd said in answer to Eva's questions. But she hadn't rung to talk about work, she'd rung to see if Eva was coping all right without her.

'So far, so good,' Eva had laughed. 'But you've only been gone two days.'

'Well, I'm just a phone call away, darling, remember that.'

The phone was ringing as Eva walked into the living room. She picked it up before the answering machine clicked into action. 'Hello, Lainey's house,' she said.

'Hi, is that Niamh?'

Wrong number, Eva nearly said. Then something in the voice sparked a memory.

'Yes,' she said tentatively. It sounded like –

'Niamh! I thought I recognised that beautiful accent. This is Greg. Lainey's friend from the dinner party the other night.'

'Greg, how are you?'

'I'm just grand, as you would say.' He gave a long chuckle.

He was still calling her Niamh. Of course he was. She was about to speak, to somehow find a way of telling him that the whole story had been complete fiction, when he spoke again.

'It's very late notice, I know, but I wondered if you might like some company while Lainey's away. I could take you out to dinner tonight, perhaps. And to a party at a friend's house in Brighton afterwards? If you haven't got any other plans.'

'I don't have any plans at all. That would be lovely, Greg, thank you.' A date with a real live Australian man. What a treat. And she could tell him the truth about the Niamh story then. Face to face.

He sounded very pleased with himself. 'I'll look forward to it, Niamh. And all my friends are looking forward to meeting you, too.'

'Are they?' she said, surprised. 'Why?'

'Well, many of them are well-known artists and designers themselves, of course, so they're always

147

interested in meeting someone as internationally successful as you. I've told them all about your sculpting and your singing. U2 and Enya are very popular here in Australia too, you know.'

'Are they?' Uh oh.

'Well then, I'll come and collect you at about seven-thirty, would that suit?'

'Perfect,' she said, her mind working at a million miles. Quick, tell him now, tell him now, one part of her said as the other part of her kept talking. 'And is it a formal restaurant? Dress-wise, I mean?'

'Oh, absolutely,' Greg said proudly. 'Dress to impress. See you tonight.'

Eva hung up. Dress to impress? And tell him the truth about Niamh? All on one date? What had she got herself into? She checked the time. It would be fine, she told herself firmly. She had hours to get ready. Hours to worry about what to wear. And in the meantime she had coffee to make and important work to do.

Out on the balcony she opened her notebook and wrote in firm letters across the top of a fresh page: 'The shop and what I would do with it'. It was like a child's essay. 'By Eva Kennedy, aged thirty-one', she added to amuse herself.

Ambrose had told her it would be her place, that she could do whatever she wanted with it. Since Lainey had gone to Brisbane, she'd been out visiting every delicatessen and food store she could find in inner-city Melbourne and gathering ideas. She'd visited small Italian delis, fragrant with the smell of rich cheese and spicy sausages. Brightly lit Asian grocery shops, their shelves crammed with pungent goods that she couldn't begin to name. Sleek, modern food stores boasting the latest in modern Australian cuisine, everything from wattleseed pasta to bush tomato salsa. Tiny shops selling only coffee or only fruit and vegetable juices or only spices. Warm, crowded bakeries filled with every kind of bread, from white loaves to olive-studded focaccia, ciabatta to heavy rye-grain rolls. Continental butchers. Vegetarian shops.

She'd picked up a few good ideas for her window displays and for new product lines. But then another, different idea for the shop had started playing in the back of her mind. Something Meg had said a week or two back had sparked it. Something about serving soup on cold winter days. About opening a little cafe in the back of the delicatessen.

It would take some renovations, of course. More than some, they'd need to install a small kitchen, probably get some sort of building approval. Redecorate. And they couldn't serve just soup, people would expect other food too. She'd need a chef, but maybe Meg would know someone. Maybe Meg would even be interested in doing it herself. She'd had the training, after all. Ardmahon House was one of the top cooking schools in Ireland.

But would a cafe work? Could it work? Eva felt like her mind was slowly stirring after a long nap. God forbid, perhaps Dermot had been right. Maybe she had been drifting along a bit, going into work, serving the customers, stuck in a routine . . . But what if all that changed? If she started doing things her way, putting her own ideas into action? She pictured the sign above the door. Camden Street Foods and Cafe. Manager: Eva Kennedy. Chef: Margaret Delaney. Or . . .

Maybe she wouldn't call it Camden Street Foods and Cafe. Ambrose had said she could do whatever she liked with it. What would he think about a name change? Eva started to smile. Now wouldn't that be a great name for a shop serving delicious cheeses, spices, breads, coffee and lunches . . . She could see the sign already: 'Ambrosia'. Nectar of the gods, indeed.

There was just one minor problem to sort out. How in God's name did she run a cafe? Running a delicatessen was one thing, but how would she decide on menus? Sort out an ordering system? Find staff? What she really needed was a crash course. A couple of weeks in other cafes, watching and taking notes, working out what to do and what not to do.

Looking over the balcony, she smiled at the thought of sitting in cafe after cafe for days, drinking so much coffee her hair stood on end and her eyes started spinning in her head . . .

Then her attention was distracted – something about the way the breeze was twisting and turning the leaves of the trees in front of her caught her eye. One moment they were silver coloured, as the breeze flicked up the underside of the leaves. The next moment they were all a deep, vibrant green. Through the branches she could see a glint of water as the river flowed past.

Tentatively at first, she started to sketch what she could see in front of her. The darkness and lightness of the tree trunks. The lattice effect of the leaves. The moving shadows. Almost thirty minutes passed before she stopped drawing, coming to as if out of a dream. She hadn't felt like that in years, completely absorbed in what she was drawing, forgetting everything around her. She had exactly captured the view in front of her. Her trained eye told her that. The perspective was perfect, the shading was assured, the leaves on the paper almost seemed real. But . . .

She pulled the page out of the book, screwed it up into a ball and threw it behind her into the apartment. 'Who are you fooling?' she said under her breath. Enough thinking about that. Enough thinking about the shop too. She stood up. She had a date to get ready for.

By six thirty Eva was in a complete state. She'd pulled all of her clothes out of the cupboard. Her bright

T-shirts and cardigans. Her skirts. Her favourite faded jeans. Several shift-style dresses, made from beautiful material. They were now all spread over the floor of her room. But there was nothing there that would impress an eight-year-old chimney sweep, let alone Greg's scary-sounding friends. She glanced at the clock. He'd be here in an hour. There was only one thing to do. Ring Lainey for help.

She caught her on her mobile just as Lainey was on the way out to dinner with the new staff of her company's Brisbane office. Eva quickly filled her in on the sudden date.

'Good old Greg, I told you he was smitten. But don't panic about the clothes, help yourself to anything of mine.'

'Thanks a million,' Eva said, hoping something would fit. She'd hold her breath, stand on tiptoes or stay sitting down all night if she had to. 'Unfortunately, the clothes aren't my only problem.'

'What else is?'

'He's still calling me Niamh.'

Lainey roared laughing. 'Of course, of course! I hadn't thought of that. Fantastic. You'll keep it going, won't you? Even without me there?'

'Lainey, I can't!'

'Of course you can. Why ever not? Who's it hurting? You haven't said you're an Irish businesswoman looking for investments, have you? You're not about to con him out of all his money?'

'No.'

'Well, where's the harm then? It's just a joke. And Greg will find it really funny when I eventually tell him the truth, I promise you.'

'It's not just Greg, it's Greg and his friends. He's taking me to a party. He's told them all about me. About the sculpting. About Galway. Enya. Even Bono.'

'This just gets better and better. Eva, stop taking it all so seriously. Sorry, I mean, *Niamh*, stop taking it all so seriously. Enjoy yourself. Enjoy all the attention. It's good for you, it's funny.'

'Oh, sure. It's all right for you, safely up in Brisbane.'

Lainey laughed again. 'Got to go. Ring me tomorrow, first thing. I'll want a full match report.'

Eva finally managed to find something in Lainey's wardrobe to wear. Thank God for little black dresses, she thought. This one was made from a beautiful fabric, clingier than she normally wore, but beggars couldn't be choosers. And it was a gorgeous dress.

Hair tied back or loose? She'd worn it down the past few days, badgered into it by Lainey, who insisted it really suited her like that. 'If you want to jazz it up, use some products too,' she'd said. 'I've got loads of them in the bathroom cupboard, just help yourself. And don't forget the silk flowers too – that one looked great the night of the dinner party.'

Eva tied it back, then left it loose again. Tied back, loose again. She actually felt different when it was untied. She associated her businesslike work personality with the plait, so if she was going to be pretending to be the creative Irish sculptor living in the wild west of Ireland, she may as well look the part. Tipping her head down, she shook it vigorously, her hair flying around. She laughed at her reflection – her hair was a mass of black waves around her face. Wild west, indeed.

How to keep it looking like that, though? Ah, Lainey's hair products. The new name for hairspray, apparently. She went into the bathroom and gathered up an armful of them from the cupboard. She read the labels. Mousse. Gel. Styling cream. Fix lacquer. Finishing spray. Imagine that, Eva thought. All these years she'd just been tying her hair back in a long plait, when she could have been applying thousands of hair products in dozens of different ways – massaging, rubbing, distributing evenly, applying to damp or dry hair, spraying lightly . . .

She took a gloopy handful of mousse from the can and scrunched it as directed into her hair. She read the words on the side of the can: 'Adds shine and texture, extra confidence and body'. All that in a handful of white foam, she thought. Who needed drugs? She finished it off with a quick blast of super-extra-firm-hold hairspray. Nuclear-hold, more like it, she decided, moving her head vigorously. Her hair stayed still.

Surely there was a risk of some chemical reaction between all these different products? She must have applied dozens of different chemicals in the past hour, between shampoo, deodorant, skin moisturiser, perfume and now all these hair products. What if one last addition – a bit of mouthspray, for example – was the missing part of the jigsaw, the final chemical formula that set off a reaction among all the other products? Boom, up she'd go in a sensational fireball.

She'd read about cases of unexplained spontaneous combustion. That would give Lainey a surprise – if she came home and found just a tiny pile of ashes in her spare room, surrounded by empty cans of hair care products. Eva waited a moment after she had applied the hairspray. Everything seemed to be quiet. No wisps of smoke coming off her hair.

Next she found the box of silk flowers Lainey had mentioned. She tried a large yellow one. No, she looked like she was on her way to a Hawaiian luau. A little blue one, perhaps. No, it looked like an insect had landed on her head. Then a medium-sized pink and white one. She pinned it just above her right ear. It looked quite nice, she thought. Jaunty.

So, to jewellery. She didn't own much but she had chosen very carefully, from young designers in Dublin. She chose her favourite heavy silver pendant, more a piece of art than a piece of jewellery, and hung it round her neck. That looked good against the black dress, she thought. Elegant. Striking even. Maybe she'd buy a little black dress for herself when she got back to Dublin.

Now, just the stockings and she was done. She heard a rustle behind her.

It was Rex, claws out, kneading holes into her new pair of stockings.

Fifteen minutes later, Eva smoothed her dress over her thighs as she settled in to Greg's car. She hoped the high colour in her cheeks had disappeared.

How embarrassing. Greg *must* have heard her roaring at Rex. He'd been outside knocking at the door, it seemed, while she had been shouting and chasing the kitten around the flat, threatening to strangle him with the stockings he had just destroyed. Rex had thoroughly enjoyed the chase, even daring to take another nip at the stockings. Eva had eventually heard the knocking and had answered it, bare-legged, her head poking around the door. Greg had been standing there dressed in a formal suit, his hair sleek with some gel or cream.

'Greg, hello. How on earth did you get in?' She'd been expecting him to ring on the entry phone.

Greg seemed taken aback at her question. 'Hello, Niamh. Your neighbour downstairs let me in. He knows me.'

'Oh, good. Uhm, are you early or am I late?'

'Actually, I'm right on time.'

'Right,' Eva said, smiling slightly hysterically.

Greg moved forward as if to come in and wait for her in the apartment. She nearly slammed the door in his face. There was no way he could come in, the place was like a tip. 'I'll meet you down in the car, will I? Won't be a moment, I promise.'

Upending her suitcase again and then doing the same thing to Lainey's drawers, she eventually found another pair of stockings and hurriedly pulled them on. Shoes, bag, lipstick, perfume. She was out of the door five minutes later.

'Bye, Rex,' she'd called. 'Be good. And don't wait up.'

CHAPTER FIFTEEN

'I MANAGED to get a booking at The Loft,' Greg said to her as he pulled out from the kerb.

'Is that a nice place?'

'It's the in place in Melbourne at the moment.' He seemed disappointed that he needed to spell it out. 'Some people wait weeks to get a booking.' The inference was, some people but not me, because I Am Very Important in this city.

It was certainly impressive, Eva thought a little later as they were shown to their table. The height of luxury. Gliding waiters. Handwritten menus. Very well-groomed customers. She didn't think she'd be getting many ideas for Ambrosia here.

Greg was a considerate host, very courteous, though he did seem to be throwing back the glasses of wine faster than might have been wise, Eva thought. Perhaps the drink-driving laws weren't as strict in Australia as they were in Ireland.

Midway into the second bottle of wine, he started to get a bit misty-eyed. 'Niamh Kennedy,' he said, gazing at her. 'Such a beautiful name. It suits you too. You and your dark Celtic hair, your creamy Celtic skin . . .'

Uh oh, she thought. What next? Her white Celtic teeth?

'So Greg, tell me about your cafes,' she said hurriedly. 'All about them.' And stop staring at my Celtic bosom, she thought.

Greg was perfectly happy to stop talking about Eva's body parts if he could talk about himself instead. For the next fifteen minutes she heard in great detail about every stage of the establishment of Four Quarters. She had just started to drift off a little when she realised something. Perhaps this was an ideal opportunity to learn how cafes were run. Was she being sneaky? she wondered guiltily as he explained how he and his chefs had decided on the menus. No, Dublin was hardly the competition, surely.

'You'll have to come down and have another look at Four Quarters.' Greg was practically purring under all the attention. 'I could show you around.'

'Actually, Greg, that would be fantastic,' she said honestly.

Then he surprised her. 'Don't tell me. You're looking for some ideas for your work, aren't you?'

She went pale and red, in quick succession. 'For

my work?' Had he guessed? Had Lainey told him about the delicatessen?

'Yes, for your sculpting. You're looking for inspiration of some kind, aren't you? Lainey said you were hoping to do some work here.'

She smiled in relief. 'Uhm, yes, that's exactly it. I'm thinking about producing a new series of urban work,' she improvised quickly. 'Moving on from the inspiration of the outdoors and the Irish landscape into a different sort of city sensibility. And what better place to get close to the heartbeat of a city than in an inner-city cafe?' She could hardly believe she'd just said all of that. Her years at art school hadn't been wasted after all.

Greg lapped it up. 'Especially one of the most popular cafes in town. Niamh, you can spend as much time there as you like. I'll let my manager know you're coming down, she'll look after you. We can set you up in one of the quarters and you can just watch and listen and get all the inspiration you need. Who knows, maybe I might even commission you to do a sculpture specially for me?'

'Oh. That would be good,' she said, her smile getting a little forced. Perhaps he'd settle for a quick sketch of the building?

'I'll be down there myself a fair bit next week. Sorting out a few staffing problems. People just don't want to work hard these days, if you ask me. They walk out after a few days, can't stick it.'

'Really? Isn't that terrible.'

'It is. We always seem to be looking for staff.'

'Really?' she said again. Her mind was racing suddenly. How would she find staff for her cafe, she wondered? Advertise? Ask around among her friends? Perhaps she could talk to his manager and some of his staff too. Just see how they managed the day-to-day running, the staffing, the ordering, everything. Maybe when she got back to Dublin she could enrol in a business course somewhere, to really top up her knowledge. She almost wanted to ring Ambrose then and there and blurt out all her ideas.

Across the table, Greg was looking at his watch. 'We'd better go, if you don't mind skipping dessert. It's a bit of a drive to the party yet. And I said we'd be there around nine-thirty.'

She noticed a slur in his voice. 'Are you sure you're okay to drive?'

'Fine, fine. Now, this is on me, okay? Don't even think about taking out your purse.' He pulled out a slimline calculator from his wallet and checked the sums. Twice. He seemed satisfied. 'I'll leave the tip too,' he said magnanimously, as if he had just left a hundred-dollar bill. Eva glanced at it. It was less than five dollars.

He noticed her expression. 'I think it's important to be careful with your money, Niamh. You might not realise that, being of an artistic nature, but I learnt the lesson very early on in life and it's got me where I am today.'

Eva smiled wanly. She'd just realised she was out for the night with Mr Scrooge.

Joseph was lying on his hotel bed reading when the phone rang. The taxi for Warner Street, Brighton, was downstairs.

'I'll be right there, thanks.' He grabbed his coat and threw it on over his black jeans and the latest of George's T-shirts, this one advertising some new London club. Aaron had said caj, so caj it was. He should bring something to drink, he thought. Some beer or wine. Maybe the taxi could stop at an off-licence on the way. Then he remembered he'd bought a couple of bottles of Australian wine in Sydney to take back as a present for Rosemary. One of those would do for now, he'd replace it later. What would he put it in? The zip-off daypack from his backpack – perfect.

It was only when they were in Brighton and the driver asked him which number Warner Street that Joseph realised he'd left the address back at the hotel. He asked the driver to go up and down the long street while they both tried to spot a party house. He'd expected lots of lights, loud music, people spilling out into the warm night air. But there wasn't a sound.

'You sure this is the right street, mate?' the driver asked.

'I think so. Can we just do another circuit, please?'

'Your money, mate. I'll drive up and down all night if you want.'

After the second loop Joseph decided to get out and investigate on foot. Maybe he'd be better able to hear any party sounds that way. Or even see someone else going into a party house. He'd do one loop on foot, and if he couldn't find it he'd just catch a taxi back to his hotel. He'd noticed a rank around the corner, so that wouldn't be a drama.

He passed a fifty-dollar bill to the driver as payment.

'Keep the change,' he said.

'That's a big tip, mate,' the driver said in amazement. 'You sure?'

'Sure,' Joseph said, climbing out.

'Mad bloody tourists,' the driver thought as he took off.

God knows what sort of party this was, Joseph thought, walking down one side of the street and still hearing nothing. Perhaps it was a slumber party and they were asleep already?

A car pulled up down the road and several people got out. Joseph watched as they crossed the road and went into a house. The door opened briefly and he heard a faint sound of music. That had to be it. He walked up and knocked on the front door.

'Hi, I'm Joseph, a friend of a friend of Aaron's,' he started to explain.

The woman who opened the door just smiled and gestured for him to come in, continuing to talk on the mobile phone clenched under her chin.

Moments after Joseph closed the front door behind him, another taxi pulled up a hundred metres down the street. A man and a woman, both dressed in jeans and T-shirts, climbed out and walked up the front path of a red-brick house six houses down.

The woman wasn't happy. 'We're not staying long, Aaron, okay? You know I don't like these friends of yours. And I don't feel like meeting this Pommie friend of Dave's either.'

'I know, I know,' the man drawled. 'You told me. We'll just stay an hour, all right? And don't worry about Dave's friend. He probably won't even turn up.'

CHAPTER SIXTEEN

THE FUNKY opening notes of James Brown's classic 'Sex Machine' blasted around the room.

Eva bit back a smile as she watched Greg gyrate around the makeshift dancefloor, enthusiastically wriggling his behind. Lainey had said he was a tight-arse. In more ways than one, it seemed. But who'd have thought he would be able to do such a fantastic James Brown impersonation? He was just hilarious, Eva thought, laughing out loud. He obviously did have a good sense of humour after all. She hadn't been too sure. But look at him, he was a natural comedian.

As she kept watching, the song changed. But Greg's James Brown dancing style didn't. Eva slowly realised that Greg's dancing wasn't an impersonation. It was just his dancing. A kind of energetic combination of groin thrusts and hip swivels, with an occasional double-handed 'Don't mind me, I'm just shaking out the mat' movement. She'd never seen anything quite like it. From the looks on some of the other partygoers' faces, neither had they. There were more than a few sidelong glances at Greg. More than a few open smiles.

She began to feel a bit embarrassed for him. Her date for the evening had turned into the party sideshow. And her daydream of a holiday romance with a nice Australian man was dissolving before her eyes. God, meeting someone was such a minefield, she thought. Such a series of obstacle courses, a series of judgements. On looks. Personality. Conversation. Behaviour.

It was like crossing a rope bridge, she decided. One tiny slip either way and you were over the edge, out of the race. She felt awful thinking it, but Greg's dancing was sending him very close to the edge of the bridge. It was a shame, Eva thought. He'd been quite nice at dinner. Well, until he'd started all the Celtic hair and Celtic skin carry-on. And started to drink too much. And did that business with the bill.

As for his behaviour in the car – he'd driven through a red light, cursed other drivers, and only slowed down after she'd practically shouted at him. She'd almost had to go into battle to get him to stop at a bottle shop so she could buy some champagne for the party.

'There'll be plenty of drink there,' he'd said, looking across at her in amazement. 'Don't waste your money.'

But Eva had insisted. She didn't want to turn up empty-handed. Greg roared into a drive-through bottle shop, keeping the car running noisily while she hurriedly chose a bottle of Australian champagne and paid for it, wincing at the noises coming out of Greg's car behind her. Afterwards, she'd sunk down into her seat, praying they wouldn't crash, sitting up only when they stopped near the party house.

Things hadn't improved when they came inside the large, stylishly decorated house, filled with beautifully dressed, confident young Melburnians. Eva had felt immediately self-conscious, very out of place. She felt like she was in a drawing from her childhood. 'Our artist has cleverly hidden an ordinary person in this room full of supermodels. Can you find her?'

Greg had started parading her around the room, reeling off her fake life story, trying to impress his friends with the company he was keeping. 'Do you know she actually lives and works in a caravan in Galway?' she heard him say. 'She sang on Enya's latest album. Bono from U2 has one of her sculptures in his garden.'

A couple of his friends had pointedly looked her up and down as if they were disappointed with her simple black dress. What had they been expecting her to wear? she wondered. A floaty green dress and an Aran sweater? A harp slung over her shoulder?

What had Lainey started that night? And what could she do to fix things now? Follow Greg around the room, apologising and explaining that actually he had it all completely backwards. Oh no, when he said Galway, he actually meant Dublin. He said I sang on Enya's latest CD? Oh, he must have misheard. I actually said I work in a delicatessen in Camden Street. You think I'm a successful sculptor? Oh no, no, no, I'm a shop assistant. But they both start with the letter 's', so I suppose it's an easy enough mistake.

No, she was hardly going to do that. Besides, she smiled to herself now, taking another sip of champagne, if the truth be told, she liked the interest these people were showing in her. And she liked the way people reacted when she was introduced as Niamh the sculptor. The way they asked her to spell her name, asked her what it meant. She certainly never got that reaction in her real life.

Greg lurched up to her, a designer beer in his hand. Another full one, she noticed. God, he was lashing them back. 'Niamh!' he shouted over the music. 'Want to dance?'

She shook her head very definitely.

'Mind if I do?'

She shook her head even more definitely. He hurled himself back on the dancefloor. He'd hardly been off it since the James Brown song had been played.

Eva stood back and drained her glass of champagne. Should she just go outside, catch a taxi at the rank they'd passed down the road? Leave him to it? No, she decided. She'd stay a bit longer. She was actually enjoying herself, the spectacle of Greg included. She liked watching people at parties, there was nothing like it for entertainment. But first she'd go to the kitchen and get herself another glass of that lovely champagne.

Joseph asked five people but no-one was able to point Aaron out to him. He began to wonder if he had the name right. Could he have misheard Dave? Maybe his friend was actually called Darren. Or Warren. Could it have been Sharon, even? A woman with a very deep voice? No, it had definitely been Aaron. He'd obviously just not arrived yet. Joseph decided to stay another half an hour, and if Aaron still hadn't turned up he'd just go back to the hotel.

The Australian definition of casual was worlds away from the London one, he thought as he walked through the different rooms of the house. He was in glossy-magazine territory tonight, from the furniture right down to the designer clothing. Even the drinks in people's hands. The television was so modern it was little more than a slim piece of metal glued to the wall. The CD system took up one side of the room. And the house was enormous. Every room seemed filled with people. He walked through, carrying his daypack, wondering where the kitchen was.

He finally had to ask for directions. On his way there, he passed through a large room that had been set aside for dancing. The music was booming through the speakers. Joseph was amazed he hadn't been able to hear it from the road outside. The windows must be soundproofed. There seemed to be some sort of performance art going on, a blond-haired man of about his own age doing a spectacular impersonation of James Brown's dancing. Joseph watched for a moment. He had to laugh. The fellow had the moves down pat, right down to the flamboyant hand gestures. Maybe he did it as a career.

The kitchen was just beside the dance room. It was like something from a film set, all sleek styling, slate floor and tall cupboards. A dark-haired woman in a short black dress was already in there, standing by the long counter, fitting a silver contraption onto a bottle of champagne. She seemed very intent on her task. Then she spoke over her shoulder. She must have heard him come in.

'Can you believe this fantastic invention I found on the bench here? I can't tell you how many times I've felt like just one glass of champagne but decided against it because the whole bottle would go flat.'

He recognised her accent. She was Irish.

'But look, if you use this thing,' she kept talking, demonstrating the silver stopper by taking it off and putting it on the bottle again, 'the bubbles stay in. Brilliant. Honestly, you ingenious Australians.'

He had to smile at her enthusiasm. It was as if she'd discovered the Holy Grail. 'I'm sorry, I can't take any credit for that incredible invention. I'm English.'

Eva heard the soft accent and turned around completely. He was tall, at least six inches taller than her. Dark hair. And beautiful dark eyes. She took it all in in just a moment, conscious she was staring at him. 'Oh. Well. Would you like a glass of champagne anyway? There's plenty.'

He smiled at her. 'You just want to try that invention again, don't you? Thanks anyway, but this is fine.' He held up his bottle of wine.

She passed him a corkscrew and glass and watched as he deftly pulled out the cork.

The kitchen door opened and a young woman came in, grabbed a glass from the counter and went out again. Before the door closed they both had a clear view of Greg on the dancefloor.

Joseph turned to Eva. 'So James Brown is alive and well and living in Australia.'

'It does look that way, doesn't it?' The champagne made her bold. 'You're not tempted to give him a run for his money? Hit the dancefloor yourself?'

'I might. Though I'm probably more of a John Travolta man myself.'

His face was solemn but his eyes were twinkling, she noticed. 'Oh, good. You can warm up the crowd for me. I'm planning quite a spectacular Torvill and Dean routine, actually.'

'Both parts?'

'Oh yes. That's where the real skill comes in.' She grinned at him.

What a fantastic smile she had, Joseph thought. It was like she lit up from inside. He noticed the flower in her hair and the heavy silver pendant she was wearing. It was very dramatic against her black dress.

The door flung open again. A tall, blond-haired man came in, wiping the sweat from his forehead. 'Niamh, there you are, I've been looking for you everywhere. You've missed some fantastic dance songs out there.'

The James Brown man. Joseph glanced over at the Irishwoman. She surprised him with a very slight wink.

The blond man was giving Joseph the once-over, taking in his clothes and the daypack he was carrying.

'Hello, mate. Haven't seen you at these parties before, have we met?'

Joseph shook his head. 'No, I don't think so.'

The blond man put out his hand. 'My name's Greg.'

Joseph shook it. 'Joseph.'

Greg moved over next to Eva and put his arm around her. 'And this, Joe, is Niamh Kennedy.'

Joseph thought she seemed very uncomfortable. 'I'm sorry, I didn't quite catch your name,' he said, looking right at her.

'Niamh Kennedy,' Greg repeated. 'It's an ancient Celtic name. The letters "m" and "h" are pronounced as the "v" sound in the Irish language, you see. So it's spelt N-i-a-m-h, but pronounced Nee-av.'

'Greg, please.' Eva felt very embarrassed. Was this a party or a spelling bee?

Greg gave her shoulder a squeeze and turned back to Joseph. 'What's that accent, Joe? English, are you?'

'That's right. From London.'

'Uh huh. And what do you do? For a living?'

As they both looked at him expectantly, Joseph realised he was tired of talking about himself. Tired of talking about his work, his designs, ergonomic principles. He'd done nothing else but that at the conference. So he kept his answer brief. 'Industrial design.'

Greg nodded. 'Right. And are you living in Oz or here on holiday?'

Joseph hadn't realised Twenty Questions was a common Australian party game. 'A working holiday, really.'

The man glanced at his daypack again. 'God, you English backpackers, you're amazing. I swear you see more of Australia than we natives do.'

Backpacker? The idea of it amused Joseph. He didn't correct him. 'Oh, yes, it's a great way to travel.'

Eva spoke then. 'Are you looking for work at the moment? Greg owns a cafe and was just saying tonight that he needs staff, weren't you, Greg?'

'Is that right? And do you employ backpackers?' Joseph asked.

Greg nodded. 'Yes. If they're legal.'

'Oh, I'm perfectly legal,' Joseph said, enjoying himself even more. This was much easier than talking about his real life. And he was legal. In a business-visa sort of way.

Greg pulled out his wallet and withdrew a business card. 'Okay, Joe. Call in and see me if you want.'

'Thanks.' Joseph took the business card and put it away without looking.

'One of the most popular bars in town, that is,' Greg said, seeming a bit put out at Joseph's lack of interest. 'I started it up less than eighteen months ago, and have seen a capital return of more than 10 per cent each month since. Now, I don't know if you understand the business world, Joe, but . . .'

Eva had heard all this over dinner and she didn't really need to hear it again. She decided to leave him to it for a while. She needed to find the bathroom in any case. 'Excuse me,' she said.

Greg continued his business report for a few more minutes, before stopping mid-sentence and picking up Joseph's bottle of wine from the bench. He squinted down at the label.

'Hunter Valley. New South Wales. Not bad, not bad. But if you're after a really good, full-bodied shiraz, you can't get any better than . . .' He stopped again, apparently losing interest in his own monologue. Swaying slightly, he walked to the kitchen door and peered out into the party instead.

'Where's she gone?' he muttered under his breath. He turned to Joseph. 'She's Irish, you know. Niamh, I mean.'

'Is that right?'

'She's a very successful sculptor,' Greg went on. 'Based in the west of Ireland. But she's here working on some commissions. Special clients. VIPs, that sort of thing. And she's a singer too, you know. She sang on Enya's last album.'

Joseph was surprised. 'Really? I thought Enya did all the singing herself.'

'That's what most people think,' Greg boasted. 'But she gets tired of laying down hundreds and hundreds of voice tracks, so she gets Niamh to come in and do some of them. She even did a sculpture for Bono from U2 recently. For his garden.'

'Who? Enya?'

'No,' Greg said, crankily. '*Niamh*.'

Eva came back into the kitchen at that moment. As she reached for her glass of champagne on the kitchen bench beside Greg, he moved to put his arm around her again. 'My Celtic princess,' he slurred.

Eva decided right then she wanted to go home. She glanced up at the clock on the wall. 'Actually, Greg, I might call it a night, I think. I'm exhausted.'

Greg looked disappointed. 'So early, Niamh? Well, look, okay, I'll just finish this beer and we can head off. Unless you want to have a quick dance before we go?'

'No, but thank you anyway.' Eva said, a little too quickly. She glanced over at the Englishman. His face was serious but his eyes were smiling at her again. She bit back a smile herself.

Just then another man pushed into the kitchen, also the worse for wear. 'Greg Gilroy, my old maaate, how are you? Diane said she thought you were in here. I haven't seen you for years, mate! How's that Irish pub of yours going?'

'Jim, maaate! Great to see you.' He slapped the new arrival on the back. 'I'm out of that Irish pub business now, Jimbo. Into cafes. Four Quarters in St Kilda, have you heard of it? I tell you, mate, best thing I ever . . .' He noticed Eva standing by the door, trying to get his attention.

She spoke quickly. 'Greg, look, I can get a cab home, I'll be grand. I noticed there's a rank just down the road. You stay here and catch up with your friend.'

Greg started to object, then the other man pulled two beers out of the fridge. He handed one to Greg and opened one himself. He ignored Joseph, who was still standing just a few feet away, watching everything.

Eva smiled over at him. 'I hope you enjoy your travels, Joe.'

That smile again, Joseph thought. It was almost luminous. 'Thanks, Niamh.' There was a pause. 'I like your pendant, by the way.'

She glanced down at it. 'Thank you.' She felt very self-conscious all of a sudden. What had got into her this holiday? Taking on false identities. Drinking more champagne than was good for her. And smiling like a lovestruck teenager at perfect strangers. 'Well, goodnight. It was lovely to meet you,' she said.

'You too,' he said.

Greg overheard. U2? Was Niamh talking about that sculpture she did for Bono? 'Mate,' he interrupted Jim's spiel about how successful his golf-buggy business was these days. 'Let me introduce you to this lovely Irish woman. Niamh, this is . . .'

He was too late. Eva had gone.

Chapter seventeen

Fifteen minutes later Eva was no further than a hundred metres down the road, still waiting at the taxi rank.

There were three groups of people ahead of her. They'd already been waiting for ten minutes before she arrived, one of them told her. Some big do at the Tennis Centre, apparently, a big rush on taxis tonight. It was ridiculous, another one of them complained. Why weren't there more taxis on the roads?

Eva was amazed. Complaining about a 25-minute wait? That was a short wait in Dublin. She'd waited nearly two hours near O'Connell Bridge one night. And it had been pouring rain.

A voice broke into her thoughts. 'Hello again.'

She spun around. It was the Englishman. She smiled at him. 'Joe, hello. Or should I call you Mister Travolta?'

'I'm sorry, I didn't realise he was a friend of yours.'

She really liked that glint of humour in his eyes. 'It didn't matter one bit, believe me.' She glanced back in the direction of the party house. 'You'd had enough too?'

He nodded. 'I tried to find the person who'd invited me, but no luck. So I called it a night too.'

'And did you manage to do your dancing?'

'I did. It was quite a spectacle, if I say so myself.'

'I'm sorry I missed it.'

'But you've seen *Saturday Night Fever*?'

She nodded.

'Well, there was no difference, really. John Travolta and I, one and the same moves.'

He was still deadpan, she noticed, even if his eyes were laughing. They stood side by side, silent for a moment, watching as one cab pulled up and picked up the first group. They all moved up in the queue and Eva turned in his direction again. 'So, are you enjoying Melbourne?'

'Very much,' he said. 'And you?'

'Oh yes.' Eva desperately tried to think of something interesting to say to him. She blurted out the first thing that came into her mind. 'The trams are great, aren't they? Really bright and convenient.'

He gave her a long look. 'Yes, they seem to be.'

She groaned inwardly. Oh, for God's sake. A whole new city to discuss and what had she brought up? Public transport. That would really get the conversation going. *Why, Eva, I've never met anyone able to speak about tram networks in such a fascinating way. What do you think about the buses?*

'And you're a sculptor and a singer, Niamh?'

She nearly jumped. He seemed to notice her surprise. 'Your friend was telling me.'

Oh, hell. When had Greg managed to give Joe the whole spiel? She'd only left them alone for a few minutes. She was about to confess that Niamh wasn't actually her name when she stopped herself. At least Niamh might have something interesting to say. The way Eva was going, she'd start talking about Melbourne's marvellous phone booths or roadside markings soon. She'd been Niamh for the past four hours already, in any case. What would another ten minutes hurt? She turned toward him and smiled. 'That's right, I am.'

'You've sung with Enya, I believe?'

Good God, had Greg been handing out detailed press releases? 'Yes, that's right,' she said, more cautiously. She needed to play it down a bit. 'Not as an ongoing thing, though. More as a guest musician. Enya's songs have so many layers, I just come in and do some of them for her sometimes.'

'Really? Just sometimes?'

He seemed really interested. Oh, God, what else could she add? 'Yes, you know, if she has to go to the shops or something, and they don't want to waste the studio time. They call me and I sing the notes for a few hours . . .'

'That's an unusual approach, isn't it?'

Was it? Uh oh. Where was Lainey when she needed her? 'Do you think?' she said vaguely.

'And are you a big fan of that sort of ambient music?'

Her tongue took off before her mind could catch up. 'I do like it, yes. It's very relaxing. In fact it can be quite hard to stay awake sometimes.'

'You've fallen asleep in the middle of recording?' The hint of laughter was back in his eyes again.

Eva decided she liked seeing it. She had a feeling he wasn't sure if she was joking or not, but it didn't really seem to matter either way. She warmed to her theme. 'Oh, it happens occasionally. Even Enya nods off sometimes. Especially when we're singing in Irish. The words are so beautiful and we're singing them over and over again, it can have quite a hypnotic effect.'

'You can speak Irish?'

'A little.' She'd learnt it at school, though she'd forgotten most of it. 'But I don't have to be too fluent. We tend to repeat the same words endlessly.'

'I've never really heard Irish being spoken. Could you give me an example? From one of the songs you sing?'

'Oh. Yes, of course.' Her mind went completely blank. Then the electricity pylon across the street caught her eye and an Irish phrase popped into her head. She started singing the three Irish words over and over, very softly, just to give him an idea. '*Bord-soláthar-leictreachas-bord-soláthar-leictreachas-bord-soláthar-leictreachas . . .*'

'It sounds beautiful. What does it mean?'

'Uhm, it's an ancient Celtic myth,' she said. 'About the search for power, that sort of thing.' That would do nicely, she thought. He didn't need to hear she'd just sung the Irish words for Electricity Supply Board.

He nodded. 'And you're a sculptor as well as a singer?'

She accepted the new topic of conversation with gratitude. 'I am. That's really my first love. My passion, really. The singing is just a sideline.'

'You feel passionate about your work?'

She really had his attention, she realised. He was looking at her as if she knew something he really longed to know. 'Oh yes, I completely love it. It's my life, really. I'm always working in some way, looking out for an unusual shape, or an interesting use of colour, wondering how I'm going to put them together.' That sounded good, she thought, pleased. Even if she was actually talking about her shop window displays rather than sculptures.

'And do you produce just one-off pieces? Or do you mass-market some of your ideas, so more people get to see them?'

An easy question, at last. Art versus commerce had been a common topic of conversation at art school. 'Oh no,' she said fervently. 'You can't mass-market art. That would be completely selling out. I think if you truly believe in what you're doing, you have to be prepared to make sacrifices for it. To live simply if you have to. Money gives me freedom, I know, but I don't want to be rich. I think it's too risky, it leaves you open to being compromised.'

'In what way?'

She warmed to her theme, really enjoying the way he was looking at her. Curious. Interested. 'I just think money can be a corrupting influence. Not just in art and music, in every industry. It can cushion people, make them soft. Or place them on a sort of treadmill, where they feel they have to keep running, keep making more, or everything will collapse around them.' Straight out of a second-year art school essay, she thought.

'But everyone needs some money. Especially if you want to travel, see the world like this.'

She thought quickly. 'I'm fortunate, I suppose. My trip has been sponsored. By people interested in my work. Commissions, you know the sort of thing.'

He nodded.

'But I still insist on doing it in a low-key way. No luxury hotels for me, I just keep it as simple as I can.'

'Oh.'

Eva started to feel a bit guilty. She was getting

worse than Lainey with her storytelling now. What next? A quick Riverdance jig on the footpath?

Another taxi pulled up then. A man climbed in and the rest of them moved up a space. A young couple walked down the road and joined the queue behind Joseph.

Eva decided it was time to change the subject. 'And you're on a working holiday, is that right?'

Joseph paused for a long moment. 'Yes. Sort of.'

'And is it easy to get holiday work here in Australia?'

Another pause. 'I don't really know, actually.'

He obviously hadn't started looking yet. 'Well, keep Greg's place in mind, won't you, when you start looking. He does need staff.'

'Greg's place?'

'Do you remember? He gave you his business card?'

'Oh yes.' He smiled at her. 'Do you think he'll remember giving it to me?'

'I'm sure he'll remember. Anyway, I'll remind him for you if he doesn't.'

'Thank you, Niamh.'

What gorgeous eyes he has, she thought. And a really lovely voice – quiet, deep. She realised she was staring at him again. She forced herself to look away.

Two taxis arrived. The second one was Eva's. On impulse she turned back to him.

'Apparently there's a taxi shortage tonight. You could be waiting for ages yet. Do you want to share this one back to the city with me?' She decided it wasn't too big a risk. In any case, she'd be safe enough with the taxi driver.

'Are you sure?'

'Of course. Which way are you going?'

'South Yarra. Chapel Street.'

She knew South Yarra. She'd been looking at cafes there. 'It's right on my way. We can drop you off first.' They climbed into the car and it pulled away from the kerb.

Back at the queue the couple behind Joseph had been listening to the exchange with curiosity.

'Lucky bloke, wasn't he?' Aaron said to his girl-friend as the taxi drove off. 'We should have asked if we could share it as well.'

In the taxi, Joseph leaned forward and gave the driver the name of his hotel. Overhearing, Eva assumed it was a backpackers' hostel. So she was surprised some minutes later when the taxi pulled up in the driveway of a luxurious hotel. Backpacker hostels had come a long way, she thought.

She was quite sorry the trip was over. She'd really enjoyed talking to him. 'It was great to meet you, Joe. And best of luck again, I hope you enjoy your travels.' She suddenly wanted the moment to last longer. On impulse, she held out her hand. He seemed slightly surprised. Then she felt his hand clasp hers. It was strong. Cool.

'Thanks, Niamh. I really enjoyed meeting you too.' They shook hands, very formally, then he stepped out of the cab and took out his wallet. 'Please, take this for my share.'

She waved away the note he was holding out. 'Not at all. You were on my way.'

'No, I insist.' Joseph put the note on the seat and quickly shut the door. With a wave he was gone.

It was only when she got home that she discovered it was a hundred-dollar note.

CHAPTER EIGHTEEN

GREG WOKE Eva at ten o'clock the next morning, full of apologies for his drunken behaviour at the party. He mumbled something about being on antibiotics for a toothache and them not mixing well with the alcohol he'd drunk.

No, I don't imagine two bottles of wine and at least six bottles of beer would mix very well with tablets, Eva thought but didn't say aloud as she twisted the phone cord just out of Rex's reach. The cord had enough little toothmarks on it as it was.

'Will you forgive me?' he asked.

'Of course.'

'And I haven't forgotten my offer for you to come down to Four Quarters. To get some inspiration for your work.'

Eva winced. She had been feeling guilty about that. It was one thing to pretend to be someone else at a dinner party. That had been just a joke. And all right, it had made it easier for her at the party to pretend to be someone else. But coming down to Four Quarters to get inspiration for her work? That was taking it too far. She'd just have to come clean. 'Greg, really, it was very kind of you. But –'

'No buts, Niamh, really. It'd be a pleasure to have you around. You can stay there as long as you like. I'll call the manager now and let her know you're on your way.'

'Greg, I –' She heard another voice in the background then Greg came back on the line.

'Sorry to interrupt you but I need to go. I'll see you again soon, then, will I? This time tomorrow, perhaps?'

'Greg –'

'I hope so. Bye, Niamh.'

He rang off. Eva sat, looking at the phone. She'd tried. She'd just have to tell him next time she saw him. She had just stood up to make a pot of coffee when the phone rang again. She picked it up.

It was Lainey. 'Every little detail, come on. What did you wear? Did he call you Niamh all night? Come on, spill the beans.'

For the next hour Eva and Lainey lay on sofas in their different cities, drinking coffee, talking about Lainey's work and going over every detail of the night before.

'Oh, well done, you. An action-packed night and you made a hundred-dollar profit,' Lainey said at the end.

'I can't keep it, Lainey. The poor man, he must have thought it was a ten-dollar note. I rang the hotel I dropped him at last night and asked to get put through to the hostel section, but they said they didn't have one. And I didn't know what his surname was either, which didn't help. Perhaps he was embarrassed about where he was really staying and just pretended he was staying in that hotel.'

'You never know, you might see him around town again. What did he look like?'

Eva opened her mouth, about to describe him. Dozens of words sprang into her mind. He had beautiful dark eyes. A deep, warm voice. A London accent. He was tall. He wore a T-shirt very well indeed, as though he worked out occasionally. And he had a particular way of looking at her. As if he was really interested in what she was saying.

'Evie? What did he look like?'

Eva didn't want to tell Lainey. She didn't know why.

Yes, you do know why. You don't want to say he was gorgeous in case she wants to meet him herself.

'Oh, dark hair. Tallish.' She quickly changed the subject. 'Lainey, can you give me some advice. I've had an idea, about the shop in Dublin. And I've got myself into a bit of a fix with Greg.'

'Oh, excellent. Tell me everything.'

Eva spoke quickly, explaining the idea she'd had about opening a small cafe in the delicatessen. 'And

Greg has offered to let me come and watch Four Quarters at work. But he thinks it's for inspiration for my sculptures and it's not, and I feel terrible – Lainey, are you laughing at me?'

'Of course I am. You should hear yourself. Oh dear, oh woe. Evie, stop taking everything so seriously. You're not trying to infiltrate the Kremlin. It's just a bit of fun. Greg gets the chance to pretend he knows a famous person and you get the chance to get some good inside knowledge for your own place. It's a win–win situation.'

'But he really believes me. He really does think I'm a sculptor and that I sang with Enya. You should have heard some of the things he was saying at the party.'

'Evie, I've known Greg for years. He will find this funny, I promise you. Eventually. It's time he stopped being so star-struck anyway. And he'll blame me, not you, so don't worry. Just enjoy yourself, spend a nice day sitting in a cafe. You can even claim all your coffees as tax-deductible work expenses. God knows, Greg won't give you one for free. Listen, I'd better go. See you at the end of the week, I hope. And enjoy yourself, okay?'

The next day, Eva arrived at Four Quarters expecting to find the manager, as she had arranged with Greg. Instead, Greg himself was already there and in a complete flap. He was pacing from one quarter to the other, speaking loudly into his mobile phone. Eva cast a glance at it. No, there didn't seem to be any inscriptions on it à la Dermot. That was a relief, she supposed.

She waved across to him and took a seat at one of the tables. It only took her a moment to recognise the music that was playing, in all four quarters of the cafe. Enya.

Greg finally finished his call and came over, all charm and manners. 'Niamh, it's great to see you again. And I'm so sorry again about the other night, you know, those tablets and all.'

Eva accepted his apology with a smile. 'Don't worry about it. You're great to have me here, thanks a million.'

'Did you recognise the music? I got one of the waitresses to go out this morning and buy it especially for you. Is this one of the songs you sang on?'

Eva pretended to listen. God, they all sounded the same to her in any case. 'Ah no, not this one,' she hedged. 'Mine are later on in the CD, I think. You seem very busy, is everything okay? Have I come at a bad time?'

Greg's smile faded slightly. 'No, it's just my bloody daytime receptionist has resigned. Walked out on me, just like that. Didn't give me any notice or anything. Money hungry, she was. But now I'm stuck, I need someone with a great voice to answer the phone and help handle the lunchtime crowds, and the employment agency is giving me the bloody runaround. Saying they haven't got time to audition everyone's voices and their best choice won't be available until later in the week. What am I supposed to do for three days? Answer the phone myself?'

An invisible lightbulb appeared above Eva's head. She could help Greg out of a spot and spend time in the cafe as well. Then she wouldn't feel half as bad. And maybe he wouldn't be half as cross when he found out she and Lainey had been playing a trick on him. 'What about me?'

'You?'

'Couldn't I answer the phone for you? Help out at lunchtime? As a favour, not for payment, that is. Until you get someone else. If my voice would be okay?'

Greg nearly swooned. 'Your voice would be perfect. Better than perfect. Niamh, are you sure?'

'I'm very sure.'

He beamed at her. 'Then it's a deal.'

CHAPTER NINETEEN

JOSEPH LOOKED at himself in the hotel room mirror. He was wearing faded jeans and another of George's T-shirts. Much better, he realised.

He'd certainly had no luck the day before. Dressed in one of the white linen shirts and dark suits he'd worn at the conference, he had called in to several hostels in the city centre. He'd tried to make conversation with some of the backpackers, get some feedback on the backpacks they were using. He wanted to be sure the modifications he was making to the design of his own backpack would be workable.

But no-one would talk to him. The first couple had thought he was trying to sell them something. Another had assumed he was from the immigration department, checking out everyone's visas. She had been out the front door in a flash. Someone else thought he was a Jehovah's Witness. Finally, the manager had come up to him and wanted to know who he was and what was he doing in there, scaring off her customers. He'd gone back to his hotel room, his notebook still empty.

Today would be different. He looked the part *and* he was taking his backpack with him as well.

He decided to avoid the city hostels and head instead for St Kilda. The receptionist downstairs had told him yesterday it was another popular spot for backpackers.

'All human life is in St Kilda,' she'd grinned.

'What do you mean?'

'Oh, you'll find out.'

With his pack on his back he walked down to the tramstop, where a tram was already in sight. He climbed aboard and within minutes had fallen into conversation with a couple of Swedish backpackers. The backpack was the perfect conversation starter, he realised. He'd become a member of a club.

'That's a great pack,' one of them said in perfect English. 'Where did you get it?'

His research was off and running before he knew it. He didn't let on he'd designed it, just spoke about the various features. In turn they showed him their packs, moaning about how uncomfortable the shoulder strap was and how the zip on the waistband kept getting stuck.

Two hours and four hostels later Joseph had talked to more than a dozen backpackers. It was just a shame he didn't have any backpacks with him to sell. He'd had two offers for his own already, and for his clothes as well.

'Cool!' A young American had stopped him in the second hostel. 'Where did you get that T-shirt?'

Joseph glanced down. It had an obscure symbol and the name of a new band. Joseph thought they might have been from Manchester. Or was it Leeds? Somewhere up north anyway. 'A friend gave it to me.'

'They are incredible live, just incredible, don't you think? I saw them in the Melkweg in Amsterdam last year. I could have died a happy man that night. That singer is *so* cool.'

'He sure is,' Joseph said, wondering who the singer was.

'Will you let me know if you ever want to sell that T-shirt? I'm staying here for a few more weeks.'

'No problem.'

Joseph walked down to the end of the street, toward the beach. The receptionist was right. All human life was indeed here. St Kilda was not only home to plenty of hostels, but it seemed to be doing a pretty good trade in drugs and prostitution as well. There was lots of legal money around too, he thought, walking past a sleek, glass-fronted cafe. Inside, the tables were filled with businessmen and women, stylish people, their mobiles and diaries and laptops placed casually on the tables. Outside, a man was begging.

Joseph kept walking along the Esplanade, following

the tram route. He noticed a multi-storey hotel right on the beachfront and stopped. That looked good. Sea views and all. Perhaps he'd move down here, rather than stay in South Yarra. He could swim, relax for a couple more days before he caught the train to South Australia.

He came to a particularly lively street. If all human life was in St Kilda, a good deal of it was based here in this street. Acland Street, according to the sign. He walked the length and back. There were bookshops, biodynamic food stores, restaurants and bars. Gift shops, clothes shops, design shops and a stretch of European cake shops, their front windows temples of adoration to cream and chocolate.

He didn't feel like sitting inside, not on a warm day like this. He kept walking until he came to the beach, and took a seat on a bench by the sand. The fine weather had lured swimmers, picnickers, skateboarders and rollerbladers to the Esplanade and nearby parks. The bay was dotted with boats and yachts and sailboats, multi-coloured sails bright against the blue water.

After a while he took out his notebook, ready to jot down ideas about the backpacks he'd seen all morning and the modifications he'd need to make to his own design if he took the job in Canada. He looked at the blank page, waiting. Nothing. He ran his fingers through his hair. Come on, Joseph, he told himself. Concentrate.

Still nothing.

Then it him like a blow from a sledgehammer. He was sick of backpacks. And not just backpacks, he was sick of ergonomic chairs and spinal-support research and weight-transfer systems. He didn't care about any of them any more.

He'd been fighting against it for months, maybe even years, he realised now. Trying to stay enthusiastic, keeping on top of everything, telling himself that he really wanted to work the long hours, have the breakfast meetings, make deals with the manufacturers. Perhaps he really had enjoyed it once, but he didn't want to do it any more.

The conversation he'd had at the taxi rank with the Irishwoman kept replaying in his head. She was clearly successful but she hadn't compromised herself along the way. She'd remained passionate about her work. Not like him. Yes, he was successful, he was rich, he had his own company, but it wasn't enough any more.

He stared out at the water. So what did he want then? He thought about it for a long moment before the answer came to him. He wanted a different life. A completely new life. Less stress. Less responsibility. More fun.

Joseph gave a soft laugh. Well, that should be straightforward. All he had to do was change every single thing about his life and he'd be happy.

Something else Niamh had said the other night

kept teasing the edge of his memory. He could almost hear her Irish accent, soft, musical. She'd said that if you truly believed in what you're doing, you had to make sacrifices. That money could be a corrupting influence, that it placed people on a treadmill. She had that exactly right. He felt like he'd been on a treadmill for years. And now he wanted to get off.

As he sat looking out at the blue water, he started remembering other things about Niamh. That smile. A dimple that came and went. The silver pendant she'd worn. A very clear mental image of it came to him suddenly. Clearer than any ideas he'd had about his backpacks.

He looked down at the blank page in front of him. Slowly, tentatively, he started to draw the pendant. It had been an unusual shape, he recalled. Not quite a square, not quite a diamond. The pen felt good in his hand. It had been a long time since he'd used a pen and paper to do his designs. Everything was done on computers now, all the weights, measurements and calculations. As he sketched, he imagined the jewellery against a woman's neck. Against pale skin. Pale skin like Niamh's. He kept drawing, his pen sure and fast on the page, adding a figure wearing the pendant. A figure with long black hair.

He looked at it closely. His memory had served him well. The drawing looked very like Niamh. And the pendant in the sketch was very like hers. But if he had designed it, he wouldn't have given it those angles. He drew it again, this time with softer, curved lines. Then another one, interlocking. And another. It was an interesting effect, he thought. Like something from nature, the texture of a pine cone or feathers in a wing. What material would he use? he wondered. Gold? Silver?

He thought back to his final year at school when he'd made the decision to go into industrial design, to channel his creative skills into a practical area. But what would have happened if he'd chosen something different? Decided to study fine art? What would he have been doing now? Would he have been just as stressed, working with a team of artists rather than industrial designers?

Or would he have been living like his father, out in the country, producing one-off pieces? He looked at the designs in front of him. He'd drawn curving shapes and interesting angles not for practical reasons, not to be used for work, but simply because they looked beautiful.

They did look good. There was something there. A sureness of line, an elegance. He felt as though a window in his head that had been shut for years was slowly being prised open . . .

It was time for a very strong coffee. Hoisting the pack onto his back he stood up and brushed the sand off his jeans. He went back to Acland Street, but all the tables in the cafes seemed to be full. He kept walking, heading back toward the hostels, where he found three of the travellers he'd been talking to still sitting outside, including the American man who had coveted his T-shirt. Joseph stopped and asked if they could recommend somewhere good for coffee.

'There's a bar-cafe down there.' The American pointed to the end of the street. 'The food's a bit iffy, if you ask me, but the coffee's good.'

Joseph tried to read the sign but it was too far away. It seemed to be a mathematical equation of some sort. 'That's great, thanks.'

'And don't forget about me and that T-shirt, will you?' the American said with a grin.

Joseph glanced down at his T-shirt. 'Do you really want it that badly?'

The man was embarrassed. 'I do. I'd love it. They're my favourite band. And I've never seen that T-shirt before. But I can't just take the shirt off your back . . .'

Joseph surprised himself as much as the other man. 'Why not?' Putting down his pack, he started to take off his T-shirt. 'Come on, we'll swap.'

'Are you serious?' The American looked down at his own T-shirt. It was just an ordinary one advertising the backpacker hostel he'd stayed at in Sydney.

Joseph nodded.

'Fan*tas*tic.' The swap was done in moments. 'My T-shirt was clean this morning, I promise,' the

American said. 'Straight out of the laundry. Thanks. This is awesome, really.'

'You're welcome. See you.' Putting the pack on his back again, Joseph set off down the street.

CHAPTER TWENTY

'FOUR QUARTERS bar and cafe, good afternoon, Niamh speaking.' Eva spoke into the phone. 'A table for four for lunch today? Of course, sir. Which quarter would you like? Casablanca. That's grand, so. We'll see you at one. Goodbye.'

Eva put down the phone and made a note in the bookings register. Was it any wonder Greg was planning on opening another Four Quarters in Melbourne? He'd certainly hit on a winning formula. This place was hugely popular. She counted the bookings under her breath. Twenty tables for lunch already today.

Twenty tables. She smiled to think if she would ever get to that number at Ambrosia. She'd have to buy the two adjoining shops and knock down a few walls to make room. If her floorplan sketch was at all accurate, she'd be looking at six or seven tables at the most. Even that would be a bit crowded.

Still, she'd already learnt plenty here at Four

Quarters about handling double sittings, getting people to move on quickly and allow other diners in, so that she'd be able to make the most of those seven tables. She was rapidly filling up her notebook with helpful information.

From her position behind the reception desk she'd been able to watch the whole day-to-day running of the cafe. In between answering the phone she'd watched the waitresses at work, seen the customers give their orders, watched the kitchen staff quickly make up the meals. It was a very smooth operation. More complicated than she had in mind for Ambrosia, especially with the four different menus, but it was better to have too much information than too little, she thought.

It had been good fun to dress up for work as well. She didn't get the chance at the delicatessen, the white shirt and black skirt almost a uniform. Today she was wearing her favourite crimson shirt, a patterned skirt, with the silver pendant around her neck. She'd worn her hair down today, pinning a flower in it again. She was really enjoying herself, talking to the mix of locals and tourists, answering the phone and writing up the bookings. And Greg had been so grateful. She'd started to quite like him again, happily accepting his offer to take her down to Phillip Island to see the fairy penguin parade the following night.

She had just made a couple more notes in her notebook when a polite cough in front of her got her attention. The first thing she saw was a T-shirt advertising a Sydney backpackers hostel. She looked up. 'I'm sorry to keep you waiting, can I – Joe! It's you. Hello!'

He recognised her immediately. It was Niamh, wearing the silver pendant he'd been drawing less than thirty minutes ago. 'Niamh, hello yourself.' He smiled at her.

She started rummaging in her bag. 'I'm so glad to see you. I've been looking for you, but the hotel said they didn't have a hostel section so I just had to hope I'd run into you again.'

He had no idea what she was talking about. She guessed as much from the expression on his face. 'You gave me far too much money for the taxi the other night. Here, you have to take it back. All of it,' she said, holding out the hundred-dollar bill she'd been carrying in her purse since the party.

'Did I give you that? I thought it was a twenty.'

'I guessed it must have been an accident. So keep it safely now, won't you?' She spoke mock-sternly.

'But I can't take all of it. You should take some for my share of the fare.'

'Joe, really, I'm sure you need it more than I do.'

Joseph felt a little awkward. He hadn't missed the money at all and probably didn't need it more than she did. But how could he tell her? Especially after all she'd said at the taxi rank the other night. *Thanks anyway, Niamh, but I'm not really on a tight budget,*

I actually flew here as the guest speaker of a national conference and now I'm staying in luxury hotels, having a holiday before I go back to London and sign a contract that could be worth several hundred thousand pounds to me, with a company which more than likely exploits its Third World workers in order to increase profits to shareholders.

No, he didn't think he'd go into that right now.

'Come on, Joe, I mean it.' She was pressing the note on him.

The moment of explanation had passed. He'd taken too long. He reluctantly accepted the money.

'You're here to talk about that job with Greg, are you? Take a seat and I'll get you a coffee. Greg's due in any minute. You might be in luck, I think there's a kitchenhand job going. One of them walked out this morning. It seems to happen a lot here.' Eva moved to the coffee machine and amidst much hissing and steam made him a coffee. 'Here you are. On the house.'

'Oh, thanks very much.'

A group of people came up to the desk to pay. She smiled at Joseph. 'Excuse me for a moment.'

She really did think he was a backpacker, he realised. That he was travelling around Australia, picking up work here and there. It actually sounded quite good, he realised. Much better than the life he had been leading, anyway. What had the dishwasher at Dave's party in Sydney said about backpacking and kitchenhand work? That it was all adventure and no stress? Fun, even? Joseph felt like he hadn't had much fun in a long time.

He noticed the background music just as she came over to him again. 'They're playing your song, I hear.'

'My song?'

'Enya.'

She coloured. He was right. Greg had put the Enya CD on some sort of automatic high rotation, telling everyone that came into the cafe that his new friend Niamh had sung on it. It was driving her batty. She opened her mouth, about to confess that she had no more sung on Enya's album than flown to the moon, nor was her name actually Niamh, when it hit her. If she told Joe the whole story was nonsense and he got a job here, there was every chance Greg would hear the truth. And he might not find it quite so funny from someone other than Lainey. Which might mean she couldn't keep working here. Which would mean she'd lose this opportunity to learn about running a cafe . . . Oh, hell. This was all getting very messy.

Then she took herself in hand. Did it really matter if Greg or Joe thought she was a singer and sculptor called Niamh? Lainey was right, she was taking all of this far too seriously. It was just a bit of a laugh, after all. She was on holiday. She'd probably never see any of these people ever again.

She made her decision. 'That's right. This one was terrible for putting us all to sleep. I'm surprised all the diners in here aren't nodding off as well.'

The front door opened and Greg walked in, his cafe manager Lisa hurrying along beside him. His face was like thunder.

Eva called him over. 'Greg, this is Joe. Do you remember, we met him at the party the other night?'

Greg's face was blank.

'Joe, the English backpacker,' Eva prompted. 'Remember you said he should call in and you might be able to give him a job?'

Joseph interrupted. This really was going too far now. He had to set them straight. 'Actually, if I could explain –'

'As it happens I do need a kitchenhand,' Greg said. 'Urgently. All right, Joe, you're on.'

'Really, thanks very much for the offer but –'

'Cash in hand, mate,' Greg interrupted again. 'Do you need the work or not?'

Joseph glanced across at Niamh. She was smiling at him. The idea of working here suddenly seemed very attractive. Fun, even. Hadn't he just decided he wanted a different life? This could be the perfect trial run. He'd do it, he decided. Just for a day or two, before he went to South Australia.

Greg was still waiting on his answer. 'Well?'

'Yes. Yes, I do need the work. I'm actually running

very short of money.' Good touch, Joseph, he thought, enjoying himself.

'And you're staying near here, are you? In St Kilda?'

Joseph thought of the big hotel on the Esplanade. He'd move down there today. 'Just down the road,' he said.

'Right,' Greg said. 'We'll see you this time tomorrow.'

The manager leant forward and whispered something. 'It's that bad?' Greg said in a low voice. The manager nodded.

Greg looked at Joseph again. 'You couldn't start now by any chance?'

He glanced at Niamh again, who was giving him that beautiful smile. 'Just lead me to that sink,' Joseph said.

Two hours later he understood why there'd been the urgency.

The kitchen was frantically busy. The four different menus were a novel idea but they created a lot of work. He'd already washed hundreds of plates and peeled what seemed like a truckload of potatoes. He was now working side by side with Bill, the other kitchenhand, preparing salad ingredients, hoping it wasn't blatantly obvious he'd not been this close to a whole vegetable for a long time. After months of living on Tesco pre-packaged meals, he'd been ready to believe vegetables came out of the ground ready-sliced.

'So you know Greg's latest squeeze, do you, Joe?' Bill asked, not looking up as he deftly sliced cucumbers.

'Squeeze? Who? Niamh, you mean? The Irish-woman at the reception desk?'

'Yeah.'

So she was Greg's girlfriend. He hadn't been sure. 'No, I don't know her at all. Why?'

Bill shrugged. 'Oh, one of the waitresses said you were talking to her a lot. We thought maybe you knew her from London. You know she's some famous sculptor and singer from Ireland, apparently? According to Greg she sings with Enya. And she's done some sculpture for that singer from U2. He keeps boasting about her.'

'Yes, he told me all about her as well.' Bill seemed very up-to-date, Joseph thought. Maybe he'd know the answer to something about Niamh that had been puzzling him. 'Why is she working here, do you know?'

Bill was indeed well informed. 'Oh, she's not officially working. Greg said she's been commis-sioned to come up with some urban sculpture or something. I don't know the right term, I don't understand art-speak. She's here to get inspiration.' He laughed. 'Imagine a sculpture based on this place! A pile of dirty plates and four crappy menus.'

Joseph nodded. She was even more interesting than he'd thought.

Toward the end of his first shift, he had just piled a frying-pan precariously on the drainer when Eva came into the kitchen. To his surprise she picked up a tea-towel from beside him and started wiping up.

She noticed his reaction and laughed. 'I can't help it. My mother drummed it into me when I was a kid. She always used to say, if you see a dirty dish, wash and dry it and it'll be done in the time you could have walked past it.'

'Thank you. No help turned down.'

Standing this close beside him, she noticed he had a crease in his cheek when he smiled.

'So which part of Ireland are you from?' he asked her, looking across as he scrubbed at another saucepan.

She was about to say Dublin when she remembered he was asking Niamh the question, not Eva. 'Galway,' she said, after slightly too long a pause. 'Have you ever been there?' She'd taken to asking people that, in case she met someone who knew more about the place than she did.

He shook his head. 'I'm sorry to say I've never been to Ireland. But let me guess, you live in a castle in Galway filled with your own artwork, hordes of adoring crowds outside?'

She noticed that spark of laughter in his eyes again. 'No, not quite. Actually, I don't live in a castle. Or even a house. I live in a caravan.' Was that what she and Lainey had told Greg that night? She wished she'd written some of it down.

'Do you really? In a holiday camp? Or is it horse-drawn?'

'Oh no, it's stationary. It's in a field, just outside the city. By the sea.' She thought quickly. 'I work with driftwood and stone and other objects I find on the beach, especially after a storm. That's why I live where I do, to be close to all that wild coastline.'

He stopped joking. 'You're the real thing, Niamh, aren't you?'

Uh oh. 'The real thing?' she asked cautiously.

'A real artist. Living the simple life, away from the city scene. Staying close to your inspiration. Working the way you want to work.'

'I guess I am,' she said carefully.

'Is it a hard life?'

'Uhm, yes, it is sometimes.' It probably would be, she thought.

'But rewarding?'

'I suppose so. I mean, yes, it is. Very.'

Joseph stopped washing up and turned right toward her. 'And what are your sculptures like? Could you describe one of them to me?'

Those dark eyes of his were quite something, she thought. She paused before she answered. She had no idea what her sculptures would be like. She'd only studied sculpture for a few months at art school. But then she pictured something in her mind's eye. An elegant shape, like a wave caught in mid-movement. Or the long graceful neck of a seabird coming out of the water. She described it to him, knowing that she had his full interest. It felt good.

'And you did a sculpture for U2, someone here was telling me?'

'You've heard that too?' The Enya story had been bad enough, but why had Lainey thrown in the U2 story as well?

He nodded. 'You're the talk of the kitchen.'

'Am I?' Oh hell, what could she do except keep making things up? 'Well, yes, I did do one. For Bono's garden. Just a little one,' she said, desperately hoping they could change the subject soon. 'Tiny, really.' She moved her thumb and forefinger until there was only about an inch of space between them.

He looked across. 'An inch-high sculpture?'

She nodded. They were both gazing at her hand. Joseph spoke first. 'It must have been very delicate work, being so small.'

She just nodded again.

Then she was saved by the sound of the bell at reception. 'Excuse me,' she said thankfully.

CHAPTER TWENTY-ONE

LAINEY'S ANSWERING machine was flashing when Eva arrived home from Four Quarters that night. She pressed the replay button. The caller sounded like a middle-aged woman.

'Miss Byrne, Patricia here from Dr Reynolds' surgery. We've had a cancellation and now have a vacancy for the operation we discussed at your last visit. It would be during one of our night clinics on the 14th. Can you please ring me back as soon as possible to confirm that you still want to go ahead with it.'

Eva was shocked. Lainey needed an operation? What was wrong with her? She certainly hadn't mentioned anything. Should she ring her in Brisbane and let her know? It could be important. She dialled Lainey's Brisbane number and waited anxiously.

Lainey sounded very bright. 'Evie, what a lovely surprise. What's up, can't you find the sugar or something? It's in the cupboard to the left of the stove.'

'No, I managed to find the sugar, thanks.'

Lainey kept talking. 'And how is my little Rexie? I hope you're still feeding him, are you?'

'Of course.' She'd been feeding him every day, choosing from the plentiful supply of cans labelled 'Prestige Food for Prestige Kittens'. What was in them? Eva wondered. Lobster? Smoked salmon? Pheasant? Other rare delicacies?

As if on cue, Rex sauntered out from Lainey's bedroom and headed in the direction of the kitchen. Eva glanced over at him, by his feeding bowl, licking something off his paws. Probably pureed white rhino, Eva thought. 'He's dining like a king,' she added.

'And how are you managing with the kitty litter tray?'

Eva's stomach heaved slightly at the thought of the kitty litter tray. She was managing to deal with it. Just. But only if she wore two pairs of heavy-duty kitchen gloves and a scarf over her mouth and nose, to ward off even the faintest suggestion of unpleasant cat toilet odour. She'd even contemplated wearing Lainey's swimming goggles. 'Just fine,' she lied. 'But Lainey, the reason I'm ringing is you've just had a message on your machine. From Dr. Reynolds' surgery. The woman said they have had a sudden cancellation and you could have your operation on the night of the

14th. And honestly, don't worry, you don't have to explain it to me if you don't want to . . .'

Lainey's roar of laughter stopped her mid-sentence. 'It's not for me, you eejit. It's for Rex. Dr. Reynolds is a vet. I really didn't expect that appointment with the vet to come up until I was back. Evie, I know this is a lot to ask, but would you be able to take him?'

'Take him? Actually pick him up and carry him somewhere?'

'You'll have to drive, actually. The vet's about ten minutes away. But don't worry, I've got one of those proper cat carrying baskets. It's a bit old but it's fine. You'll just need to coax him into that and the vet will do the rest.'

'What will be occurring,' Eva chose her words carefully, 'at this said visit?'

Lainey whispered into the phone. 'He's being neutered.'

'*Neutered?* Oh Rex, did you hear that? Do you know what the word neutered means? Do you know what your cruel and heartless owner has got planned for you? Oh Lainey, you daughter of Satan.'

'Eva, don't be awful. Poor little kitten, but I've no choice, it's the best thing to do for an indoor cat. You will take him, won't you?'

Rex looked at Eva. Eva looked at Rex.

'Eva?'

She relented. 'Of course I'll take him. I'll ring the vet right now.'

'Thanks a million, Evie, I owe you one. The number's on a card on the fridge. Now, how is your sightseeing going? I did tell you about the fashion-clearance shops down the road, didn't I? And that lovely cafe with the cheese room just down from there? And which tram to get if you want to go into town?'

Eva laughed. 'Yes, Lainey. You told me all of it.'

'Oh good. See, born to be a tourist guide. Listen, I'd better go. Talk to you later. Thanks again about the vet. And give Rex a pat from me, won't you?'

'Of course.' What with? A glove on the end of a long stick? Hanging up, Eva noticed Rex, just a few metres away, sitting watching her. He almost looked like he had a half-smile on his little kitten face.

She laughed, despite herself. 'How are *you* coping with Lainey, Rex? At least I knew what to expect when I came to visit her. You poor thing, you wouldn't have had any idea, would you? Taken from your mother at such an early age, given a weird name like Tyrannosaurus Rex. Treated like a child, not an animal. What else is she planning for you, Rexie? School? Piano lessons? Cat scouts?'

Rex just flicked up his tail and sauntered back into the kitchen. As she watched, he put one back leg up behind his head and started licking his –

She grimaced. 'Rex, *please*. If you don't get some

manners I'm telling the vet you don't need any anaesthetic.'

Later that night, Eva was in bed fast asleep when something woke her, all of a sudden. She looked at the clock. Three a.m. She turned on the bedside lamp and jumped in fright.

Rex was curled up asleep at the end of her bed. He must have crept out of his basket in the middle of the night, hopping up on her bed and curling himself around her feet. She'd never had a hotwater bottle with four legs and a tail before.

She sat up quickly now, creating a ripple with the quilt that sent the kitten sliding gently onto the floor. He just yawned, then sauntered out of the room, his tail flicking. She listened again. Surely it hadn't been Rex's cat snores that had woken her? No, it was a voice coming from the living room. Someone, a young woman, was sobbing.

Eva sat still, rigid with fear as the tearful voice floated down the hallway. In her half-awake state, she started to think the worst. Was the apartment haunted? Lainey certainly hadn't mentioned it . . .

Then Eva realised that the voice was Meg's. And it was coming from the answering machine. She leapt out of bed in a bound and had just started running down the hallway when she stopped and gave a sudden scream. Rex had been lying in wait for her and had made a lunge for her feet as she ran past.

'Rex, you brat!' Eva roared, hopping on one foot. She could still hear Meg's voice, weirdly amplified through the speaker on the answering machine. 'Sorry, Evie, I hope I haven't ruined everything, I don't even know what time it is there, but I had to talk to you before Ambrose did, anyway, so, uhm . . .' Another sob.

Eva limped the last few metres and snatched up the phone. 'Meg, I'm here, don't hang up, it's me, Evie. What on earth is wrong? Are you okay?'

It took Meg a few tries to speak again. 'There was an accident at the shop this morning,' she finally managed to say. 'I've only just got home. We've been trying to clean up all day.'

'What? Meg, for God's sake, what's happened? Is Ambrose all right?'

'He's fine. No-one was hurt. Just the back of the shop.' Meg was in tears again. 'And it was all my fault, Evie.'

Eva coaxed the whole story out of her. Meg had helped Ambrose tidy the storeroom several days previously, getting completely dirty in the process. Ambrose had suggested she tidy herself up in the spare bathroom upstairs above the back of the shop. So she had, filling up the basin and washing the dirt off as best she could. Then she'd heard Ambrose's call for help with a sudden rush of customers and had hurried back downstairs. 'And that's when it started, Evie.' She was in tears again.

'What started, Meg?'

'I mustn't have turned the bathroom tap off properly. Or taken the plug out. And I just forgot all about it.'

Eva shut her eyes. Oh God. She knew that Ambrose only ever used the front stairs to his flat. He wouldn't have noticed the water. There was a staff washroom downstairs too, so Meg wouldn't have needed to go upstairs again either. Which meant . . .

Meg's next words confirmed her thoughts. 'So the tap just kept on dripping and the basin over-flowed and then the floor flooded and the water ran into the ceiling, the plumber thinks. For days. Until it all got too waterlogged and a whole section of it just collapsed.'

'And Ambrose's flat? How badly was it damaged?'

Meg sobbed. 'That's okay, they think. It's the bath-room and the back of the shop that are completely ruined.'

Eva soothed her as well as she could from this distance, her mind working furiously even as she spoke lots of calming words. Oh, poor Ambrose. This would be the last thing he needed. There was nothing else for it. She'd have to cut short her trip and go home and help him clean up.

'Listen, Meggie, don't worry about it. It was an

accident, do you hear me? I'm sure Ambrose understands that. I'll give him a ring now and see how things are with him. All right now? Don't worry, I mean it, I'll sort it all out with him.'

'What will you do?'

'I'll come back and give you a hand clearing up, of course. And don't worry, I've had a great holiday already, I don't mind a bit.'

There was a long sniff from Meg. Eva guessed that was exactly what Meg had hoped she'd say. The poor thing, she was only a baby really. And Ambrose could sometimes seem much scarier than he was.

'Go on, Meggie, go and make yourself a cup of tea, and I'll ring Ambrose at home now and talk to him about it. And I'll see you soon, okay?'

'Okay,' Meg answered in a small voice.

Eva made herself a strong cup of coffee to wake herself up completely before she rang Ambrose. Her thoughts were tumbling. Did she mind about going back to Dublin so quickly?

She realised she did. She wasn't ready to go home yet. She liked what was happening here. Seeing Lainey. The fun of being Niamh. Being at Four Quarters. Meeting Greg. Meeting Joe. She didn't want to leave Melbourne yet, but she couldn't leave Ambrose to clean up a mess like that himself. She'd have to go back.

Trying to ignore Rex, who was prancing around on the top of the sofa and making little forays up and down the curtains, she picked up the phone again and rang Ambrose's number.

'Come back to Dublin? Cut short your holiday? Are you mad, Eva?'

'But Ambrose, you can't do all that cleaning up on your own. I can't just leave you like that.'

'Of course you can. What are you going to help me with here? Hammering nails and replacing rotten floorboards and ceilings? Eva, there won't be work for any of us. The place will be crawling with plumbers and builders instead of customers for the next few weeks anyway.'

'But Meg made it sound as though the whole shop was in ruins.'

Ambrose actually laughed. 'Yes, well, Meg can be a little excitable at times. Excellent worker, but really, what an imagination. It's not half as bad as she thinks, but she couldn't be told. She's too busy blaming herself to see that it isn't the end of the world.'

'So it's not that bad?'

'It's not that bad. Just a section of the back ceiling and a few broken pipes. Everything's very wet, too, but nothing that can't be dried or replaced. And I'm insured of course.'

Eva's spirits started to lift again. 'So you really don't want me to come back?'

'No. Really. But I know you would, Evie, and I'm very touched. And you know that if I really did need you here, I'd say as much. But truth be told, stay right where you are. In fact, stay right where you are for even longer. Take another week off, if you can change your ticket again at this short notice.'

'What?'

'I'm serious. There's no point rushing back here, the shop will be shut. Take some more time off. Enjoy yourself. You might come back with even more ideas for the shop.'

'So your offer still stands?' She'd hardly dared to ask.

Ambrose was relaxed. 'Of course. I hope you've had a chance to think about it, have you? Though I suppose you've been busy enough with Lainey and all that sunshine and sightseeing. It's just with the rebuilding that we'll need to do out the back, well, if you had any major ideas, now could be the time to . . .' He trailed off at the silence from Eva's end. He had a sudden feeling that she was going to tell him she didn't want to work in the shop at all any more. Or that she had decided to emigrate to Australia. So he was astonished at her next words.

'Ambrose, I have been thinking about what you said. About your offer. Actually, I've been thinking about it all the time.'

He settled back in his chair. 'And?'

She sounded tentative. 'I've had an idea. You said that I could think about changing it, doing something different?'

'And I meant it, Eva.'

'It was something Meg said a few weeks ago. I wondered if it would work if I opened a little cafe. At the back of the shop. Just serving lunches and coffee and cake. As well as the delicatessen at the front, of course. I've looked at lots of places here in Melbourne, and I think it could be done. I mean, I know there'd be lots of work. Building approval, I suppose. And renovations, of course. I pictured it in the back left-hand corner of the shop –'

'No,' Ambrose interrupted.

Eva's heart sank. 'No? That wouldn't work?'

'I don't think so, Evie.'

She should have guessed it was a mad idea. Ambrose had realised straight away. She should have checked with him before she started running around, doing all her research, imagining it –

Ambrose spoke again. 'I think it would work better in the right-hand corner. That's where the water damage is, so we'd have to rebuild there anyway. And you'd need to set up a small kitchen, wouldn't you? The gas pipes are on that side, so that would be more efficient. How much room would you need, did you think? And what about the storeroom? You could move that out into the yard, there's enough room out there, I think.'

Eva felt her spirits fly again. Her skin tingled. 'You think so? You really think it would work?'

Ambrose was very matter-of-fact. 'Evie, I think it would all work. I think it's a wonderful idea.'

'Ambrose, have you got a pen and paper handy, if I was to describe to you what I had in mind? It's early days, I know, but I was thinking we could . . .'

In Dublin, Ambrose was smiling as, directed by Eva, he drew a sketch of her proposed new floorplan. This was even better than he'd imagined. He even laughed out loud at her suggested name, Ambrosia. He said it aloud a few times. He'd think about it, he said. He certainly didn't dismiss it out of hand.

He settled back in his chair and looked down at the sketched plan again. 'Right, now, go on. So where did you propose to put the tables?'

CHAPTER TWENTY-TWO

JOSEPH CAME into the kitchen with a pile of dirty plates. He was about to tip all the leftovers into the bin when Bill the kitchenhand came up behind, saw what he was doing and stopped him with a sudden yell. 'Mate, don't throw them out.'

Joseph was puzzled. 'But they're leftovers.'

Bill peered at the contents of the plate and picked out several uneaten prawns. 'Just give them a quick wash and put them back in the fridge.'

Joseph was appalled. 'What?'

'You've heard of recycling, haven't you? That's what we do here. The boss insists.'

A shout from the head chef interrupted them. 'Bill, three new prawn salads and make it snappy.'

'No need to be so crabby, you shellfish old bastard,' Bill whispered under his breath. 'You do them, Joe, would you? Use those recycled prawns.'

'But that's disgusting.' Joseph couldn't believe this.

Bill shrugged. 'You want to work here, you work the way Greg wants you to work.'

'But people could get sick.'

Bill just shrugged again. 'So? How do they prove something from here caused it? They can't. People get food poisoning the whole time and have no idea that's what it is.' He noticed Joseph's expression and laughed. 'Joe, come on, mate. It's not that bad. Isn't there too much waste in the world as it is?'

By the end of the day Joseph had resolved never to eat out again. He'd never seen such penny-pinching in his life. The British government should hire Greg as a consultant, he thought. The budget would be in surplus within months.

Greg's cafe used every cost-saving trick in the book. The supposedly high-quality extra-virgin olive oil on the tables was in fact cheap oil poured into new bottles. The chicken described on the menu as free-range and corn-fed had arrived in a carton clearly labelled as factory-processed. The bread apparently freshly baked on the premises was day-old leftovers from the bakery three streets away, sprinkled with water and revived in the oven. As for the prawns – Joseph was practically on speaking terms with one of them. It had now appeared on three different plates. He felt like adopting it and taking it back to his hotel. Or at the very least wrapping it in a serviette. It would catch its death going in and out of the fridge like this.

Out in the cafe collecting some more dirty dishes, he glanced around at the crowded tables. He felt sorry for the people who had eaten everything on their plates. Greg should be giving away free antacid tablets rather than peppermints at the reception desk, he thought.

As he looked over at the desk, he gave Niamh a smile and received a dazzling one in return. What was it about her smile? he wondered, going back into the kitchen laden with dirty dishes. It was the contrast, he decided, after giving it some thought. She could look so solemn and then the sudden smile would light up her whole face. It was a lovely effect.

At the end of her shift Eva came into the kitchen to pick up her bag from the staff locker-room. Joe was there, as she'd hoped he would be. She'd caught herself looking out for him all day. 'Hello again. How are you enjoying it here, Joe? Not too drastic a change from industrial design, I hope?'

She'd remembered what he did. 'No,' he said. 'This is much more straightforward. Someone dirties their plate, you wash it and then it's clean again. Simple.'

'So what sort of designing do you do? Bridges? Buildings?'

He didn't want to talk about his work. He wanted to forget that life for a little while. He decided to keep it uncomplicated. 'Smaller scale. Furniture, that sort of thing. Very boring.'

She was about to ask more when Greg came in. He ignored Joseph.

'Niamh, there you are. I'm really sorry, I won't be able to take you to Phillip Island tonight after all. I've got a major problem with the architect at the other premises, could be an all-nighter the way things are going.'

'That's fine,' Eva said, hiding her disappointment. 'I'll go another time. Thanks for the offer anyway.'

Greg's mobile rang. He snapped out his name then started barking into it. 'Okay, okay, I said I'm on my way.'

'Goodbye, Greg,' Eva said, looking after him as he went striding out of the kitchen.

'You were going to go to Phillip Island tonight, to the fairy penguin parade?' Joseph asked. 'Sorry, I couldn't help overhearing.'

'We were. Never mind. As I said, there's always another time.'

Joseph made a sudden decision. 'I was actually thinking about going to see the fairy penguins tonight myself. The backpacker hostel runs tours. Would you like to come with me instead?'

She didn't even have to think about it. She looked up at him and smiled again. 'I'd love to go with you, Joe.'

The Phillip Island bus was parked in front of the hostel when she met Joe at six o'clock that night.

'Are you staying in this one now?' she asked, looking up at the brightly coloured building.

'No, I'm over that way,' he said, pointing toward the Esplanade.

The driver arrived, collected their money and waved them all into the bus. 'It's like a school excursion, isn't it?' Eva said as they took their seats at the back, very conscious of how close they were to each other. Except she'd never felt like this on any school excursions. Nervous, but oddly excited as well. It was a strange combination. Like being filled with helium gas and having lead weights on your feet, all at the same time.

'It is,' he agreed. 'Are you thinking about leading a singalong?'

'Of Enya songs?' she said, trying not to laugh at the mental image that produced. 'Well, yes, I will if you promise to do your John Travolta routine again.'

'It's a deal.'

The bus was crowded, the other travellers of all ages speaking in lots of different languages, only half-listening to the driver who told them they were heading to see one of the top five tourist attractions in Australia.

Joseph spoke in a low voice. 'Australia does a very good line in wildlife, doesn't it? I think it's the first country I've been to where you can visit the national emblem in a zoo in the afternoon and then eat it for dinner that night.'

'You ate kangaroo?'

'Actually, no I didn't. I drew the line at that. And crocodile. And emu. I'm keen to try a fairy penguin burger tonight, though.'

She tried to look appalled and then laughed. 'And have you done a lot of this sort of tourist thing?'

'No, this is the first, really. But it's growing on me.'

'It'd be a pleasant way to live, wouldn't it? Being ferried around all day, told where you're going, what you're looking at. Like being a baby in a pram all over again.'

'But you'd have to make sure there was something special, like these swimming penguins, at the end of each trip, wouldn't you?' he said in a thoughtful voice. 'Perhaps Buckingham Palace should follow this example. It would certainly get British tourism up and running again.'

'What, get your royal princes and princesses to swim home up the Thames each night?'

'Exactly. Wouldn't that do them good? They could pick out the rubbish along the way, really earn their keep.'

'Just as well we don't have an Irish royal family then. They wouldn't last an hour in the Liffey, especially the stretch near my house. Too busy dodging all the shopping trolleys in there.'

'The Liffey? I thought that was in Dublin.'

'It is.'

'But you live near Galway, don't you?'

She gazed at him. This was it. This was the time to confess all. No, she didn't live in Galway. She lived in Dublin. And her name was actually Eva, not Niamh. And just by the way, she wasn't actually a sculptor, she was a very ordinary shop assistant.

But at that moment she realised she didn't want to tell him the truth. She liked the way he called her Niamh. She liked how interested he was in her sculpture. How curious he was about where her ideas came from. How he really listened to her when she answered his questions. She was liking lots of other things about him too. His clever, kind face. His great smile. It seemed to start in his eyes before it reached his lips.

And she felt she had lots to talk to him about. As Niamh, that was. Ordinary old Eva would have found it much harder, she was sure of it. She would have felt awkward. Tongue-tied. But pretending to be Niamh made her feel different. It was like slipping on a confidence cloak, an invisible shield between her and the rest of the world. If she told him the truth now it would only change things, wouldn't it? Spoil their trip? She didn't want to do that.

He was still waiting on her answer. She made her decision. 'Sorry, I meant to say when I used to live in Dublin. Years ago. I went to art school there.'

As the bus drove through Melbourne's suburbs she started to relax. She really didn't have to keep up the Niamh charade all the time, she realised with relief. There were plenty of safe subjects. They talked about their impressions of Australia. He talked about London. She talked about Ireland. She told him about her parents and much older sister. He told her he was an only child, that his parents had divorced years before. He talked about university, she talked about art school. They talked about the sort of music they listened to, books they'd read. He wanted to read a book of Australian short stories that she had and she offered to lend it to him. She wanted to read the Bill Bryson book he had, so he offered to lend her that.

'You like reading, Niamh?'

'I love it,' she said. Truthfully again. 'I keep picking books up at markets and things, thinking, Oh, I must read that one, oh here's a classic I haven't read. I'm hoping for a long retirement, I think, a chance to catch up on them all. Or a broken leg, even. Something that keeps me bedbound for a few months. It's my only hope of catching up on my reading.' She was surprised at the sudden smile he gave her.

The more they talked, the more he listened, the more confident she became. He asked her lots of questions, listening closely as she described her childhood and her adventures with her friend Lainey. She told him that Lainey had emigrated to Australia, that she was staying with her now.

'You're not staying with Greg then?'

'With Greg?' she said, puzzled. 'No. Why would I stay with him?'

'Isn't he your boyfriend?'

'Oh, no,' she said firmly.

She thought she felt a sudden, subtle change in the mood between them.

They reached Phillip Island just as the sun was setting. Their bus group joined many other groups of people strolling along the beachside boardwalk to a kind of open grandstand facing the ocean. As the sun disappeared into the horizon, sending bright pink and orange light into the sky, the seats filled completely. There were hundreds of people sitting there.

Eva shivered, the cardigan she was wearing not much protection against the sea breeze.

'Are you cold?' Joseph asked.

She turned toward him and shook her head. 'No, it's not too bad, really. I'll be grand.'

He had taken off his coat before she had time to protest. 'Please, wear this.'

'But you . . .'

He gave her that slow smile again, the one that did odd things to her heartbeat. 'I'm fine. Please, you wear it.'

He helped her put it on. It was still warm from his body. She could smell the subtle aftershave he wore. Then someone called out from behind them. 'Look, here they come!'

Eva was glad of the distraction. Completely conscious of Joe sitting close beside her, of the feel of his coat around her, she gazed out to sea, trying to sight any penguins in the water. There were just a few at first, all under two feet high, surfing the waves into the beach and waddling up the sand, past the grandstand packed with people and up to their burrows in the sandhills behind.

As the minutes went by, there were dozens more, each one funnier than the last. There were small darting penguins, in a big rush to get back to their burrows. Slow-moving, plump ones, their tiny wings outstretched as though they were carrying invisible and very heavy suitcases. Several indecisive ones, coming halfway up the beach before changing their minds and starting to head back to sea. There was a very round, comical one that Joe pointed out to her. She indicated a tall, thin one. 'Ally McBeak,' she whispered. He gave a quick, low laugh, an amused look in his eyes.

Soon there seemed to be hundreds of penguins, the sea alive with them, the beach crowded with small waddling bodies. As another few dozen birds ambled by, so close they could have leaned over and touched them, Joseph leaned over and spoke in a quiet voice.

'Do you suppose there's a penguin tourist industry operating at the bottom of the sea as well?'

She was puzzled. 'What do you mean?'

'You know, maybe word's got around among the penguins. "Come on, let's all go to this beach, just on the edge of this little island near Melbourne. It's incredible. Night after night, there are hundreds of humans just sitting there, looking out to sea. It's really worth a look."'

Eva's sudden burst of laughter brought a sharp glance from the guide.

Their bus was back at the hostel by ten o'clock. Stepping off it, they stood side by side. Eva felt a little awkward. She didn't want the night to end yet. Summoning her courage, she was about to ask if he'd like to have a drink when he beat her to it.

They walked along the Esplanade, coming to a big white hotel, crowded with people. A blackboard out the front advertised several bands. A poster on the door read: 'Cabaret tonight in The Gershwin Room.' 'Would you like to try that?' he asked. 'Not too noisy?'

'Oh, I do like to come in out of the Celtic mists now and then.'

They walked into a back room, dodging the crowds, the carpet sticky under their feet. At the door a young woman was packing away a tray of money. She waved them in. 'The band's doing their final set, you're just in time.'

The room was like an intimate club, darkly lit, a coloured mirror ball throwing drops of light onto the walls. On stage a five-piece band was doing cover versions of classic songs. The male singer, dressed in a beige lounge suit and rollneck jumper, was crooning into the microphone like a young Dean Martin. The small dancefloor was crowded.

They found a vacant table at the side of the room. 'Can I get you a drink, Niamh? Wine? Beer?'

'Red wine. But let me.'

He stood up. 'No, I'll get it.'

She watched him as he went over to the bar. He was tall enough that she could see him over the crowd, talking to the barmaid. He had such beautiful manners, she thought. Greg should take some lessons.

He came back with their two glasses of wine just as the band finished a funny, extravagant version of 'What's New Pussycat'. The band was very slick, three guitars, a keyboard, drums. The singer was only young but with a strong, pure voice, taking the microphone from the stand and moving out into the crowd, speaking in a patently fake American accent, playing up to the audience. He moved smoothly into Frank Sinatra mode with 'Night And Day' and 'Fly Me To The Moon'.

Then he introduced the final number. 'Last chance for the dancefloor, ladies and gentlemen. Last chance to dance.' The band started the distinctive introduction to Burt Bacharach's 'Anyone Who Had

A Heart'. The singer went down on one knee, his voice low and sexy. Eva smiled. It could have been Luther Vandross himself singing. She felt a touch on her arm. She turned. It was Joe, looking very serious.

'Our last chance to dance. Will you, Niamh?' He held out his hand.

The colour rushed to her face. She hoped the low light hid it. 'Dance?'

The singer used a break in the lyrics to repeat his words. 'Your very last chance, ladies and gentlemen. The dancefloor awaits.'

Around them several other couples got up, smiling at the singer's patter.

Joe was waiting, the amused look still in his eyes. 'Our last chance, Niamh,' he repeated.

She stood up then. The wine and the dim lights and the music seemed to be having a strange effect on her heartbeat. It was racing. She followed Joe to the dancefloor. They stood still for a moment, just inches from each other.

'I did tell you I was the British ballroom-dancing champion as a child, didn't I?' he whispered.

'I had wondered about that number pinned to your back.'

He gave her a sudden smile, then took her hand in his. She put her other hand on his shoulder. It felt firm, muscular. The music was slow and sensual. Slowly they began to move round the dancefloor. She was intensely conscious of the feel of his hand on her waist. The realisation that he was so much taller than her, that his aftershave was having an odd chemical reaction with her blood. She saw the crease in his cheek again, this time from very close range. He had laughter lines around his eyes. And she noticed in the light that his hair was going just slightly grey.

She closed her eyes briefly. The dancefloor was very crowded now. She felt his hand around her waist, the slight pressure. His body, close to hers. It felt good. Better than good . . .

Then it was over. They sat down, the applause for the band sounding around them. But it took a while for her heart to stop beating so quickly.

The main lights came on too soon, too bright and revealing, the taped music jarring after the smooth sounds of the band, changing the mood. They joined the rest of the crowd filing out into the night air, squelching over the sticky carpet again. She didn't want to go home yet. They started walking, heading toward the pier by unspoken agreement. She glanced at him. He didn't seem to want to go home yet either.

They walked along the wooden boards, talking softly, passing other people, some fishing, others just standing there talking in low voices. They stopped before they got to the cafe at the end of the pier and leaned against the barrier. A wind had whipped up, the air suddenly chilled. She shivered.

'Would you like my coat again?' he asked, his voice low.

'That's not fair. Then you'll get cold.'

His eyes were dark in the moonlight. 'We could share it.'

As she came toward him, he opened his jacket and folded it close around her. She felt the warmth again, the feel of his chest close against her own. There was a long moment when they were still. She felt all her senses wake. She could hear the waves hitting the beach, feel the breeze against her face, smell the salt in the air. The touch of his hands on her back. He leaned toward her, his lips touched hers. It was the softest of kisses. A gentle exploration, tentative. She closed her eyes, feeling the warmth of his body, the feel of his arms behind her, holding the coat against her. It felt safe and beautiful and sensual all at once.

After a long while she pulled away, overwhelmed with how she was feeling. His eyes were dark, his expression as serious as she knew hers was. The next kiss lasted even longer, soft and slow. Eva closed her eyes tight, feeling the caress of his fingers on her back. She moved closer against him.

'Niamh,' he breathed her name.

Her eyes snapped open. He'd called her Niamh. He was kissing Niamh, not Eva. Had she taken complete leave of her senses? What had got into her on this holiday? She had to slow all this down, she had

239

to tell him the truth. She stopped the kissing then and took a small step back. 'Joe, I'm sorry . . .'

'It's all right, really. I understand.'

'You understand?'

'It's all happening too quickly?'

She gazed up at him. Hating herself, hating her cowardliness, she nodded. 'That's it, I suppose.'

He kissed her forehead. 'Will we go back?'

Slowly, arms around one another, they started to walk back along the jetty. Eva felt self-conscious again. It did seem to be happening too quickly, and she didn't know quite what to do now.

Halfway along, it started to rain. By the time they reached the Esplanade it was pouring down. A taxi pulled up beside them, two people jumping out and running across the road to the hotel. The driver wound down the window and called out to them. 'You waiting?'

Eva felt like she needed to press a pause button for a moment, take all of this in, before anything else happened. 'Yes, please,' she called to the driver.

'I think I should go home,' she said, turning back to Joe.

'You're right. It's late. And we do have work tomorrow.'

She smiled at that. 'Would you like to share the taxi again?'

'No, I can walk from here. It's not far.'

She needed to leave but at the same time she didn't

want to go. 'Thank you, Joe. I really enjoyed tonight. The penguins, the pub, the band, everything.' She sounded like a polite child, she realised, embarrassed.

'Thank you, Niamh,' he said, just as politely. 'So did I. I'll see you tomorrow.' Then, just before the taxi drove away, he kissed her quickly again.

Eva let herself into Lainey's apartment and walked into the living room without turning on the lamps. The red flashing light of the answering machine caught her attention. She pressed it. Lainey's voice filled the dark room.

'Evie, it's me. Where are you, darling? Listen, I'll try again later. Heading out myself now for another work dinner, so I'll talk to you later, okay? Bye.'

There was a second message. Lainey again.

'Still out, Evie? God, you've got a better social life than me. Are you out with Greg again? I'll try again later.'

The phone rang again as Eva stood beside it, making her jump. It was Lainey once again. She had just started to leave a message when Eva picked it up.

'Lainey, it's me, I just got in.'

'Evie, at last! Are you okay? I've been trying all night. When I kept getting the machine I got a bit worried that something had happened to you. Are you okay? What have you been doing?'

Eva sat down on the sofa with a bump, still

holding the phone. Oh yes, she felt okay. She felt better than okay, she felt . . .

'Evie, are you there? Hello? Don't say the bloody phone has packed up.'

'Sorry, Lainey, I am here.' Eva snapped out of her thoughts.

'So what *have* you been doing tonight?'

Eva sat down, still dazed. 'Having one of the best nights of my life, I think.'

CHAPTER TWENTY-THREE

GREG WAS waiting behind the reception desk when Eva came in the next day. She smiled at him. She'd woken up feeling like she was in love with the whole world.

'Hello, Greg. Have you come to present me with my gold watch for long service?'

He just stared at her blankly.

'It's my last day,' she prompted him. 'Remember? Your new receptionist is starting tomorrow.'

'That's right, so she is.' He paused. 'You went to see the penguins last night after all, I hear?'

'I did.' One of the waitresses must have told him. She smiled broadly. 'Aren't they the gassest things? The way they walk. And there were so many of them. We were expecting a couple of dozen at most, but there –'

He interrupted her. 'You went with that Joe? That kitchenhand?' He made 'kitchenhand' sound like another word for leper.

'Yes, with Joe.' What in God's name was Greg's problem? Was he *jealous*?

'I was going to take you,' he said, almost sulkily.

He *was* jealous. Well, if he was going to behave like a child, she'd talk to him like a child. 'Yes, Greg, you were,' she said in a patient voice, 'but you had to work. And Joe offered. And I am only in Australia for a little while, so I accepted his invitation.'

That seemed to satisfy him. 'So are you free tonight? For dinner with me?'

She hoped she wasn't. She wanted to see Joe again. That morning she'd lain in bed thinking about him. She'd decided she really wanted to see him again. Talk to him again. Kiss him again. And most important of all, tell him everything. About her real name, her real life and her real job.

'Niamh?' Greg prodded.

'I'm not sure yet,' she hedged. The phone rang. As Eva moved to answer it, Greg walked away to speak to the manager, his face stony.

It was Lainey. 'Listen, Evie, can you talk? I've got a crisis.'

She looked around. Greg had gone into the kitchen. 'What's up?'

'My landlord's just rung on my mobile. He's finally agreed to build new cupboards in my bedroom but only as long as his brother-in-law does them. And his brother-in-law can only come and measure up tomorrow night, when he's up from Wangaratta or some place out in the bush.'

'So you want me to be there to let him in?'

'No, he's got a key. It's just that I really don't like him to be there when I'm not. He came up once before to do the kitchen cupboards and I swear he went through my things. Could you . . .'

'Be there when he comes? Of course I will. What time?'

'He can only make it in the early evening. After work.'

Eva pulled out her diary. Written across the page in question were two words. 'Rex. Vet'. 'Oh Lainey, I can't. I'll be taking Rex to the vet then. Unless you want me to postpone that?' she asked hopefully.

'Oh God no, that's much more important. Poor little Rex needs that done as soon as possible. Oh, damn. Let me think for a second . . .'

Beside her Eva heard a cough. Greg was in front of the desk, waiting for her. 'Just a moment, Greg.' She smiled politely at him.

Lainey overheard. 'Is that Greg there? Greg Gilroy? Can I talk to him?'

Eva handed the phone over to a surprised Greg. She watched as Greg listened to Lainey for a few minutes. He pulled out his diary. 'Sure, I can. What, round six o'clock? No worries, Lainey. Happy to help. I met Niamh because of you, after all. Heh heh. Yeah, see you.'

He passed the phone back to Eva, who was shuddering a little inside. 'Lainey?' she spoke into the phone.

'All sorted. Greg will go to the flat for me. He's great on all this renovation and building business, too. And I even remembered to call you Niamh when I was talking to him, aren't I great?'

Eva pressed the phone closer to her ear, hoping Greg hadn't heard. She was pleased when he moved away.

Lainey kept talking. 'So is that all okay with you too, *Niamh*? You could leave a spare key out for Greg to let himself in while you take Rex to the vet. Then he can wait for the landlord's brother and just let himself out afterwards.'

No wonder Lainey was doing so well in her job, Eva thought, feeling slightly streamrolled. But these arrangements did seem to make sense. 'That all sounds fine,' she said.

She had just hung up when she saw Joe come in through the front door, carrying a bag. Her stomach gave a funny kind of leap at the sight of him. 'Hi.'

'Hi.' He gave her that slow smile. 'Thanks again for last night. I really enjoyed it.'

'I did, too. Very much.' Eva wanted to stand there smiling at him all day.

'Are you free tonight? To see that film we were talking about last night?'

She nodded. 'I'd love to.'

He reached into the bag he was carrying. 'I brought you that book we were talking about, the Bill Bryson one.'

'And I brought one for you too. The short stories.'

Greg came over just as they were exchanging the books. 'What is this, a book club?' He picked up both of them. 'Never heard of them. More of a Stephen King man myself. Know his stuff, do you, Joe?'

'I do,' Joseph said.

'Like them, do you?'

'I do. They're terrific. Real page-turners.'

Greg looked ostentatiously at his watch. 'You'd better get to work, Joe. Another busy day.'

Joseph turned toward Eva. 'See you tonight,' he said clearly.

Greg stared back and forth.

'We're going to see a film,' Joseph explained, very nicely. He gave Eva a quick wink, then went into the kitchen.

Ten minutes later Greg came into the kitchen. Joseph was at the sink washing a large pile of saucepans. Greg didn't meet his eye, just spoke in a loud voice. 'Had to make a change to the roster, mate. I need you to work a double shift today, all right? Through till ten-thirty.'

'No problem at all, Greg,' Joseph said. The film they wanted to see didn't start until eleven. He turned back to the saucepans.

CHAPTER TWENTY-FOUR

'REX, PLEASE come out. This isn't funny any more.'

Eva lay down on the floor and peered under the cupboard again. She could just make out a kitten's silhouette in the shadows. 'Rex, come on, it'll be great fun at the vet's, really. I promise you.'

Eva had spent the last hour and a half trying to coax him into the basket. She'd already had to ring the vet twice to say she'd been delayed. The receptionist hadn't seemed to mind. 'The vet's doing a few of these procedures this evening, so we can just move little Rex to the end of the queue.'

There were going to be lots of pre- and post-neutered cats at the vet's surgery? She'd already been told she'd need to wait for a while after the operation, to be sure that Rex had fully recovered. It would be like sitting in some kind of kitten purgatory, she thought. There were some times she wished Lainey wasn't her friend.

'Oh, Rex, please. It's Lainey's fault, not mine.' She reached under the cupboard, sliding her hand from side to side. This method would mean she might actually have to touch him, but if it was the only way – '*Owww*!' She pulled her hand out swiftly. There was a long red scratch down the back of it.

He must have guessed what was going to happen to him. Eva couldn't blame him. She'd be hiding under a cupboard if she was being neutered today too. She tried another tactic. 'Rex, I'd actually be perfectly happy if you stayed a male cat, but all the research shows it just won't make you happy. This is just the best thing all round, physically and psychologically. So would you please just get in that basket? Not for Lainey, not for me, but for yourself.'

Nothing. Not even a hint of movement.

The intercom buzzed. Eva jumped, hitting her head against the cupboard. Oh hell, that would be Greg. She'd hoped to have left the spare key out for him and been well gone by the time he arrived. He'd been at Four Quarters the previous night, entertaining a table of businessmen, when she had arrived back there to meet Joe after his shift finished. He'd been watching as they left together, Eva had realised. And he hadn't been happy about it.

The intercom buzzed again. Twice. 'Coming!' she called.

'Okay, Rex, please stay right where you are,' she spoke under the cupboard before going to the door.

At least if the kitten stayed there she'd know where to find him. She'd already wasted thirty minutes chasing him from room to room.

'Hello,' she said cheerfully, as she let Greg in. 'I'm sorry the key wasn't left out for you. I'm just running a bit late, still trying to put Rex into his basket.'

Greg walked in past her and made his own way through to the living room. He smirked when he saw the basket on the floor in front of the cupboard, with an assortment of cat toys and lures scattered in front of it. 'Having a few problems?'

'Just a few,' Eva admitted. 'It's a bit hard to catch a cat when you're not used to them.'

Greg seemed to find it funny. 'They're very simple creatures, Niamh. Really. Like women. All they care about is their food and comfort.' He smiled as if to say, no offence, I'm only joking of course.

Fortunately he had gone into the kitchen and didn't see the expression on her face. I'll stick *you* in the basket and take you to the vet, you sexist pig, she thought. Only the fact that this sexist pig was going to pick up the soon-to-be-castrated cat made her bite her tongue. What was Lainey doing hanging around with people like this? Disobedient cats. Sexist pigs. She'd really fallen into bad company since she'd emigrated.

Greg came back with a tin of opened catfood. With a condescending 'Watch this, you might learn something' kind of smile, he tilted the tin in Rex's direction and let the smell waft under the cupboard. Nothing happened for a few seconds. Then one little black paw appeared. The top of a little black head. Then half a kitten body. In seconds Greg had scooped Rex up and dropped him in the basket, tin of catfood and all. He quickly shut the lid.

'There you are. Simple.' He was very pleased with himself.

'My hero,' Eva said with a fake smile.

Greg glanced at the cat basket. 'You know that the clasp is broken?'

Eva hadn't noticed. 'But it still closes, doesn't it?' she asked hopefully.

'Seems to,' Greg said, trying it again. 'Anyway, he won't be in it for long, will he? Just the drive to the vet. Then he'll probably be a bit dopey on the way back, so it shouldn't be a problem.'

Eva gingerly picked up the cat basket, holding it away from her body. A black paw came out through the plastic bars and made a grab for her T-shirt. She held the basket even further away. 'Well, thanks for that, Greg. I'll have to leave you to it, I'm sorry, I'm late enough as it is.'

Greg nodded. 'So did you enjoy yourself last night?' His jealous-and-hurt voice was back again.

She nodded. 'I did, thanks.' She'd really better get going, especially if she was going to leave time to get lost on the way there, as she knew she would. 'Thanks again, Greg. You're happy to let yourself out?'

He was already settling on the sofa with a newspaper. She left before he had a chance to suggest dinner or a film tonight. She'd decided there was something about him she really didn't like. And it wasn't just his dancing.

Outside, Eva quickly packed Rex and his basket into the back seat of Lainey's car. She wound the seatbelt around the basket to hold it secure, spent a few minutes working out her route, then drove off. As she turned onto the freeway and settled back to enjoy the driving, she started thinking about the conversation she'd had with Lainey that morning.

'I can't believe it, I leave you alone for a second and look what you get up to. So what's Joe like? Does he like you? Do you like him?'

'Lainey, I don't know. We've only just met each other.'

'But you've been on proper dates with him, haven't you?'

'Not really. We just went to see the penguins together. And a band. And a film.'

Not that they'd seen the whole film the night before. Midway through, Joe had leaned over and whispered to her, 'Have you seen enough?'

'What?'

'Have you got the general idea?' he whispered. 'Do you want to leave? Go somewhere we can talk rather than just sit beside each other?'

She'd nodded. That was exactly what she'd like to

do. So they'd crept out of the cinema, bumping against other patrons, and practically ran down the road to a small bar. And there they'd stayed, talking and drinking wine until it shut at two a.m. and they were asked to leave.

Lainey was roaring laughing. 'You don't call those dates? Of course they're dates. If they look like dates, walk like dates, they are –'

'Lainey, shush.' Eva interrupted, laughing too. She'd changed the subject then.

Eva thought about it now. Lainey was right. They *had* been sort of dates. But not like any she'd ever had before. There'd been no awkward silences, for a start. She and Joe had found plenty of things to talk about. She kept finding more and more things about him that she liked. His hands. The way his black hair stood up in tufts now and then when he ran his fingers through it. His body. She liked the things he noticed. The remarks he made. The way he made her laugh. The way he kissed her.

She felt relaxed with him. Completely herself. Except for one small problem. She wasn't herself when she was with Joe. She was Niamh Kennedy, the sculptor.

She glanced at her reflection in the rear-view mirror. She didn't look like a woman harbouring a secret, did she? Like someone living a lie? No, she didn't look like one. But she was one.

She *wanted* to tell him. She'd rehearsed it all in

her head. But the right opportunity had never presented itself. She couldn't tell him just before they went into the cinema, there hadn't been time. And they'd been laughing so much when they'd crept out that that wasn't the right time either. And in the bar there had been too much else to talk about. The last thing she'd wanted to do was change the mood, ruin both their evenings.

The worst of it was she didn't have any excuse not to tell him the truth, not any more. She'd finished working at Four Quarters now. She didn't have to worry about Greg finding out from someone other than Lainey. There was nothing standing in the way of telling Joe the truth. Except one small obstacle. The possibility of Joe deciding the real Eva wasn't half as interesting as the fake Niamh.

It was Niamh's life that intrigued him, she already knew that. Her stories about her lifestyle in Galway. Her sculptures. Her inspiration. He had wanted to hear all about it last night. They had talked about lots of other non-Niamh things, though, she consoled herself. But it had all been within the pretend framework of Niamh's life. It couldn't go on like this. She knew that.

As she pulled up in front of the vet's surgery, she made her decision. Again. The next time she saw him she'd tell him the truth.

Joseph sat in a cafe on Acland Street thinking about Niamh. A conversation he'd had with her the previous night kept replaying in his head. It had started when he'd come back to their table in the wine bar with two more glasses. She'd looked up and given him that beautiful smile. 'I really admire you, Joe, do you know that?'

He'd nearly spilt the wine. 'Admire me? What for?'

'Your courage, I suppose. Your adventurous spirit. The way you've just packed up and come over here, all on your own. Just travelling around, taking things as they come.'

He'd started to protest but she'd interrupted. 'No, I really mean it. I know lots of people do it, young ones especially, but when you're as old as we are, in our thirties –' She'd smiled at him. 'Things are harder, don't you think? You can't be as impulsive. But you have been. I think it's great.'

He'd felt like walking out of the door in shame. Impulsive? Taking things as they come? Him? She couldn't be more wrong. It had been planned for months. Rosemary had looked after all his travel bookings. This trip was about as impulsive as a military campaign.

He should have told Niamh the truth there and then. Confessed everything. But he hadn't.

Because it had felt too good to see her on the other side of the table, smiling at him, telling him how much she liked something about him. It had felt uncomplicated. Good. Right. It was just a shame she had it all wrong. He wasn't a carefree, impulsive, adventurous backpacker. He wasn't what she thought he was.

He hadn't set out to mislead her in any way. It had just happened. Then, as time had passed, it had seemed too awkward to backtrack, to fill in the details. *Actually, Niamh, I'm not a backpacker, I'm a business traveller staying in luxury hotels. I don't work for a company, I own a company. I'm not running out of money, I'm rolling in the stuff.*

But he'd let it go on. Too long. As he took a final sip of coffee, he made a decision. He'd call her, ask her to have dinner with him. And then he'd tell her the truth.

Chapter twenty-five

The carpenter packed away the measuring tape and stood up. 'Well, that's the lot. I'll make up the cupboards at home in Wangaratta and we'll get them fitted in a month or so.'

Standing at the doorway to Lainey's bedroom, Greg nodded. 'Thanks. Lainey will be very pleased.'

From the front door he called out as the carpenter went down the stairs. 'And don't forget that place I told you about. Four Quarters in St Kilda, yeah? Bring all your mates, you'll love it.'

'Righto, mate.'

Shutting the door, Greg came back into the apartment. It had taken less time than he'd expected. He checked his mobile. No calls missed. His next appointment wasn't until nine that night. He'd make another coffee, have a break. Maybe even have a nap. He'd been having a lot of late nights lately.

As the kettle boiled, he went for a roam around

the flat. He'd been here several times before, for Lainey's dinner parties and to collect Niamh that night, of course, though she hadn't let him in for some reason. Nice apartment, he thought. Great location too.

He'd already been in Lainey's bedroom with the carpenter. He wandered down the corridor toward the second bedroom. This must be Niamh's, he thought. He opened the door and had a quick look round – it was very tidy. Good. He liked a tidy woman. He'd half expected sketch books and uncompleted sculptures to be lying around. Maybe even some early versions of the work she'd been researching at Four Quarters. He planned to invite her out for dinner again, ask her all about it. If she could spare him a night, he sniffed, instead of spending all this time hanging around with that backpacker. God knows why, he thought. Maybe she was getting some research material from him as well.

She must have some of her work here, Greg thought. Didn't artists spend their whole time sketching and coming up with ideas? Maybe she kept it locked away. He was about to open one of the wardrobes when he heard the phone ring. It was probably Lainey. The answering machine was just clicking into action as he came into the living room. Lainey's recorded voice broadcast into the room, brisk and businesslike.

'Hi, thanks for ringing. We can't talk right now, please leave your message after the tone.'

There was a click, then the caller started leaving a message. 'Hi, Niamh. This is Joe.'

What was he doing ringing here? Just how friendly was he with Niamh? Greg kept listening.

'I saw an Italian restaurant in Prahran today, I thought you might really like it. We could go there tonight perhaps? Around eight? I'll ring back again and see what –'

Greg snatched up the phone. 'Hello.'

'Hello? Who's that?'

'Greg Gilroy.' Greg spoke in his deepest voice.

'Oh, hello Greg. Could I speak to Niamh please?'

'She's busy.'

'Busy?'

Greg thought quickly. 'Sleeping.'

'At six-thirty?'

Greg pitched his voice low. 'Come on, mate, you know how it is.' He laughed in a bloke-talking-to-bloke way. 'She's worn out. In bed. We had a bit of a, what would you call it, a marathon session.' That laugh again.

'You what?'

Greg smiled into the phone. Good. Joe was sounding suitably shocked. He kept his voice low as though he was afraid of being overheard. 'Actually, mate, I owe you a favour. Niamh and I had been going through a bit of a rough patch. Then she started flirting with you to make me jealous, and I don't need to tell you, it certainly worked. Pulled me into line, that's for sure.'

'You and Niamh? Since when?'

Greg spoke very confidently. 'Oh, a while. I guess you could call me her patron. Of sorts.' That suggestive laugh again. 'You know these creative types. Head in the clouds most of the time. She needs someone like me around her. Someone who understands the business world, who can advise her.' The inference was clear. Not someone like you.

'You're her business adviser? Haven't you just met her?'

Greg gave a contemptuous laugh. This scruffball could back right off – he'd seen Niamh first. 'Is that what she told you? That she just met me? She's extraordinary. We met last year, when I was in Ireland. That's why she's out here. So do you want me to give her a message? When she wakes up?'

There was a long pause.

'Tell her I rang to say goodbye.'

'You're going somewhere?' Greg asked, pleased.

'To South Australia. On the train tonight.'

Greg put on his best boss voice. 'Tonight? You seem to have forgotten something, mate.'

'What?'

'You're rostered on to work tomorrow morning.'

'Am I? Then you saved me the phone call. I resign. Goodbye.'

Greg smiled. Too bad. Backpackers were a dime a dozen. And then he remembered something else. He hadn't paid Joe yet. Even better.

It was past eight o'clock as Eva parked Lainey's car in the underground carpark and came up the stairs to the flat carrying a dozing Rex in his basket. The operation itself had been straightforward enough. It was the waiting around afterwards that had been traumatic. For her, not Rex – all those poor cats in baskets everywhere she looked.

She walked into the apartment, turning on the living-room lights as she came in. To her astonishment Greg was stretched out on Lainey's sofa, fast asleep. Putting down the basket, she dropped the car keys with a clatter onto the table. The noise woke Greg immediately. He opened his eyes and stretched. He didn't seem at all uncomfortable to have been caught making himself so at home.

'Sorry to wake you, Greg,' she said sweetly. 'I thought you'd have left by now. Hasn't the carpenter been yet?'

'Oh yes.' Greg stretched again. 'That was all fine. I kept a close eye on him.'

'Oh good, thanks.' Then why are you still here? Her question was unspoken.

He seemed to guess what she was thinking. 'I just thought I'd wait until you got back. To see how Rex was, in case he had to be lifted out of the basket. I know you don't like touching him.'

That was thoughtful of him. 'Thanks very much. But the vet said I should just leave him in the basket. He can get out himself when he feels better.'

'And how did the operation go?'

Greg was behaving very oddly. Like he had a secret. Oh no. Had he been through her room while she was away? She'd tidied up in a big hurry, making sure nothing too incriminating was lying around. But he wouldn't have gone through her cupboards, would he? Would he?

'Uh, the operation – it went fine, I think. As far as these things go. I mean, it can't be pleasant having your . . .'

'No, I suppose not. You had a phone call, by the way.'

Joe, Eva thought. 'And you answered it?'

'Just by instinct, sorry. I was standing right by the phone.'

'Who was it?'

'Oh, just that English guy, Joe. The kitchenhand. He was ringing to say goodbye to you.'

'*Goodbye?*'

'Yes, he said something about going to South Australia tonight. On the train. Leaving me in the lurch at the cafe, thank you very much. Just as well I haven't paid him yet.'

Eva didn't want to hear about Four Quarters. She

wanted to hear about Joe. 'Sorry Greg, can you just say that all again? Joe said he's catching a train *tonight*?'

'That's right.'

Eva couldn't believe her ears. 'Did he say anything else?'

'No.' Greg looked at her innocently.

Eva was astonished. And very hurt. She sat down, speechless.

Greg smiled at her. 'So I guess you're at a loose end tonight? Perhaps I could take you out to dinner somewhere nice again?'

Eva didn't want to go out to somewhere nice with Greg. She wanted to be somewhere ordinary – somewhere anywhere – with Joe. She tried to smile, trying to be polite. Greg was Lainey's friend, after all. 'No, but thanks anyway, Greg. I actually don't feel very well. I might just have an early night tonight, I think.'

'Tomorrow night then?'

'Perhaps.' Eva wished he'd leave. She stood up as if to guide him toward the door. 'I'll call you, will I? If I'm feeling better?'

'Any time, Niamh, any time.' He turned and went down the stairs, two at a time. Good, he thought as he climbed into his car. A job well done, Greggie boy. He wasn't a successful businessman for nothing.

Inside the apartment, Eva sat down on the sofa again. Joe was going to South Australia? Just like that, without saying goodbye to her in person?

I mean, of course he can, she told herself. We've only just met. He doesn't have to check with me before he does anything. But to just leave like that? Was it something she'd said to him? Something last night? The night before? The day before that? She rewound it all, running through it quickly in her head. No, they'd had great times. And it was he who had suggested they go out again tonight. He'd even said he'd choose somewhere and would call and let her know where.

Maybe Greg had been mistaken, she thought hopefully. Maybe that hadn't been Joe on the phone at all. Maybe it had been another friend of Lainey's. Eva went over to the answering machine again. Maybe miraculously she had imagined everything Greg had said and there would be a lovely message from Joe waiting for her, inviting her out.

The light wasn't flashing, but she couldn't help herself. She pressed the play button. Her heart leapt as Joe's voice came out of the machine. 'Hi, Niamh. This is Joe. I saw an Italian restaurant in Prahran today, I thought you might really like it. We could go there tonight perhaps? Around eight? I'll ring back again and see what –'

The message stopped there. The phone had obviously been picked up by someone.

The phone had obviously been picked up by Greg. So Greg had spoken to Joe. And told him what? Something that had made Joe decide to go to Adelaide tonight.

Eva switched off the machine, instantly raging at Greg. Who did he think he was, sticking his nose into her business? God only knows what he'd said to Joe. She had a mind to ring him there and then, have it out with him, find out what sneaky lies he had –

A voice piped up in the back of her mind. *Isn't that the pot calling the kettle black? You telling Greg off for being deceitful? You've hardly been Miss Honest, Straight and True yourself, you know.*

Oh shut up, she told the voice. Greg was the least of her worries in any case. It was Joe she cared about. She didn't want Joe to leave just like that. She wanted to see him tonight, tomorrow night, lots of nights. Damn Greg. Damn him for whatever it was he'd said. He'd ruined everything.

She sat down in the armchair, landing right on top of a hardback book. She picked it up. It was Joe's book. She hadn't even had a chance to return that to him either. How could she contact him? Track him down and explain? Then she remembered he'd told Greg he was catching the train to Adelaide. But which train? From where? And what time?

Several quick phone calls later she knew. The overnight train to Adelaide was leaving from Spencer Street station in the city in less than an hour.

Would she have time to get there? The traffic in the city centre would be heavy. Her sense of direction wasn't the best and Lainey's car wasn't the fastest. But she might just make it.

She was halfway down the stairs when she remembered Rex. Napping in his basket. What if he woke up hungry, distressed, and no-one was there? More to the point, what if Lainey heard that he had woken up hungry, distressed, and no-one was there?

She turned and ran back up the stairs before she had time to think. She picked up the basket, trying not to bump Rex around too much. She was nearly out the door again when she remembered she'd promised to ring Lainey and give her a report on Rex's operation. Oh hell. Did she have time?

She dialled Lainey's mobile number. 'Come on, come on,' she said, impatiently. It rang several times, then switched to Lainey's message bank. She was probably in a meeting, Eva thought. She listened to Lainey's businesslike voice on the recorded message, waited for the beep, then quickly left her own brief message. 'Lain, it's me. Just to let you know Rex is fine. It all went well. He's a star patient. I'll give you all the gory details later, okay? Bye now.' She hung up, then ran out of the apartment and down the stairs.

Five minutes later she was on the road.

On the Overland train at Spencer Street station, Joseph walked into his first-class sleeper cabin. It was fine. Compact, clean. Good.

His mind was clear. Businesslike, even. The conversation with Greg had served that purpose at least. He must have been living in some strange dream world the past few days. Spending time with Niamh. Talking to her. Laughing with her. Kissing her. Having fun. But he'd been mistaken. She hadn't been interested in him after all. It had all been to get at Greg. And he'd been taken in so easily. It was as well he'd discovered the truth now, before he started feeling even more . . . He stopped his thoughts there.

He needed to forget about Niamh. Think about Lewis instead. And Kate. He looked at his watch. It was a good time to ring London. He stepped off the train and dialled her number on his mobile. He hoped the battery would last. He hadn't charged it for a few days.

'Hello, Kate.'

'Joseph! How are you? I've been thinking so much about you. Is the trip going well?'

'It's going fine,' he said briefly. He thought about what a different answer he might have given if he'd spoken to her yesterday. Yesterday he'd felt optimistic, on the verge of something great. As though his life was about to change from black and white into colour. Today he felt . . . Today he just felt like himself again.

'And where are you? In Sydney still?'

'No, at the railway station in Melbourne. I'm on my way to see Lewis.'

'Oh Joseph, I'm *so* glad. Thank you.'

'Should I call him, let him know I'm on my way . . .'

She interrupted. 'No, no you don't need to do that. I'll call him for you. He'll be very pleased to see you, whenever you arrive. I know that.'

'And is there anything I should know before I meet him?'

There was a long pause. 'Yes, there is a lot you should know. But you shouldn't hear it from me. It's time you heard things from Lewis.'

He was surprised at the depth of feeling in her voice. 'What things?'

'Talk to Lewis, Joseph. Please. And I'll be thinking about you both, I promise you.'

'Are you okay?' Her voice sounded odd.

'I'm fine, I'm fine. And I love you very much. Never forget that, will you?' She hung up before he had a chance to answer.

Two hundred metres away, Eva was cursing as she drove round and round the short-term carpark. Had *everyone* in Melbourne decided to catch a train today? To hell with it, she decided. She'd park in the long-term area, pay the extra fee. At least there were spaces there.

It was a warm night. Humid, even. Eva pulled into a parking space and quickly wound up the window, leaving it open an inch or two to give Rex some fresh air. She peered in at him in his basket in the back seat. He looked back at her, eyes shining through the bars. Poor little fellow. She hoped he wasn't feeling too uncomfortable. 'It was for your own good, Rexie.'

She locked the car doors and had just turned to go into the station when she stopped again. She couldn't leave him in that warm car. Lainey would be furious if she heard. She'd be cross enough that Eva had left him alone, but if she cooked him as well? She quickly unlocked the door again.

'Come on, Rexie, come and see the lovely train.' With the basket in one hand and her handbag and the Bill Bryson book in the other, she headed for the entrance. Now all she had to do was find the right platform. She hoped she'd be in time.

Back in his cabin, Joseph took out his notebook and tried sketching some more designs. Nothing. The door to his imagination seemed to have locked tight again.

He stared out the train window. The station was crammed with people. Last-minute passengers running down the platform. People wheeling trolleys piled with luggage. Couples having tearful farewells.

Niamh carrying a shopping basket in one hand and what seemed to be his book in the other . . .

Niamh?

He looked again.

It *was* Niamh. Peering into each carriage window as if she was looking for someone. Him?

She drew level with his window. He watched as her face cleared and a smile of relief came over it. She waved the book, then quickly walked out of sight. Seconds later she was at the entrance to his cabin.

She put the basket on the floor and stepped inside. 'Joe, thank God I found you. I was sure the train was about to start moving.'

He was very surprised to see her. 'Why *are* you here?'

She paused, then held out the book. 'I wanted to return this to you.'

'Oh. Thank you.' He took one end while she held the other. It was almost as if they were holding hands. She let go first. Then they both spoke at the same time.

'Joe, I can only guess what Greg said to you . . .'
'Niamh, Greg told me . . .'

They both stopped. 'You first,' he said.

'No, after you.'

'Please.' His voice was firm.

She glanced at the clock on the platform. She was running out of time. 'Joe, I don't know what Greg said to you, but all I know is that you rang to talk to me about going out tonight and the next thing I knew you were going to South Australia. So I'm assuming it was because of something he said.'

'Niamh, it's fine. I should have realised you and Greg were a couple.'

'Me and Greg? Is that what he said? That we're a *couple*?'

Joseph nodded.

'Oh no, Joe. That's not true,' she said passionately. 'He's a friend of Lainey's. My friend Lainey. The one I'm staying with. She needed someone to be at the house while a carpenter came. Because the carpenter had been through her cupboards last time he was there on his own and it gave her the creeps. I couldn't because I had to take her cat to the vet's, so she got Greg to do it instead. I only know Greg through Lainey. He's not even my friend. Not really. Let alone anything else.' She knew she was talking too much but she wanted him to know all the facts.

'So you didn't meet him in Ireland last year?'

'He said that as well?'

Joseph nodded again.

'No, I didn't. I only met him here, in Melbourne, nearly two weeks ago. I can't believe he said all that. Was there anything else?'

Joseph paused. 'He said you'd been using me to make him jealous.'

Eva's face showed her dismay. 'Oh Joe. That must have made you feel *awful*.'

He gave a ghost of a smile. 'Yes, it did, actually.'

A voice came over the PA system, making them both jump. 'Five minutes to departure. Would all non-passengers please leave the train immediately.'

Eva started talking even more quickly. 'Joe, it was all lies, everything Greg said. I don't know why he said what he did and I wouldn't go out with him in a million years, I'd much rather go out with –' She blushed and tried again. 'Go out to dinner with you.'

This time he did smile. Properly.

Since she had gone this far, Eva decided she may as well keep going. 'I felt sick when I guessed that he'd done something like this, and I couldn't let you go without saying goodbye.' She came to a halt, thrown by the look in his eyes. The warmth again. And something else. 'I'd better go, you're about to leave, but I just wanted you to know the truth.' About Greg at least, she realised with a heavy heart. This was hardly the time to tell him the truth about Niamh. She turned to pick up Rex's basket.

Behind her Joseph spoke suddenly. 'Come with me, Niamh.'

She spun around. 'What?'

'Come to South Australia with me. Tonight. It's just an overnight trip.'

'To South Australia?'

'You're on holiday, aren't you? Do you have to be in Melbourne tonight? Or tomorrow?'

She thought quickly. Lainey wasn't coming back for a few more days. Did she need to be in Melbourne? The train was creaking. 'No, I don't. Not really.'

He spoke quickly. Persuasively. 'Then come with me, on the train tonight. I'm just going to South Australia for the day. We could fly back to Melbourne tomorrow night.'

Go to South Australia just for one day. Fly back?

'I've got thousands of frequent flyer points,' he lied. 'Let me cash them in for you. My treat. The train trip as well, I insist.' She needn't know he didn't have a frequent flyer point to his name, he couldn't be bothered with them, but he'd happily buy her a hundred flights and a hundred train tickets if she'd come with him.

She shook her head. 'Joe, I can't.'

'Why not?'

'I haven't got any clothes. A toothbrush.'

'I'm sure you could buy a toothbrush on the train. Or in Adelaide. I can loan you a T-shirt tonight if you need it. But you look lovely in that dress. I don't mind seeing it all day tomorrow as well.'

Eva glanced down at her simple shift dress. He thought she looked lovely in it?

'Will you come with me?'

Very, very tempted, Eva was about to nod when she remembered something else. Rex. Down at her feet, he was asleep in the basket.

The train gave a jolt. 'Oh Joe, I'm sorry. Of course I can't come with you. There's Rex.'

'Rex? *Another* man?'

Eva laughed and pointed down to the basket. 'No. That Rex. Kitten Rex.'

She had a kitten in there? He'd heard of kitten-heel shoes. But kitten baskets?

A whistle sounded on the platform. The train gave another jolt and slowly started to move. Joseph felt very light-hearted again. He didn't care if she had an alligator in that basket. 'Great. Bring him too. And then over a bottle of wine you can tell me exactly why you're carrying a live kitten around Melbourne.'

'Over a bottle of wine?'

'In the bar. On this train. Tonight.'

Eva blinked at him. Was she going completely mad? She couldn't just jump on a train like this, could she? With a near stranger and a post-surgery cat. Even if it did feel like the most wonderful, stupid thing in the world to do . . .

She looked out of the window. The platform had disappeared. The train was moving very quickly. It seemed she didn't have any choice.

Joseph had realised the same thing. 'Welcome aboard,' he said.

CHAPTER TWENTY-SIX

THE CONDUCTOR was very put out about his extra passenger.

As Eva listened to a lecture about the inconvenience to both him and the catering staff of not booking in advance, she thought it was probably just as well he didn't know about Rex. The kitten and the basket were hidden away in the tiny bathroom in Joseph's cabin. It had seemed the safest option.

The conductor hummed and hahed, as he checked the bookings sheet. There were quite a few empty sleeper cabins on the train but he didn't want them to know that. Yet. He stared at them both, standing in the corridor smiling like two cats that had got the cream. What did they have to be so happy about?

'So, do you want another cabin or will you be sharing this one?'

There was a split-second awkward pause, then

Eva leapt in. 'Oh, another one please.' She felt she should explain why. 'We've really only just met, you see.'

They'd only just met but they'd decided to go on an overnight train trip? Why didn't they just go and have a drink together like normal people? Looking down at his booking sheet one more time, the conductor finally relented. 'Well, luckily there does seem to be one empty cabin. Two carriages down. So, cash or credit card?'

He watched with some bemusement as the couple had a spirited discussion about who would pay. First the English man insisted it was his idea, so he would pay. Then the woman – Scottish, was she, or Irish? – insisted it had been her decision, so she would pay, and she could probably afford it as much if not better than he could. The conductor couldn't believe his ears. What had happened to the days when women did exactly what they were told? He blamed Germaine Greer.

Finally the woman agreed to let the man pay as long as he agreed to let her pay for their lunch the next day. And any drinks tonight. The conductor hoped to God this pair would never think about getting married. Their pre-nuptial agreement would take years to sort out.

He took the credit card and started to write out the ticket. 'Name?'

Eva was on the verge of saying Eva Kennedy

when she stopped herself. Oh hell, it would have to be Niamh again. This was certainly no time to break the news to Joe. And the conductor seemed cranky enough as it was. She couldn't imagine him standing there patiently while she explained about her real name and her real job and her real address . . .

Finally it was sorted. A single ticket to Adelaide. A cabin booked, two carriages down. Yes, there was a bar on the train. Yes, there was food available. Possibly there was a seafood roll or a tuna sandwich, he answered, in response to the woman's sudden question. And certainly she could get a glass of milk from the bar. What was she on? he wondered. The Eat Like a Cat Diet?

Mad bloody tourists, he thought as he went on his way.

Joseph shut the door as the conductor left.

'Was I too obvious?' Eva asked at once. 'Do you think he guessed?'

'That we had a stowaway kitten?'

She nodded.

'No, of course not. I'm sure lots of people are as interested in fish and milk as you were.'

'Lucky he went when he did, then. I was about to ask if he had any toy mice.'

Joseph unlocked the door to the small bathroom and retrieved the basket. Rex was awake, peering out through the bars, bright-eyed. Eva watched as Joseph opened the hatch, reached in and gently lifted Rex out. He stroked the kitten's head. 'He's a nice little fellow.'

'Actually he's not any more. Not since about two hours ago.'

Joseph winced. 'Ahh. That's why you were at the vet's?'

She nodded.

Joseph held Rex even more carefully. 'So he's been in that basket since then?'

'He has, I'm afraid. We've had a hectic afternoon.'

'And do you usually carry him around with you everywhere you go or is this a special occasion?'

'It's a bit of a long story.'

'Later, yes? Over a glass of wine? You'll tell me everything then?'

'Everything, I promise.' More than you're expecting, Joe, she thought with a sudden sinking heart.

Just then Rex leapt out of Joseph's hands and made for the bathroom. He seemed to be walking quite gingerly. No wonder, Eva thought, given what he'd been through that afternoon. As she watched in some horror, the kitten crouched in a corner of the shower cubicle. An unpleasant noise was followed by a very unpleasant smell. Seconds later Rex stepped delicately out of the cubicle, sat down and started to give himself a good wash, all over.

Eva was mortified. 'Oh God, Joe, I'm so sorry. If I'd known he was going to do that I would have made him do it in my cabin.'

'It's fine,' he said, laughing. 'I had a cat when I was a kid.' He leaned into the bathroom, lifted Rex out, turned on the shower to full strength and heat and firmly shut the door. He was trying not to smile. 'We'll let it run for a while, what do you think?'

She nodded, too embarrassed to smile back. 'I think that's a very good idea.'

Half an hour later, Eva had forgotten all about Rex's bathroom habits. She was sitting with Joe in the lounge car. They had enjoyed a glass of complimentary champagne and shared some sandwiches. A good portion of the filling was now wrapped in a serviette in her bag, ready to be fed to Rex, who was now in his basket in her cabin.

They sat opposite each other, a bottle of red wine between them. Outside, the countryside lay in darkness, interrupted occasionally by the lights of a town or a car on the nearby highway. The noise of the train was like a soundtrack to their conversation, a constant reassuring clacking sound. The other tables were filled with passengers, their talk and laughter a constant hum around them.

'Did you have something in South Australia you really wanted to see tomorrow, Joe? I hope I haven't spoilt your plans.'

He shook his head. 'Oh no, you haven't spoilt my plans at all.' He'd wondered how to bring this up.

'Actually, I need to go to one of the wine regions. To the Clare Valley. It's a couple of hours' drive from Adelaide.'

She smiled. 'You *need* to go to the Clare Valley? It's a burning ambition? A dare?'

He wanted to tell her why. He wanted to tell her all about his father. But it would change the mood between them, surely. And the fact of the matter was, he didn't want to say or do anything that might change what was happening right now. He had that lovely drifting feeling back again. Some of it was the wine, but most of it was the feeling that he and Niamh were floating slowly toward each other. Getting closer and closer. He wanted to kiss her. Touch her . . .

He realised he hadn't answered her question. 'No, it's not a dare.' He thought quickly. 'I've just heard the wine is really good.'

'All this way to buy some wine? You are keen.'

'I'd like to see where it comes from, I guess. Like buying milk from a farm, rather than a supermarket.' He stopped there. 'Would you like to do that, come to the Clare Valley tomorrow?'

'I'd love to,' she said. The way she was feeling she'd visit a canning factory with him.

She had never felt this alive in a man's company. This was a million miles from how she had felt with any other boyfriend she'd had. And it was a trillion miles from how she'd felt with Dermot. As for telling him the truth about the Niamh story tonight – well, she'd ruled that out completely. They'd gone beyond talking about what she did for a living, or what he did for a living, for that matter. Or where they lived. He hadn't been talking to fake Niamh tonight as far as she was concerned. He'd been talking to Eva, who just happened to be called Niamh at the moment. So there was absolutely no reason to change the mood and bring up a subject like that, was there? No reason at all.

Yes, there is. It's called the truth.

She ignored the voice. 'And after that, Joe? Is there something else you'd like to do on this trip?'

He didn't say anything out loud. But she instantly felt as though she could read his mind. *I'd like to touch you. Kiss you. Make love to you.*

At that moment she became completely physically aware of him. She felt like her skin was sending off vibrations in response to his. Every part of her had sprung to life. It was as though an electric current had been switched on between them. She knew he was aware of it too. His expression had changed from the warm, interested look she had enjoyed all evening. His eyes had darkened, his face was still.

She knew she wanted to kiss him. She'd had to stop herself all night from leaning forward to touch his arm. But she hadn't expected this . . . This what? she wondered. This absolutely intense longing for him.

Their next moves were all unspoken between them. He asked for the bill. She paid, as she had insisted she would, and he didn't protest. Didn't speak. They weren't communicating to each other in words any more.

The walk back to her carriage was tense with anticipation. Eva led the way, conscious with every part of her of Joseph's closeness behind her. They still hadn't touched. They moved along the narrow curving corridors, crossed over the swinging join between each carriage. They still hadn't spoken.

They reached her cabin. She turned to him. She could see the longing in his eyes. 'Will you come in for a coffee?'

He knew she didn't have any coffee. He didn't want any coffee. 'Yes, please.'

Her hands were shaking as she unlocked the door. She had folded down the bed before she went to dinner, telling herself she was just being organised, knowing that she hoped exactly this would happen. That Joe would come into her cabin with her.

She switched on the lamp and jumped in fright. Rex had managed to get out of his basket. He was stretched full length in the middle of her bed, fast asleep.

The charged mood between them relaxed slightly. Joseph smiled. 'Would you like me to pick him up?'

'Do you mind?'

Shaking his head, Joseph picked up the sleeping kitten and draped him over his right shoulder. Rex wriggled, then fell asleep again.

How could he do it? Eva thought. But at least Rex had got them past the first awkward moment.

She felt unsure of what to do next. What to say. 'Would you like a seat?' The polite enquiry was ridiculous, she knew. They were standing in less than two metres of space, with the bed the most dominant feature.

Joseph sat down on the edge. Eva sat beside him. They were both looking straight ahead. The only thing to look at was the bathroom door. Then they both turned toward each other to speak at the same time. Their faces were just inches apart.

And then much closer.

And then even closer still.

For a long moment she couldn't speak. She looked into his eyes, the dark irises getting darker as she watched. She gazed at his skin. His lips. He met her halfway.

The first kiss was soft as silk. Just a brush against each other's lips. They both pulled back. There was another long look. Then they leaned in again. Eva put her hand to the side of his face, loving the feel of his skin, of his hair, bringing his face closer to hers, his lips harder against hers. She felt like her blood had turned effervescent. They moved closer against each other, their bodies pressing tight.

Then Eva yelped and sprang back. She'd felt sharp teeth on her ear. Rex. Still on Joseph's shoulder, the kitten had been squashed between them. He was now hissing, his nails dug into Joseph's shirt. Now Joseph yelped.

'Sshh.' Eva was relieved to be laughing, her head still spinning from the kiss. 'The conductor will hear you.'

Joseph was trying to untwist Rex's claws and was laughing now too. 'You'll have to help, Niamh.'

'I can't,' she said, hardly able to speak for laughing. 'I can't touch him.'

Joseph finally untwisted the kitten's claws. Eva had the basket ready and Rex was unceremoniously dropped into it. She'd have to try and fix that broken latch in the morning. Basket and cat were moved into the bathroom again, the door left slightly ajar to give him air.

Eva and Joseph were back to square one, sitting side by side on the bed. Joseph turned to her and spoke in a quiet voice. 'Can we try that again? Without Rex?'

She nodded, her eyes closing in pleasure as she felt his hand stroke the side of her face, come around to her neck and move her face closer to his. The kiss was silk again. Long and slow and languorous. Then a little harder, faster. Eva felt herself move slowly back against the bed, felt the beautiful heavy weight of Joe on top of her. Their lips stayed together, her arms wrapped tightly around his back.

The blood seemed to be rushing in her ears. She felt every sense start to shimmer, felt her body start to open toward him as the kiss went on and on, slow and strong. She wanted this. It was all happening quickly but it felt so right. The barest touch of his hand on her arm sent a shiver of pleasure through her. She heard herself moan as he moved his lips from hers and started to gently kiss her neck.

He gasped as she worked her hand under his shirt, her fingertips hot against his bare skin. Then they both heard a hammering at the door.

'Good evening. Conductor.' Another sharp knock.

They both sprang up, feeling like teenagers caught out by their parents.

'What does he want?' she whispered.

'I don't know.'

There was another sharp knock. 'Conductor.'

'Just a moment,' she called. She stood up, straightening her dress. Turning around, she saw Joe, lying there, watching her every move. It was all she could do not to ignore the conductor and fall straight back into his arms. She touched the side of his face. His hand came up to meet hers. The electric charge rippled between them again.

Smoothing her hair, she opened the door.

'Evening, Miss,' the conductor said. He looked beyond Eva to Joseph, now sitting upright on the bed. 'Evening, sir.'

'Hello there.'

'Sorry to disturb you, Miss. But I didn't get your order for the morning.'

Eva tried to get her thoughts straight. 'My order? For breakfast? Uhm, toast? Eggs?'

'Breakfast is served in the lounge car, Miss. I supply just the tea or coffee.'

'Oh. Good.'

'Well?'

'Sorry?'

'Which would you like?'

'Oh. Tea, please. No – coffee, please. Either.'

He gave her an odd look.

'Coffee,' she said firmly.

'The time?'

Eva was puzzled. She wasn't wearing her watch. 'I don't know, I'm sorry.'

The conductor sighed. 'I mean, what time would you like your coffee? We arrive at Adelaide at seven-thirty. Do you want to be woken at six, six-fifteen, six-thirty or six-forty-five?'

Each of them. Anytime. Not at all. I don't mind. Could you please just leave us alone? About to answer him, she realised that the conductor was staring over her shoulder. He seemed to have lost interest in her waking time. Eva turned around to see what had caught his attention.

On the bed, Joseph turned to look too.

Coming out of the bathroom was a small black kitten.

CHAPTER TWENTY-SEVEN

THE CONDUCTOR ruled his train like a fiefdom. And a serious fiefdom rule had been broken. No live animals in the carriages.

'Madam, it is not only completely unhygienic to have a cat in your cabin, it is against the law.'

Eva was no longer Miss, she noticed. She was madam. For a moment she thought about pretending that the conductor was having hallucinations. *Cat? What cat?* Or perhaps she could say she'd never seen that cat before and couldn't begin to imagine how it got there.

Then Rex came up and started winding between her legs, purring loudly, as though she had hand-reared him from birth. She took the defensive option instead. 'He's not really a cat, he's just a kitten. And he's just had a very serious operation.'

'On his deathbed or not, he will have to travel in the goods carriage. It's not ideal but it's the only option. And there will of course be an extra fee. There could even have been a fine but I'm prepared to waive that, on account of the animal being a small one.'

Just as well Lainey didn't have a pet elk, Eva thought.

Behind her, Joseph stood up from the bed. It was getting very crowded in the small cabin. 'Niamh, do you want me to look after this? Take Rex down?'

'Thanks, but no. I'll take him and get him settled myself.'

The conductor was standing there waiting to escort her, as though she was a criminal. He was clearly displeased that Joe was here too. Would he send Joe down to the goods van as well? No live animals and no funny business in my carriages, young lady.

Eva desperately tried to communicate as much as she could to Joe in just a long look. *I wish we hadn't been interrupted. I want to keep kissing you all night. Please wait here and I'll be back as soon as I can.*

But it seemed Joe was no mind-reader. 'You're sure I can't help? Carry the basket or something?'

'No, really, I'm fine. But thanks.' He couldn't come with her. She was going to have to pay Rex's travel fee by credit card and she couldn't risk him seeing her real name. She decided to throw all subtlety out the window. 'Will I meet you later?'

Joseph smiled. 'In my cabin?'

She nodded.

Behind her, the conductor was sighing, without any subtlety at all. 'If you could put the cat back in the basket, madam, and follow me?'

Joseph noticed Eva's expression and stepped forward. 'Let me help.' He picked up Rex and put him in the basket, quickly withdrawing his hand out of way of the grasping claws.

As the conductor headed down the corridor, another long look passed between Eva and Joseph.

'See you soon.'

'Yes.'

Eva felt like she was doing a Walk of Shame as she followed the conductor through every carriage, past curious eyes in the lounge car, past people sitting looking out from their cabins. It took nearly five minutes to reach the goods van at the end of the train. The conductor unlocked the door with a flourish, rattling the keys like a jailer. A dim light in the middle of the van roof showed shelves filled with neatly stacked suitcases, mail bags and parcels. Several bicycles were leaning against the side of the van, their pedals rattling with the movement of the train. Rex started mewing.

'If you'll put him there, madam.' The conductor pointed to a space beside the bicycles.

'But he'll be terrified of the noise,' she protested. 'He's just a tiny kitten. And he's had a terrible shock today.'

'Madam, he shouldn't even be on the train. You're lucky I'm not reporting you to the RSPCA. Now, please, put him there. It's by the vent. He'll be able to breathe at least.'

'Please, can't he go over there?' She pointed to the other side, among the mail bags. 'He'll be nice and cosy there. And there's another air vent.'

The conductor relented. 'Okay. That's fine.'

Eva placed the basket on the floor, put a small parcel on top to hold the clasp down, then joined the conductor at the doorway. She dared to look back. Rex was pawing at the side of the basket, doing his silent mewing trick. She couldn't leave him like that. She imagined Lainey's voice. 'You left him? On his own? With just bikes and parcels for company? Oh, Evie, and I *trusted* you with him.'

Then Eva thought about Joe. Waiting in his cabin for her. But she couldn't just leave Rex. 'Can I have one more minute with him?' she begged.

The conductor practically counted to sixty under his breath as Eva crouched beside the basket, muttering to Rex and feeling self-conscious. 'You'll be fine, Rexie. It's just for one night, and I'm very sorry. But Lainey doesn't need to know about any of this, okay? This can be our secret. A sort of bonding exercise, what do you think?'

Weirdly, it seemed to work. Rex settled down in the far corner of his basket, curled up in the scrap of blanket and fell asleep.

'Thank you,' she said to the conductor, most politely. 'I can just collect him from here when we get to Adelaide?'

'You can. There is of course the small matter of payment. I would prefer to settle that now, if you don't mind.'

Oh hell. Eva cursed herself. She'd left her handbag in her cabin. They'd have to go all the way there again. The minutes were ticking away fast. Joe would wonder where she had got to. 'Would the morning be okay?' she asked hopefully.

'No, madam, I'm afraid not. I find people tend to be a bit forgetful in the mornings.'

Back at her cabin, the conductor seemed to take enormous pleasure in ever so slowly processing her credit card. Ever so slowly writing out a receipt, even though Eva said she didn't need one. Then giving her a long lecture about the diseases cats could spread to humans.

Half an hour must have passed since she and Joe had parted. It was nearly midnight. Would he still be awake?

Of course he would be. Of course he wanted to see her again. And she dearly wanted to see him again. To kiss him again.

After she'd finally said goodnight to the conductor, she was overtaken by a surprising fit of nerves.

She wished she had a full suitcase of clothes with her. Some make-up. A stylist, hairdresser and couturier.

He doesn't mind what you look like, the voice said. *It's you he likes.*

It's Niamh Kennedy he likes.

That's sort of you.

Good try, she answered.

She looked at herself in the mirror. Quickly washed her face. Took her hair out of the plait. Put it back in. Took it out again. It would have to do.

Shutting her cabin door quietly, she made her way to the carriage two down from hers and knocked lightly at the fifth door.

No answer. She knocked again. Still no answer. 'Joe?' she whispered.

Nothing. 'Joe, it's me. Niamh.' Nothing again.

A noise to her left nearly made her jump out of her skin. It was a middle-aged couple, a bit the worse for wear. She smiled politely, pressing herself against the wall to give them room to pass. They stared at her curiously.

'Lover's tiff?' the man asked sympathetically.

'Something like that.' She tried to smile.

One more knock. Still no answer. It was all Rex's fault. It had taken so long Joe had fallen asleep.

In his cabin four carriages down in the other direction, Joseph lay on his bed.

Surely she would have come back by now? She'd been more than half an hour already. How long did it take to find the goods van and put a cat basket in there? He wanted her here with him. Now. In his arms again.

He smiled. He couldn't help himself. She had felt wonderful. Beautiful. 'Come on, Niamh,' he said under his breath.

By half-past midnight he'd given up waiting. His heart was heavy. She'd obviously changed her mind.

For a moment he thought about going down to her cabin. But no. If she'd wanted to see him, she would have come back to his. And she hadn't. With that unhappy thought he fell asleep.

Eva tossed and turned. Had she come on too strong? Should she have played harder to get? But she hadn't wanted to be hard to get. She wanted to kiss him. Be in bed with him. Now. But she wasn't.

With that unhappy thought she fell asleep.

CHAPTER TWENTY-EIGHT

JOSEPH WOKE before six. It took a minute to work out where he was.

Then he remembered everything. Niamh was on the train too, and she was supposed to be with him now, here. But for some reason she'd decided not to come back last night.

He lay there for a moment. It was no good. He had to talk it over with her. He got up and quickly dressed.

Eva woke. She remembered everything, straight away. She was on a train. With Joe. And she wanted to *really* be with Joe. In his cabin. In his bed. In his arms.

She lay there for a minute. It was no good. She wanted to see Joe again. Now. She was going to talk to him. Morning face or not, bed-head hair or not.

She pulled on yesterday's shift dress, all she had with her.

She had just stepped into the corridor when she met him. They spoke at the same time. 'Joe, about last night –' 'Niamh, I'm sorry that –'

The door beside them opened and an elderly man peered out. 'Oh, sorry. I thought you were the conductor. I'd kill for a cup of tea.'

They smiled apologetically and moved down a little way. Eva tried again. 'Joe, I just wanted to . . .'

Two children emerged from another cabin and tried to squeeze past them.

Joseph touched her arm. 'Niamh, will you come back to my cabin and talk? It's a bit busy out here.'

She nodded, then watched, puzzled, as he walked away from her. 'Joe, where are you going?'

'To my cabin.'

'Isn't it down that way?' She pointed in the opposite direction.

It was his turn to look confused. 'No, I'm in the front of the train.'

He watched as she went a bright pink then a very pale cream. 'Not back there?'

'No.' It dawned on him the same time it dawned on her. He spoke first. 'You *did* actually come to what you thought was my cabin last night?'

'Yes, of course. As quickly as I could.'

They were instantly back to where they'd been the

night before. Eva moved closer to him. She felt his hand caress the side of her face.

'*Excuse* me, please. This is a public thoroughfare. And a public place.' It was their friend the conductor, carrying a tray of cups.

There wasn't the time or the opportunity to recapture the mood. The conductor delivered their coffee and tea and practically shooed them down to the lounge car for breakfast. The carriages filled with noise as people woke up, got ready and walked up and down the corridors. The view changed outside their windows from hillsides and trees to the outskirts of Adelaide, houses and roads and shopping centres. They sat together in Joseph's compartment, close beside one another.

He broke the silence between them, stroking her hand and looking at her with a smile. 'Next time I'm tying a big yellow ribbon to my door.'

She laughed. 'And I'm leaving a trail of breadcrumbs.'

At the railway station they reclaimed a wide-awake Rex and found the hire car Joseph had pre-booked. They drove into the Adelaide city centre along a wide tree-lined road, past a museum, art gallery and elegant sandstone university buildings. Eva did the fastest shopping trip of her life, buying clothes and toothpaste, a toothbrush. Even if Joe didn't mind seeing her in the shift dress again, she felt much happier. She usually took more than a cat with her on an overnight trip.

By mid-morning they were on the main road heading north out of Adelaide toward the Clare Valley. Eva glanced at the back seat, checking on Rex. He seemed happy, in an expressionless kitten-faced sort of way. Lainey would be pleased at how quickly he'd recovered. Lainey. Oh God, she'd forgotten to ring Lainey. How on earth was she going to explain all of this?

'Joe, I'm sorry, can you stop at a phone box? I need to ring my friend Lainey. Let her know about Rex.'

'Of course.'

Five minutes later she was in a phone box on the side of the road, in the shelter of some gum trees.

The phone was answered on the third ring. 'Lainey Byrne speaking.'

'Lainey, it's me.'

'Evie, hi! I'm so pleased to hear from you! How is the poor little fellow? I tried to ring you last night but the answering machine wasn't working. Were you out on the town again?'

Not so much on the town as out of town, Eva thought. 'Uhm, yes, I was out. But Rex is fine. Absolutely fine.' The phone beeped and she quickly fed in some more coins. It was gobbling up her money.

'Are you in a public phone box?'

'I am,' Eva admitted.

'With Rex?'

'He's close by, yes.'

'Is there something wrong with the phone at home?'

'Uhm, no, I don't think so.'

There was a pause on Lainey's end. 'Then why are you ringing from a phone box?'

'It was the closest phone.'

'The closest? To what?'

'To me. The closest one I could find.'

'Eva, where on earth *are* you?'

She swallowed hard. 'In Adelaide.'

'*What!*'

'I'm in Adelaide. South Australia. With Joe.'

'Joe?'

Eva kept her voice low. She didn't think Joe could hear her, but the car was close by. 'The English backpacker,' she whispered.

'Why are you whispering? Is he holding you captive or something?'

Eva laughed. 'Oh no. No, I really want to be here.'

'But what about Rex?'

'He's here too.' Eva held the phone away from her ear as Lainey made a high-pitched sound.

'Have you gone completely mad? Poor Rex has just had the most traumatic event of his life and you've flown him to Adelaide?'

'Uhm, no, actually we didn't fly.'

'You *drove*? You kept him in a car for eight hours?'

'No.'

'Then how on earth did you get there?'

'On the train.'

Lainey's screech nearly smashed the phone-box window. 'Is he all right?'

Rex had been dozing in the basket most of the morning. 'He seems very happy.'

There was a long pause from Lainey's end. 'Eva, enough joking around. What is going on? Is Rex safe? Are you safe, more to the point? When in God's name did you decide to do this? You don't even know this man. It's complete madness.'

'Lainey, I'm fine, I promise. Better than fine. Rex is fine. And we'll both be back in Melbourne tonight.'

'You've gone all the way to South Australia just for one day?'

'Yes.'

'And how are you getting back? Cycling? Skateboarding, perhaps?'

'No. This time we're flying.'

'Evie, I really am very worried about you. Come on, be sensible.'

The phone beeped again. Eva had run out of coins. She spoke quickly. 'Lainey, I promise I'm fine. I know what I'm doing. And I promise I'm looking after Rex.'

The call cut out then. As Eva hung up and came out

of the phone box, she thought about it. Be sensible? She was sick of being sensible. Being un-sensible was much more fun.

They drove north through the dry countryside of South Australia. At first there was plenty of conversation, before the car radio and the changing landscape around them slowly took their attention. To a soundtrack of classical music, they gazed out at bare hills covered in yellow stubble, dwarfed by the enormous blue sky. Occasional clumps of trees, some with bark peeling and twisting from their trunks, sent long black shadows across the road.

The Clare Valley was like a sudden oasis. The first curving rows of vineyards stood stark against sunburnt hills. They passed through several small towns, the road twisting and turning through the low hills. Soon there were vineyards as far as they could see, the leaves coloured with a hint of autumn reds and yellows.

They were just on the outskirts of the town of Clare when Eva noticed a sign: LORIKEET HILL WINES: NOW ENJOYED IN IRELAND. OPEN FOR LUNCH.

Joseph slowed the car. 'Enjoyed in Ireland? Would you like to try it? Have some lunch perhaps?'

Rex gave a sudden plaintive mew from the back seat. 'I think the mews have it,' Eva said. Joseph parked the car next to a number of others in the gravel carpark. As they got out and stretched, Eva breathed in the fresh air, taking in the scenery. The trees all around the winery had strangely black trunks and particularly bright green leaves. Another odd Australian species? she wondered.

Joseph had noticed them too. 'It looks like they've all been burnt, doesn't it?'

The trees on the hill across the road looked like that too. There must have been a big fire here in recent years. A tree-lined path led away from the carpark. They followed it, Joseph carrying Rex's basket, ducking his head as they passed under a garden arch. In front of them was an ivy-covered stone building. It must have been a house once, Eva thought, noting the chimney and the symmetrical windows. It reminded her of the stone cottages in the west of Ireland, with its low roof and white walls.

They walked inside, blinking for a moment as their eyes adjusted to the dimness of the light. They had just glanced at the photographs and reviews on the wall when a tall, smiling woman greeted them, coming out from a small room to the back. 'Hello there, I'm Gemma. Welcome to Lorikeet Hill.'

Eva smiled back. 'Hello, we were wondering if we could get some lunch?'

'Of course you can. Would you like to sit inside or outside?'

'Outside, please.' There was Rex to think of. And

the verandah seats looked tempting in any case, shaded by a huge walnut tree. 'I'm sorry if this sounds a bit strange, but we're actually travelling with a kitten. Do you mind if he sits with us? He's in a basket.'

'You've brought your kitten wine-tasting?'

'It's a long story.'

'I'd like to hear it,' the woman laughed. 'Don't tell me, is that an Irish accent? It is? I was there for my honeymoon two years ago. Where are you from?'

That explained the Ireland mention on the sign, Eva thought. She was about to say she was from Dublin when she remembered. 'Galway,' she said, very conscious of Joe beside her.

'Oh, I loved Galway. My best friend lives in the west of Ireland too, in County Clare. She runs a –' A bell rang, summoning the woman back to the kitchen. She smiled at Eva. 'Sorry, excuse me, we're short-staffed today, I need another three pairs of hands and a less chatty mouth! Make yourselves comfortable, won't you, and my husband will be out in a moment with some menus. If I get a minute, I'd love a chat. Any excuse to reminisce!'

Twenty minutes later Joseph and Eva were each sipping a glass of flavour-packed shiraz and sharing a big platter of food, listed on the menu as the Lorikeet Hill lunch plate. It was a selection of ten or more different fresh tastes, everything from cheese and olives to smoked chicken and little pies.

'That was really good, wasn't it?' Eva said afterwards. 'Fantastic ingredients. Especially the cheese.'

'How can you tell?' Joseph asked.

'Lots of ways. The texture. See?' She picked up a leftover segment. 'You can tell it's a good one by the way it crumbles. And the olives are very high quality. You can tell that by their firmness and the colour of the skin. And the taste of course.'

Joseph was impressed. 'You know all about food as well as art?'

'A little,' she said. She probably knew ten times more about food than art, if it came down to it. She needed to change the subject. 'Is there anywhere special you need to visit here? One of the wineries in particular?'

This was the moment, Joseph realised. He was glad it had arrived. He wanted her to know the real reason they were in the Clare Valley. 'Niamh, I need to tell you something. Something important.'

She was thrown by the sudden change in his mood. He looked very serious.

'Tell me,' she said quietly.

So he did.

Half an hour later the mood was gentle between them. She leaned over and touched his hand. 'I'll stay here and look after Rex. You go to your father now, take as long as you like. I'll wait here for you.'

'Thank you, Niamh.'

She watched as he walked back up the gravel path to the car.

Five minutes later, Joseph came out of the petrol station down the road, the directions to Spring Farm Road clear in his mind. As he drove onto the main road, he thought back to his conversation with Niamh. She had been so understanding, listening so intently, asking the occasional question. He had told her everything he knew about Lewis and about his mother.

But he still hadn't told her the truth about his own life. He knew it was time he did. As soon as he could. It was becoming very important. For now, he focused his attention on the road ahead. He slowed as he saw a white pub, turned left and followed a curving road past more vineyards, a cemetery, an old church and a winery. Then the bitumen ran out and he was driving on dirt, a cloud of dust around the car.

There were no people around, no other houses, just vineyards. Ahead he saw a road sign: SPRING FARM ROAD. He slowed, checked his scribbled map and turned right, the wheels spitting out stones, the noise loud. He caught sight of a wooden sign on the fence ahead. Another dirt road stretched away from it, leading to a house with a cluster of sheds around it. He brought the car to a stop and read the sign: LEWIS WHEELER, CRAFTSMAN. OPEN DAILY.

He sat in the car for a moment, gazing over at the house before he climbed out. He looked around. The rough dirt road was lined on both sides by newly planted trees. On his left was a vineyard, the green of the leaves tinged with orange and red. To his right was a rocky hill, a huddle of sheep gathered around a dam in the middle. Above him the sky was blue and cloudless. There was now just a driveway between him and his father.

Back at the winery, Eva sat on the verandah, staring out at the garden. She felt wretched. Joe had shared a very personal secret with her, and in return she was still feeding him lies. It had to change. But was today the day to break something like that to him?

She tried to imagine what it would be like for him to meet his father for the first time. Her head filled with images of her own father, the easy relationship they had, the regular contact. What would it have been like to meet him as an adult, without any of the love and familiarity of shared lives? Would she have liked him? Known him differently? Been able to talk to him?

She was startled by the arrival of the waiter. 'Sorry, I was miles away.'

He smiled at her, his sunburnt face creasing into dozens of lines. 'Don't worry, that's what we like to see. People relaxing.'

'Do you mind if I stay here until my friend comes back? You don't need the table?'

'Of course we don't mind. But perhaps you'd like to stretch your legs? I'm happy to mind your kitten for you. He's probably ready to try a cheeky little shiraz now, is he?' He grinned. He'd been very taken with the idea of the wine-tasting kitten.

'No, he's had quite enough, thank you. But I'd love a walk in a little while, if you're sure you don't mind looking after him?' She needed to sort through her thoughts.

'I don't mind at all.' He pointed to a narrow path leading from the winery shed down through the vineyards. 'The Riesling Trail's down there. It follows the path of the old railway line. It's beautiful. Very peaceful.'

It sounded perfect. 'Thanks a million.'

Joseph walked up the dirt road. The only sound was his own footsteps. He jumped when a bird took off from the tree in front of him, its bright pink feathers vibrant against the sky.

The driveway felt like it was three miles long. At the end was an old house made from wooden logs with a large stone chimney to the side. There were two corrugated-iron sheds behind it. It was simple. Neat. Joseph wasn't sure what he'd been expecting. A tent daubed with rainbow symbols? A cave in the woods? He nearly laughed aloud. It was the new century. Of course his father would have left the seventies behind by now.

He went up three worn steps onto a verandah and knocked on the front door. Once. Twice. No answer. Brilliant. His father wasn't at home.

He waited a moment, wondering whether to try around the back door when he heard a scrunch of gravel behind him. He turned around. An elderly man was walking up the path toward him. Fit-looking. Short grey hair. A weathered face. The man from the photo.

'Lewis.'

'Joseph.'

They were statements, not questions.

Lewis took him into the kitchen. 'I wasn't sure when you might arrive, so I just got something simple in,' he said, as he took bread, cheese and salad out of the fridge.

'Thanks anyway, but I've just eaten.' Then he thought that sounded impolite. 'It looks good, though. Did you make this yourself?'

'The cheese? And the bread?'

Joseph nodded.

Lewis had an amused look in his eye. 'Like all good hippies should?'

Joseph realised his father was teasing him. Lewis

continued. 'No, it's from the supermarket in Clare, but I think some of their food is organic.'

Joseph nearly smiled, then stopped himself.

'Will you have a glass of wine with me then, while I eat? It's a local riesling, very good. Best in Australia.'

'Just a small glass. Thanks.'

They talked about the weather. The scenery. Joseph's conference in Sydney. His impressions of Australia. Joseph began to feel as if he was in an elaborate chess match. One move from Lewis followed by one move from him. He was searching for any resemblance between them, while trying not to be too obvious about it. The shape of their faces, maybe. Their hands. Not their voices, anyway. It was strange to hear the beginnings of an Australian accent coming from his own father. His own father. He decided then he needed more than small talk.

Lewis was by the kitchen sink, putting the plate on the draining board when Joseph spoke up. 'Lewis, was there anything in particular you wanted to talk about?'

Lewis stopped still for a moment, before turning around. 'Well, yes, I suppose there are a few gaps about your life I'd like to fill in.'

'A few?' Joseph felt a rush of unexpected anger, at Lewis or at his mother, he wasn't sure which. A few gaps? Like thirty-four years worth, perhaps?

Lewis seemed to guess what he was thinking but

didn't take the bait. He sat down slowly in the chair opposite Joseph and took a sip of his wine. 'I did want to ask why you went to the university in South London, rather than that good one just near home. And the award you won? Was that in your third or fourth year? And did it take you long to find the Wheeler Design offices in Hoxton? And have you found anyone else since you and Tessa broke up?'

Joseph was speechless. Had his father been tailing him all these years?

Lewis stood up. 'Come with me.'

Joseph followed him outside, through the garden and back into his workroom, an old shed on the side of the property. It was full of wood. Planks and slabs of rich-coloured timber. One whole wall was covered in sketches and photographs of tables and detailed close-ups of knots and burls in trees. In the centre of the shed was a long, half-finished table. As Joseph stood still, not sure what to say or look at, his father picked up a cloth and began rubbing oil into the wood.

The swish of the cloth was like a soothing rhythm. The gentle movement made Joseph even more aware of how tense he was.

After a moment his father began to talk. 'Your mother and I were very unhappy when we divorced, Joseph. I'm sure you know that much at least. I'm not certain how much else you know, if there is anything you remember at all. But it was a very difficult time.'

There was a long silence before Lewis spoke again. 'Kate and I knew it wasn't possible for us to get together again. I had already decided to come to Australia, but before I left we came to one agreement. Kate would send me a photo of you once a year, on or around your birthday, with a brief note. That would be the only contact between us.'

He moved from the table. Going to a cupboard at the back of the shed, he took out an old photo album and laid it on the table, moving a chair in front of it. He gestured at Joseph to take a seat.

As Joseph sat down, Lewis opened the album from the back. Joseph glanced at the colour print stuck in the centre of the page. It was a photo of him in his mother's front room in Kensal Green, taken just three months ago. He remembered Kate taking it. She'd said she wanted to use the last film in her camera.

Joseph turned back another page. A photo taken in his new apartment. Kate had called around to see it. He remembered her taking that photo too. He turned back another page. Him in the Wheeler Design offices. Another page. With Tessa at a restaurant in Camden Town. Then another. There was a photo on every page, all of him. Each had a short caption, written on a small piece of paper or a postcard, in his mother's handwriting. Graduation. Award night. Current girlfriend. A few extra details here and there. Some newspaper and magazine cuttings. It was a photo story of his life.

Lewis had moved away from the chair and gone back to rubbing the table. The slow swish of the cloth and the oil against the wood and the noise of the pages turning were the only sounds in the shed for a while.

Finally Lewis broke the silence. 'Do you have any memories of me at all, Joseph? From your childhood? Of living in Scotland?'

Joseph thought hard. He didn't know if what he remembered were his own memories or if they'd become confused with what his mother had told him.

'I don't know,' he answered honestly. 'I don't think so.'

He wanted to ask his father what memories he had of him as a child. But he wanted to finish the album first. He turned the pages quickly and finally reached the first page. It was a black and white photo of himself, two or three years old, with curly black hair, holding a baby. There was no caption.

'This photo at the front, Lewis. Who's the baby I'm holding?'

Lewis put down the cloth and came over beside him. He looked down at the photograph. 'No, Joseph, the baby is you.'

'Then who's that holding me?'

The shed was quiet for a long moment.

'Lewis?'

'Your brother, Joseph.'

Chapter twenty-nine

Joseph felt like he'd been punched. Winded.

He looked around as though a grown version of the boy in the photograph was about to appear, here at his father's house. 'Did we get divided up, is that it? One child for each of you? And I never knew?' His anger rose quickly, sharp, white hot.

Lewis was very still. 'No, Joseph. Alexander died. Nearly thirty-five years ago.'

'I had a brother who died? Why wasn't I ever told?'

'It was my fault, Joseph.'

'I don't care whose fault it was no-one told –'

'No, Joseph, you misunderstand me. It was my fault your brother died.'

Joseph didn't move.

'I want to tell you the whole story. And I know Kate wants you to hear it from me too. Do you want to hear it? Now?'

Joseph nodded mutely. He didn't trust himself to speak.

At first Lewis spoke directly to him. Then, as he kept talking, his gaze shifted out the window. 'It happened when we were living in Scotland. Outside a small village. You were only tiny, eight months, less perhaps. Your mother had taken you into the village, I can't remember why – to visit the doctor, perhaps.'

'I was at home working, minding Alexander. He was nearly three. I'd planned to wait until your mother and you got home before I gave him his bath, then I thought no, I'll surprise her, have him bathed and ready, the dinner on.

'Alexander loved baths, he would sing away to himself, play, splash water all around. The bathroom was always soaked when he'd finished. It was this day too. He'd splashed so much the towel I'd had ready for him was soaked. So I said, "Hold on there Allie," I liked to call him Allie, not Alexander, "hold on there and I'll get you a dry one, then we'll get you out and drying by the fire by the time your mum and your little brother get home." So I was out of the bathroom for a minute, not even that.'

Lewis didn't speak again for some time. 'When I came back in he had slipped somehow. He was face down in the water. I tried to resuscitate him but I didn't know how. We lived out in the country, Joseph. We didn't even have a phone. Your mother had the car. I ran with Allie to the farm down the road but no-one was there. And it was too late any-way. I knew he was dead.'

He took a sharp breath. 'Your mother came back with you then, just as I was running along the road with Allie in my arms. She knew immediately what had happened. We got in, she drove, but it was too late. He had gone.'

Joseph didn't look up at Lewis. He kept his eyes firmly on the photograph. His brother Allie. In his mind he played an image of the scene his father had just described. 'Why didn't Kate ever tell me this?' he said at last.

'You were just a baby when it happened, a tiny baby. We knew you wouldn't remember Allie. Your mother was devastated. We both were. She blamed me and so she should. It was my fault. I've been over and over it a thousand times, a million times, in my head. If I hadn't gone out at that moment to get the towel. If I hadn't left him alone. If I'd come back more quickly . . .

'And your mother blamed herself too. If she hadn't taken you into town, if the car had been there, if we'd been able to get to the doctor's more quickly. If, if, if. We fought about it, all the time. If I hadn't been an artist, if I hadn't insisted we live out in the wilds, if I had had a proper job, this wouldn't have happened. If we weren't crying, we were fighting.'

'So you and Kate split up when you moved to London?'

'No, we tried to get through it. To stay together. We tried for nearly eighteen months, but she couldn't trust me with you, Joseph. She was so scared to let you out of her sight. To let me hold you, even. It got worse the closer you got to Allie's age when he died. She wouldn't let me near you. In case I did the same thing again. In case I killed you as well.'

Joseph reacted to that. 'Lewis, it was an accident.'

'Killed. Accident. Just words, Joseph, and they mean the same thing in the end. A dead child. It's taken more than thirty years to accept that awful, hard fact. For your mother and for me. There was nothing like counselling back then. Not that it would have done us any good, I don't think. We were too raw with anger and guilt, we wouldn't have let anyone near us. We had to be apart, we were just feeding each other's misery. Too many things shattered that day and we knew we would never be able to put them back together. Not in the same way. So you and your mother stayed in London, and I started travelling.'

Hundreds of memories of his childhood started flashing through Joseph's mind. His mother crying, not able to talk about his father. Not able to answer questions about him. Joseph had invented a father in his head, he realised. A good-for-nothing artist. He'd invented all the reasons he and Kate had split up. Fights. Arguments over money, perhaps? Over ways of life? Everything but this. He had never imagined this.

'Why didn't Kate tell me?' he asked again.

'Where would she start? What would have been the right age to tell you? Five, six years old? Just as she was starting to mend? Telling you would have opened it all up again, ripped open the wound. We've been writing about this in our letters to one another lately. And talking about it on the phone. She deeply regrets it now, not telling you. We both regret a lot now. That's why it was so important to her that you came to see me, and why she wanted you to hear it from me.'

'But why didn't she tell me herself? After you'd spoken about it?'

'Because I asked her not to, Joseph. Yes, in my heart I know it was an accident. A terrible accident. But it was still my fault, no matter which way I look at it, no matter how many years go past. Your brother died because of me. Your mother knew she'd painted a false picture of me to you – that I abandoned you both, started a new life out here in Australia, wanted nothing to do with you. That was the only way she could cope, I think. Then when she and I made contact again and we talked about it, she felt she couldn't add one more terrible thing to that story. We both decided you had to hear it from me.'

Joseph felt he needed to check every detail. 'How long have you and Kate been in touch again?'

'Nearly twelve months. Apart from the photos

of you each year, of course. They always arrived as regular as clockwork, with just that brief note about you, nothing more. Nothing about her. Until last year. She enclosed a letter telling me about her cancer. I took it as a signal she was ready to talk to me again. So I wrote to her, and she wrote back. You know the rest, I think.'

'Why didn't you ever come looking for us, Lewis?' Looking for me, he didn't say aloud.

'When I said that your mother couldn't trust me with you as a baby, I didn't tell you the whole story. I didn't trust myself with you either. Anytime I held you, I kept thinking I would drop you, hurt you in some way. I tried to bath you once but I just couldn't do it. I had you in my arms, the bath full of water, and it all came back to me. Every detail of the day Allie died. Kate heard me cry, she'd been just outside, trying to trust me with you. But she couldn't either. She came into the bathroom, took you away from me, did it herself. That was the last time I tried to bath you. But I lost confidence with every part of looking after you. I couldn't feed you, in case you choked. Couldn't play games with you, in case I hurt you.

'I realised I couldn't be a parent again. No child can grow up with an adult watching their every step, terrified to let them climb anything, do anything. Kate and I stopped fighting, stopped blaming each other for long enough to realise that we were starting

317

to damage your life. We'd lost one son and now we were ruining a second son's life.

'So I left. Kate didn't try to stop me. We knew that's what had to happen. After our divorce came though, I travelled for a while, then I ended up in Western Australia. I met a woman, we married. She wanted children but I couldn't do it. It was always a source of disagreement between us, I know that. She and I finally separated and I moved here. But all that while Kate and I kept in touch, through those photos of you.'

There was silence for a long moment. Then Joseph spoke, his voice quiet. 'What was he like, Lewis? What was Allie like?'

'Allie?' Lewis gave a slow smile. 'He was great fun. He liked doing things. Being busy. He was always wanting to take things apart, and trying to put them together again – his toys, things around the house, whatever he could get his hands on. And he liked to laugh. Really laugh. I'd never have expected a child that young to have a sense of humour, but Allie did. He –' And then his father started to cry.

Before he thought too much about it, Joseph went over to him. Then, awkwardly, slowly, he put his arm around his shoulders.

It was some time before Lewis could speak again, and when he did he changed the subject completely.

'Tell me about your work, Joseph. About your designs.'

Slowly, and initially with difficulty, Joseph talked about his years at university, his first designs, setting up his own company, the exciting early days.

Then, prompted by his father's questioning, he spoke about what his work had now become. A mass of meetings and schedules. Markets and deadlines. A world away from his imagination.

Lewis nodded and was silent again. Then he said, 'The imagination is everything, isn't it? I have to have the entire image of my finished work in my head, even before I've picked up a pencil or a tool. I can spend weeks, months even, imagining each piece, thinking about every detail, every knot and turn of the wood, every join. The finish, the look and the feel of it. It's all made up here,' he tapped his forehead, 'finished to perfection before I've even chosen the piece of wood.'

What Lewis said was strangely familiar to Joseph. It was how he had felt when he thought about the jewellery he imagined for Niamh. Complete in his head before he had so much as touched some silver or gold.

He watched as his father stood up again, went back to the table and once again started slowly, rhythmically oiling the wood. He thought how far this world of design was from his own in London. Here it was his father and a piece of wood – nature becoming art. What was his own design life now? Production schedules, meetings with manufacturers, chasing clients. A long way from his hands and mind coming together to produce something really beautiful, like his father was doing now, right in front of him. Joseph had a sudden flash again of the jewellery he had imagined. And another flash of Niamh wearing it.

'Can you make a living, Lewis? Working like this?'

'I get by. Some years I get by very well indeed. Other years are leaner. But oddly enough, the more we move into technology, the more people long for hand-crafted objects in their homes.' He gave a sudden grin. 'Like my tables, fortunately. I have the occasional exhibition, just ship one or two pieces up to Sydney expos or to a gallery, and I usually get enough orders to keep me going for the next year or so. Anyway, I have to keep it small. Each one takes me weeks, sometimes months, as it is. So yes, it's a struggle at times.'

Joseph realised again the craft involved in each table. The time his father spent on them. The meticulous work involved in making each piece of wood fit so perfectly. The eye for beauty. These weren't just pieces of furniture, they were works of art.

'I could help you, Lewis.'

Lewis was puzzled. 'Help me with my work?'

'Help you sell your tables. Overseas. In London.

I know people, magazine editors, gallery owners, manufacturers even . . .' He trailed off.

'I know you do.' Lewis glanced across at the photographs, then back at Joseph. 'But no, thank you. I'm fine.'

Joseph was glad his help had been turned down. He wasn't sure why.

He decided to leave soon after. He wanted to get away, think everything over. He wanted to get back to Niamh too.

They walked back to his car together. At the end of the driveway, Lewis turned to Joseph. 'Will you come back again? Come to dinner tonight perhaps? You're welcome to stay too. I have plenty of room.'

'I have a friend with me . . .'

Lewis smiled. 'Your friend is very welcome too.'

'Thanks, Lewis.' Then he remembered something. 'About my friend, it's a bit complicated, but she doesn't actually know about my company. Or the conference. She thinks I'm a backpacker on a working holiday.'

Lewis nodded. 'I see. And does she know your name or is that a secret too?'

Joseph smiled. 'She does know my name, yes. She calls me Joe, actually. Not Joseph.'

'Your mother wouldn't like that. I remember when we named you, she insisted you were to be Joseph, not Joe. If she wanted you to be a Joe, she would have called you Joe, she used to say.'

Joseph was strangely moved by the thought of Lewis and Kate discussing his name.

'And does your friend have a name?'

'She does. It's Niamh, it's an Irish name. She's from the west of Ireland. Galway. She's an artist too, a sculptor. And a singer.' Joseph realised he was sounding like Greg from Four Quarters. Worse, even.

'She sounds very interesting. I'll see you both later then? Around seven?'

'That sounds good.'

'Thank you, Joseph.' His father didn't hug him. He just placed his hand firmly on his son's shoulder and pressed, as if he was leaving an imprint of his hand.

Eva walked slowly along the Riesling Trail, breathing in the smell of the eucalypt trees lining both sides. The only sounds were the occasional birdcall and the faintest murmur of traffic in the distance. She'd been walking for a long time. It was probably time to head back. She turned and had walked just a short way when she saw a figure in the distance coming toward her.

It was Joe. She stopped and waited until he met up with her.

'Hello, Niamh.'

'Hello.' She searched his face for a clue to how it had gone.

'Can we keep walking?' he asked. 'Just for a while?'

It was some time before he started to talk. 'He lives in a beautiful place,' he said. Slowly, choosing his words carefully, he described the house, his father, his work shed, his tables.

Eva didn't ask many questions, just walked alongside listening to him. But she could feel there was more than he was telling her.

They had just passed through a shady part of the trail when he stopped walking. He turned to her and she could see pain and hurt and something else in his face.

'Joe? Is everything all right?' She moved forward and took him into her arms without speaking. She held him close for a long while, just feeling the beat of his heart against hers. She stroked his face, held her palm flat against his back. He didn't speak, but she felt as though something very deep, very big was settling inside him.

Some time later he pulled away from her and kissed her forehead gently. They started walking again.

They were nearly back at Lorikeet Hill when he told her about Lewis' invitation to go back for dinner and to stay the night. 'You don't have to stay if you don't want to. I can drive you back to Adelaide now, take you and Rex to the airport if you'd rather.'

She didn't want to leave him. 'I'd like to stay. If you're sure I wouldn't be in the way.'

The look in his eyes touched her deeply. 'No, Niamh. You wouldn't be in the way at all.'

CHAPTER THIRTY

As THE plane to Melbourne took off from Adelaide airport the next afternoon, Eva touched Joseph's hand. 'Are you okay?'

He nodded, taking her hand and holding it tightly. 'I'm fine,' he said, before turning to look back out the window, deep in thought.

She closed her eyes, her mind drifting back to the night before. She'd been nervous but Lewis had been immediately welcoming. When they first arrived they'd stood on the verandah of his house, watching the hills around them change colour from yellow to purple as the sun faded right away, and listening to the sounds of magpies and kookaburras.

She'd immediately noticed small similarities between father and son. A facial expression here and there. Their laughs. Their hands. Over a simple meal Lewis had asked her about her art and her singing. She'd answered as briefly as possible, feeling a cloud of guilt around her, changing the subject as quickly as she could. There was such a gentle, early trust between Joe and Lewis, she felt as though her fake life would spoil things. Taint it somehow. She felt uneasy, bringing her lies into the room when they had been sharing truths all afternoon.

Rex had helped lighten the mood. They'd let him out of the basket soon after they arrived and he'd entertained them by darting around the room, chewing at their shoelaces, before finally falling into a round bundle of sleep in front of the fire Lewis had lit.

'It's not quite cold enough,' he said, 'but I like it.' After they'd eaten, they moved in front of it. She'd sat quietly, watched and listened to them talk. Then she'd gone to bed early, in the spare room Lewis had made ready for her. 'I'm happy on the couch,' Joe had said quickly, before there had been any awkwardness.

She'd lain in bed listening to the murmur of voices from the living room, finally falling asleep with the sound still drifting into her bedroom.

They'd left the Clare Valley early next morning, soon after breakfast. She hadn't listened to their farewell, feeling intrusive enough as it was. She'd said goodbye to Lewis first and carried Rex, in his basket again, down to the car at the end of the drive. She couldn't hear what they were saying to each other. But she saw Joe hug his father, and she saw Lewis hug him just as firmly back.

They had been driving for an hour, back down the long straight road to Adelaide, when Joe had started to talk about it. Eva had pointed to some trees further ahead. A parking place. They had stopped the car, got out and walked to an old tree stump. Sitting there side by side, he told her all his father had said. About his brother, the real reason his parents had divorced. She hadn't interrupted.

He'd kept talking about what it had been like to grow up not knowing his father. How he had felt a part of him wasn't complete. It wasn't that he missed it, he'd never had a father so he didn't know what it was like. But now he felt that he'd had a glimpse of what might have been.

'And is that better or worse?' she had asked him softly.

He turned and looked at her. 'It's both.'

The look in his eyes had nearly broken her heart. Gently, slowly, she'd put her arms around him. Kissed his face. And then she'd held him closely for a long time.

It wasn't until they reached Adelaide airport that she'd remembered to phone Lainey again. While Joe took care of their tickets and checked Rex into the baggage section, she'd tried three times, getting only Lainey's voicemail on her mobile. On the fourth try she'd left a message.

'Lainey, it's me. I'm on my way home and everything's fine, I promise. With me and Rex. We'll be back at the flat in a few hours, so I'll try you again then.'

Thinking about it now, Eva realised she'd been glad to get Lainey's machine, not the real thing. She wasn't in the mood for Lainey's questions, or disapproval. It had been like that enough when they were children. She was thirty-one years old now. Not six. Not fourteen. Not twenty-three. And something about Lainey's tone on the phone yesterday, and her questioning of her judgement, had been bothering her. As they started descending into Melbourne airport, she shook the thought away, feeling disloyal. This was Lainey she was thinking about. Her oldest friend.

Half an hour later they were in a taxi going into the city, Rex safely on the floor at Eva's feet. She directed the driver to Spencer Street station, where she hoped Lainey's car was still waiting. They sat side by side in the back of the taxi, speaking little. She knew he was still far away in his own thoughts but it didn't feel strained between them. She felt . . . what was the word? Connected to him.

At the entrance to the railway station carpark, she opened the taxi door, holding Rex's basket. Joseph spoke quietly.

'Niamh, can I ring you later tonight?'

'I'd like that very much.'

He gently touched the side of her face. 'Thank you.'

'Thank me? For what?'

He kissed her on the lips. A strong, firm kiss. 'You know what.' He got back in the taxi and it drove away.

At that exact moment at Melbourne airport, Lainey was waiting at the baggage carousel, tapping her foot impatiently.

She'd just checked her voicemail messages. Thank God there had been one from Eva saying she was on her way home, that she was all right. Lainey had been up the walls with worry all night, ringing her Richmond apartment and not getting any answer.

Lainey's boss had been very understanding about her need to fly back to Melbourne. 'Of course you can go home, Lainey. You're nearly finished in Brisbane in any case. And it does sound urgent. Has your friend had these psychological problems for years?'

'On and off,' Lainey had answered, crossing her fingers behind her back and silently apologising to Eva.

But Eva definitely had *some* sort of problem, Lainey thought. Taking off on this mad jaunt across the country with Rex and a complete stranger. She always had been a bit innocent. A bit too trusting. It was her lack of confidence – she didn't have a lot of faith in herself and her own judgement and was easily taken in. Look how easy it had been for that Dermot fellow. Surely anyone else would have been a bit wary of all that sudden attention? But Eva hadn't. She just had a bit of a blind spot when it came to men, Lainey decided. And it looked like it was happening again with this backpacker. Joe, or whatever his name was.

Lainey's suitcase came sailing past. She quickly grabbed it. As she walked up to the taxi rank, she knew she'd made the right decision. She'd be home in less than an hour. Then she'd sit down with Eva and have a good old heart-to-heart chat.

Eva and Rex had been back at the Richmond apartment less than half an hour when the phone started to ring.

She answered it. 'Hello, Lainey's house.'

'Niamh?'

'Joe? Are you okay?'

'I can't wait until tonight. Can I come and see you again. Now?'

She didn't even pause. 'Yes.' She gave him the address and put down the phone. 'Hurry,' she said aloud.

There was a long queue at the taxi rank. Lainey wanted to shout in impatience. 'Let me go first. I need to go and see my friend who has lost her mind.' Three taxis came. She moved up the queue, giving her suitcase a nudge with her foot to move it along. The lock sprang open, clothes and other items spilling out.

That bloody case. Lainey wanted to kick it into the gutter. She'd only bought it last year. Three people went past her in the queue while she tried to stop her undies from blowing all over Melbourne airport. She put a foot on top of the case to make sure it didn't spring open again and counted the people now ahead of her in the queue. Six, maybe even seven. Damn. She'd be here for ages yet.

Eva had just about worn a hole in the carpet between the living room and the front door. Rex thought it was some new game and was trit-trotting happily behind her as she paced back and forth.

She had never felt like this in her life. So full of anticipation. So physically conscious of her own body. The urgent longing she'd felt for Joe on the train had come back. Tenfold.

The doorbell finally rang and she pressed the intercom button. 'Hello?'

'It's Joe.'

At last, Lainey thought. She helped the driver lift her broken case into the boot of the taxi, then came around and climbed into the front seat.

'Where to, love?'

'River Street, Richmond, thanks.'

Eva opened the door and Joseph followed her into the muted light of the living room, the sunlight blocked by the blinds. They were some distance apart but the electric current was strong between them again. She swallowed, so nervous she could barely speak. 'How are you?'

'Good, thank you.' He closed the gap between them. He took one of her hands, then the other. Holding them tight he pulled her gently toward him. She lifted her face. He lowered his.

She shut her eyes as their lips touched. She didn't want to see anything. She just wanted to feel. His lips brushed against hers. Soft. Strong. She pressed closer against him.

The kiss seemed to last for hours. She felt like she was dancing. Like they were swapping leading positions. The music in her head got harder and faster and suddenly their kisses weren't feather-light any more. Standing like this, pressed up against each other in the middle of the living room, wasn't even near to being close enough.

The dress she was wearing had a long zip down the back. She shivered as he took hold of the clasp and slowly pulled it down. The barest hint of air ran down her back as the dress opened. With sure hands, Joseph moved the dress down, baring her shoulders, baring the tops of her breasts. She breathed in sharply as he slowly, gently traced her skin, traced the line of her lace bra. His eyes were dark with desire.

Eva's head swirled. No man had ever gazed at her like that. Touched her like that. His hand moulded her curves. For once she didn't feel self-conscious. She was glad of her body, she could feel that he liked it. She moved closer to him, standing on tiptoes, reaching up to his face to kiss him again. The feel of his jeans, the cotton of his shirt against her naked skin, was the most sensual thing she had ever felt.

She pulled the shirt out from his waistband, feeling his skin. She unbuttoned it, pressing a kiss against his chest, touching the silky skin of his back. Her breasts in the lacy bra were pressed close against his chest.

Then they both heard the sound of the front door opening.

'Why is it so dark in here? Hello? Is anyone home?' There was the sound of a flick of a switch, then a bright fluorescent light filled the living room.

'Bloody hell,' the voice said.

It was Lainey.

CHAPTER THIRTY-ONE

SHE LOOKED at them both and spoke slowly and calmly. 'I'm going to go outside again for a few minutes, what do you think about that?'

'I think that's a very good idea,' Eva said, pulling up her dress. 'That's my friend, Lainey,' she said to Joseph after Lainey had gone back outside.

'So you know her? That's a relief.'

Eva reached up and kissed him. 'I'll be right back.'

Lainey was sitting out on the steps with Rex purring on her lap. Her feet were up on her broken suitcase. 'That was quick. Would you like me to do up the zip properly?'

Eva gave Lainey an embarrassed smile. 'I'm so sorry. If I'd known you were about to walk in I –'

'Would have kept your clothes on for a few more minutes?'

'Lainey, you're not making this any easier.'

'That's Joe the English backpacker, I presume?'

'It is.'

'You certainly seem to have hit it off.'

'Lainey . . .'

'I'm just trying to make you feel better. Can I come in now?'

'Of course you can. And it's fantastic to see you. I just wasn't expecting you.'

'I gathered that.'

As she walked ahead of Lainey through the front door, Eva stopped so suddenly that her friend bumped against her back. 'Lainey, I need to ask a huge favour,' Eva whispered.

'What?'

'I need you to call me Niamh in front of Joe.'

'What? Are you still keeping this up?'

Eva nodded sheepishly.

Lainey frowned. 'But why with him, Eva? I mean, I thought it was funny with Greg, but surely you haven't been telling everyone you're Niamh?'

Eva shook her head. 'Not everyone. It's a long story. A really long story. And I'll tell you everything, I promise. But would you just go along with it for now?'

Lainey didn't look happy about it. 'Okay,' she said, after a moment.

Joseph was standing by the window in the living room. He turned as Eva and Lainey came in. Lainey moved Rex onto her shoulder and held out her hand. 'It's lovely to meet you, Joe. Did Niamh tell you I'm chronically short-sighted? I can't see a thing unless it's just a few centimetres away from me.'

He gave a quick grin. 'That must come in very handy sometimes.'

'When you least expect it, actually. Please, sit down.'

The three of them sat. Joseph and Eva felt like they were being interviewed.

'So, Joe. Niamh's told me a lot about you. You're travelling around Australia, I hear.'

'I am, that's right.'

'And you're an industrial designer?'

'Yes, I am.'

'Are you enjoying Australia?'

'Very much.'

Lainey glanced at her watch. 'Well, isn't this nice. Tell you what, why don't you stay for dinner, Joe. Or better still, let's all go out together. What do you think?'

'Joe?' Eva turned toward him.

'But Lainey has just arrived, are you sure I'm not in –'

'In the way?' Lainey said cheerfully. 'Of course not. It'd be great to get to know you a bit better. I've heard so much about you from Niamh, haven't I, *Niamh*?'

'Yes, Lainey.' Eva wasn't at all sure of her mood. 'Joe, please come out to dinner with us.'

He glanced from one to the other. 'Then thanks, I'd like to do that.'

Lainey stood up, putting Rex on the ground. 'Niamh, could you give me a hand with something before we go? My suitcase has broken and I'll need some help. Excuse us, Joe, won't you?'

'Of course.'

Lainey picked up her suitcase and went into her bedroom. Eva was barely inside before Lainey shut the door firmly behind her, dropped the suitcase and put her hands on her hips. 'Evie, what on earth is going on here?'

Eva was taken aback. 'You don't need help with your suitcase after all?'

'Of course I don't. Eva, I'm serious. What in God's name has got into you?'

'Nothing has got into me. Why?'

'You hardly know this man. A visit to see some penguins is one thing, but going off to Adelaide with him just like that? With my cat? A one-day driving tour of South Australia? Flights back to Melbourne? And now passionate lovemaking sessions – in a standing position, if you please – in my front room? Anything could have happened. And it's not just about your personal safety. I don't want you to get hurt again. Like you were with –'

'Dermot.' Eva interrupted. This was no time to bring up anyone else. 'Lainey, I won't get hurt. This is nothing like it was with Dermot. With anybody I've ever gone out with before.'

'But you don't know the first thing about Joe.'

'I do. I know plenty of things about him.'

'Like what?'

'All the things I've already told you on the phone. He's thirty-four. He lives in London. He's backpacking on a working holiday around Australia. Isn't that enough to be going on with?'

'A backpacker on a working holiday, is he?'

Eva nodded.

'Who takes spur-of-the-moment one-day trips to South Australia?'

Joe's meeting with Lewis wasn't her story to tell. She didn't answer for a moment, hating how Lainey was making her feel. 'He had to get some wine,' she finally blurted out.

'Get some wine? What, he can't buy it in London? Or here?'

Eva shifted uncomfortably under the force of Lainey's questioning. 'I don't know. Maybe. Maybe not. He just liked the idea of getting it straight from the winery.'

'And did this Joe happen to know the people at this winery? Were they expecting him, do you think?'

Eva had just about had enough. 'No, the people at *this winery* didn't know *this Joe*. What exactly are you getting at, Lainey? Because I don't like your line of questioning one bit.' Eva felt her cheeks go red. She rarely stood up to Lainey.

'Oh come on, Evie. Don't you think it's all a bit weird? I'm sorry, but I think you have to be a little more wary than that these days. You can't take people on face value any more. He's a backpacker who was working in Four Quarters because he was running out of money, is that what you told me?'

Eva nodded.

'So how did you get from Adelaide to the Clare Valley?'

'He hired a car.'

'And how did you get home?'

'We flew.'

'Who paid?'

'Are you an immigration officer, Lainey?'

'Evie, who paid?'

'He did. He had those frequent flier points, he said.'

'Oh, did he? Don't you think that's a bit suspicious? A bit unusual? For a backpacker? I read a very interesting article in the newspaper a week or two back about drug trafficking in Australia. How it's quick and easy money for the right people. And how they prey on innocents, get them to do the dirty work. He hasn't given you any parcels or anything, has he? To take back home with you?'

'Now you're saying Joe's a *drug smuggler*?'

'No, I'm not saying anything for sure. I'm just not taking everything at face value, like you have. Come on, how much do you know about him? Really?'

Eva was defiant. 'Lainey, Joe is exactly what he seems. Why would he be anything different?'

'What does he call you?'

There was a long pause. 'Niamh.'

'What does he think you do for a living?'

'He thinks I'm a sculptor. And a singer.'

'And that you live where?'

'In Galway. In a caravan. Oh, stop it, Lainey, you know exactly what he thinks. You're the one that started this whole thing.'

'I know, I know. For one night. I didn't expect you to start living your whole life around it. I'm just trying to say that things aren't always what they seem. And you need to be a bit wary sometimes. I mean, meet him for a drink, fine. Dinner, maybe. But a spur-of-the-moment trip to South Australia? A day in a car with him in the middle of nowhere? It could have been so dangerous.'

'But it wasn't, was it? Lainey, stop this, please.'

'Look, I'm not trying to be difficult, but I feel very responsible for you. I invited you over here, after all. What if something were to happen –'

'For heaven's sake, Lainey, I am *thirty-one years old*. I wanted to come to Australia. I wanted to go away with Joe. You're not my mother. In fact, you're behaving worse than a mother. Please, don't spoil this. For once I've felt free with someone, that I'm really being myself, that I –'

Lainey made a strange noise. 'Oh yes. You're really being yourself. With your fake name and your fake caravan and your fake successful career.'

That was enough. 'Shall we go to dinner, Lainey? I don't want to be any ruder to Joe than we've already been.' She walked out of the room.

Twenty minutes later they were in a restaurant that Lainey had chosen down the road from the apartment. 'Modern Australian cuisine, I think tonight. What do you say, Niamh?'

Lainey was mad with her, Eva knew that. Well, too bad, because she was mad with Lainey too. 'Perfect,' Eva had said with a fake smile.

Another twenty minutes and she was regretting having agreed to go out to dinner. Regretting urging Joe to come along. Regretting coming to Australia in the first place. She wasn't mad with Lainey any more. She was furious.

Lainey was performing, there was no other word for it. She was behaving like an actress, a celebrity, glittering at all and sundry. She had insisted on changing before she came out, emerging from her bedroom in a very figure-hugging dress. Eva had immediately felt like a postulant nun beside her, her previously lovely shift dress metamorphosing in her imagination into something from the scrap basket. She was Maria von Trapp beside the baroness. Cinderella beside her stepsisters.

Since they'd arrived at the restaurant Lainey had flirted with the waiter, the barman, the two men at the neighbouring table. And now she was flirting with Joe. She was like someone in a How to Flirt documentary. All twinkling eyes, hands on her chin, tinkling laughter and just that bit longer than necessary eye contact.

Eva had only seen Lainey in full flight like this once before. In Ireland, eight years ago. She hadn't liked it one bit then and she liked it even less now. She felt like Lainey had drained all her personality away. She'd hardly opened her mouth, yet Lainey was in top form, telling anecdotes about her early days in Australia, what it had been like when she first went back to Ireland, tales about Melbourne. And was Eva imagining it, or was Joe laughing at every single thing she said?

Lainey leaned across the table again now. 'So tell me, are you enjoying Australian food, Joe?'

'I am, yes. There seem to be some great restaurants here.'

Lainey gave a deep sigh. 'Oh, there is, isn't there? I have to say, nothing makes me happier than being in a kitchen or a restaurant. I worked in a deli for a while, it was heaven, all the wonderful tastes and smells.'

Eva blinked. What was Lainey talking about? She'd never worked in a deli.

Lainey turned toward her now. 'I had all sorts of ideas to open a cafe or something too, didn't I, Niamh?'

Joseph glanced between the two of them again. 'But you didn't?

Lainey gave an elegant shrug. 'No. I guess I was just too scared that it wouldn't work. So I didn't even give it a try. And now I'll never know for sure, I suppose, will I, Niamh?'

Lainey was playing with her, Eva realised. She just glared back at her without answering.

Joseph stood up. 'Could I get you both another glass of wine?'

Eva nearly toppled the table in her haste to stand up as well. 'No, Joe, let me get it.'

'Please, let me.'

He was barely out of earshot when Eva turned on Lainey and hissed, 'That's enough, Lainey. Stop it.'

Lainey smiled innocently. 'Stop what?'

'You know what. All that stuff about the deli. Everything you're doing.' *The flirting*.

'It's just a joke, Evie. You're not being you, so I thought I'd be you for you. That way you can see if Joe likes the real you, can't you? He seemed quite interested in the idea of the cafe, don't you think?'

'It's not funny, Lainey.'

'What's not funny?' It was Joseph with the glasses of wine.

Lainey smiled up at him. 'Niamh and I were just talking about the price of wine in restaurants these days, it's just not funny how expensive it is. Thanks for getting these, aren't you great?' She put her hand on his arm for a moment.

That was it, Eva thought, rage overtaking her. Enough. More than enough. She felt like she was twenty-three years old all over again. Worse than that time, even. She stood up, her eyes flashing. 'I do apologise if I've been in the way tonight. Have a lovely night together, won't you?'

She snatched up her bag and walked out of the restaurant.

CHAPTER THIRTY-TWO

EVA WALKED three hundred metres before she stopped, overcome with embarrassment.

What a stupid, childish thing to have done. And now what would she do? She certainly couldn't go back in there, feeling like this. Disappointed with Joe and raging with Lainey.

She started walking again, dodging the groups of people going in and out of the restaurants and bars all along the street. She felt sick. What could she do now? Go home? She didn't want to. She didn't think she ever wanted to see Lainey again.

She'd gone another hundred metres when she heard her name being called. Her false name. She stopped and turned around.

'Niamh, wait. Please.' It was Joe, walking quickly toward her.

She stood, embarrassed and angry at once, waiting for him.

He came up beside her, his face very serious. 'Are you all right?'

She felt her breathing quicken. What on earth could she say? *No, Joe, I'm not. I thought something wonderful was happening between us and then you met Lainey and responded to her just like every other bloody man that ever meets her responds to her. And I can't handle it and it makes me sick with jealousy and I couldn't stay another minute and I know it was childish but she's done it to me once before and I couldn't watch her do it again.* No, she couldn't say that. She shook her head.

'What did you mean you were in the way tonight?

'I can't talk about it yet, Joe, I'm sorry.' She couldn't. Her mind was too jumbled, filled with fury at Lainey, shame for her own behaviour. She had been so happy. Things had been going so well. And then Lainey had arrived in the middle of it and ruined everything, just as she'd done before.

His eyes searched hers. 'Do you want to come back to the restaurant? Or do you want me to walk you home?'

Go back there? Or go home? Lainey would be there either way, eventually. She shook her head. 'No. I'm sorry, Joe. But I think I need to be on my own.'

'Are you sure?'

She nodded, fighting a sudden longing to go into his arms, to kiss him.

'Can I ring you later? I'd like to know you're all right.'

His words nearly brought her to tears. But she had to get away. She nodded. 'I'm sorry, Joe. Goodnight.'

He watched her walk away for a moment, then he turned and went back to the restaurant.

Eva walked steadily for ten minutes, her anger and distress keeping her moving, until she realised she'd passed all the restaurants and cafes. She was now in a much darker part of town and there were very few people around. She'd just begun to feel nervous when she recognised where she was. At the intersection of Lainey's road, with the petrol station on one corner and the motel on the other.

The motel. Before she could think too much about it, she'd opened the door and walked up to the reception desk. 'A single room for tonight, please.'

What on earth are you doing?

What does it look like? Booking into a motel room.

But what will Lainey think when you don't come home? She'll be worried sick.

She won't even notice I'm not there. She's probably about to invite Joe back to her house. No point all that flirting going to waste, is there?

Don't be ridiculous. Of course she'll be worried if she gets back and you're not there.

Good. She wanted Lainey to worry. Eva wanted Lainey to feel as bad as she was feeling now.

But –

I'm not listening to you, she said, as she passed over her credit card.

In the restaurant Lainey sat at the table, not sure what would happen next. She'd been very impressed when Joe had stood up and gone after Eva. She felt a bit guilty about her behaviour. She had been flirting a little bit, she knew that. Been a bit mean to Eva. And all right, a bit jealous of her too. In Melbourne for such a short time and finding this lovely man.

She looked up as Joseph came back in again. 'Is she all right?' she asked.

He didn't sit down, just took his coat from the back of the chair. 'She's gone home. To your apartment.'

'Oh,' Lainey nodded. 'She's overtired, probably.'

'Do you think so?'

Lainey glanced up, unsure of his tone.

'I think I'll call it a night myself. And I'll take care of the bill.'

'No, Joe, you don't have to do that.' Lainey started to stand up.

'I insist,' he said.

Five minutes later, they said goodnight in front of the restaurant and walked in separate directions.

Less than a kilometre away, Eva lay on the motel bed in the darkness, watching the passing car lights flicker against the wall. She was still angry. Furious. About tonight and about eight years ago. She'd been wrong all along. It hadn't gone away. It had just been lying in wait, like a dragon, waiting to be awoken.

And tonight Lainey had woken it. By trying to do with Joe exactly what she had done with Martin eight years ago. Ruin things.

Eva rolled over, feeling the memories rush into her mind again. Martin had been her first boyfriend. She'd been just twenty-three years old, still living at home with her parents in Dunshaughlin, working in the local newsagent. He was the first man she'd been in love with, the first man she'd ever had sex with. She and Martin had been together for five months, Eva in dreamland for most of it. Her friends had teased her about being lovestruck. She hadn't minded any of it. She was the luckiest woman in Ireland, she thought. Her very first boyfriend, her very first lover, and he was the kindest and most gentle man in town. Perhaps he didn't like talking about their future together as much as she did, but sure, weren't all men like that? Everyone knew that it was women who did all the organising, got things done in relationships. And there was plenty of time anyway. They were getting on just fine, weren't they?

Then Lainey had arrived back from Australia on holiday. She'd radiated sunshine and confidence, had

348

been full to overflowing with funny stories about Australia, about her studies at business school. Martin hadn't minded the two of them becoming the three of them, at the pub, on trips into Dublin. How could he mind, he said, with two gorgeous girls to go out with?

Lainey had been a prize flirt back then too. She knew all the tricks. Looking up at him through her lashes. Touching him on the arm. Laughing at his jokes. At first, Eva had been confident enough in Martin to point it out. 'Lainey Byrne, are you flirting with my boyfriend?'

'Eva, such accusations,' Lainey had laughed. 'I'm just practising my womanly wiles. You don't mind, Martin, do you?'

'Ah no, practise away.'

Then things started to change. Lainey and Martin seemed to have lots to talk to each other about. They'd stop when Eva came in. She started getting suspicious. Finally, she'd confronted Lainey. 'Is something going on between you and Martin, Lainey?'

'Of course not. He's your boyfriend.'

She seemed to be telling the truth. Eva relaxed again. But she couldn't help noticing Martin was changing too. As though he was slowly shutting windows into himself that had once been wide open to Eva.

Lainey went back to Australia. Then, one week

later, Martin called around and told Eva he was leaving Dunshaughlin. Leaving Ireland. And therefore, it went without saying, leaving her. She had been too shocked to cry. 'But why?

'I want more than this, Evie. More than living here for the rest of my life. I'm not ready to get married, have kids, buy a house, any of it.'

'It's Lainey, isn't it? She's put these ideas into your head. Is that where you're going? To Australia? To her?'

'No,' he'd said quickly. Too quickly? she'd wondered. 'I'm going to England first. Maybe Australia later, I don't know. I just know I want to go somewhere that's not here.'

After he'd left, Eva sank into misery. Several weeks later, her mother had snapped, 'Eva, that's enough. You have to lift yourself out of this. If it's a broken heart, then I'm sorry, but you'll have plenty more of those before you're through with your life. If it's more serious than that, we'll make an appointment with the doctor and get you sorted out. Because I know one thing for sure and that is your father and I are tired of seeing you moping around day after day. You're twenty-three years old, not ninety. It's time you grabbed life again, do you hear me?'

She'd come to her senses. In a fit of energy she'd turned her life upside down. She'd decided to move to Dublin, to apply for art school. If Martin was going to make something of his life, so was she. She'd pulled together all the work she'd done over the years, especially the dark, angst-ridden ones she'd painted since Martin had left. She'd survived a long, gruelling interview with the head lecturer, who had uhmed and aahed over her work, before saying that, yes, there could be something there and, yes, she was in.

Ambrose offered her a part-time job in the delicatessen. She decided to study part-time and work part-time, to be as self-sufficient as she could. She lived in a series of bedsits until her cousin moved to London and asked her if she wanted to rent his house in Stoneybatter. And all the while she ignored any letter and phone message she got from Lainey.

Eva shifted position on the bed. She wondered sometimes if Lainey had even noticed that she'd stopped writing to her for nearly a year. They'd never talked about that either.

You didn't talk about that either? Well, how astonishing.

She sat up on the bed, miserable, angry, disappointed. She'd come to Australia with such high hopes, seeing Lainey again, cementing their friendship, finding the time to think over Ambrose's offer. But look at the mess she'd made of it all. Not only had she started living a false life, telling lies, but she'd let Lainey do it to her again.

Do what to you again?

Interfere. Take over. Just like she always has.

When we were young. When she came over to Ireland. And tonight, with Joe.

Well, why do you let her?

You just do with Lainey. How can anyone fight that sort of personality? All that spark and energy she has.

And what are you, a slug at the bottom of the sea?

Compared to Lainey I am.

Oh rubbish. You're talking like a four-year-old. You're thirty-one. Lainey hasn't lived in Ireland since you were a teenager. You've hardly been in a coma since then, only wakening whenever Lainey's around.

No, but –

You managed to get yourself through school, didn't you? Get a job in the newsagent after school? Get into art school? Make the decision to go part-time? Work with Ambrose? Lainey hasn't been there beside you weighing out olives and cutting cheese, has she? That's been you smiling at customers, hasn't it?

Yes but –

Are you still jealous of her, is that it?

Jealous? I'm not jealous. Lainey's my friend. You can't be jealous of a friend.

Of course you can. And this jealousy goes back years. Right back to Martin. Tonight had nothing to do with Joe and everything to do with Martin. You've never spoken to her about it, so it's been locked away in a vault in your mind. Until Joe came

*along and accidentally unlocked it. And now he's
had to deal with the consequences.*

No, it's not just about Martin. Lainey is trying to
ruin things between me and Joe.

How has she done that?

By planting doubts in my mind about him. Telling
me what I should and shouldn't do with him.

*So? Tell her thanks for the advice but you're
happy to make up your own mind. Unless you've
been programmed to only do what she tells you, is
that it?*

What about tonight, then? The way she was
behaving tonight? Talking and laughing and flirting.
That's exactly what she did with Martin when she
came back to Ireland that time.

*Well, it's just as well she was talking tonight,
wasn't it, with you sitting there like Lot's wife,
struck dumb. There wasn't a peep out of you.*

I couldn't get a word in, that's why. She's trying
to take him away from me. Like she did with
Martin.

*But you still don't know if you and Martin broke
up because of her. Because you've never asked
Lainey what actually happened between them. You
just assumed that's what it was. Assumed that every
conversation and every joke the pair of them had was
Martin plotting to get away from you. And you still
don't know for sure because you've always been too
scared to ask Lainey. Like you're too scared to try*

353

and run the shop. Too scared to try and paint again. Too scared to tell Joe who you really are.

Yes, all right, I am scared.

So what is it exactly you're scared of with Lainey? Why haven't you asked her about it?

I'm scared of finding out that Lainey had fancied Martin. That Martin and I broke up because of her. In case that's the end of our friendship.

You don't want your friendship with Lainey to end?

Of course I don't.

That's why you haven't asked her about this before now?

Yes.

So you've been happier to spend all these years nursing this hurt, feeding it and helping it to grow bigger and stronger, rather than learn the truth and face up to what actually might have happened?

Which might have been what?

Couldn't Martin have been telling you the truth? That he just wasn't ready to settle down? That he didn't want to live in Dunshaughlin and get married? That he wanted to see the world? That hearing Lainey talk about Australia planted a seed in him, made him realise there really was a big world out there?

Yes, I know that's what he said –

Well, doesn't that all sound fairly reasonable? Where's Martin now, anyway? In Africa, isn't he?

Still travelling? Sounds like that's what he really wanted to do, doesn't it? But rather than find out once and for all, ask Lainey if anything actually happened between them, you've tucked it away, let it grow right out of proportion. You've tried poor Lainey and found her guilty before she's had a chance to defend herself.

Poor Lainey? What's poor about Lainey? She's got everything going for her. Everyone loves her. People just flock to her. Everyone at school did. Martin did. Joe did tonight.

What was Joe supposed to do? Ignore her? Only talk if you spoke to him? Only laugh at your jokes, not Lainey's? You were out to dinner, the three of you. When people are out, they have conversations. That's another name for people talking to each other. You reacted as though they'd been playing footsies under the table. Exchanging phone numbers. Kissing –

But what about Lainey's carry-on about the deli?

Try and look at it from her point of view. She flies home from Brisbane to see her oldest friend, here all the way from Ireland, and walks into a love-fest in the middle of her living room. Not what she expected to see, I imagine. Don't you think she might be feeling a little displaced herself?

I don't know how she feels.

Well, why don't you ask her? Start facing up to some of these things? Start having the courage to actually ask people if there's something you need to know.

*More to the point, tell people the truth about how you
feel? And how about starting now?*

Now?

*Right now. Look at you, this is ridiculous. You fly
across the world to see your friend, then you throw
a tantrum and book yourself into a hotel five minutes
from her house. Don't you think that's a bit silly?*

Yes, but –

*You go down to reception right now, check out
again. Then you go around that corner and see
Lainey and talk to her. Now.*

But –

*Eva, you are a smart, capable human being. You
have many friends. You have people who love you.
You have something new and exciting waiting for
you in Dublin. You've started something with a
lovely man that might get even nicer if you dare to
tell him the truth too. But you have to start somewhere, and Lainey's the closest to hand.*

Eva got off the bed and went into the bathroom.
She stared at herself in the mirror for a long moment.
Her hair was down again. She'd been wearing it like
that most of the time she'd been in Melbourne, since
Lainey had told her it suited her like that. Eva
realised something then. She didn't like wearing her
hair down. If she had done, she would have been
wearing it down for years. But it got in her eyes,
that's why she preferred to wear it in the plait. And
she thought it suited her better like that, anyway.

So wear it in a plait. Since when was Lainey the Hair Police?

Eva quickly plaited her hair.

Good. Step one, hair fixed. Now step two, Lainey.

Eva stopped her train of thought right there. Step two was going to be a bit harder to fix. And she didn't want to even think about step three.

CHAPTER THIRTY-THREE

EVA QUIETLY opened the front door to Lainey's apartment and jumped as a shadow moved in front of her. It was Rex.

'No, Rexie,' she whispered. This was no time for an escape bid. She closed the door and waited. She heard Lainey's voice and stiffened. Was Joe in here with her? Oh God, she couldn't handle that. She had turned back to the door when the voice inside her spoke again.

Go in there. Sort this out.

Lainey was on the phone. 'I know it's only been two hours, but she's just an innocent. God knows what might have happened to her, can't you just drive around? Or put out an alert or something?'

Eva put down her bag with enough noise to make Lainey spin around. Her expression changed rapidly. 'It's all right, sergeant, she's here.' She hung up and stood up. 'Oh, thank God, you're okay. Bloody hell,

Eva, you've had me worried sick. I've been onto the police, the hospitals – where the hell were you? Joe and I were both worried about you.'

Joe and I? It was Joe and I? Eva's good intentions disappeared in a flash. The reasoned conversation she'd planned disappeared. She was instantly as angry as she'd been before. 'You noticed I was gone? I'm surprised you could see through all the fluttering eyelashes.'

'What?'

'Don't be coy, Lainey. We're adults now, remember. Responsible for our own actions. You were flirting with him.'

'With Joe? I was not.'

'You were, Lainey. Are you pleased with yourself? Doing your best to ruin another relationship for me?'

'I don't know what you're talking about. Have you been drinking? Taking something?'

'It's all right for you, isn't it? Miss Confident. Miss Successful. Miss Gorgeous. You were flirting with him. You think I didn't notice? Why? Just to see if you could wreck my happiness again?'

Lainey blinked. 'What the hell is this about? I expected to come home to Melbourne, have a laugh and a drink with my old friend Eva, not be attacked like this.'

'You don't remember, do you?'

'Remember what?'

Eva went into the kitchen, rage giving her speed,

and grabbed the framed photo from the side cupboard. The one of the three of them, her and Lainey and Martin. She thrust it at Lainey. 'His name was Martin Conroy, Lainey.'

Lainey glanced at the photo. 'Oh, that's right, so it was.' She was wary, puzzled. 'Do you want me to write his name somewhere. Is that it?'

'Stop it, Lainey.'

'You just wanted me to remember him, is that it? Well, yes, I do now. Martin, that fellow you went out with for a little while.'

'I didn't just go out with him for a little while, I was in love with him. I had slept with him. For the first time. My first time. Maybe that wasn't a big deal for you, but it was for me. And I thought he liked me back. Loved me, even. And he did. Until you came along and turned his head. Turned him off me.'

'Me? Eva, I didn't do that. I was just being friendly.'

'You weren't just being friendly. You flirted with him. It was so easy for you. Talking, laughing, bewitching him.'

'Stop it! If I was talking to him, being friendly to him, it was because he was your friend. And I do remember now, I remember it all. He was talking about leaving Ireland the whole time I was there. He was always going to leave, he said. He'd tried to talk to you about it as well, he told me.'

Eva stood like a statue. Unbidden, she remembered

360

Martin raising the subject with her too. Several times. But she'd ignored it each time, or changed the subject.

Lainey continued. 'He was trying to decide whether to go to England or try Australia. He asked me to keep it secret. His parents would go mad, he said. And he didn't know how to tell you either. He wanted me to do it for him. He even asked me if I would, but I said that it wasn't up to me to tell you.'

Eva remembered lots of things from that time. Walking in on the two of them talking and seeing them spring apart, looking guilty. 'That's what you were talking about? All those times I came in and the two of you seemed guilty about something?'

'Well, I wouldn't have felt guilty. I had done nothing to be guilty about.'

'You didn't try and break us up? You didn't fancy him yourself?'

Lainey stared at her. 'Of course I didn't. I'm your friend. He was *your* boyfriend. Have you gone mad? Why would I have done that?'

Eva's temper flared again. 'The same reason you put on that display in the restaurant tonight, I suppose. With Joe. Is that what a friend would do?'

A shadow crossed over Lainey's face. 'Evie, I was cross with you, I'm sorry, I admit it. You came to Melbourne to see me and first thing I know you're off gallivanting with this fellow. I didn't like it, I didn't want to like him. I was testing him a bit, I guess.'

'Testing him?'

'To see if he'd flirt back. I guess I wanted to make sure he was good enough for you.'

'Good enough?'

'You know what I mean. It's always been like that with us. I look out for you, you need it. You know that yourself, look how easily Dermot took you in. I just didn't want it to happen to you again.'

'This is how you think of me? As some mindless waif? Then let's just call this friendship off here and now, will we? Because clearly you think I haven't a brain in my head.'

'Of course I know you have a brain. You know I think you're great. But come on, you're always the first person to say you don't know what to do or which way to go. I suppose I just got used to giving you advice.'

'It may come as a surprise to you, Lainey, but not all of us ordinary mortals have your endless well of self-confidence to draw from. Some of us out here in the real world find life a bit difficult sometimes. We don't all breeze through it like you seem to.'

'That's rubbish, it's not like that for me. I've worked bloody hard for what I've got, you know that better than anyone. And anyway, you're a fine one to talk. You're not exactly on the scrap heap yourself, you know. You've got a great life. Parents who dote on you, who don't parade you around like a prize poodle like mine do. You've just been offered a whole business to run. You can sing, even though you don't. You've got artistic talent.'

'No, Lainey. I haven't.'

Lainey dismissed her. 'Yes, you have. I know, I know, you haven't finished your degree but you will one day.'

Eva's face was a mixture of defiance and misery. 'No, I won't.'

'What are you talking about? You went to art school for three years, remember? Until Ambrose's wife died. Remember?'

'Of course I remember. But I'd made my decision before Sheila died, I just hadn't told anyone.'

'What decision?'

'To leave art school. Before I was kicked out.'

'What are you talking about, being kicked out? I thought you just postponed your study.'

'I know that's what you thought.'

'But you were going to be kicked out? Why?'

'Do I really need to spell it out?'

Lainey stared at her blankly.

'I wasn't good enough, Lainey. I wasn't going to pass. I was just average at art, nothing special.'

Lainey was taken aback. 'But I thought you'd put your studies on hold because you wanted to help Ambrose.'

'That's what everyone thought. And I was feeling so ashamed and embarrassed about being a failure as an artist, I didn't tell anyone the truth.'

'I don't get it. You *are* great at art. I remember those paintings you did of the Hill of Tara that time. They were brilliant.'

Eva managed to laugh. 'Lainey, that was more than fifteen years ago. I was good technically. But I don't have that extra something. The spark. Whatever it is that separates the ordinary from the excellent. That's exactly what the head lecturer told me.'

'That's just one person. Couldn't you have got a second opinion?'

'I got five second opinions. I took my work around to some galleries and each of them backed up what the lecturer had said. I was just average. Nothing special.'

Eva remembered the week she'd done that, traipsing from gallery to gallery. The last one had been the hardest. That's when she'd known for sure. After the gallery owner had delivered his verdict, blunt and charmless, she had gone outside and burst into tears. The man's secretary had followed her out and found her crying. She'd been kind, kinder than anyone else. She'd taken her for a coffee, listened as Eva had poured out her heart. Eva had got the feeling she wasn't the first failed artist the woman had consoled.

She took a breath. 'I was about to tell my parents and Ambrose and Sheila what I'd decided. That I was leaving art school, was going to rethink my life. And then Sheila died, and poor Ambrose needed help so badly. And because I wasn't going back to study I could help him. I was really happy to help him, but then it backfired. I got all this credit for something I didn't deserve.'

Lainey was trying to take it all in. 'Is that why they had that party for you? That one you told me about? At your ma and da's house?'

Eva remembered every second of that party. Her parents had held it in their house in Dunshaughlin, a year after Sheila had died. A surprise party. They'd found all of Eva's paintings and hung them up on the walls. Invited all the family friends. Her sister Cathy had sent a video message. Her father had made a lovely speech. Ambrose had spoken too, saying how grateful he was that Eva had come to work for him full-time, that she had left art school to come and help him out. 'One day she will have her own exhibition. Until then, I now declare the Eva Kennedy exhibition open.'

Eva looked at Lainey now. 'What could I say? Thanks, everyone, but in fact all the paintings on these walls are rubbish and I never will have a real exhibition. I just didn't say anything. I didn't lie, I just didn't tell the whole truth. And I've paid for it ever since. And now this, Ambrose wanting to give me the shop in gratitude for something that I didn't ever really do. I don't deserve the shop.'

'Evie, you do deserve it. You didn't have to go full-time four years ago. You could have done something else. Anyway, whether you were there wholly and solely because you felt sorry for Ambrose or because you were glad to have something else to do while you licked your wounds about art school, the outcome is the same. You worked in the shop, didn't you? Side by side with Ambrose. I bet that's exactly why he's offering you the shop, because he knows you'd be good at it.'

There was a long pause as Eva's revelations settled around them. Then Lainey spoke again. 'So what about your singing? With that band? Was that real?'

'No, that was all dubbed.' Eva managed a wry smile. 'Yes, of course it was real. I loved the singing. But I couldn't take time off to sing with the band, not when everyone was praising me so much for helping Ambrose. I felt guilty enough as it was.'

'Oh Evie, I just wish I'd known all this before now, that you'd told me all of this. Not just about the art school, but about Martin, all of it. I hate the idea that you've been angry about all this for years, bottling it all up. What am I going to do with you?'

Eva's temper gave one final flash. 'Lainey, please, you don't have to do anything with me. I'm thirty-one. You're not responsible for me any more.'

Lainey gave a sheepish grin. 'All right, I won't boss you. I'm sorry, I know I do it. It's part of my charm, don't you think? But I can advise you now and then, can't I? Push you gently in the right direction? Like good friends do?'

Eva tried not to smile. 'Yes, you can make a suggestion. But you're not allowed to give me a time limit for when I take it up, okay?'

'Okay.'

'Go on then. What is this suggestion?'

'I really think you have to tell Joe the truth. If this is serious between you, if you do really like him.'

'I know. Of course I know. I've wanted to tell him the truth since I first met him. I've just been waiting for the right moment. But each time something keeps stopping me.'

'What thing?'

'Can't you see? Everything he likes about me is a lie. If I tell him the truth, there's nothing left of me to like.'

'Oh, for God's sake. You and Joe don't talk about sculpting and your singing the whole time, do you?'

'No, of course not. Hardly at all any more.' She thought about it. They didn't. There seemed to be too many other things to talk about.

'And you weren't paying him to kiss you today, were you?'

'No.'

'And have you . . . ?'

'Have I what?'

'You know.'

'Lainey! It's none of your business.'

'Then you haven't. But you want to, don't you? And he does too. I've seen the way he looks at you.'

'Lainey, please! What do you want, tickets to the event?'

Lainey laughed. 'Seriously, Evie. You have to tell him the truth. When does he go back home?'

'Soon.' She hated the word.

'And have you talked about what might happen then? When you're both back home?'

'No. But I know I want to see him again. I *really* want to see him again.'

Lainey gave her a long look. 'This isn't just a holiday romance for you, Evie, is it?'

Eva shook her head. 'No, Lainey, I don't think it is.'

The phone rang, making them both jump. Lainey answered. 'Yes, she is. No, don't worry, we were still up. Yes, she's fine. Hold on.'

She held out the phone. 'Niamh, it's Joe.'

CHAPTER THIRTY-FOUR

THE NEXT day Joseph parked the hire car outside the Richmond apartment. The back seat was covered with everything he'd gathered to bring on their trip to the Great Ocean Road. He had spent an hour that morning in the food hall of a large department store. After loading up the car, he'd returned to his hotel room. He'd glanced at his mobile, lying on the desk, its battery flat. It had gone from being a high-technology communication tool to a useless bit of plastic.

He still hadn't rung Kate. He would. Tonight, or tomorrow perhaps. He was still letting all Lewis had told him sift through his mind, letting everything settle into place. He knew Lewis was going to phone her, tell her that the meeting had gone well. Better than well.

In the meantime there were other important things he needed to do. Like spend the day with

Niamh. And tell her the truth about himself. He still hadn't managed to do it. He wanted to talk about some other things too, about the way he was feeling about her. And about what might happen when they both went home.

He got out of the car and looked up at the sky. It was still heavy and grey. He spoke into the entry phone. 'It's Joe.'

The door buzzed and he went upstairs.

Up in the flat, Eva turned to her friend. 'Lainey, you're sure you don't mind me going like this?'

'I don't mind at all,' Lainey said, almost truthfully. They were still stepping a little gingerly around each other.

'Really?'

'Evie, I know how important this is to you. You don't have to ask my permission. Remember our new rule?'

'I know that. But you flew down to see me specially. I'm here to see you.'

'Evie, honestly. I'm exhausted, I'm probably going to sleep all day anyway. And I get to see you tonight, don't I?'

'I'll be back for dinner, I promise.'

'Excellent. Listen, could you quickly pass me that phone book there, before Joe gets up here?'

Eva passed it over. 'What are you looking for?'

Lainey flicked through the pages. 'I want to see if I can hire any drug-sniffer dogs. To check Joe out when he brings you home tonight.'

Eva threw a cushion at her just as they both heard a knock at the door.

Lainey gave a mischievous smile. 'He awaits. Go, my child. Go to this man who calls you.'

The rain was pelting down by the time Joseph and Eva got to the car. A sharp wind gusted around them. They climbed in and turned to each other. 'Joe, we need to talk.' 'Niamh, I think we need to talk.'

Eva swallowed. 'Could we drive on a bit, do you think?'

'Of course.' He pulled over just a few minutes away, in a parking area overlooking the River Yarra. The rain was heavy on the roof. He gave her a searching look. 'Niamh, what happened last night?'

She took a deep breath. 'It was something between Lainey and me, something from years ago and I'm afraid you got caught up in the middle of it. I'm sorry.' She wanted to tell him more about it. More about how she felt. 'I thought you . . .' She stopped. 'I was jealous of her. I have been for years, I've realised.'

'Why?'

Wasn't it obvious? 'Lots of things. Everything about her. Her looks. Her confidence. Her . . .' She was faltering, thrown by the expression on his face. A mixture of amusement and something else.

'Niamh, Lainey seems very nice. She's very lively, very entertaining. But she's not you.'

She turned around in her seat completely. 'And is that not too boring? Too ordinary?'

There was a look in his eyes that made her shiver and tingle at once. 'Too boring? You? With your sculpting and the life you lead in Galway and the way you look at things?' He smiled. 'No, Niamh, it's not too boring. Not in a million years.'

He leaned over and kissed her, his lips soft against hers. 'I'm glad you told me that. Told me what had been wrong.'

'Are you?'

'You're very straightforward, aren't you? There's no pretence with you.' He touched her cheek. 'Now, can I please take you away for the day?'

She nodded weakly. Straightforward? No pretence? If he only knew the half of it.

An hour later they were still stuck in city traffic. There were traffic diversions in place all over the city. A visiting head of state, an irate cab driver had shouted in answer to Joseph's question.

The windscreen wipers were working hard against the lashing rain. A sign ahead of them pointed to something called the Dandenongs. What were they? Eva wondered. They sounded like body parts.

The news came on the radio, followed by a long sports report, then the weather. A low off Bass Strait was causing extensive heavy rainfall and fog throughout Melbourne and surrounding areas. Drivers were warned to take extra care, particularly in coastal regions.

Joseph made a decision. 'I promised you a picnic, didn't I? With ocean views?'

'You did.'

'I can't go back on a promise. Will you trust me if I change part of the plan?'

'Of course.'

He turned the car and drove back in the opposite direction. Twenty minutes later, they were parked outside the big hotel on the St Kilda Esplanade.

'Will you wait here?' Joseph asked.

She nodded.

'Shut your eyes for a minute.'

She did and heard a rustle of bags and paper from the back seat. Then his voice again. 'I'll be back very soon.'

'You'd like to book another room with us, Mr Wheeler?'

'The best room you have, please. And it has to have sea views.'

The receptionist nodded. There was a click of keyboard keys. 'The penthouse suite is available. It's got a superior-sized bedroom, a living area, bathroom with spa –'

'That sounds perfect. I also need a few other bits and pieces, I wonder if you could help me.'

The receptionist didn't blink. 'Certainly, sir.'

Ten minutes later, Eva jumped at the sound of a voice at her car window. Joseph was standing there with an umbrella. 'If you'd like to come with me, madam?'

'I would indeed.'

He sheltered her as they walked from the carpark into the foyer. She expected to be taken into the bar area, or into the restaurant section. But instead he led her straight to the lifts.

'Am I allowed to ask questions?'

'Of course. But I won't answer them. This is a surprise.'

She watched as he pressed the top-floor button. The lift reached its destination in seconds. Eva stepped out first and turned to Joseph, unsure what to do next.

'Look down. There's a clue.'

She looked down at the floor. At first she thought it was an odd pattern. Then she thought someone must have dropped something. Finally she realised what it was.

A trail of breadcrumbs. Leading from the door of the lift, down the corridor.

She got it immediately. She'd mentioned it on their train trip. 'I should follow this?'

He nodded.

She followed the trail along the carpet, turning left, not lifting her eyes until it finally ran out. She was standing in front of a door. A yellow ribbon had been stuck to it.

He smiled. 'After you, Niamh.'

The room was beautiful. Except it wasn't a room, it was a suite. An enormous suite.

They had stepped from the hotel corridor into a living room. One whole wall was windows. Outside was a balcony. On a beautiful day the view would be incredible. Even this morning, with nothing but grey skies and lashing rain to look out onto, it was amazing. Far below was the beach and the sea. Eva could see the wind buffeting the sails of boats moored in the marina to the left. A few people hurried along on the footpath, their clothes billowing around them.

She turned away and gazed around the whole suite, aware that Joe was watching her every move. To her left was the master bedroom. She couldn't help but notice that the breadcrumb trail led in there. Her stomach gave a little lurch.

This must have cost him a fortune. How generous.

How romantic. She knew she should be over the moon. Ecstatic at this gesture. But instead Lainey's words kept flashing into her head. *Drug smuggler. Quick and easy money for the right people.*

She knew it was ridiculous. Lainey had nothing to back up her suspicions, nothing at all. But now the thought was there, she couldn't get rid of it. She had to bring it out in the open. Now.

'Joe, I have to ask you something.'

He waited.

'Are you a drug smuggler?'

'I beg your pardon?'

'Are you a drug smuggler?'

'Of course I'm not. Why on earth would you think that?'

'This. This room. Your travelling. The train trips. The flights. The hire cars. Lainey was worried for me. She just thought it was all a bit suspicious.' Eva spoke quickly, feeling more and more foolish. 'Joe, I'm sorry to even have to ask it.'

He interrupted her. 'Niamh, believe me, I am *not* a drug smuggler. I really am an industrial designer in London. And I am on a working holiday. My first holiday in many years. I promise you that all of this has been paid with my hard-earned savings, not criminal profits. But there is some–'

'Joe, that's all I need to hear.' He'd told her enough. Now it was her turn. She couldn't wait another moment. 'But there's something I have to tell you, too. I have to clear the air. You think something about me that isn't strictly true.'

He waited.

'It's about Enya. You know, the singing I told you about?'

He nodded.

'Joe, I'm sorry, it's not true. Lainey and I just made it up. As a kind of joke on Greg, really. I do sing, but I've never sung with Enya.' She watched and waited, feeling like she was at an execution. The knife was hanging over her neck.

To her astonishment, he started to laugh. Really laugh. 'And he fell for it? We all fell for it? Oh, Niamh, you know he was telling everyone? His customers? All his staff?'

'Yes, I gathered he was.' She smiled wanly.

'I should have guessed. Especially after what you'd said about everyone falling asleep in the studio. But I just thought you had a fantastic attitude to it all. I should have realised then you were making it up.' He laughed again.

He didn't mind, she realised. He really didn't mind.

'So what do you normally sing? If you don't actually sing Enya lullabies?'

She grinned. She could answer him honestly, she could tell him the truth. The wonderful, simple truth. 'Anything. Everything. I used to sing in a cover band around Dublin. But I haven't done a lot of it lately.'

'I guess not. It's a long way to drive from Galway to Dublin for a gig, I suppose.'

Oh dear, she thought. It's not over yet.

She was saved by a knock at the door. Joseph answered it. It was room service, with a bottle of champagne in a silver ice bucket. Eva's mind was racing. That had gone okay. One lie down, only a few to go. Did she really need to tell him the whole thing all at once, though? Wouldn't that be a bit overwhelming?

No. Tell him now.

But I've told him the truth about Enya.

Now tell him the rest.

I will.

Joseph closed the door and came toward her, carrying the ice-bucket.

'Joe –'

'That really is very funny. Poor Greg.' He was still smiling.

'You don't mean that at all.'

'About poor Greg? No, I don't. Now, madam, that's enough talking from you at the moment. We've established two things. I'm not a drug smuggler and you didn't sing with Enya. Can we have our picnic now?'

She nodded, very relieved. She'd done as much confessing today as she wanted to.

Chicken.

Oh, shhh.

Joseph took her hand and led her along the

breadcrumb trail into the bedroom. It was another beautiful room with tall windows looking out onto the stormy sea. He had lit the two lamps. They sent a warm, orange light into the room.

They stopped at the foot of the bed. In the middle of it was a tray with a colourful array of food laid out in pairs. There were two plump olives. Two wafer-thin ginger biscuits. Two handmade chocolates. Two slivers of camembert cheese. Two artichoke hearts. Two pieces of Turkish delight. Two fine slices of smoked salmon. It was like a culinary version of Noah's Ark.

Joseph was watching her reaction. 'I'm sorry about the weather. I did expect we'd be eating this on the beach.'

Her heart felt like it was flying around inside her rib cage again. 'This is lovely, really. Much better without all that sand.'

'Please, sit down.'

She did. He sat just a small distance away from her. 'I took a crash course in picnic food. Can I show you what I learnt?'

'Of course.'

He picked up an olive. 'These are called olives. From the Barossa Valley in South Australia, I believe. The hot climate there is very conducive to olive growing.'

'Is that right?' she said, just as seriously.

He held it out to her. She opened her mouth and he carefully placed it between her lips. She felt a drop of salty brine run down her chin. He used his finger to catch it and put that in her mouth as well. She gently sucked it.

'And this is cheese. From a place called King Island. Best served at room temperature.' He picked up a sliver and held it out.

Again she took it from his fingers and slowly savoured the taste. 'My turn now?'

He nodded.

She chose a chocolate. 'This is chocolate.' Her voice was soft. 'Handmade, by the looks of things?'

He nodded.

'I'll taste it first, will I? To check that it's okay?'

He nodded again.

She took a bite, then held out the rest to him. He took the chocolate from her fingers, then he moved closer. They were only inches apart. Then they weren't apart at all. They were kissing, their mouths soft and hot against each other, the chocolate flavour strong and sensual.

The kiss seemed to last for a long time. Slowly, reluctantly, he pulled away from her. 'Are you still hungry?' he asked, tracing her face with his finger, touching her lips again.

'Not at all.'

He stood up, took her by the hand and pulled her up beside him. He picked up the tray of food and put it to one side. She moved into his arms, into a long kiss. She shivered with pleasure at the feel of his fingers stroking her back. She felt sure that this was what she wanted, all of this, all that was about to happen.

Moments later she stood in front of him in her bra and knickers. Lacy. Sexy. She helped him take off his T-shirt, loving the feel of his chest under her hand. They kissed again, slow and beautiful. She had just touched the waistband on his jeans when he pulled away from her.

'Joe? Are you all right?'

She watched, puzzled, as he moved into the living room, opened the main door and hung the Do Not Disturb sign on the doorknob. Then he locked the door. Pulled the curtains. He came into the bedroom again with a serious expression. 'There is still an air vent, but I'm going to take a gamble no-one gets through it. I don't think I can handle another interruption.'

She laughed. And then she wasn't laughing. She was kissing him again. He was kissing her. Then they were lying on the bed, both of them naked. The feel of his body against hers was almost too much. The feel of his lips on her face, on her neck. On her breast. The feel of his skin under her fingers. His thighs.

There was something urgent about it, but there was something slow and sensual and gradual too. There was more kissing. More slow, sensual stroking. She could feel that he was ready. Her body had opened up completely to him too.

And then there they were, at the contraception moment. He whispered softly in her ear, 'I have some condoms here with me. I was hoping we might need them.'

She whispered back, 'So have I. I was hoping too.'

And then they didn't need to talk any more.

Later she lay in his arms while he gently stroked her back. It had been beautiful between them. Unsure at times, tentative even. But warm and loving and full of promise. She wanted to just lie here. Just hold him. Feel him holding her. But now she'd confessed some of the truth, she wanted to confess it all. She wanted to be in his arms as Eva, not as Niamh.

'Joe, I need to tell you something else. It's about my sculpting.' She felt him kiss the top of her head. Felt his fingers start to stroke her lower back again.

His voice was low. 'I think I already know what you want to tell me.'

She pulled herself up from his chest and looked at him, alarmed.

'You didn't really do an inch-high sculpture for Bono's garden, did you?' he said.

She realised he was trying to fight a grin. She shook her head. 'No, I didn't.' She couldn't believe it. He didn't seem to mind about that either.

He was laughing out loud again. She could feel the movement beneath her. 'I thought that was completely weird. Who on earth would have an inch-high sculpture in their garden? You'd only ever see it in autumn, surely.' He laughed again. 'Don't tell me. You and Lainey made that one up too? To fool Greg?'

Eva smiled, hugely relieved. 'Well, the sculpture itself was her idea. But no-one had ever asked any details about it, until you, that day in the kitchen. And you caught me on the spot.'

'Oh, poor, poor Greg.' He didn't sound in the least sympathetic.

'Poor Greg,' she agreed.

'So what else?' he said, moving onto his side and taking her with him. Their bodies were close against each other, their faces just inches apart.

'What else what?' What else had he guessed?

'Surely it doesn't stop there? Let me think. I know, you're not really Irish, are you? That beautiful voice isn't real. This beautiful skin isn't real. These eyes. This nose. This neck. This? And this?' He was kissing her as he said each word.

'No, they're all real,' she managed to say before her body surrendered to waves of feeling again.

Well, she'd tried, she thought as his lips moved lower down her body. As she gasped at a rush of pleasure, two thoughts crossed her mind. Maybe it wasn't too late to take a sculpting course. Or move to Galway.

CHAPTER THIRTY-FIVE

IT WAS six in the evening. Joseph lay alone in the bed, looking out of the window at the last of the light playing on the water. He thought about Niamh. About the afternoon they'd had together. About her beautiful body, her soft skin. He'd never felt such an overwhelming passion for a woman before. Not just when he was touching her, kissing her, making love with her. But talking to her. Being with her. And he felt as though she wanted to be with him as much as he wanted to be with her. He just hoped what he was about to tell her, about his company and his real life, wouldn't change anything.

He glanced over at the bathroom door. As soon as Niamh came out of the shower he was going to tell her everything.

The bedside phone started to ring. He picked it up.

'Joseph?'

'Yes.'

'That is Joseph Wheeler?'

'It is.'

'Joseph, it's Rosemary.

Rosemary?'

'Oh, Joseph, thank God I found you.'

'How did you, if you don't mind me asking?'

'It's been extremely difficult.' His PA sounded quite distressed. 'I've been trying your mobile for the past two days but there seems to be something wrong with it. So I rang your mother, in case she'd heard from you. And she told me you'd been to South Australia but she understood you were going back to Melbourne. So I've been ringing all the Melbourne hotels I could find on the Internet. I finally hit it lucky with this one. They even told me you had two rooms booked there. But I've found you, thank heavens.'

'Rosemary, what is it? Is it about the Canadian offer?'

'No, it's not about Canada. It's much more urgent than that.'

'How urgent?'

'Maurice has disappeared.'

'He's what?'

'Maurice has disappeared. With all your money.'

Joseph sat up straight. Was he hearing right? His accountant had done a runner? 'Rosemary, is this a joke?'

'No, Joseph, it's not. The auditor discovered it. He thinks Maurice has been siphoning off money for the past two years. Not just from you, from all his clients.'

'What? How could Maurice have got away with it?'

'He covered his tracks very well. Last year's auditor didn't notice a thing. But we used a different firm this year.'

'And Maurice?'

'He's just vanished. He's not home any more, he's not anywhere. Even his wife doesn't know where he is. She's devastated. I'd had emails from him until two days ago, that we assumed he was sending from home. He could be anywhere by now. Spain. South America. The police are trying to track him down.'

'I can't believe this. How did he do it?'

'He used every trick in the book, the auditor thinks. Fake invoices, payable to him. A separate Wheeler Design bank account with him the sole signatory.'

Joseph shut his eyes. Two years ago he'd made Maurice the sole signatory on any transactions under ten thousand pounds. Maurice had advised him it was the most efficient way of handling things. 'It'll save me bothering you with every little matter,' he'd said.

Rosemary was still talking. 'It was that bank account that gave it all away. The auditor spotted it.

Maurice had been channelling funds into it. Five thousand pounds here. Ten thousand pounds here. Lots of small amounts but it all added up.'

'To what, Rosemary? How much has he taken?'

'We don't know yet. Hundreds of thousands of pounds. Maybe more.'

'More?

Rosemary didn't say anything.

'Is the auditor still there?' Joseph asked.

'And the police as well. We had to call them in. It's a criminal investigation now. You'll have to come back, Joseph. I've got you booked on a flight leaving Melbourne tonight.'

Joseph thought of Niamh. 'Tonight? But I can't leave tonight.'

'Joseph, I'm sorry, you'll have to forget your holiday. The police are here. They need to interview you as soon as possible.'

The carefree life was over. 'Okay, Rosemary. I'll be on that flight.' He wrote the details down and said goodbye. Then he just sat there in the bed, shocked.

Eva came out of the bathroom to find him still holding the phone, staring into space.

'Joe, what is it? Is it bad news?'

He wanted to tell her everything. The truth about him and his company. But he couldn't do it now. He couldn't tell her he'd been lying since they'd met, then get on a plane and expect it to be all right next time he saw her. In London. Galway. Wherever it happened to be.

She came around in front of him. She was wrapped only in a towel, her shoulders bare. He reached up, touched her, stroked her skin, still without speaking.

'Please tell me what's wrong. Are you sick? Is it bad news from home? Your family?'

He thanked her silently for the excuse. He nodded, hoping he could lie convincingly. Another lie. 'It is. It's my grandmother. She's seriously ill.'

'Oh Joe, what is it? What's wrong with her?'

His mind went blank. Both his grandmothers had died before he was born, and he couldn't remember what they'd died from. So he said the first thing to come into his head. 'Heart trouble. It's touch and go, they think.'

'Oh God. Do you need to go home?'

'I do.'

'As soon as you can?'

He nodded.

'Can I ring the airport? Get you a flight?'

'No, it's all organised. My flight leaves in three hours.'

Three hours? she thought in disbelief. He was leaving in *three hours*.

He took her hand, pulled her closer to him. 'Niamh, I'm sorry. This is the last thing, the very last thing I want to do.'

She didn't want him to leave her yet either. Not after today. Even before today. But his poor grand-mother . . . She steeled herself. 'You haven't much time then. You'd better start packing. Is there anything I can do to help?'

'Will you come with me to the airport?'

'Of course I will.'

Two hours later they were standing in the departure lounge at Melbourne airport. He'd checked in, grateful that Niamh wasn't standing at the check-in desk beside him. That might have taken some expla-nation. Mercy flights home for ill grandmothers weren't generally business class, he guessed.

One more deceit. The past two hours had been full of them. She had stayed in the penthouse suite while Joseph had gone three floors down and hur-riedly packed his bags. He hadn't told her that was where he was going. He knew she assumed he was going to the backpacker hostel down the road.

As he handed over his credit card at the reception desk he'd wondered anxiously if he had the money in his account to pay for this any more. Or had Maurice cleaned all that out as well? He'd know soon enough.

Now he looked up at the television monitor. His flight was boarding. He turned to her. 'I didn't want it to end like this. But can I see you again when you get back to Ireland?'

He'd said it. He wanted to see her again. 'Yes. Please,' Eva said.

He smiled at her formal answer. 'Can you give me your phone number in Galway?'

It hit her then. No, she couldn't give him her number in Galway. Because she didn't have a number in Galway. Because she didn't live in Galway, she lived in Dublin. But he still didn't know that. And this was absolutely no time to tell him.

She thought quickly. Could she arrange a phone number in Galway? Get it diverted to Dublin somehow? Buy a mobile phone and try and figure out how to use it? Or could she tell him the truth now? *I'm so sorry about your grandmother and the fact you have to rush back to London like this but by the way my name is really Eva Kennedy and I work in a shop and live in Dublin and here's my home number.* No, that would be so unfair to him at a time like this.

'Joe, I'm sorry, I don't have a phone in Galway. In the caravan. It's too isolated. But can I ring you in London?'

'Of course.' He quickly wrote his phone numbers down and gave them to her.

Eva looked at the piece of paper. Three numbers, work, home and a mobile. She felt like she was holding a treasure map. She glanced at the work number. 'What's the name of the company you work for? I don't think you ever mentioned it.'

It was out before he could help himself. 'Wheeler Design.'

'Wheeler? Your own surname?' She smiled, trying to lighten the mood. 'A family company, is it?'

Tell her. Tell her. Tell her. He saw the clock on the monitor behind her. There wasn't time. And he didn't want the last thing he said to her to be an admission of lies and half-truths. 'In a way,' he said.

They stood there, looking at each other for a long moment.

'I'd better go,' he said. 'You'd better go,' she said.

There was just time for one long kiss. Then he went.

Lainey was in the kitchen stirring a saucepan when Eva came home. She ostentatiously looked at her watch. 'You've broken your curfew, I'm afraid. I'm going to have to ground you.' Then she noticed the expression on her friend's face. 'Evie, are you all right? Did you tell him? Is that what's wrong?'

'No. He's gone.'

'Gone? Where?'

'Back to London.'

'Just like that? Today was that bad?' She realised Eva wasn't in a joking humour. 'I'm sorry. Tell me what happened.'

'He got a call from London in our hotel room. His grandmother's been taken ill.'

Lainey ignored the news about the grandmother. 'Hotel room? I thought you were on a picnic?'

'The weather was so bad, we went to that big hotel in St Kilda instead.'

'That beachfront hotel? What's a backpacker doing staying there? You're sure it wasn't one of the groovy backpacker hostels?'

Eva was in no mood for Lainey's suspicions. 'Yes, Lainey, I'm sure. It was that hotel. The penthouse suite. And he paid for it with pure cocaine.'

Then she burst into tears.

Chapter thirty-six

Kate was waiting at the arrivals gate at Heathrow when Joseph came out. 'Rosemary told me which flight. I wanted to meet you.'

'I'm glad you did.'

She looked at him intently. 'And are you all right?'

He knew she was talking about Lewis, not Maurice. 'I'm more than all right. How are you?'

'Is that a how *are* you or a how are you?' She tried to smile but suddenly started to cry. She put her arms around him and hugged him close to her. 'I'm so sorry, Joseph. We're both so sorry. For not telling you the truth about what happened. For not telling you about Alexander.'

He was fighting tears himself. 'I know that. I know that now. It's okay. Really. It's okay.' And it was, he realised as he stood there, comforting her. It wasn't perfect. He wished it could all have been different. All of it. But this was where they were now, and he knew they would be okay.

They talked more about his visit to Lewis as Kate drove him to his office. 'He said you had a friend with you.'

Joseph gave a half-smile. 'Yes, I did.'

Kate waited for him to say something more. When he didn't she looked over at him quickly. 'Lewis said she was lovely.'

'She is.'

'She's Irish, I believe.'

'That's right.'

Kate laughed. 'You're not going to tell me anything else, are you?'

'No, not just yet. So what about you? Are you still planning your trip to Australia?'

She nodded.

'It's a beautiful place. You'll like it there, I think.'

'Yes, I think I will.'

Rosemary was waiting in the Wheeler Design offices for him. So was the auditor, and two detectives. Joseph wondered for a moment if this was some sort of jetlag hallucination. He blinked. No, it was real.

He accepted the big cup of coffee Rosemary was holding out. 'So tell me, is it as bad as you thought?'

The auditor answered him honestly. 'It's worse.'

Five hours later he knew most of the facts. It had been going on for nearly two years. Maurice had indeed used every trick in the book – not just the false invoices and separate bank accounts, but a complex web of shelf companies and off-shore accounts as well.

Rosemary tried to console him. 'It's not your fault, Joseph. Maurice was very clever. And he had sole responsibility for the finances as well. It was easy for him.'

Joseph knew it was his fault. He was the one who had given Maurice that responsibility. He was the one who had only half listened during Maurice's financial reports. 'Maurice, that's what I hire you for.' His words kept coming back to haunt him.

No wonder Maurice had always been so cheerful. He had been happily salting away thousands of pounds each month. Building a nice nest egg for himself, and slowly ruining Wheeler Design at the same time.

The auditor was blunt. 'All the royalty agreements he set up for you when your designs were sold to manufacturers are still intact. He didn't touch those for some reason. They could cover your overheads – the rent here, your operating costs, the wages for your designers, Rosemary's wages.' He nodded in Rosemary's direction. 'So, plainly speaking, Mr Wheeler, you are still a wealthy man. Not in the poorhouse yet. But it's the capital that's gone. Your savings, if you like.'

'The property portfolios? The shares?'

'Did you ever notice they're not actually in your name?'

'Maurice said it made more sense tax-wise to put them under other company names . . .' He stopped there. Yes, of course that would have made more sense to Maurice.

'You may get them back. We may be able to track him down. It just depends how far he's got and how much unravelling of all your accounts we need to do when we do find him. And not just yours. You're not the only client he's stolen from, of course.'

'So what are my options?'

'As I said, you still have those royalty cheques coming in. It's really your decision what you do. You could just close the company down, of course, that would be the most drastic measure. But I think you could trade through it. It's a matter of checking your overheads – the rent of these offices, for example. You may find it makes more sense to move. You have enough in the short term to cover any money outstanding to creditors, suppliers, and the like. And your employees' salaries and entitlements. I understand from Rosemary that the other designers are all on contract, is that right?'

Joseph nodded. 'We're nearly at the end of a project. Two or three more weeks.'

'That's lucky. And I also understand from Rosemary that you've been offered a consultancy in Canada. That may be another stroke of luck, in fact. You've accepted it, no doubt?'

'No, I haven't.'

The auditor went back to his notes. 'Well, when you do, you may find that the best option, payment-wise, just to get you through the initial period, might be to –'

Joseph interrupted. 'No, I won't be accepting the Canadian offer.'

'You won't?'

'No.'

'Oh. I see. You're going to do something else instead?'

Joseph realised right then that he was. And he knew exactly what it was.

'Yes, I am.'

It was nearly eleven o'clock by the time Joseph got home. He was desperate for sleep. The figures on the paperwork the auditor had been showing him had begun to swim in front of his eyes. He couldn't take in any more, between the jetlag and the shock of it all still.

He wanted to sleep. But he wanted to make a phone call first.

In Melbourne Eva put down the phone and came out onto the balcony. Lainey looked up from her deckchair. 'So? Any news?'

'His grandmother is much better, so that's a relief,' Eva said as she sat down on the wooden bench. 'But it sounds like he's walked into some crisis at work that's worrying him just as much. They've discovered the accountant was fiddling the books for the past two years, maybe more. Creaming off all the profits. And now he's done a runner, with hundreds of thousands of pounds.'

Lainey frowned. 'He'd been doing this for years and Joe's boss didn't notice?'

'No. He didn't suspect a thing, Joe said.'

'What sort of eejit is this boss?'

'He didn't really mention him, but he sounded very tired. He'd been in there for hours going through the paperwork.'

'With his grandmother lying sick in hospital?'

'His grandmother is fine, Lainey. This problem with his boss seems to be what's really worrying him.'

'Yes, I've heard those Colombian drug lords are a worry to work for.'

'Would you give that drug stuff a rest? Please?'

Lainey winked over at her. 'Only joking, really.' Was she though? Lainey wondered. Perhaps her suspicions had all been unfounded. Maybe Joe *was* everything he seemed. Just a nice ordinary designer having a nice ordinary holiday in Australia until his nice ordinary grandmother had fallen ill. Forcing him to leave the penthouse suite of one of Melbourne's most exclusive beachside hotels to rush back to London. Where his grandmother miraculously improves, just as hundreds of thousands of pounds go missing from Joe's workplace . . .

Stop it, Lainey, she thought. But she couldn't help herself. She just didn't take anyone at face value. That's why she was so good at her job. People didn't get away with anything when she was around.

But she supposed a real drug smuggler wouldn't have rung Eva from London the way Joe had done. A real drug smuggler would have slipped away never to be heard from again, surely? And a drug smuggler wouldn't have had this effect on Eva, would he? Since that day in the hotel room she had been practically glowing with happiness. She hadn't given many details, but whatever had happened had been lovely, Lainey could tell. This was certainly no holiday fling.

A shame Eva hadn't managed to tell him the whole truth yet, Lainey thought. But she'd made a start on it at least, by the sound of things. And it seemed Joe hadn't minded that she hadn't sung with Enya or done a sculpture for Bono. That was good. She wondered what he would think when he learned Eva's name wasn't Niamh, though. And that she didn't live in Galway. And that she worked in a delicatessen . . .

Lainey decided to keep her thoughts to herself and her mouth tightly shut. She didn't want to jeopardise her friendship with Eva, after all. Let some man come between them again.

She stood up. 'Come on, Evie, let's go for a drive somewhere. You've only got a few days left here, no point wasting them hanging around here. Are there any more cafes you want to visit?'

'No, that's it for me and work. It's holiday time now.' Her notebook was filled with sketches of how Ambrosia might look. Suggested menus. Even the lettering for the sign. All she needed to get started. 'What I'd really like to do is take you out to lunch somewhere. Somewhere very smart. Your choice. The best place in town, if you like.'

Lainey smiled. 'What a brilliant idea. I'd love that. Have you noticed what you're doing, by the way?'

'What do you mean?'

'Look down.'

Eva did. Rex was lying in the sun beside her, and she was patting his little head. She shrieked. Rex leapt in fright.

Lainey roared laughing. 'We've a way to go yet, I think.'

CHAPTER THIRTY-SEVEN

THREE DAYS later Eva and Lainey were standing in the departure area of Melbourne Airport. Eva hugged her. 'Thanks, Lainey. For everything. For more than you know.'

'You'll come back again, won't you?'

Eva nodded. She would, too. 'And you'll come back to Ireland soon, won't you?'

'We'll see. If the weather improves, maybe. And you'll say hello to Joe for me, won't you? When you see him.'

'I will.' Eva had spoken to him that morning, just before she and Lainey left for the airport.

'Will you go to London to see him or will he come to Ireland to see you?'

'I don't know. It'll depend what happens with Wheeler Design.'

'Wheeler Design?'

'The company he works for.'

Lainey hadn't heard the name of the company before. 'Wheeler? That's his surname too, isn't it? Is it a family business?'

Eva shook her head. 'In a way, he said. Perhaps it's an uncle or something.'

Lainey tucked the name away in the back of her mind. She should have thought to ask Eva the name of his company before now. They could have looked it up on the Internet perhaps. Never mind. Eva would find it all out soon enough in any case.

'I don't want to say goodbye to you, Evie. But you'd better go. It's boarding.'

Eva's eyes filled with tears. 'Goodbye, Lainey. And thanks a million.'

'Don't you start crying or that'll be me gone, as well. Anyway, I should thank you. For coming all this way. And for the beautiful present. I'll think of you as I lie there covered in mud.'

Eva laughed. She'd given Lainey a thank-you gift of a full day in one of Melbourne's beauty spas – luxury massages and facials from dawn to dusk. 'And thank *you* for letting me look after Rex. For that shock treatment of my cat phobia.'

'Oh, my pleasure. I know exactly what you got up to with him, by the way. I had security cameras on you the whole time. Now go, will you? Before I start bawling and have to go into work with mascara everywhere, not good for my image at all. Ring me, won't you? Email me. Write to me. About everything, okay? Especially Joe.'

'As long as you don't start telling me what to do.'

Lainey looked outraged. 'Me? Tell anyone what to do? Of course not.'

'And you'll tell Greg I'm sorry about the Niamh business, won't you?'

'Oh, I will indeed.'

Two hours later, Lainey was in her office at work with a big pot of coffee beside her. She stretched her legs out under the desk and wriggled her feet. Poor Eva, she thought, twenty-two hours stuck in a plane. The sooner someone invented instantaneous travel, the better. You could already send emails around the world in an instant. Surely humans were the next step?

She looked down at her in-tray, still piled high with paperwork that had come in while she was in Brisbane. She had masses of work to catch up on. Phone calls to make, files to read, events to plan . . .

But all of that would just have to wait. She wanted to do a bit of searching on the Internet first. A bit of searching about a company called Wheeler Design. She pressed several keys and waited as her computer screen blinked into life. Moments later she was connected to the web.

She'd start with the most obvious details, she

decided, and then whittle it down from there. There could be lots of companies with the words Wheeler and Design in their titles, not just in London but all over the world. She'd have to use all her Internet searching skills.

She keyed several words into the search subject area and pressed enter. There it was, just like that, seconds later. The Wheeler Design website address.

She clicked on it and was connected to the site in seconds. She was surprised at the speed. It usually took a few minutes to log on to a website. Lainey took a sip of coffee, running her eye over the home page. She put down her cup. Leaned forward. There it all was. In black and white. And colour. And moving pictures. Background information on the company. Client testimonials. Newspaper and magazine articles. And a very detailed biography and close-up photograph of its managing director.

Joseph Wheeler. Also known as Joe.

Lainey clicked the mouse button and enlarged the photograph. Yes. It was definitely him.

'Well, well, well,' she said under her breath. 'Well, well, bloody well.' He certainly wasn't a drug smuggler, she'd determined that at least. But look what he was instead. A very successful businessman. An award-winning designer. A company director. Who for some unknown reason had been masquerading as an impoverished backpacker in Australia.

Lainey couldn't help it. She started to laugh out

loud, shaking her head slowly from side to side, speaking under her breath. 'She's not what he thinks she is. And he's not what she thinks he is.'

She threw back her head and laughed again. 'They're *made* for each other!'

As Eva walked the long corridor at Heathrow to her Dublin connecting flight, she made some important decisions. She'd done plenty of thinking during the long economy-class flight home. She'd been almost glad she hadn't been upgraded again. It was time she started living her real life, after all.

She was going to tell her parents and Ambrose the real reason she hadn't gone back to art school four years ago. Tell them how sorry she was that she hadn't told them the whole story before now. And tell them how determined she was to make a success of the delicatessen and cafe. She was going to ring Jillian, the manager of the cover band she used to sing with, to see if maybe it wasn't too late to start singing again, even just as a fill-in, now and again. She'd make time for it somehow.

Her parents were going to collect her from the airport. They'd said they were really looking forward to hearing all about her trip. They'd be hearing more than they expected, she thought. Then, after they left, she was going to ring Joe. And if things were still all right with his grandmother and he sounded like he could take some more bad news, she was going to tell him the truth as well.

'You knew? All this time?'

Her mother nodded. Eva looked at her father, sitting opposite her in her living room in Stoneybatter. 'You knew too?'

He nodded as well.

'Since when?'

'Since about a month after you left art school.'

'How did you find out?'

'Do you remember the woman who took you for a coffee?' her mother asked. 'At that gallery? I went to school with her. When you told her your name and said you were from Dunshaughlin, it rang some bells. But it wasn't until after you'd gone that she wondered if you and I were connected.'

Eva shut her eyes. Could you do anything in Ireland without someone noticing? Apparently not.

'She rang here to see if she'd been right and to ask after you. I guess she thought we'd know all about it, about you deciding to leave art school and what the gallery owners had said to you. But you hadn't mentioned it. We waited to see if you would, and then Sheila died and everything turned upside down for a while.'

Her father took up the story. 'We knew for sure that you weren't going to go back to art school when you went full-time at the shop. And we thought it was such a shame that you were going to miss out on an exhibition, after all those years of study. So we decided to give you one. At home in Dunshaughlin. We still thought your work was wonderful, even if it wasn't exactly what the galleries wanted.'

'That's why you had that party?'

They nodded. Eva thought about it again. All the neighbours in the house. Her paintings hung on the walls. The speeches her father and Ambrose had made. Her feeling so guilty, carrying her secret. And all the time her parents had known.

'Why didn't you tell me you knew?' She was nearly whispering.

'Why didn't you tell us you'd decided to leave the art school?'

'I didn't want you to be disappointed in me.'

Eva's mother smiled across at her. 'Eva, we've never been disappointed in you. We love you, whether you work in a shop or in a gallery. Whatever you do.'

Eva was glad of the jetlag. She could blame it for all the confused thoughts tearing around inside her head. She looked at her mother and father. She knew her eyes were filling with tears. She couldn't help it. A lovely feeling of relief went through her. She felt four years of tension slowly lift away from her shoulders. 'I've been an eejit, haven't I?'

They nodded.

An hour later, Eva hung up the phone from talking to Joe and caught sight of her reflection in the window. She wasn't just an ordinary eejit, she realised. She was the Queen of the Eejits.

She'd spoken to him for more than half an hour. It had been so good to hear his voice, to hear that his grandmother was very well and that his boss was getting on top of the problems at work. But had she told him the truth about herself, as she'd vowed she would? No. And just to make matters worse, she had invited him to come and visit her as soon as he could. In Galway.

Shame you don't live there, isn't it? Don't suppose you could hire a caravan from somewhere? Hire some sculptures? Hire some people to call you Niamh?

She didn't need that voice to tell her what to do any more. She knew it all herself. She had to ring him back. Tell him again that she would love him to come to Ireland, but this time she'd ask him to fly to Dublin instead of Galway. She'd explain why when she saw him.

She would meet him at the airport. Bring him home here to Stoneybatter. And tell him the truth. Not over the phone – where she couldn't see his face, couldn't properly judge his reaction – but face to face. And it would feel wonderful. And he wouldn't mind at all. She hoped.

She had just reached for the phone when it rang loudly. She nearly leapt out of her skin. 'Hello.'

'Evie, it's me. Lainey.'

She sat down. 'Lainey! I'm hardly in the door here –'

Lainey wasn't in the mood for traveller's chitchat. She'd been counting down the hours until she knew Eva would be back home in Dublin. She interrupted. 'Have you got a pen and paper?'

'Yes,' Eva answered, a little put out.

'I want you to write down this website address. And I want you to go and look at it. Right now. Okay?'

'Okay.' Eva was very puzzled.

Five minutes later, sitting in front of her computer, she wasn't puzzled any more. She was bewildered. Shocked. Surprised. Joe wasn't just Joe, not according to this. He was Joseph Wheeler, Managing Director of Wheeler Design.

And Joseph Wheeler was no ordinary designer. He was a very clever, very successful designer, who owned his own very successful company. It was all there. His biography. Photographs. She read everything, studied every picture.

She turned away from the computer and took a deep breath. Oh my God. She felt angry and stupid for being taken in. All this time she'd thought he was just an ordinary person on a backpacking trip around Australia. Dozens of conversations flashed into her mind. Her insisting he take the job at Four Quarters. Asking him about his work. All the things she had said about money being a corrupting influence. And all the time he'd been having her on. Pretending to be someone else.

Eva stopped there. All the time he'd been doing to her exactly what she had been doing to him. And if she was feeling this angry and hoodwinked and stupid, then how was he going to feel when he heard the truth about her? They had lied to each other, that definitely changed things. But there was one big difference. Joe had made himself smaller, made himself less than he was. And she had tried to make herself bigger.

She paced the room. Which was worse? Did knowing all this about Joe make it easier to tell him the truth about her? Or did it make it harder? She didn't know yet. But she did know two things right now. She was going to make herself a cup of very strong coffee. Then she was going to ring him.

Chapter thirty-eight

JOSEPH WAS just leaving his London flat when the phone rang. 'Kate, good timing, you just caught me. I'm on my way into work.'

'On the weekend? Are things still that bad?'

'I know the extent of it all now, at least.' Maurice had been a very busy man, they'd discovered. He'd be up for all sorts of charges if they ever managed to find him.

'I wanted to be sure you're eating all right, so I've cooked some meals for you. Can I drop them over?'

He laughed. 'I'm fine. You didn't have to do that. There's a Tesco's down the road.'

'I wanted to do it. I know I can't help you with your company business but I can do this.'

'But it's a long trip in the car for you.'

'I like driving.'

He was touched. 'If you're sure?'

'I am. And you left the spare key for your apartment

here, didn't you? I'll bring it so you won't have to wait around for me.'

'That's good. I don't know how long I'll be at work, but I'll ring and leave a message for you. We can go and have a coffee or something later, perhaps?'

'I'd like that very much.'

Joseph locked his front door, walked down the stairs and out into the street. He was touched by Kate's gesture. She seemed different since he'd come back from Australia, he thought. Two nights before they had met for a meal. She had needed to talk, to tell him everything. He'd hardly asked her a question, just sat quietly and listened as she told him all she could about that time. He now had a very clear picture of what Allie had been like. And an even clearer understanding of how difficult his death had been for Kate and Lewis. It seemed a lot of things were becoming clearer to him these days.

A gust of icy wind hit him square in the face. The memory of Australia's sunshine was fading fast. He walked the block to where his car was parked.

As he pulled out from the kerb, back in his flat the phone started ringing again. The answering machine clicked into action and the tape started recording.

'Joe, this is Niamh. I must have just missed you. I'll call back again later.'

Eva hung up the phone. Damn, damn, damn. It wasn't supposed to work like this. There she was, in full confessional mode and with a million questions to ask him, and he was nowhere to be found.

She roamed around the house for a while. Maybe he'd gone into work. Or to the shops. Or to visit his grandmother. She didn't know what Joe did on a weekend in London. Yet. But she wanted to. She wanted to know everything about him. And she wanted him to know everything about her.

She had his mobile number, but she didn't want to have a conversation like this with him while he was walking along the street or driving in his car. She went over to her computer and looked at the Wheeler Design website again. She just couldn't understand it. He was so successful. He had no reason to pretend, did he? She had a sudden recollection of some of the things she had said to him that night at the taxi rank. She'd been up on her artistic high-horse, pretending to be Niamh the pure artist, talking about art versus commerce, how money corrupted. What must he have thought?

All these questions – she had to get some answers. She had to start somewhere. Tell him the truth about herself. And then? She didn't know what would happen then.

Perhaps he was at work. He was the managing director, after all. He was the boss, she realised now. The financial problems were his financial problems.

And he had the worry of his grandmother too – or did he? She wondered then whether the story about the grandmother was true. Certainly she seemed to have made a miraculous recovery.

She decided to try his work number. Just in case he was there. Steeling herself to hear his voice, she dialled the number for Wheeler Design.

In his office Joseph noticed a light flashing on the telephone console.

Would he pick it up? No, who'd be ringing the office on a weekend? Either a crank caller or a journalist, and he didn't want to talk to either of them.

He let it go through to the answering machine.

Eva shut her eyes as the Wheeler Design answering message started to play. Should she leave a message on this machine? No, she decided, just as the beep sounded. Not at his work. She replaced the receiver.

She had to do something. Could she leave a message on his home answering machine? Tell him the whole story about herself? At least get the truth ball rolling? She wished she wasn't feeling so jetlagged. She wasn't sure if she was actually thinking sensibly. Then she remembered what else she'd done when she hadn't been thinking sensibly.

She'd taken a spur-of-the-moment train trip.

Taken a temporary job at a Melbourne cafe. None of those things had been particularly sensible. But she wouldn't have changed a thing.

She decided to do it. She'd say everything into his answering machine at home. He could listen to it as many times as he needed to. And then he could decide what he wanted to do next.

She sat down and dialled his home number again and the machine clicked into action. His message played, the tone sounded. She was on.

'Joe. It's me. Niamh again. I'm sorry, but I think I'm about to use up all your tape. I've got a fair bit to say. And I need to say it to you before you come to Ireland. Before we see each other again.'

She crossed her fingers. 'Joe, I've just seen the Wheeler Design website. I know who you are. I know all about your company. Everything. You're the boss, aren't you? And that's why you had to come back so quickly? I don't know why you didn't want to tell the truth about it. I know you must have had your reasons. And I can hardly complain, Joe, because you haven't heard the truth about me, either. But I think it's time you did.

'My name's not Niamh Kennedy, it's Eva Kennedy. I don't live in Galway, I live in Dublin. You already know that I didn't sing with Enya or do a sculpture for U2. I did go to art school but I failed. I work in a delicatessen, Joe. I'm a shop assistant. I can't really tell you how the whole Niamh-the-sculptor business started. Just as a bit of a joke really between Lainey and me. And then I let it get out of control, and I didn't know how to stop it.

'I'm sorry to be so cowardly. To just leave the real story on your machine like this. I've been trying to tell you the truth since we met but I was worried it would change things between us. And I didn't want that to happen.'

She paused. She felt like she was standing on the edge of a cliff. Then she jumped. 'Joe, I've fallen in love with you. That time I spent with you in Australia was the best time I've ever had in my life. That's really blurting it out, isn't it? And I don't know where this leaves us now. What you will think. But I hope it's nothing terrible.' She paused again. 'I do have phone numbers. In Dublin. It's up to you if you want to ring me, after all I've just told you.' She slowly gave her numbers, at home and at the shop. 'Joe, I won't call you again but I hope you'll ring me. Because –' The tape ran out then.

Eva hung up. She felt sick and relieved all at once.
Well done, the voice said.

Kate Wheeler drove around the block again. How on earth did Joseph put up with this? She couldn't find a parking space *anywhere* near his flat.

Ten minutes later she finally found one, a block away. It took her three attempts to get into it, then five minutes to lock up her car safely. She was a bit nervous in other parts of London, felt much safer on her own patch. She took the containers of food from the boot of the car. There were enough meals to last Joseph a couple of weeks at least.

His flat was surprisingly tidy, she thought as she let herself in. Mind you, there didn't seem to be a lot to get messy. For someone so successful, Joseph didn't go for the trappings very much. He took after Lewis in that respect. Lewis had never been one for status symbols either.

She noticed that the answering machine was flashing. Joseph, ringing to let her know how he was going, as he'd promised. She pressed the play button. A female Irish voice filled the room. 'Joe, this is Niamh. I must have just missed you. I'll call back again later.'

Then moments later, a second message. 'Joe. It's me. Niamh again. I'm sorry, but I think I'm about to use up all your tape. I've got a fair bit to say. And I need to say it to you before you come to Ireland . . .'

Kate listened. Oh God, it was the Irish woman. The one he had met in Australia. And this sounded private. Very private. She shouldn't be hearing this, it was definitely for no-one's ears but Joseph.

She picked up the answering machine, quickly turning it around, trying to find the stop button. She touched it. The voice stopped. Good. Then she noticed the tape was still going round. She'd obviously just hit the volume control. She touched the button again and the voice echoed around the room.

'. . . you. That time I spent with you in Australia was the best time I've ever had in my life. That's really blurting it out, isn't it? And I don't know where this leaves us now. What you will think. But I hope it's nothing terrible. I do have phone numbers. In Dublin. It's up to you if you want to ring me, after all I've just told you.' The Irishwoman slowly called out two sets of numbers. 'Joe, I won't call you again but I hope you'll ring me. Because –'

The voice stopped. Kate watched through the window on the machine as the tape clicked, stopped, then started rewinding again. What was it going to do now? She'd just picked it up again when the phone started to ring, startling her. She dropped the machine with a clatter and watched, horrified, as it kicked into action.

The tape started rolling again. The caller's voice filled the room. It was a London accent, a young woman speaking clearly and slowly. 'Good afternoon, Mr Wheeler. This is Susie from Shoreditch Health and Fitness ringing on Sunday afternoon. I was actually hoping to catch you at home. This is just a courtesy call, hoping that everything's fine with you. Our records show that you joined nearly two months ago but you haven't actually been to the gym yet. Now, there's no need to be embarrassed about it.

It happens a lot more than you might think, for all sorts of reasons, but the thing to remember is that we are here to help. Perhaps you'd like to discuss your membership with one of our trained fitness instructors? We could help you work out the best way to achieve your fitness goals. Please don't hesitate to call me and we will do our utmost to help you. Because, as our slogan says, a fitter person is a happier person. Hope to hear from you soon. Bye now.'

Kate thought the woman was never going to stop talking. She wanted to shut her up but she didn't know how to stop the tape running. As she stood there watching, the cassette clicked and started to rewind. It finally stopped. Unconsciously holding her breath, she pressed the play button again, fingers crossed that the Irishwoman's voice would come back on.

It didn't. The only sound was the chirpy London accent of the gym receptionist. 'Good afternoon, Mr Wheeler. This is Susie from Shoreditch Health and Fitness . . . Oh *no*, Kate thought. The new message had obviously wiped out the other one. The important private message with the phone numbers. Which she couldn't remember if her life depended on it.

She knew that Joseph would hate the idea she had heard even a bit of that message. He'd always been so private. He hadn't even told her he'd split up with Tessa until three months afterwards. What did she do now?

She could just say nothing and hope the Irishwoman rang back again soon. But there had been enough hidden secrets between her and Joseph over the years. They had a clean slate now, she wasn't going to start filling it again. She picked up the phone and rang Joseph's mobile number.

Chapter thirty-nine

The answering machine was flashing when Eva arrived home after work the next day. Her heart lifted. Joe. At last.

She'd been a bag of nerves since she'd left the message the day before, waiting for her home phone to ring. She hadn't even gone around the corner to the shop. She'd just sat within easy reach of the phone, pretending she was doing something other than waiting for it to ring.

But it hadn't. He must be thinking about it still, she'd decided. Or perhaps he'd been caught up at work or somewhere, and had decided it was too late to call her when he got in. In which case he was bound to call early in the morning. Before she went to work.

But he hadn't. Of course he wouldn't have, she'd reasoned. He couldn't be sure what time she'd leave for work, so he would have decided it was best not to ring in case he got her just as she was going out of the door, in a hurry. That wouldn't be the right time for the sort of conversation they would need to have.

So he was probably going to ring her at work. That wouldn't be ideal but it would be fine, she'd decided. She would be able to take the call in the storeroom, the most private place in the shop. She'd just have to hope the builders weren't using their drills or electric saws when he rang. Or their hammers. The noise was a little overpowering.

But the phone hadn't rung for her at work. The only calls had been from suppliers, wanting to find out from Ambrose when the shop would be re-opening and whether it was true they were starting a cafe at the back.

But here it was at last, she thought now. The message from him. She pressed the replay button. It wasn't Joe. It was Jillian, the band manager. 'Eva, it was fantastic to hear from you. I was thinking of you just the other day when I was walking past your uncle's shop. What are you up to in there? It looks very exciting. I'd love to talk to you about you doing some singing. I'm actually managing a couple of bands these days, playing for the tourists in a few pubs around town. And there's always a spot for someone with a voice like yours. Try me again, will you? We've got a few gigs coming up in the next few weeks. Maybe it could start sooner than you think?'

It was good news. Exciting news. But Eva still felt terrible, because Joe still hadn't rung.

Lainey was just coming out of her apartment. It was barely six a.m. and she was hardly awake.

She was about to shut the door when she noticed the lace on one of her running shoes was undone. As she crouched down to tie it, Rex slipped out through the open door and made a dash for the stairs.

'Rex! No, Rex! You're not allowed down there.' She stood up quickly and ran down the stairs just in time to see a little pointy tail flick around the corner of the landing.

'Rex! Come here!' She jumped the final two stairs to save time. As she landed she heard a loud crack and felt a searing pain. Her leg gave way beneath her. 'Owww!' she screamed. The noise stopped Rex in his tracks ten stairs down.

Doubled up, she clutched at her ankle, rocking and muttering to herself. 'Ow-ow-ow-ow-ow.'

Someone came up the stairs below her. It was Adam, her downstairs neighbour. He picked up Rex as he came past. 'Lainey? My God, what's happened? Are you all right?'

Her face was tight with pain. 'I think I've broken my ankle.'

Joseph put down the phone and crossed out another number on the long list in front of him. There had to be a better way to find her. Over the past three days he'd rung hundreds of Kennedys in Ireland. He'd started with Galway, then moved out to all the counties surrounding Galway. He'd spoken to old women, young men, teenagers, children. But none of them had heard of a sculptor and singer called Niamh who had just got back from a holiday in Australia.

If only Kate had been able to remember the numbers Niamh had left. But she had been so embarrassed about hearing any of Niamh's message, it was hardly surprising the two numbers hadn't stayed in her mind. 'I'm so sorry, Joseph, I only heard snatches of it. I remember she said that the time she spent with you in Australia was the best time in her life. And I think she said it was up to you to ring her if you wanted to talk to her again.'

He very much wanted to talk to her again, but he couldn't find her. She must have an unlisted number, there was no other explanation. But Kate had said she'd left two numbers. So what could the second number have been?

He ran his hand through his hair. Then it came to him. Of course. How could he be so stupid? It must have been Lainey's number in Melbourne. Perhaps she'd left a message with Lainey for him, which was why she'd left that number on his answering machine. But she hadn't needed to. Because he already had it.

He picked up the phone again and dialled Lainey's number.

At that moment, Eva was on the phone to Lainey in Melbourne.

'Crutches for a fortnight? At least? Oh Lainey, that's terrible. You poor thing. How on earth are you managing the stairs to your apartment?'

'I'm not. I tried once and nearly fell head over heels again. I've moved back home with Mum and Dad. Me and little Rex. Just until the swelling has gone down a bit and it isn't complete agony every time I move. My brothers are carrying me everywhere, doing my every bidding, it's brilliant. And Rex loves it, all this company and attention.'

'So are you picking up messages from home or should I ring you at your parents' number?'

'At my parents'. Or this mobile number. I turned the answering machine at home off. There was no point people leaving messages thinking I'd get back to them when it could be days before I even heard them. Besides, everyone who knows me has my mobile number.' Then Lainey's tone of voice changed. 'So, Evie, any word yet?'

Eva's tone changed too. 'No. Not yet.'

'It *has* only been a few days.'

Only? They'd been the longest few days of her life.

Lainey went on, 'He might have been called away for work. Or maybe his grandmother had a relapse. Or maybe –'

'He heard my message and decided he didn't want anything else to do with me.'

'Stop that. You told me what you said on your message and it was great. It was perfect. I'm sure he'll ring you. Maybe he's just thinking it all through. He's not free of blame either, you know. Maybe he's really embarrassed that you caught him out. You can't possibly know. But I'm sure he'll ring, I saw the way he looked at you.'

Eva was a little consoled. 'Thanks, Lainey.'

'No worries. Just be patient, okay?'

In London the next day, Rosemary picked up the final page from the printer. Number after number was listed on the pile of pages.

She knocked on the door of Joseph's office. 'Excuse me, here are those numbers you're looking for – every art gallery in Ireland, is that right?'

'That's right, Rosemary.' He took the pages. 'Thank you very much for doing that, I really appreciate it.'

'You're welcome,' she said. She waited, half hoping for an explanation, but Joseph had turned back to his computer screen.

Puzzled, she walked back to her own desk. She'd never known him to be interested in art or sculpture before. And he'd certainly never mentioned Ireland. It was all very odd.

In the delicatessen that afternoon, Eva stood back as Meg dragged the sample table and chair across the wooden floor. She and Ambrose winced as the metal tips of the chair legs screeched.

'I'm sure we could fit in another table, Evie. Look, if we squashed this one up against the wall here. And moved these chairs in tight here. Plenty of room.'

'No, I don't think so. There'd hardly be room to move. And no-one wants to sit tight up against some-one else, feeling their every word is being overheard. Let's stick to seven tables and that's it. Now, how are your menu ideas coming along?'

Meg beamed at her. 'Well, I'm definitely sure about soup. Several different varieties every day, I thought, served with crusty white bread. And what about big thick sandwiches with plenty of fillings. And some hot dishes, of course. Like Thai chicken curries or vegetarian lasagnes. Gourmet pizzas, per-haps, with smoked salmon, fetta cheese and spinach leaves. And what about salads, with lots of crispy vegetables and fresh herbs? And shall we have some really good desserts as well? Like rich chocolate mudcakes? Or caramelised apple tarts? I love making cherry almond biscuits. And pancakes are quick and delicious – What? What did I say?'

Meg stopped and looked back and forth between Eva and Ambrose, who were both openly laughing. Eva reached over and tousled her hair. 'What you said was brilliant, Meg. Just brilliant.'

That morning Eva had told Ambrose the whole story. Explained to him the real reason she'd left art school four years previously. She'd waited anxiously for his reaction.

'Do you really think it matters, Evie? Because it doesn't change a thing as far as I'm concerned.'

She'd looked at him. Then she'd smiled in relief. 'You're right, Ambrose, I don't think it does matter any more.'

The following day, Joseph put the folder of business papers to one side and turned his attention back to another pile of paper on his desk. He picked up the phone and dialled a number in Ireland.

'Oh, good afternoon,' he said politely when a young woman answered, 'I wonder if you can help me. Do you happen to represent a sculptor by the name of Niamh Kennedy? No? Are you sure? Do you happen to know anyone who does? No? Well, thank you anyway.'

He drew a line through that name, then dialled the next number on the list.

Two nights later, Eva knocked on the door of the rehearsal room at the back of a big house in Mountjoy Square.

Jillian answered. She beamed at Eva. 'The

prodigal daughter returns. Welcome back, Eva. Come in.'

Eva followed her into the room. The floor was crowded with instrument cases, packing crates doubling as stools, boxes of sheet music and a few small speakers. Six people smiled at her. She smiled nervously back.

'Okay,' Jillian said in a businesslike tone when the introductions were over, 'let's get cracking. Eva, you might as well throw yourself right into it. We're really playing for the tourists these days, I should warn you. Cover versions of everything from The Corrs and The Pogues to Van Morrison to U2. Even Boyzone at a pinch. Can you cope?'

She nodded. 'Can I just check one thing? You don't do Enya covers, do you?'

'No. Why, would you like to?'

Eva shook her head. 'No. No, I wouldn't.'

'Okay, let's go. "Dirty Old Town", on the count of three. One, two, three . . .'

Joseph put down the phone yet again, mystified. Who was she, the Scarlet Pimpernel? She seemed to have disappeared without trace.

In between meetings with the auditor and hours of paperwork, he had been ringing the galleries on the list Rosemary had given him. He'd had no luck there either. He'd discovered there was a well-known potter in Ireland called Shauna Kennedy. And an up-and-coming tapestry artist called Niamh Brogan. But no-one had heard of a Galway-based sculptor called Niamh Kennedy, even when he described the work she did, based around ocean and beach images. One of the owners had thought it sounded very interesting. She'd actually asked Joseph to get this Niamh to phone her, to perhaps come in and show some of her work.

Niamh's friend Lainey had disappeared as well. He'd tried her number at all different hours, morning in Australia, night-time in Australia, lunch-time in Australia. But there was never any answer, not even the answering machine. He didn't understand it at all. It was as if they had both just disappeared off the face of the earth.

He tried Lainey's number again now, just in case she was there.

Lying on the couch in her parents' living room, Lainey called out to her brother in the kitchen. 'Hugh, can you make that two slices of cake, please? I'm a bit peckish tonight. It must be part of the recovery process.'

'Recovery process? Lady Muck-itis, more like it,' Hugh said, coming into the room carrying a tray of coffee and cake.

Meanwhile, in her flat across Melbourne, the phone started to ring again.

Eva lay in bed, trying to get to sleep. It was a little difficult with all the noise Meg was making packing downstairs.

She couldn't begrudge her. It was all very exciting, and very generous of Uncle Ambrose to offer the first-floor flat to her, rent-free, while she worked as the chef at Ambrosia.

'You might want to wait until the cafe is up and running before you move in,' Eva had suggested. 'You're welcome to stay with me until then.'

But Meg was too excited to wait. 'It's been great with you, Evie, but I'm going to move in as soon as I can. Furniture or no furniture. My own flat, this is incredible!'

Eva turned over in bed, wincing as she heard something go crashing downstairs. Holy God, was Meg ripping the cupboards off the walls and taking them with her?

The house finally fell quiet but Eva still lay there, looking up through the skylight at the night sky. She was too anxious to sleep. Not just about the cafe. Slowly but surely, it was coming along, but there was still such a lot to get done. More than she'd expected. Tables and chairs to order. Kitchen equipment to buy, install and test. Final menus to decide on. Extra staff to interview. And the delicatessen to keep running in the meantime. Oh yes, she had every right to be a bit anxious about the cafe, but that was nothing compared to how she was feeling about Joe. It had been ten days now since she'd left the message on his machine.

And it was starting to seem that he was never going to ring her back. He'd found out she'd lied to him and now he didn't want to know her. It was as simple as that.

Joseph put down the last pile of paperwork, then stood up and walked to the window. The Hoxton bars and restaurants below were filled with people as usual, designers, artists, writers, computer programmers, all making deals, discussing plans.

He'd been part of it all once, when he'd started his own company. It had taken ten years to set it up. Ten years of long hours, late nights, risks, hard work, to get it to where it was today. He looked back at his desk. And it had just taken him less than half an hour and several signatures to officially close it all down.

He'd expected to feel something. Regret. Disappointment. But he hadn't felt anything like that. Just relief. And optimism. He hadn't felt that for a long time.

It had been surprisingly simple. A friend with a graphic design business two offices down had already offered Rosemary work. But Rosemary wasn't even sure if she wanted it. She'd started to think seriously about retirement, she'd told Joseph.

Or a long holiday, at least. He'd make sure she received all her entitlements, either way.

The designers were just days away from completing their projects. They all had plenty of other work lined up, too. A website design company was happy to take over the lease on this building. He'd contacted all his other clients and explained that he was closing Wheeler Design down but would still finish the designs he was contracted to do. He just wouldn't be working from London.

He went back to his desk and picked up the brochure again. He'd spoken to a few people about it and they'd all agreed this was one of the best art schools in Europe.

He turned to the section on jewellery design and started reading it again. It sounded good, better than good. He pictured the designs in his head – they were coming thick and fast these days, despite everything going on around him. And then he tried to picture Niamh again. In Galway somewhere. On a coast, maybe. Or the beach, perhaps. The wind in her hair. Working on her sculptures . . .

She had to be there somewhere, he knew that. He was determined to find her.

Eva sat at her dining table, surrounded by architects' drawings and builders' quotes, nearly pulling her hair out in frustration. How could one carpenter charge four hundred pounds and the other only ninety-five? Either the expensive one was trying to rip her off, or the cheap one was terrible and was planning on using substandard material.

As for the council approvals – there was so much red tape. She was planning on opening a small cafe, not the Taj Mahal.

Oh God, maybe she should have become a sculptor after all. It would have been a lot simpler than this.

The following morning, Joseph looked at his phone. He was sick of the damn thing. He was beginning to feel it had been grafted onto his ear. But he'd had a flash of inspiration during the night. This was the last person he wanted to call, the last person he wanted to ask, but things were getting desperate.

He checked his watch. It would be late afternoon in Melbourne. It might be a good time. He dialled the number.

A well-modulated Australian voice answered. 'Four Quarters, St Kilda, Lisa speaking. Can I help you?'

'Could I speak to Greg Gilroy, please.'

'Who's calling, please?'

'Joseph Wheeler. Of Wheeler Design. I'm calling from London.'

'Just one moment, sir.'

He waited, listening to the funky hold music. Then a brusque male voice cut in. 'Greg Gilroy.'

'Greg, hello. This is Joseph Wheeler speaking. From London. You might not remember me –'

'The Pommie kitchenhand who left me in the lurch? I remember you very well.'

Joseph kept his temper in check. He needed Greg's help, no point getting him off side. 'I'm hoping you can help me with something. I'm trying to contact Niamh Kennedy or her friend Lainey, but I'm not having any luck with the phone numbers I have.'

'Aren't you?' Greg said in a pleased tone of voice. 'That's a shame. Can't help you, mate. Sorry.'

'You don't have a mobile number for Lainey? Or an email address?'

'No, mate, sorry.'

Greg was smiling. Joseph could hear it in his voice. He knew without doubt that the bastard did have a mobile number for Lainey, and that there was no way he was going to give it to him. He spoke again, in a different tone of voice. 'So Greg, I understand you're opening a new cafe soon, is that right?'

Greg sounded suspicious. 'Yes. Yes, I am.'

'Got a name for it yet?'

'I'm sorry?'

Joseph was relaxed. 'Names are so important, don't you think? What do you think of the name Cats, for example?'

'Cats? What are you talking about?'

'You could call your new cafe Cats. Your food has nine lives, after all.'

'What the hell are you talking about, mate?'

Joseph's tone was chatty, even conversational. 'It was extraordinary, Greg. Before I worked those few days in your cafe, I had no idea prawns could be re-cycled like that. Or that chicken could be served three days after its use-by date. I'm sure the Melbourne health authorities will be just as fasci-nated too, when I give them a ring. Just as soon as I hang up from you, in fact. Thanks for your help, Greg. Goodbye.'

Joseph hung up. Would he ring the Melbourne health authorities? No. But Greg would never know that.

At home, Eva put a cushion on top of the phone. Then a newspaper. Then a rug. She just couldn't bear to look at it any more.

Lainey was being carried up the stairs to her apart-ment by Brendan and Hugh. Perched on a makeshift seat formed by their linked arms, she was having a big fit of the giggles. 'Never join the fire and rescue service, will you?' she said, shrieking again as they nearly tipped her over the side of the stairs.

They finally reached the landing on the third floor. She stood on one foot as she scrabbled in her bag for her keys.

Brendan was looking out of the landing window at the pub just down the street. 'Fancy a beer, Hugh? While Lainey gets her stuff?'

'Oh, you two. I'm just picking up some clothes and some of Rex's toys. I won't be a minute.'

Hugh rolled his eyes. Lainey was *sick*, the way she treated that cat. Like it was her child or something.

Brendan knew his sister well. 'Your minute is an hour in normal human time. We'll just have the one. Anyway, you'd be surprised how quickly we can drink a beer.'

'No, I wouldn't,' she said wryly as she unlocked her front door.

Joseph made a decision. He'd try Lainey's number one more time, for the last time. He would drive himself mad otherwise. He dialled the number. He knew it off by heart by now.

Lainey had just hopped into her living room when her phone started ringing.

Joseph almost fell off his chair when the ringing stopped and a breathless voice answered. 'Hello, Lainey speaking.'

'Lainey! Hello. This is Joseph Wheeler and I'm looking for –'

'Joe? Backpacker Joe? That Joe?'

'Yes, that Joe. Lainey, I'm looking for Niamh. A phone number, can you help me?'

'Phone number? But haven't you got one already? She left them both for you, didn't she? On her message.'

Lainey knew about the message? 'Yes, she did. But I didn't get them.'

'You didn't get her message?'

'No, not exactly. I know she left one but I didn't hear it. It's a long story. All I can tell you is that she rang nearly three weeks ago and I haven't heard from her since. Is she all right?'

'Is she all right?' Lainey repeated. 'Uhm, yes, she's fine.' Her voice sounded calm but her mind was working at a million miles an hour, trying to take all this in. Joe was still calling her Niamh, not Eva, so he couldn't have heard her message. Or her phone numbers. Which explained why he hadn't rung her back. But he'd obviously been trying to find her. This call was proof of that. So he was obviously still keen. That was a good thing.

But the bad thing? The bad thing was that he still didn't know the truth about Eva, even though Eva had tried to tell him. This was tricky, all right, Lainey thought. Then again, she did specialise in sorting out tricky situations.

But was this one her situation to sort out? It was in a way, she decided firmly. She was the one who had started this whole Niamh mess, so she had every right to clean it up, didn't she? She made her decision. 'Joe, are you sitting down? Good. I've got quite a lot to tell you.'

CHAPTER FORTY

EVA WALKED down Camden Street on her way to work, thinking over the night before, her first singing gig in four years.

After just the first few songs, she'd known the session in the city-centre pub was going to be a good one. She'd forgotten the way it could happen so unexpectedly. It took a particular combination of things – the right mix of people in the audience, the right mood in the air. All of the singers and musicians coming together, watertight with their harmonies, fluent with their melodies, guessing what the other was about to do at the split second they did it. Last night had definitely been one of those nights. The band had played Irish reels and jigs, ballads and modern songs, switching from one to the other, the crowd joining in with Eva and Lorna, the other singer.

She'd been nervous at first, glad the stagelights meant she couldn't see out into the audience. But the crowd had been enthusiastic from the start. She'd sung a solo, a long traditional song that she'd known since childhood, starting with slow sad notes and ending in a fast, sweet tumbling tune. There'd been loud applause at the end.

A voice broke into her thoughts. 'Morning, Eva, love.'

Eva turned to the woman setting up her fruit and vegatable stall. 'Hi, Brenda.'

'Howya, gorgeous.'

'Hi, Sean,' Eva called over. 'How's my favourite fourteen-year-old?'

'Pining for you.'

She shook her head at him as she walked into the delicatessen. You see, Eva, she told herself. You can have a normal life again. It'll just take time. 'Morning,' she called.

Ambrose poked his head from behind the new partition. 'Good morning, Eva, how are you this lovely day?'

'Grand, thanks.' He seemed very bright this morning. She put her coat in the temporary store-room and glanced over at the cafe area at the back of the shop. It was really coming together. It had been a good idea of Ambrose's to open the delicatessen again, even before the cafe was ready. Customers were looking at the menu Meg had drawn up, promising to come and have lunch once everything was up and running in a few weeks' time.

Ambrose come over, 'We've had a phone order this morning, I wonder if you could look after it for me?'

'Of course,' she said, going behind the counter. 'Who's it for?'

'A new customer, actually. It's a picnic lunch for two people.'

Eva started putting the order together. Three kinds of cheese, she decided. Olives, crusty bread, ham, a selection of the handmade chocolates . . .

'Morning, Evie,' Meg called over as she came downstairs.

'Hi, Meg.' She was all smiles too, Eva noticed. What had got into the pair of them this morning?

Meg peered into the cardboard box Eva had taken out. 'Oh, is that for that picnic order? Maybe we could offer picnic baskets as part of Ambrosia's service, Evie. Especially in the summertime, what do you think?'

'I think it's a great idea.' The delicatessen was packed with food perfect for a picnic. All they'd need to do was get some nice little baskets, some serviettes – it could work very well.

The memory of the picnic she and Joe had shared that day in the hotel room flashed into her mind. Is this what it would be like from now on? Little things reminding her of him all the time? The day before, she'd seen a tall, dark-haired man in the street and her heart had leapt. Then he'd turned and she'd

442

realised he was nothing like Joe. She'd been glad and disappointed all at once.

The phone rang. 'I've got it,' Ambrose called. Eva could just hear his voice. 'Lainey, how are you? Still having that good weather Eva was telling us about? Good, good, yes, she's right here, hold on a moment.'

He held out the phone to her. Eva put the box down and came over, puzzled. Lainey rarely rang her at work. And they'd spoken only two days before. 'Lainey? Is everything all right?'

'Everything is brilliant, Evie. But I need to tell you something, and you're probably going to be cross. So before I tell you I just want you to know that everything I said was with your wellbeing in mind and that our friendship is very, very important to me, okay?'

'Lainey, what on earth are you talking about? Have you been drinking?'

'Not a drop. But I have been talking. To Joe.'

'To *Joe*?'

'He rang my house the day before yesterday.'

'*What?* Where is he, Lainey? Why hasn't he rung me?'

'He didn't ever get your message. The one you left him, explaining everything. The one with all your phone numbers.'

'He didn't hear any of it?'

'His mother accidentally erased it or something, it's a long story, apparently. But it doesn't matter. The point is, he hadn't heard your numbers so he couldn't ring you. And he knew you were waiting to hear from him but he couldn't get in contact with you. He's been trying to find you for days and days.'

'How is he? Is he all right? How is his grand-mother?'

'He doesn't actually have a sick grandmother.'

'He doesn't?'

'That wasn't true. He had to go back to London suddenly because of the business problems. It's all a bit complicated. But he didn't ring me to tell me about his grandmother, he rang to talk about you. And I'm sorry, Evie, I hope you don't mind, but I told him everything. About Niamh. About the dinner party. How it all started. How we made it all up just as a laugh. And that you'd been trying to tell him the truth for a long time. I also told him that you'd seen the website, that you knew the truth about him as well.'

'You told him all of that? Oh, Lainey –'

'I know, I know I promised not to interfere ever again. But he was so concerned, Evie, and I just felt he had to know everything. And I felt bad because it was my fault in a way that all of this happened, and I wanted to do anything I could to put it right. I hope you're not mad, are you?'

Eva wasn't mad at all. She was just so relieved that Joe had been trying to contact her, that he still wanted to talk to her. She wanted to talk to him. Now. She spoke quickly. 'Of course I'm not mad. I'll ring him now, is he at home or at work, do you know?'

'He doesn't want you to ring him.'

'He doesn't?'

'He wants to see you. Talk to you face to face.'

'Face to face? Where is he? Is he in Dublin?' Her pulse quickened.

'I don't know where he is. All I know is he asked me not to phone you until today. He said he had to get organised.'

'Get what organised?'

'I don't know, I'm keeping right out of it from now on. I just wanted to ring and wish you luck. And just remember what a lovely woman you are. And what a good man he is. And how perfect you are together. My child, I give you my blessing.'

Eva laughed. 'Lainey, what are –' It was too late. Lainey had hung up.

Ambrose walked past. 'Everything all right, Evie?'

It was better than all right. Joe wanted to see her again. Face to face. Oh God, was he about to walk into the shop? What did she look like?

'Everything's fine, Ambrose. I'll be back in just a minute.' She nearly ran to the little bathroom to look in the mirror. Her hair was back in the plait, a few stray strands coming loose already. She tucked them away, fumbled for her lipstick and quickly reapplied it. Did she look tired? She hadn't had that late a night, she'd been home by midnight. But what about her clothes? The white shirt and black skirt? They weren't the sort of clothes he'd seen her in in Australia. Did she have time to go home and change? No, what if he came into the shop while she was gone?

She heard the faint sound of the front doorbell ringing and her heart leapt. Was it him? She peered around the door. No, it was another customer. Meg was dealing with her, chattering away about the cafe.

Eva took a last glance in the mirror then came back into the shop.

'You're looking very well,' Ambrose said surprisingly.

'Am I? Thanks, Ambrose.' Was it just her imagination or was he behaving a little oddly today?

The doorbell rang again. A short, red-haired man came in.

Eva went in behind the counter. 'Good morning, can I help you?'

'Good morning. I'm here about that picnic order.'

She picked up the container. 'Here it is. All ready to go.'

'Are you Miss Kennedy?'

Eva nodded.

'Do you want to bring a jacket or anything? The wind is fierce this morning.'

'Pardon me?'

'You should bring your jacket, it's cold out there.'

'But I'm not going out.'

'Yes, you are. That's what I was told, anyway. Go to the delicatessen on Camden Street, pick up the picnic basket and Miss Kennedy. Oh, and give you this. Sorry, I forgot.'

Eva took the envelope the man was holding. With shaking hands she opened it and read the words, written in firm black handwriting. 'Please come. Joe.'

'You need the day off, Evie, do you?' Ambrose had come up behind her.

She spun around. 'You know about this?'

'Just a little. Enough to know you need the day off.'

'You've been talking to Joe too?'

'That would be telling, Evie. Now, off you go. You don't want to be late.'

'Late for what?'

He smiled. 'Oh, I can't really say for sure.'

'But I can't leave you here.'

'Meg and I can handle the shop between us. It'll do you good to get out in the fresh air.'

Eva looked from Meg to Ambrose. They were both smiling at her. 'Where am I going?'

'If you leave, you'll find out,' Ambrose said. 'Goodbye now.'

She picked up her bag and coat and the box of picnic food and followed the taxi driver outside. His car was double-parked.

Sean was leaning against the railing, looking on with interest. 'Evie, where are you off to?'

'I haven't a clue, Sean,' she answered honestly. She got into the front seat and waved to Ambrose and Meg in the doorway. As the car moved into the traffic, she turned to the driver. 'Do you know where I'm going?'

'I know where I'm taking you. I don't know where you're going from there.'

They drove down Camden Street and on towards Dame Street, then left along the quays. Where was Joseph waiting? In the Phoenix Park? At her house in Stoneybatter? Then she realised. 'We're going to Heuston station, aren't we?'

'That's it.'

'What do I do when I get there?'

'It's a railway station – perhaps you could catch a train somewhere.' He grinned at her.

Eva felt the beginnings of excitement rise in her as the taxi pulled up at the station. She opened the door, getting a scent of malt from the Guinness brewery nearby.

'Don't worry about paying me, that's all been looked after. And your ticket's waiting at the booking office,' the driver said matter-of-factly. 'Have a nice journey.'

Journey to where? she wondered. She knew there was no point asking the driver. Everyone seemed to have signed a code of secrecy today.

She went into the station and looked up at the destination board. Cork. Limerick. Ennis. Tralee.

Waterford. Westport. Ballina. And Galway. She started to smile. She was right. Her ticket to Galway was waiting at the booking office. The train was leaving in fifteen minutes.

She walked the length of the platform, then climbed into the first carriage and found a window seat. She was still clutching the box of food. As the seats around her slowly filled, she thought back to the last time she'd been on a train. With Joe. She'd been blocking all of those memories, becoming more and more sure that he wasn't going to ring, that it was all over between them before it had properly begun. But now she allowed a glimmer of hope to rise inside her. Please come, he'd written.

She leaned her head back and shut her eyes as the train slowly pulled out of the station. It was a three-hour trip, straight across the country. The noise of the wheels on the track brought back more memories. She thought of meeting him at the party. The conversation at the taxi rank. The penguins at Phillip Island. Dancing in the pub. Working together at Four Quarters. Meeting Lewis. The day in the hotel room.

It had all happened so quickly between them. But holiday time wasn't like normal time. It had a different quality to it. She gazed out the window as the houses gave way to green fields, interrupted occasionally by small towns, lakes, woods. The sky was heavy with clouds. She was looking out at Ireland but her thoughts were in Australia.

She had a rush of panic as she thought of the whole Niamh pretence. How could she even think about the future when their entire past together, so brief but intense, was built on a foundation of lies? That was no way to start a relationship, was it? She wished she could put all her doubts at bay, have confidence, know for sure that everything would be all right. But she didn't have that certainty.

No one does. The voice again.

Yes, they do. Most people know exactly what they're doing. I'm one of the odd ones out.

No, you're not. Everyone feels uncertain. Some people are just better at hiding it than others. You just have to learn to trust your own instincts. Believe in yourself. And trust and believe in other people too.

Eva thought about it. She hadn't done much of that. She hadn't trusted Ambrose's belief in her when he had offered her the shop. But it looked like that might just work out. Of course, it was early days, there was still a lot that could go wrong. But there was also a lot that could go right.

Exactly.

She thought about Lainey. All those years she had misjudged her, thought that she had somehow spoiled things with Martin. And she'd thought Lainey was doing the same thing with Joe. She'd been wrong about that. Lainey was a good person, a great friend. Eva realised how glad she was to have her friendship. And how nearly she had lost it by not trusting her, by looking for the worst rather than the best.

She thought about Dermot too. She'd known in her heart that he hadn't been right for her. But she'd ignored her own instincts.

And then she thought about Joe again. His clever, kind face. The warm, amused look he'd get in his eyes. His soft London accent. His curiosity. His gentleness. The way he kissed her . . .

She started to worry again, thinking over what could happen next with him. Then she stopped herself. There was no point worrying, she just had to wait and see what happened.

She was about to find out, in any case.

A voice on the PA announced they were coming into Galway. Eva looked out the window at the crowded platform, trying to see him among the groups of people. She waited for the other carriages to clear first. Her heart had started beating faster again.

She stepped off the train, waiting to hear her name being called or to see him.

The platform gradually cleared until she was the only person left. She just stood there, still clasping the picnic box, not daring to think that it all stopped here. That it was some joke. That it had all gone wrong.

'Miss Kennedy?'

A voice behind her. She turned around. It was a woman wearing a blue shirt with a Galway Taxis logo. 'Sorry I'm a bit late, you can never be too sure what time that train will get in. Are you ready to go?'

She felt the relief. 'Yes. Yes, I am.' She followed the woman, who was striding quickly back along the platform. 'Would you be able to tell me exactly where it is I'm going?'

The woman spoke over her shoulder. 'I don't know the exact name of it, but it's not far. If you'd like to come this way, the car's just here.'

Eva stepped out of the station and glanced around. They were just on the edge of Eyre Square. The Great Southern Hotel was in front of her. She looked up. The light was bright, reflecting off the sea close by.

The taxi driver didn't speak as she drove through the system of one-way roads. They were soon clear of the city, driving on the coast road past Salt Hill. On their left was the sea, the Aran Islands easily visible in the clear light, the sea a shifting pattern of blues and greys. The sky was filled with clouds buffeting through the air, revealing quick glimpses of blue.

Fifteen minutes later, the car pulled off the main road and drove down a narrower, bumpier road. Eva looked ahead. The road led to a small field which ran right down to the sea. There was a figure standing on the rocks by the shore, looking out over the water. A tall, dark-haired man, dressed in a black coat. Joe.

The driver smiled over her shoulder. 'Here you are, Miss.'

'Thank you.' Eva climbed out. The ground was springy beneath her feet, the air damp with sea spray. She stood there for a moment, waiting as the taxi turned and drove away. Then she pulled her coat in around her body and started walking, still carrying the cardboard box.

As she came closer, he stepped over the rocks, until he was just a short distance away. She searched his face, overwhelmed by how good it was to see him. He was looking at her just as intently. Part of her just wanted to go to him, to hold him close, kiss him. But she held back, still uncertain.

'Hello,' she said.

'Hello.'

'I brought your lunch.' She held it out.

He smiled then. 'Thank you. It's very good to see you.'

'It's very good to see you too.'

She felt like she was in an English-language training video. She waited, not sure what was going to happen next. What was this mood between them? Wary? Careful?

'Did you have a good trip?'

'I did, yes.' She'd turned into Miss Manners.

'Thank you for bringing me here. You've gone to a lot of trouble.'

'I thought it was safer than calling you. You and I don't seem to have a lot of luck with telephones.'

'No, we don't.' She smiled briefly, then looked around. The taxi had gone from sight. It was just the two of them now, alone by the sea. The only sound was the waves hitting against the stony beach, the occasional birdcall.

'We need to talk,' he said.

She nodded. She had so many questions. But there was something important to say to him first. Right now. 'Joe, I know you've heard it all from Lainey already, but I want you to hear it again from me. I want to tell you myself. I'm not a sculptor. I don't live in Galway, I live in Dublin. I work in a delicatessen. I'm about to open a cafe. I've just started singing in a band again, but not with Enya.'

'Yes, I know. You have a beautiful singing voice.'

'You know? How do you know?'

'I was there last night.'

The beautiful voice turned into a high-pitched shriek. 'In the pub? In Dublin?'

He nodded. 'I flew in from London last night. Lainey told me where you were singing. So I went to see your band, then I drove across here afterwards.'

Eva wanted to hear more about that. But not just yet. 'Joe, I really need you to explain something to me. I saw your website, I read all about you. Your company. Your life. You're a success, why didn't you just stick to the truth? Why did you have to pretend to be someone else?'

There was a long pause before he answered. 'It wasn't a deliberate thing. It just started to happen. People made assumptions, assumed I was just an ordinary traveller having an ordinary holiday. And I began to realise I actually preferred it like that. That I wanted a life like that, a simpler life. I met you, then I met Lewis. And I knew it for sure then, that I wanted to change the way I lived. I'd known for a long time that something had to change, I just hadn't realised it would have to be me.'

'Why didn't you tell me all of that?'

'I wanted to. I wanted to tell you everything. But there didn't ever seem to be the right time.'

'It was like that for me too, Joe. I wanted to tell you the truth a hundred times.'

'So why didn't you?'

She forced herself to look right at him as she spoke. 'Because I was too worried that you wouldn't like me if you knew how ordinary I really was, if I was being the real me. And it was very important to me that you liked me.'

'You don't think I met the real you?'

'No.'

'Lainey said as much. That you were worried about telling me the truth because you thought the real you wasn't good enough. That's why I wanted to talk to you here. Not in Dublin. Not in London. Tell me, is this where you imagined that caravan to be?'

She looked around. The field was green, as she had described. The hills of Connemara were visible. There were long beaches stretching out either way, littered with shells and pieces of wood, bleached white by the salty water. She nodded.

'You're here now, not in Australia. But what's different about you? The way you feel? The way you look?'

She paused. 'No.'

'The things you notice?'

'No.'

'Your sense of humour?'

'No.'

'Your stories about your childhood? The books you've read? The films you've seen? The music you listen to? That was all true, wasn't it? That was all you?'

She nodded.

'I thought so,' he said. He pointed a few metres away. His backpack was lying on the ground. 'And if I was wearing that now, would that change the person I am?'

She didn't have to answer.

'It wouldn't. I'm just the same person, whatever I'm wearing. You see, I think I did meet the real you in Australia. And I know that you met the real me, even if we were upside down at the bottom of the world. What we were on the outside didn't count. I think we got to know each other from the inside out. The real us.'

She took a step toward him. 'I should have told you, Joe. Should have told you I wasn't a sculptor –'

'It doesn't matter to me what you do for a living. Where you live. None of that changes you. And I've realised the same thing about myself. What I am is not what I do for a living or where my house is, it's the way I think, the way I feel.'

'But your company?'

'I don't have a company any more. It's a long story – you know some of it, I think, but that part of my life is over. I've closed the company down.'

'But what are you – ?'

'Going to do now?' He smiled. 'I've you to thank for the inspiration, actually. That pendant of yours sparked something in me.'

She felt for the pendant around her neck and took it in her hand. It felt warm from her skin.

'I'm going to art school. To study jewellery design.'

'To art school? Where?'

'Dublin.'

'You're coming to live in *Dublin*?'

'For three very good reasons. Would you like to hear them?'

She nodded slowly.

'The art school there is very good, I believe.'

'Yes, it is,' she said.

From the look he gave her she knew that Lainey had told him about all of that too. And it didn't matter that he knew about it, she realised. It wasn't important any more.

'And I don't know yet for sure, but I might be needing some part-time work. Apparently there are lots of cafes in Dublin. You don't happen to know anyone that might be looking for a part-time kitchen hand, do you?'

She tried not to smile. 'Oh, I might.'

'I can give you some good references.' Then he thought about it. 'Actually, no, I probably can't.'

She saw the laughter in his eyes. 'I don't think I'll need any references.'

'No?'

'No, I think I trust you.'

There was a long moment while they looked into each other's eyes. Eva felt as though the wind that was sweeping around them was taking her last worries and carrying them out to sea.

As he moved closer to her, she surprised him by putting a finger on his lips. 'You haven't told me the third reason you're moving to Dublin.'

'You haven't guessed?'

She shook her head.

He gently tucked a piece of hair behind her ear, caressing the side of her face. 'I'm in love with a woman who lives there.'

The touch of his hand was beautiful. 'Really? What's her name?'

He smiled. 'It took me a while to find out, actually.' Then he leaned down and whispered, his lips close against her ear. 'Her name is Eva Mary Kennedy.'

EPILOGUE

Three months later

'Now, Mrs Lacey, let me just read that order back so I'm sure I've got it right. You'd like the Ambrosia Platter with extra smoked cheese, and your friend would like the Asian noodle salad, is that right?'

Mrs Lacey nodded vigorously on behalf of herself and her friend.

'With the caramel pancakes to follow for the both of you? That's grand.' Eva smiled. 'It won't be long.'

'Thank you, Eva,' Mrs Lacey said graciously. She wriggled comfortably into her chair and leaned across the table. 'It really is excellent service here. And the food is something special, Dorothy. You're in for a treat.'

Dorothy looked around appreciatively. 'It's certainly a lovely room, isn't it? So bright and welcoming.' The late July sunshine was streaming through a high window on the back wall, illuminating the original artworks dotted along it.

Mrs Lacey nodded. 'Yes, it's quite the hottest spot on Camden Street these days. I've been a loyal customer of the Kennedys' delicatessen for years, of course. So they always make sure there's a table free for me.'

Heads would roll otherwise, Dorothy thought, wisely saying nothing. Instead she leaned over and whispered. 'And that lovely young woman with the plait who served us? Who is she?'

Mrs Lacey lowered her voice. 'That's Eva Kennedy. The manager here. She set up this whole cafe herself, took over when her uncle Ambrose retired. He's on holiday in Spain at the moment, I believe.'

'And is she the chef as well? It's a wonderful menu, isn't it? I had great difficulty choosing, there were so many things I'd like to try.'

Mrs Lacey was thoroughly enjoying being the font of all knowledge. 'No, the chef is Eva's cousin. See, that little one in the kitchen there, you can just see her through the door. She's a marvellous young lady. Very enthusiastic.'

Just then the front door of the cafe opened. A tall, dark-haired man came in, casually dressed in jeans and a T-shirt.

Mrs Lacey whispered across the table again to her friend. 'Do you see that man? That's Eva's boyfriend, or partner or whatever word they use these days. His name's Joseph. He's from London but she met him in Australia, of all places.'

'Really? How romantic.'

They watched as Eva caught sight of him. Her face lit up. They had a quick conversation, then she laughed and reached up to kiss him. As he took a seat at the counter by the front window, he was smiling too.

Mrs Lacey leant forward again. 'He's studying to be a jewellery designer, I believe,' she whispered.

Was there anything Mrs Lacey didn't know? Dorothy wondered. 'Really? How fascinating.'

Then their conversation was interrupted by Eva's arrival with their lunch.

Six months later . . .

Lainey lay on the sofa watching the late-night music videos on television. Rex was fast asleep, a heavy weight on her lap.

A tall blond man came out of the kitchen carrying a newly opened bottle of shiraz. 'More wine, Lainey?' He read the label. 'Lorikeet Hill, from the Clare Valley.'

'Oh yes please, Adam.' She held out her glass and smiled. Who'd have thought her downstairs neighbour would turn out to be such a lovely man? She looked at him fondly, remembering the conversation she and Eva had had, all those months ago. What was it she'd said to Eva? Something about waiting for the man who would make her weak at the knees, make her heart skip and her stomach swirl. Could Adam be Mr Cholera himself? He certainly gave her some of the symptoms. He was Mr Flu, perhaps. Lainey gave Rex an extra-special pat. It was all his doing, after all.

She had just wriggled along the sofa to let Adam in beside her again when the phone started ringing. Adam looked at his watch. 'It's after one. Who on earth would be ringing at this hour?'

Lainey had a fairly good idea. She stood up, Rex hopping off the couch behind her. He'd taken to following her around like a shadow. Ever since they'd stayed with her parents for that month, he'd been completely disoriented. She picked up the phone just as the answering machine was about to click into action.

It took her a moment to calm the excited voice on the other end of the line. 'Evie? That is you, isn't it? Are you all right? Do you know what time it is here?'

Sitting beside Joseph on their sofa, Eva just laughed. 'I'm fine, Lainey, really. And I'm sorry about the time, but I had to ring. To ask you something very important.'

Lainey waited.

'It's about you and that pink taffeta dress . . .'

Lainey's shriek down the phone was all the answer Eva needed.

A TASTE FOR IT

Monica McInerney

Maura Carmody's off on the trip of a lifetime. A talented chef, she's travelling around Ireland for a month to promote Australian food and wine.

Maura's expecting a straightforward business trip. But what she gets is a whirlwind of mishaps, misunderstandings, rivals and revelations – and Dominic Hanrahan, who's giving her *plenty* of food for thought.

Set in Ireland and Australia, *A Taste for It* is a warm, funny novel about following your heart and pursuing your dreams.

AN EXCERPT FROM THE BESTSELLING *A TASTE FOR IT*

'The Diner, the *OzTaste* magazine food critic, is coming here today.'

'What! The Diner! How on earth does Joel know that?'

Maura sat down. 'He was calling from the *OzTaste* office. He just happened to see a confidential list of the critic's restaurant visits this month. And he just happened to read it closely and notice we're the lucky one for today. Apparently The Diner's travelling around the country with his wife reviewing regional restaurants.'

Nick looked worried. 'That's really bad news, isn't it? Isn't he the one who closed down Gemma's restaurant?'

Maura nodded. Several years previously her friend Gemma had opened a small bistro in Sydney. All had gone well until The Diner had visited and written a vicious – and factually incorrect – review. Overnight it had destroyed her trade.

'Did Joel have any good news?' Nick asked.

Maura smiled broadly. 'Today's review will never be published. *OzTaste* magazine is closing down. Joel's heard the publisher's been taken over by some international magazine group and there's going to be a big change in direction. But it's still hush-hush and The Diner wouldn't have heard the news yet.'

'So he'll soon be out of a job?'

'Just like Gemma was when he closed her restaurant.'

They were silent for a moment.

'If this is going to be his last free meal, we really should make sure it's one to remember, shouldn't we?' Maura said thoughtfully.

'Make sure he never forgets us, do you mean?'

'Pull out all the stops,' she grinned.

THE WOULD-BE WIFE

Andiee Paviour

The night Claudette Columbine meets Gary King, she knows her life will never be quite the same. But what she doesn't bargain on is the catastrophe it becomes. Gary is tall, handsome and dark. He also happens to be the husband of Claudette's new best friend.

For Claudette, who delivers singing telegrams by night, mixes cocktails in Gary's edgy Bondi bistro by day and dreams of elusive Hollywood stardom, an affair with her boss is just another thing she can't control. For Gary, as it turns out, it's something else entirely.

Set in the Sydney of nightclubs, beach houses, fashion boutiques and very bad telegram lyrics, *The Would-be Wife* is the hip, funny and heart-wrenching story of a party girl who suddenly grows up.

PANTS ON FIRE

Maggie Alderson

When London editor Georgia Abbott comes to Sydney to work on *Glow*, a glossy women's magazine, she has high hopes for a bright new start. Leaving behind a broken heart (her own) and a philandering ex-fiancé, she's looking forward to immersing herself in the Tim Tam-eating sisterhood of women's mags. Not to mention being whisked off into the dusty Australian sunset by a suntanned, Akubra-hatted fantasy man.

At first, things seem promising, as Georgia is swept up in a whirl of A-list parties, dancing, dinners and debauchery. But while Australian water may go down the plughole the other way, Australian men are starting to look all too familiar. And then there's the chaotic bunch of women Georgia works with on *Glow*, to whom every relationship disaster is a potential article, not least of all Georgia's, whose quest for love is fast becoming headline material.

What to do when all the blokes you've found are either gay, married, unfaithful, unable or just plain unworthy?

GIRLS NIGHT IN 2
GENTLEMEN BY INVITATION

Edited by Jessica Adams, Chris Manby and Fiona Walker

Following the phenomenal success of *Girls' Night In*, you're invited to spend another night in with the hottest women authors in town . . . and some fellas as well (under strict supervision, of course).

Over forty of your favourite writers have written stories specially for *Girls' Night In, Gentlemen By Invitation*, making it the chunkiest and funkiest book around. And since all of the proceeds go to the charity War Child, by buying this book you've made a difference to the lives of children devastated by conflict.

Guaranteed to make you laugh, cry and . . . blush, *Girls' Night In, Gentlemen by Invitation* contains bedtime stories that your parents never told you.

PRAISE FOR GIRLS' NIGHT IN

The perfect girls' night in
VOGUE

Curl up with a glass of wine and enjoy the choicest cuts from contemporary female writers
NEW WOMAN

An enchanting and insightful collection featuring anyone who's anyone
ELLE